# FAST WOMEN

Maggie Hudson was born in Bradford and now lives in London with her husband and three dogs. Writing under the name Margaret Pemberton, she is the author of many successful novels including the bestselling *White Christmas in Saigon*, *The Flower Garden* and *A Multitude of Sins*.

# MAGGIE HUDSON

# *Fast Women*

HarperCollins*Publishers*

This novel is entirely a work of fiction. The names, characters and incidents portrayed in it are the work of the author's imagination. Any resemblance to actual persons, living or dead, events or localities is entirely coincidental.

HarperCollins*Publishers*
77–85 Fulham Palace Road, London w6 8jb

www.fireandwater.com

Published by HarperCollins*Publishers* 2000
3  5  7  9  10  8  6  4  2

ISBN 0 00 651154 6

Typeset in Sabon by
Palimpsest Book Production Limited,
Polmont, Stirlingshire

Printed and bound in Great Britain by
Omnia Books Limited, Glasgow

For Linda Britter. With love.

# ACKNOWLEDGEMENTS

I would like to thank my agent Caroline Sheldon; her cohort Samantha Finlayson; my editors, Rachel Hore and Anne O'Brien. They are special ladies all.

Other thanks, too, are in order: to Ronnie in Rio, Tina, Bry and JV.

And remembering Joe Beveridge, 1936–1998.

# Prologue

It wasn't the funeral Bryce Reece might well, in life, have expected. There were none of the traditional trappings customary when a big-time South London gangster made his last journey. The hearse was a sleek Mercedes, not a flower-laden carriage drawn at walking pace by plumed black horses. The Bermondsey streets in which he had played as a child – streets once lined with small shabby terraced houses and now overlooked by high-rise council flats – were not knee-deep with the pruriently curious. It was almost as if those who had known Bryce Reece were reluctant to acknowledge the reality of his death.

'Which, under the circumstances, isn't too surprising,' Chief Constable Leslie Somerville said drily to his CID companion. 'Even half the Met think he's cosily tucked up in the sun with a new face and a new identity and police protection for the rest of his natural. That was the deal, after all.'

Detective Chief Inspector Victor Roberts grunted as, shoulder to shoulder with Somerville, he edged as unobtrusively as possible into the rear of the packed crematorium chapel. Bryce Reece never had been a man for honouring any deals he might have made with the forces of law and order. That death had overtaken him before the deal he had made with them could be fully implemented on their side was absolutely typical of him. The new identity had been set up – the best plastic surgeon in the country had been studying photographs of him for weeks – and,

1

though it wasn't likely that having grassed once he would grass again, whilst he remained alive and under police protection there was, at least, hope that he would do so.

From his rear-view vantage point Victor looked over the sea of heads. Though the upper echelons of London's criminal fraternity hadn't paid Reece the honour of walking with bowed heads behind his hearse, they hadn't completely flunked paying their respects. At the end of his life Bryce may have committed the most cardinal of all sins, that of grassing on a fellow crim, but the crim in question had been scum of mega proportions. No one, not even his henchmen, had been sorry to see Frankie Briscoe go down on a thirty-year stretch – especially so when they remembered Tricia Reece and the way she had died.

The September sun streamed in mellow shafts through the stained-glass windows. The coffin had not yet been carried in and the tension was palpable. Feet shuffled. More than one woman was weeping. Victor, who had known Bryce since they'd been ragged-arse kids playing on Bermondsey bomb sites together, forced memories of Bryce's step-daughter to the back of his mind and made a wry moue. Women had always shed tears over Bryce. Love 'em and leave 'em had been Bryce's motto, and he'd loved and left more than he, or anyone else, cared to count.

'Who is the girl, fourth row down, second left?' Somerville whispered in plummy tones as music began to play and, instinctively, those who had been seated rose to their feet.

Victor tensed himself against the appearance of the coffin, looked in the direction Somerville had indicated, and frowned. For all of his professional life he'd prided himself on knowing more about Bryce Reece than Bryce did. He didn't know the identity of the girl Somerville had singled out, though. He only had a partial view of her, but it was obvious she was no more than nineteen or twenty. Tall and wand-slender, her satin-straight hair was the most amazing shade of wheat-gold. Gathered in the nape of her neck and tied with a black velvet ribbon, he would have staked good money that the colour was natural.

'I don't know,' he whispered back tersely, his scalp prickling as a taped version of Frank Sinatra's 'My Way' filled the chapel and the pallbearers entered, Bryce's casket on their shoulders.

Whoever the girl was, of all the mourners squeezed together cheek by jowl, she looked the most out of place. As the casket passed within a hair's breadth of him and he plunged clenched fists deeper into his raincoat pockets, Victor reflected that her doing so was no easy feat. Two rows from the front a government minister was seated next to a man only recently released after serving time for the Great Train Robbery of 1963. A little behind them a well-known peer of the realm was rubbing shoulders with a gnome-like figure who, in his heyday, had run with both the Krays and the Richardson gang and, solo, had been more influential and dangerous than either. There were famous representatives of the boxing fraternity present, an ominous sprinkling of journalists, more than one South London publican, several internationally known pop stars, a whole gamut of local people incongruously inter-mixed with Kensington and Knightsbridge types and, last but not least, there was the police presence in the shape of himself and Somerville.

It wasn't uncommon, of course, for coppers to be in attendance at the funeral of a big-name crim. Sometimes they'd be there because they'd been ordered to be there. It was always useful to see who would emerge from the woodwork – or from Spain – on such occasions. Sometimes they'd be there by choice, drawn by the complex bond often forged between copper and criminal. It was unusual for men of the rank of Chief Constable to put in an appearance, though. He took a quick look at Somerville's impassive, granite-hard features. What Somerville's off-duty relationship with Bryce had been

3

Victor didn't know. He only knew what his own had been – and it had been painfully deep.

He returned his attention to the pallbearers. They were all major-league crims; four of them were South Londoners, one was a Scot and one an American. Despite Bryce's grassing Frankie Briscoe, when it had come to the real crunch his comrades in crime hadn't been prepared to see him be carried on his last journey by the employees of a funeral director. Black-suited and wearing mirrored shades they looked as if they'd stepped straight off a Hollywood film-set, not the Old Kent Road.

'Taken altogether, that little lot should be going down for three hundred years minimum,' Somerville growled. 'A bomb chucked in here would wipe organised crime out in a stroke.'

Victor wasn't listening to him. He was trying hard not to look at the casket. Decked in white roses and now set on a purple-draped catafalque it overwhelmed the small chapel just as, in life, Bryce had so effortlessly overwhelmed everyone he had come into contact with. Bryce hadn't been Jewish but it was a Jewish word that best summed up his swagger and charm and warmth and attitude: *chutzpah*. That was what Bryce had possessed, and he'd possessed it in spades.

'Dear Friends and Family,' the crematorium's resident chaplain began over the sound of muffled weeping, 'this is not to be a religious service. Bryce Reece was not a man who espoused religion in life and he expressly requested that, at his funeral, no prayers be said nor hymns sung.'

The woman who had been weeping for as long as Victor and Somerville had been seated tried, unsuccessfully, to stifle the sound with a handkerchief.

Victor's jaw clenched. How many years had it been since, as a small boy, he had lain in the dark in his bedroom in Swan Row listening to the sound of Sandra Parry crying herself to sleep in the little terrace house

4

next door – the house sandwiched between his home and Bryce's? Twenty-five years? Twenty-eight? The sound was as distinctive as some people's laughter. He would have known it anywhere and, just as he'd longed to do years and years ago, he wished he knew a way of bringing her tears to a hiccuping finale.

'As the spirit moves you,' the chaplain was saying encouragingly, 'perhaps you would like to come forward and express your thoughts and feelings and your memories of Bryce Reece who, I'm sure you will all allow, was a most . . . unusual man.'

One of the pallbearers, the heavily built Italian-looking American, rose from where he had been seated and, as the chaplain vacated the lectern, swaggered unerringly towards it. 'Mafioso,' Victor thought and could feel Somerville's attention sharpening.

His own attention wandered. It was impossible for it not to do so when, everywhere he looked, there were reminders not only of Bryce's life, but of his own life also. Rusty was there and, looking at her, it was hard for him to believe she was a day older than she'd been way back in the early sixties when he'd busted her for soliciting. She'd become famous shortly after that, of course. Famous and rich. One of the first of the Pirelli calendar girls, she'd turned stripping and nude modelling into a genuine art form. Just looking at her made even his prick stir.

As svelte as ever, dressed in a greeny-gold silk suit with a skirt so short it left no one in doubt that the perfection of her legs still reached to the top, Titian-red hair skimming her shoulders and white-framed sunglasses hiding her eyes, she was seated as befitted her status as an ex-wife in the centre of the front row on the left-hand side of the aisle.

The second ex-Mrs Reece was seated in the centre of the front right-hand row. She'd been Nina Denster, the only daughter of Sir William Denster, all of seven-teen years old and a pupil at Benenden when she and

Bryce had first become an item. Now, wearing a black satin suit with broad shoulders and a narrow waist, a white silk blouse tied in a loose cravat at the neck and sporting a double rope of priceless black pearls, she was Mrs Eduardo Patino. To say that a lot of water had passed beneath the bridge during the intervening years was, Victor reflected, an understatement of mammoth proportions.

'I fink I'll always remember Bryce as a bloke who 'elped people out,' a well-known South London 'face' was saying, his voice unsteady with emotion. ''E 'elped people out of Pentonville and 'e 'elped people out of Park'urst.'

'And he helped that particular bugger out of Wormwood Scrubs,' Somerville whispered darkly, wondering for how much longer he was going to have to listen to the eulogies.

Victor grimaced, remembering Bryce's own flamboyant escape. There'd been a woman involved, of course – a woman who was seated not a dozen yards away. Wherever Bryce was, there were always women. He'd had a libido that would have done a bull proud. 'Fast women, slow horses – the story of my life,' he'd said once with self-deprecating humour. Victor had laughed but hadn't been convinced about the horses. From what he'd seen of Bryce's gambling habits, luck clung to him like shit to a shoe.

'He was the best mate, the best fun, the best everything.' The speaker was one of the Costa del Crime expatriates, though not, unfortunately for Somerville and Victor, one with a warrant out for his arrest.

Thanks to the seat that had been temporarily vacated Victor could now see Sandra clearly. Though there couldn't have been more than half a dozen years between her and Rusty, it seemed more like a lifetime. Where Rusty had become even more sleek and svelte with age, Sandra had become dumpy and frumpy. The fake fur she was hunched into did her no favours and, instead of looking elegantly funereal, her black-seamed stockings and black suede shoes merely looked tarty.

'. . . Bryce was so mad 'e didn't give a toss that the Roller was 'is own,' one of the Bermondsey-born pall-bearers was now saying, a chuckle in his voice as he remembered a long-ago evening out. ''E leapt on to the bonnet shoutin' and hollerin' at the bloke in front. Eighty-five thou that car cost and you ain't never seen damage like it.'

In a release of nervous tension everyone began to laugh, even those who, a few seconds ago, had been weeping. There'd always been laughter when Bryce was around – great, roaring gales of it – and suddenly his spirit seemed to fill the small chapel.

'I remember when . . .' someone else was now saying, beginning yet another outrageous anecdote.

Victor closed his eyes. With the exception of Sandra his links with Bryce went back further than those of anyone else present. If he'd wanted he could have told stories, lots of stories, but he wasn't going to. Not now. Not ever.

He opened his eyes, looking towards the girl with the wheat-gold hair again. Who the devil was she? She wasn't family, he knew that. A girlfriend, then? He rubbished the idea almost instantly. Apart from Nina, Bryce had never gone in for cradle-snatching. Nina had been the only exception to that rule – and it hadn't escaped his attention that Nina was just about the only person present who had, so far, remained dry-eyed.

He caught the government minister looking across at her with a frown, and his own puzzlement deepened. As was nakedly clear by the wide variety of class and profession at his funeral, Bryce's life had been lived on many different levels. That the mystery girl wasn't from the level occupied by the government minister was obvious, if a little surprising. From the moment he'd clapped eyes on her, Victor had had her marked down as a debutante making a novelty visit south of the river.

'And now the coffin will be committed.'

It was the chaplain again and, with a stab of shock, Victor saw that the coffin had been moved from the catafalque and was now in position before the curtains that would close behind it as it slid from view en route to the crematorium burners. Christ, but he hated funerals! He wasn't going to watch the coffin slide away. He couldn't watch.

There was no laughter now from anyone, only stunned disbelief that Bryce's flamboyant, incident-packed, reckless life had come to this – and that the same unspeakable fate lay in wait for them, too.

'Goodbye, Bryce. God bless, mate,' someone, a man, called out.

Victor wished the last farewell had come from him, but it had been impossible. His throat was too tight for speech; it was so tight he was terrified he was going to start blubbing like a woman.

With his jaw clenched he remained standing next to Somerville as the mourners began to dazedly rise from their seats and file from the chapel. As they did so, low in the background, Frank Sinatra began to sing of regrets too few to mention. It was certainly apt – though Victor doubted that Bryce would have had a single regret.

With the exception of the government minister, who had walked quickly off in the direction of his car, and the peer of the realm, who was engaged in conversation with a famous show-business figure, people had now begun milling together in small groups.

'It's a fucker, Victor love, ain't it?' Rusty said, ignoring Somerville, whose attention was on the Italian-American, and speaking in the South London accent she still, on suitable occasions, lapsed into.

8

'It's a bugger,' he agreed, his own accent slipping likewise. 'Especially under the circumstances.'

She remained silent as, like him, she remembered just what the circumstances were.

Victor felt his gut tighten as it always did when he was in close proximity to Rusty. Telling himself she must now be close to forty didn't help. She didn't *look* to be close to forty. Christ, she didn't look to be close to thirty! For as long as he'd known her she'd radiated accessibility and untrammelled sex and, slender and supple and still the same measurements she had been when she'd first begun modelling, it was evident she was going to unnervingly retain those qualities lifelong.

'Who was the girl?' she asked as he caught, yet again, the evocative fragrance of Chanel No. 5.

It was a question that brought him sharply back to his senses.

'I don't know,' he said, not wasting time asking which girl she was referring to; knowing all too well. 'I thought you might.'

She shook her head and her hair swung silkily, the sunlight glinting the Titian-red to gold.

'Nope. She's new to me. I thought at first Sandra might know her, but there's not been a glimmer of recognition between the two of them.'

He said nothing, not remotely surprised. He knew everyone Sandra knew. For years, because of Bryce, he had made it his job to know.

'Fancy a drink, Vic?' Rusty asked, tilting her head and looking at him speculatively. 'For old time's sake and all that?'

Close to, he saw that her suntanned skin was beginning to betray fine lines at the corners of her eyes and mouth. They didn't detract one iota from her sexiness.

'Nah,' he said, wondering if he was mentally certifiable, 'I'm not here in a private capacity, Rusty. I'm on duty.'

9

She sucked in her breath sharply, as he had known she would, her matey friendliness changing in an instant to open hostility. '*Fuck you*!' she spat, her green-gilt eyes flashing fire.

As she spun on her heel, walking away from him as swiftly as if he had had the plague, a stab of amusement leavened his feelings of regret and frustration and shame. Coming from Rusty, the language had been nursery-book mild.

'You won't believe me when I say I'm sorry, but I am.' The crystal-cut voice came from behind his left-hand shoulder and the speaker was Nina Patino. He turned reluctantly to face her.

'If you're referring to Bryce's death, then you're right,' he said bluntly. 'I don't believe you.'

She shrugged, as indifferent of his opinion as she was of everyone else's. 'I'm here, aren't I? All the way from sunny Colombia.'

Her hair, the same raven-black as her suit, was cut in a short, geometrically straight bob. The uncompromising style emphasised the beauty of her high cheekbones and full, wide mouth. Her lips and nails were a singing red. Her light-coloured eyes, wide-spaced and dark-lashed, were hard as flint.

He glanced across to where her chauffeured limousine was waiting and beyond the limo to the plain-clothes boys from the drug squad who were waiting to see where the limo would next take her. Claridge's, probably. Wherever it was, the drugs boys were on to a loser. Though wife to the biggest known drug baron in South America, Nina remained impossible to touch.

'So, where have the great and the good stashed Bryce away?' she asked, uncaring of the many hostile glances being cast in her direction from the South London contingent. 'Brazil? New Zealand?'

'It would have been Brazil,' he said, seeing no reason

10

now, with Bryce dead, for the information to remain top secret. 'But he's dead, Nina. Stone dead. Real dead. Dead beyond any mistake or connivance. That being the case, I don't think even for poetic reasons Bryce would expect us to send his ashes to Rio, do you?'

It wasn't said nicely. He knew Nina Patino and what he knew he didn't like. Nina was money-hungry to a degree that put most of the villains he knew to shame – and Bryce had had money. Lots of money. Victor's eyes narrowed as he remembered how many questions were still to be answered about the bizarre way Bryce had died.

'I was in Colombia,' she said, reading his mind. Though she had turned her head to avoid meeting his eyes, Victor detected a bleakness in her voice that was undeniably genuine.

He remained silent, his thoughts and assumptions shifting; surprised that someone with her contacts should have even half-believed the funeral to be a sham. The tautness of her body, though, as she continued to look away from him, told its own story. Unless he was very much mistaken – and he very rarely was – she really had believed that Bryce, the ultimate survivor, had survived yet again; that with police assistance he was lazing beneath a foreign sun complete with a new face and a new identity.

Looking at her, as she held herself together against what appeared to be inner disintegration, his jaw clenched. Why did he find it so surprising that she hadn't accepted the reality of Bryce's death? Christ alone knew the difficulties he'd had in accepting it, and he'd had the benefit of seeing every piece of official documentation pertaining to it.

'Who is the girl?' There was an odd note in her voice. It was as if she'd switched to automatic pilot having retreated to a place deep within herself; a place suspended in time where, impaled on the past, she was paralysed by the present and unable to conceive of the future.

'I don't know.' He released the tension in his jaw

11

slightly. Somerville was walking across to members of the drug surveillance team, obviously about to have a few words with them. Some of the small cliques of mourners had begun moving off in the direction of the long row of parked cars. From a point a little distant from the chapel the girl with the wheat-gold hair was taking what appeared to be a last, sweeping view of everyone. 'But I soon will,' he added and, hands deep in the pockets of his Burberry, he walked away from her, leaving her to the hell she was so obviously inhabiting, heading in the mystery girl's direction.

She saw him coming and, even though he was so unmistakably a policeman, didn't turn away. His eyes narrowed. As far as anyone knew, Bryce had left a cool two million pounds unaccounted for when he had met his repugnantly grisly end. So far, despite the number of high-profile villains and top-drawer businessmen in attendance at the funeral, he hadn't heard so much as a whisper, nor detected the slightest frisson, which could be interpreted as referring to it. Was the girl someone he should be taking a professional interest in? And just what part in Bryce's complex and complicated life had she played?

'Detective Chief Inspector Roberts,' he said, not beating about the bush. 'I don't believe we've met.'

'No.' Her voice was pleasant and had a faint North American intonation. Puzzling the conundrum of who she was and why she was there he waited for her to proffer her name. She didn't do so.

'And you are, Miss . . . Miss . . . ?'

Unfazed by his prompting, green eyes met his; green very different from the feline green of Rusty's eyes, green the colour of cool northern seas.

'I was a fan, Detective Chief Inspector,' she said, turning away from him, still not answering his question. She opened the door of the Aston Martin she had been

12

standing against, a black wool coat buttoned high to her throat. 'I'm sorry my presence has disconcerted you.'

Her unruffled composure sent a flare of anger through him. Who did she think she was talking to? A bobby on the beat? Deep in his pockets his hands tightened. By the end of the day he'd know all he needed to about her – and more.

'I didn't have you marked down as a gangster groupie,' he said acidly.

She turned the key in the ignition and the Aston snarled into life. 'No.' Her eyes met his. 'But then, you didn't have me marked down at all, did you, Detective Chief Inspector?'

There was something in her eyes that, for all his years of experience, he couldn't quite decipher; something that was smothered almost instantly. What had it been? Triumph? Amusement? Or another emotion entirely – an emotion not far removed from pity?

As she drove off at a speed blatantly exceeding the limit allowed in crematorium grounds, he walked over to his Wolseley, reaching through the open window for his radio hand-set. 'I want twenty-four-hour surveillance on the girl driving the Aston Martin, licence number MUW 639S, now heading towards the east exit,' he said into it tersely. 'Have you got that? Let me know the name the car is registered in the minute it comes through, and for Christ's sake don't stint on the numbers covering the girl. This is top priority, OK?'

Other cars, thick and fast, were now beginning to leave the crematorium grounds. He felt a tightness in his chest that scared the living daylights out of him. If it had indeed been pity he had glimpsed in the mystery girl's eyes, it had been pity well directed. What the hell was he going to do with himself now that Bryce was dead and Frankie Briscoe was banged up for what was likely to be the rest of his natural? It was a question he couldn't answer and,

13

stepping off the gravel to stand under the shade of a tree, he watched morosely as the South London element piled into the fleet of cars that would take them to the pub where the funeral booze-up was to be held.

On the other side of the chapel's concourse a still weeping Sandra was being helped by a local publican into the passenger-seat of a Ford Granada. Rusty, accompanied by the living legend who had helped rob the Glasgow to Euston mail train, was walking across to a Mark-II Lotus Cortina. Nina, hidden from view behind the smoke-tinted windows of her black stretch-limousine, was long gone. Soon, only Victor remained.

There was a slight breeze now and the sickly sweet scent of the scores and scores of floral tributes was almost overpowering. He turned up the collar of his Burberry. This was it, then. This was when he said his last goodbye and walked away to his car.

For the next few seconds he stood very still and then, as he looked towards the crematorium chimneys, his expression changed and a pulse began to pound at the corner of his jaw. It was his imagination, of course – it had to be – but he could hear familiar laughter. Bryce's laughter. And the bastard wasn't laughing with him. He was laughing at him.

# Chapter One

*June 1945*

'*K-i-ll*!' Bryce Reece hollered as, with a gang of mates pounding in his wake, he raced down Swan Row hard on the heels of his arch enemy Frankie Briscoe and the mob of younger brothers and cousins Frankie led.

Wearing a holey jumper, short shabby pants and battered plimsolls, he held a bayonet high above his head as he ran. Scavenged from the local ammunition dump it was his pride and joy; impaled upon it, streaming in the breeze like a captured enemy flag, were a pair of bloomers nicked from Roy Clarkson's mother's washing line.

'*K-i-ll*!' he yelled again as he veered out of the bottom end of Swan Row, leading his triumphantly whooping cohorts down the narrow cobbled street the Briscoe mob had raced pell-mell into.

'*They're 'eading fer the bomb site, Bryce*!' Victor Roberts, nine years old and six months his senior, yelled from immediately behind him.

Running down the centre of the road, uncaring of the intermittent traffic, Bryce didn't waste his breath in replying. He knew very well where Frankie Briscoe and his gang were heading and he wanted to catch up with them before they reached it. Having taken the time and trouble to waylay them when they weren't armed to the teeth, which had been as they were leaving the local baths with only damp towels and swimming trunks tucked under their arms, he didn't want them arming themselves with bomb-site rubble. His own gang, following his example,

15

were pretty dirty fighters, gouging eyes and using their feet with the same enthusiasm as they used their fists, but they weren't dirty fighters on the level that the Briscoes were.

With the Briscoes, carrying weapons was a family tradition. One of Frankie's older brothers was in the nick for slashing a man with a razor in a pub fight, and one of his uncles was doing time for manslaughter. Frankie carried half a cricket stump with him nearly everywhere he went, while his younger brothers and cousins were just as bad; billiard cues, chair legs, bicycle chains, home-made knuckle-dusters – if it meant winning a fight then they used it.

Not this time, though. *'If we cut through the butcher's we'll be able to come at them from the front before they get to the bomb site!'* he shouted back to Victor.

His second-in-command grinned and, as Bryce let out a blood-curdling war whoop that would have done a Zulu proud, followed unhesitatingly with the rest of the gang as he led them in a sharp right across the oncoming traffic. A bread delivery van screeched to an emergency stop to avoid them. A motorbike and sidecar slewed into the kerb. Other motorists cursed in their wake as the boys tore on, regardless.

*'Ch-a-a-a-rge!'* Bryce bellowed as, leading from the front as always, he took advantage of Tucker & Bros' ever-open door and stormed into the sawdust-floored shop, his eight-strong gang hard behind him.

'Clear off! Get out!' Old Man Tucker roared, brandishing a meat cleaver from behind the safety of his butcher's block as his half-dozen customers, ration-books in hand, surged against his counter so as not to be trampled underfoot.

*'Ch-a-a-a-rge!'* Bryce bellowed again, making a beeline for the door at the rear of the shop that led out into a delivery yard, pretending, as he did so, that he and his troops were in Italy, storming Monte Cassino.

16

'I've broken two eggs thanks to you, Bryce Reece!' Hilda Clarkson screeched after him as she failed to get out of the way in time and her net shopping bag began dripping smashed yolks. 'You wait till I tell your mother!'

'Will yer tell 'er 'e's using your knickers fer a flag?' little Georgie Craven queried breathlessly as he sprinted past her, bringing up the gang's rear.

Hilda Clarkson's scream of outrage could have been heard in the Old Kent Road but Bryce and his gang were uncaring. Desperate to cut off the Briscoes before they reached the rubbled haven of the bomb site, they were clearing Old Man Tucker's delivery yard fence with a mixture of front vaults, back vaults and good old-fashioned dives.

'Bloody hooligans!' Harold Tucker raged, emerging from behind his butcher's block to stand in the back doorway, shaking his fist after them as they cleared his property. 'I know every last one of you and I've got your cards marked!'

He had, too. Bryce Reece was from number 6 Swan Row. Victor Roberts from number 10. Curly Craven – whose blond hair was as straight as a die – and Curly's younger brother, George, were from number 20. Billy Dixon's mother owned Swan Row's corner shop. Gunter Nowakowska was a Polish airman's offspring, and the Wilkinson brothers, Robert, Richard and Jack, were the local milkman's boys. Apart from the Polish kid's dad, who'd lost a leg when shot down in the Battle of Britain, and Stan Wilkinson, the boy's dads had either been killed in the war or were awaiting demob. He'd make sure their mothers knew about their hooligan-like behaviour, though, and he'd make sure their mothers gave them a good larruping – they'd have to, because if they didn't they'd never get black-market meat off him again.

As Bryce pounded towards the junction where his gang would hopefully take the Briscoes by surprise, he held up his free hand to indicate there were to be no more war whoops. If the Briscoes heard them and cottoned on that they were running into an ambush they'd hare off in another direction and the whole exercise would be pointless.

The Briscoes, who had a stash of weapons hidden in one of the bomb site's many derelict cellars, were too intent on reaching their cache to take on board the fact that Bryce and his gang were no longer behind them. They were all wearing boots and the clatter as they pounded the cobbles masked the sound of the plimsolled feet fast approaching on the far side of the blind corner.

If Bryce and his gang had been lying in wait for them all along, the timing couldn't have been more perfect. Heedlessly and at full pelt Frankie led his younger brothers and cousins in a charge out of one street into another. As they did so, and without losing a second's momentum, Bryce and his cohorts raced smack into them.

'*What the bleedin' fuck*?!' Frankie roared in the brief moment before Bryce's fist slammed into his mouth and the blood spurted.

For the first time ever in an encounter with the Briscoes, Bryce's gang had the advantage and they seized it ruthlessly.

The fight between Frankie and Bryce was personal and as they began to slog it out, fists and feet flying, no one barged in on it. Victor took on Ginger Briscoe, whose dad was in the nick for manslaughter. Both were tall for their age, and fearless scrappers. Bone connected with bone; flesh split flesh. Gobbing blood from a split lip, Ginger desperately tried to knock Victor to the ground. Victor, knowing full well the battering he would then receive from Ginger's booted feet, dodged and lunged and stayed resolutely upright.

Ginger's brother, Terry, tried to give Curly Craven a whack but Curly stepped aside and got one in first. Terry

18

went skidding backwards into the road and Curly did a rugby flying tackle on top of him. It wasn't a particularly pleasant experience because, like all the Briscoes, Terry stank to high heaven, but Curly had perfected the art of breathing only through his mouth when engaged in such close combat.

His little brother Georgie was putting his lack of inches to good use. Fearlessly he lit on Jimmy Briscoe who was much taller than him and, taking advantage of their difference in height, got good momentum as he leaped up, nutting Jimmy on the bridge of the nose. Jimmy howled, clapping his hands to his face, blood spattering between his fingers.

The Wilkinson boys weren't quite as fortunate as the Cravens. The Briscoes' swimming trunks and towels had gone flying every which way and, as the brawl spilled into the narrow road, Richard Wilkinson had tripped over one of the sodden bundles and gone crashing down into the gutter, a pile of kicking and gouging Briscoes on top of him.

His older brother, Robert, and his younger brother, Jack, did their best to come to his aid, but those Briscoes not being beaten to pulp by Bryce and Victor and the Cravens weren't having any of it.

'Smash 'is 'ead in!' Tommy Briscoe, the smallest of the clan, exhorted from the periphery of the fight as his brothers and cousins pulverised the living daylights out of the vainly struggling Richard.

A fortunate combination of events saved Joan Wilkinson's favourite son from being battered senseless. Ducking and diving through the mêlée, Billy Dixon and Gunter Nowakowska launched themselves like terriers on to Richard's attackers. Together with Robert and Jack, eye gouging and biting and kicking, they forced Richard's attackers to cease beating the shit out of him and, instead, to begin pitching into them.

19

Bryce, meanwhile, had landed a punch to the gut that had winded Frankie so badly he was rolling over and over on the cobbles in a curled ball, unable to fight on. It was an affliction several other participants in the brawl were also beginning to suffer from.

'*Bastard*!' Frankie gasped, still clutching his stomach and making no attempt at further retaliation.

'*Squint-eyed fucker*,' Bryce rejoined, sitting on the kerb as a meat van trundled down the street between them, dragging air into his own lungs only with the greatest difficulty.

'Our Frankie's got a cast, not a squint!' Tommy Briscoe yelled at him indignantly from a safe distance. 'An' when our dad 'ears what you've called our Frankie, 'e'll do fer your dad, Bryce bloody Reece, just you see if 'e don't!'

Ignoring him, resting his arms on his splayed knees, hands hanging limply, Bryce said wearily to the still prone Frankie: 'Say you're sorry about the cat.'

'Are you sixpence short of a shilling? The cat was bleedin' *dead*.'

With their respective leaders no longer going at it hammer and tongs the fight was obviously over. Even the Briscoe/Wilkinson faction had lost impetus, flopping down in two separate camps at either side of the narrow road to nurse their wounds and get their breath back.

'I know the cat was bleedin' dead,' Bryce said through gritted teeth. 'Mr Wilkinson accidentally ran over it with his milk lorry. The point is, my gang had it first. It was *our* dead cat and you nicked it.'

Frankie painfully hauled himself into a sitting position. 'If yer want a dead bleedin' cat I'll get yer a dead bleedin' cat,' he said belligerently. 'But yer can't 'ave the one we nicked. It's fallen apart.'

Bryce's eyes narrowed. A cat killed accidentally was one thing. A cat killed on purpose quite another.

'You needn't bother,' he said, his elbows sticking out

of the holes in his jumper. 'Just say you're sorry for raiding us.'

'Bollocks.' Frankie bullishly spat out a bit of broken tooth and a gobbet of blood. 'I ain't apologising ter no one for nuffink, not ever – and I 'specially ain't apologising ter *you*. Me dad would skin me alive.'

Things were beginning to look distinctly dodgy again and there was a subtle flexing of muscles amongst the Briscoe camp. Bryce's gang looked uneasily at each other. Were they all going to be up and at it again in another moment? The mere thought had Richard Wilkinson, more battle sore than a straightforward street fight warranted, looking white about the gills.

The gang leaders eyeballed each other, Bryce still squatting on the kerb edge, his feet in the gutter, Frankie several yards away from him in the road, his arms hugging grazed and filthy knees.

'Your dad would 'ave to come home first if 'e was going to skin you alive,' Bryce said tauntingly. ''Ow long has 'e bin on the run from the army? Three years? Four?'

On either side of the street, feet began to shift. They were all knackered and ready for home but another brawl was clearly on the cards.

From beneath glowering brows Frankie continued to hold eye contact with Bryce. A gobbet of phlegm followed the gobbet of blood, this time travelling a quite remarkable distance in Bryce's direction.

'Our dad thought it was more important to feed us kids than ter fight the Germans,' he said, repeating the line his mother always took whenever her husband's absence from home and army was derogatorily commented on by her neighbours. 'So that makes 'im a better dad than all your poxy dads put together.'

There was a glint in Bryce's eyes that Frankie would have done well to have heeded. Seeing it and recognising what it portended Victor tensed his muscles, ready

21

to spring once more into violent action. Curly Craven, remembering rule number one – always hit first – did the same.

'Yer reckon that, do yer?' Bryce's tone of voice was dangerously affable. 'Yer reckon 'e's better than Billy's dad who was one of Monty's Desert Rats and died fighting the Krauts in North Africa? Yer reckon 'e's better than Gunter's dad who flew a Spitfire in the Battle of Britain an' who carves animals and birds from blocks of wood?'

The bayonet, still flaunting Hilda Clarkson's now torn and grubby bloomers for a flag, was laid flat on the ground beside him. As if doing so absentmindedly, not moving from his slumped sitting position, his fingers curled around it.

'Or the Cravens' dad,' he continued as if genuinely perplexed. 'Yer reckon 'e's a better dad than a bloke who's spent nearly all the war in a submarine being chased and torpedoed in the North Atlantic?'

'Don't come all that heroic shit with me,' Frankie scoffed. 'Those thickos in the army and navy are just workin' for guvnors, for officers wiv posh accents. Our dad would rather be dead than 'ave a guvnor bossing 'im about. *No one* tells our old man what ter do. Not even Winston bleedin' Churchill.'

'Christmas!' freckle-faced Billy Dixon said devoutly from where he was standing on the pavement, a foot or so behind Bryce. 'If everyone thought like 'im the whole bloody country would be in German slave camps by now.'

Coming from Billy it was a surprisingly valid comment but Bryce didn't pursue it. Instead he said in the same deceptively casual manner, 'And my dad, Frankie? Do yer reckon my dad's a thicko?'

Still with his arms hugging his knees Frankie rocked backwards, cracking with laughter. 'Your dad, Bryce? Your dad's a commando! That means 'e ain't just thick – he's bleedin' brainless!'

22

Frankie wasn't completely stupid. He knew his goading would provoke retaliation and, now he'd got his breath back, believed himself to be ready for it. What he wasn't ready for, though, was a near-death experience.

The bayonet seemed to come out of nowhere at him. Bryce hadn't even leapt to his feet in order to throw it.

'*Bleedin*' *Christ*!' Frankie shouted, throwing himself sideways as the savagely hurled weapon sliced through the air towards him. '*Yer a fuckin*' *lunatic*! *Yer fuckin*' *divvy*!'

The bayonet impaled itself spear-like between the cobbles in the exact spot where, till a brief second ago, his crotch had been, wobbled uncertainly and then clattered to the ground.

White-faced, Frankie scrambled to his feet. '*This is war, Bryce Reece*!' he yelled, backing away, his voice cracking with the force of the shock he had received. '*This is all-out, total, and annihilating WAR*!'

From where he was still seated on the kerb Bryce shot his enemy a face-splitting grin. 'It's a war you'll never win, Frankie! You ain't got the brains! And that ain't a cast in your eye – it's a soddin' ugly squint!'

'So there it is,' he said later that day to his little acolyte, seven-year-old Sandra Parry, 'my gang's at war with the Briscoe gang. That means no other gang will even dare to have a go at us. It means we're the business. Get it?'

'Not really, Bry.' Sandra hitched herself into a slightly more comfortable position. They were sitting astride a branch in the only tree Swan Row possessed, and it wasn't easy. 'I mean, the Briscoes *hurt* people, don't they? Why are you so pleased their gang is out to get yours when it means they'll always be trying to hurt you? It doesn't make sense to me.'

Bryce sighed heavily. Sandra's drawback as an admirer

23

was her sex. No boy would have seen the situation so negatively.

'Bein' a tough gang is what bein' a gang is all about,' he said patiently as Tigger, Sandra's little dog, yapped at them from the ground, anxious for their company. 'If we've got the Briscoes runnin' so scared they've declared war on us, it means we're a gang to be reckoned with. Understand?'

Sandra wanted to understand. Having Bryce as her best friend was very important to her. None of the other girls in her class had a boy for a best friend. 'W-e-ll,' she said, trying to think of a response that would please him, 'if it's what you want Bry, then I s'ppose it's good, isn't it?'

'Yeah.' As the conversation was obviously going nowhere Bryce did what he always did when things were unsatisfactory; he cut his losses. 'Me dad'll be 'ome soon,' he said, his eyes lighting up, his grubby face shining with fierce anticipation. 'Me muvver ain't 'eard from 'im fer a while, but Roy Clarkson's uncle is in the commandos, like me dad, and Mrs Clarkson told me muvver she's 'ad a letter from Roy's uncle sayin' he already 'as a date for 'is demob.'

As Tigger's yaps turned into yowls, Sandra sucked in her breath, her eyes rounding. 'Does that mean my dad will be home soon as well?' she asked, her tummy turning a giddy somersault. 'My mum hasn't said. Do you think she's keeping it secret as a special surprise?'

This time it was Bryce's turn to shift uncomfortably on the rough bark. 'Nah,' he said, not happy about sending her hopes crashing to the ground. 'Your dad's out in Burma, Sand. The war ain't over out there – the Japs 'aven't surrendered like the Germans 'ave. The Wilkinsons' dad says they probably won't surrender fer years and years.'

The radiant elation on Sandra's face vanished. 'That's . . . not fair.' Her eyes filled with tears as he had known they would and her bottom lip began to wobble. 'Your dad's

24

been home lots of times on leaves and my dad hasn't been home ever. If anyone's dad is coming home soon, it should be mine.'

As Tigger began vainly trying to climb the tree Bryce sighed and pushed a tumbled fall of dark hair away from his eyes. Sandra couldn't remember ever seeing her dad, he'd been away fighting in the war for so long. There was a framed photograph of him, of course, on the Parry's sideboard, but unlike the photograph of his father that his mother had on their sideboard Sandra's dad's face was blurred and indistinct and it was hard to tell what he really looked like.

'Victor's dad is with the 14th Army as well,' he said, trying to make her feel not so left out. 'I 'spect when the war with the Japs is over his dad an' yours will come 'ome together.'

Sandra wiped her tears away on her cardigan sleeve. 'Yes. I suppose.' With great effort she forced a gap-toothed smile. 'At least your dad'll be home and that'll make your mum happy.'

Sandra liked Bryce's mum. Nell Reece was her mum's best friend and, though she wasn't her real auntie, Sandra called her Auntie Nell. The friendship between their mums had been forged when they'd both been evacuated to the same Somerset village in the early days of the war.

She could remember nothing about the experience but Bryce had told her it had been horrible. The farmer they had been billeted on hadn't wanted them and the quiet of the countryside had nearly sent his mum demented. The minute they'd been able to they'd all returned to London. Even when the Blitz was at its height and she and her mum had been bombed out of their Islington home, they hadn't returned to Somerset. Instead they had moved into Swan Row to be comfortingly near to Bryce and his mum.

From then on they had become almost like one family. 'Bryce will look after you while I go down the shops,' or

25

'Bryce will come and sit in with you while I pop out for five minutes,' her mum would say, and the responsibility had been one he had always taken seriously. When she had first started school he had taken her there and back each day, just as if she had been his little sister. During the last months of the war, when Hitler's V-I rockets had screamed down on London faster than the speed of sound, he'd helped her not to die of fright. Though she couldn't be a member of his gang – no gangs had girls in them – he was just as much her friend as he was Victor Roberts' or Billy Dixon's or Gunter Nowakowska's or the Wilkinsons' or the Cravens'.

A nearby bedroom window was rammed violently upwards on its sashes and Effie Craven, the Cravens' mum, leaned dangerously far out of it, her hands splayed on the windowsill in order that her beefy arms could take her weight. '*Shut that perishin' dog up before I slaughter it*!' she bellowed, her peroxide blonde hair scraped into metal curlers. '*If Hitler 'ad 'ad that thing as a secret weapon 'e'd have won the bleedin' war*!'

Bryce said a word his mother didn't know he knew and, grasping hold of the branch with both hands, swung himself down from it, dangling in mid-air for a second or so before dropping, parachute-landing fashion, to the pavement. Sandra took a slower but safer route, clambering arduously down the same way she had climbed up.

'I don't think I like Mrs Craven,' she said as her feet touched the ground and Tigger, a cross between a Yorkshire terrier and something that should have known better, bounded around her in frenzied delight. 'She told Billy Dixon's mum she thought my mum was stuck up.'

'That's 'cos your mum doesn't go in any of the local pubs an' she doesn't go up the West End the way Mrs Craven and Ginger Briscoe's mum do.'

'Do you mean when they go out of a night, swinging their handbags?' As she began walking with him down

26

Swan Row, towards their homes, her forehead was creased in perplexity. *There go Effie Craven and Ginger Briscoe's mother again, swinging their handbags*, her mother would say in a very odd tone of voice whenever she saw them dolled up to the nines setting off for a night out in the West End.

It was an expression Sandra couldn't for the life of her understand because Mrs Craven and Mrs Briscoe always had clutch bags tucked beneath their arms; they could wave them – though Sandra couldn't imagine why they would want to – but you couldn't swing them.

'Yeah. I s'ppose.' Bryce was deliberately off-hand. Ginger Briscoe's mum was a prossy and, ever since her husband had been drafted into the Merchant Navy, Effie Craven had been earning money the same way. Aware that Sandra hadn't a clue as to what prostitution entailed, and having only a hazy idea himself, Bryce changed the subject. 'I'm goin' down the bomb site to look for shrapnel,' he said, tearing Hilda Clarkson's tattered bloomers from the point of his bayonet and stuffing them in his pocket. 'D'yer want to come?'

There were other things Sandra would have enjoyed doing more but she didn't say so. An unspoken condition of their friendship was that she happily fell in with all his suggestions.

'There won't be any new bomb sites now, will there?' she asked as she broke into a little run in order to keep up with him. 'Not now the war is over.'

'Nah.' It was an aspect of the peace that seriously disgusted him. He'd wanted the war to be over because it meant his dad would come home. What he hadn't wanted, though, was for life to become dull. Without the excitement of German bombers winging in over the Thames and V-1 rockets whistling down out of nowhere, that was exactly what it looked like becoming.

What was his gang going to do with no fresh bomb

sites to play on and to excavate for shrapnel? Even the ammunition dump he'd scavenged his bayonet from had closed down, which meant there'd be no more nicked jack-knives and German, English, American and Italian helmets.

For kids with brothers freshly demobbed or on their last leave, there were compensations: the returnees often brought back war souvenirs. The Cravens' older brother had come home with an American pistol and an Italian machine-gun, making Curly and Georgie the envy of Swan Row. The Briscoe clan was rumoured to have amassed quite an arsenal of such souvenirs and, as some of Frankie's uncles and cousins had yet to be demobbed, it was an arsenal that would, no doubt, grow even bigger.

Bryce, however, stood no such chance of adding to his weapon collection. He had no older brothers or cousins or uncles, and if his dad did bring any war souvenirs home he'd be sure to keep them safely under lock and key.

As they neared the bomb site, passing the place in the road where, such a short time ago, he had hurled his bayonet straight at Frankie Briscoe's crotch, his bad humour vanished. He would rather have his dad home, even if he didn't bring any weapons with him, than have a million trillion new bomb sites to scavenge.

'I always wonder if I'll find another little dog like Tigger when we're searching a bombed-out building,' Sandra said, breaking in on his thoughts as, with Tigger bounding happily in front of them, they began picking their way amongst the jagged shells of brickwork that had once been a pin-making factory.

'There'd been 'ouses on the site where you found Tigger,' Bryce said practically. 'I expect 'e used to live in one of 'em. There won't be the same chance of finding a dog on a factory bomb site, 'specially when it's an old bomb site.'

'There won't be much shrapnel now, either, will there?' By pointing this out to him Sandra was hopeful that he would soon give up on their present search. Shrapnel wasn't only dirty and dangerous; it was also heavy and cumbersome to carry. It didn't matter too much for Bryce. His short pants were always in a fairly filthy condition and had been patched so often there was hardly any of the original material left in them. Her mother, however, wasn't the usual run of Swan Row mum, being very particular about neatness and cleanliness. If she went home with a torn and dirty dress her mum would be very upset.

'I want to get down to the cellars,' Bryce said, well aware they'd be lucky to find shrapnel on a site his gang and the Briscoe gang had gleaned so often. 'The Briscoes 'ave a secret stash of weapons 'ere somewhere.' He negotiated a pyramid-like mound of rubble and slithered down the far side of it on his backside. There came the ominous sound of material ripping.

Sandra, who had kept up with him so far only with great difficulty, made no attempt to follow him further. There would be spiders in the cellars and, even worse, rats.

'Come here, Tigger,' she said protectively, unaware that it was Tigger's presence, where the rats were concerned, that Bryce was counting on.

'Yorkshire terriers were bred for ratting, Sand.' There was exasperation in Bryce's voice as he so clearly read her mind. If Sandra was going to prevent Tigger from going with him into the cellars then he might as well not have come. He stood at the top of a flight of broken steps, looking down into dingy dankness. The factory bomb site's rats were notoriously large – which was one reason why he and his gang had never done a proper recce of the cellars. The sign which had warned DANGER! KEEP OUT, was, thanks to his own gang, long gone, as was the protective barbed wire the ARP wardens had thrown across the top of the steps in the days immediately after the factory's destruction.

He wondered what the chances were of being able to come back on his own with Tigger, and knew they were slim. Sandra had found Tigger whimpering with fear amid the ruins of a still smoking bombed-out house and the two had been inseparable ever since.

'Let Tigger come wiv me fer ten minutes, Sand,' he said, careful to keep his voice nonchalant, knowing from American gangster films that gang leaders *never* asked but only gave instantly obeyed commands.

'I'd rather not, Bry.' Sandra was squatting on the pyramid of rubble beside Tigger. Her arms tightened around his neck. 'I think Tigger might be frightened of the dark and . . .'

*'Bryce! Bryce! You've got to go 'ome quick! There's a bloke in army gear at your 'ouse an' I fink it's yer dad!'* Billy Dixon hurtled towards them, slipping and sliding on the rubble. *'He ain't got a kitbag wiv 'im, but 'e's wearing a commando's beret an' . . .'*

Bryce didn't wait for him to finish. He spun away from the steps so swiftly a couple of shattered bricks toppled and went clattering downwards. 'Me dad's 'ome!' With shining eyes he scrambled back up the mound of broken masonry towards Sandra and Tigger, his face blazing with happiness. 'Mrs Clarkson said 'e'd be 'ome soon, Sand, and 'e's 'ome now! Fer good!'

Even though it was hard to move at speed on the bomb site he began to run. Leaping and slithering, he'd cleared the rubble and was on the cobbles of the road before Sandra had even begun to follow him and certainly before Billy had got his breath back.

Never in his life had he run so fast. With his heart bursting in joyous anticipation he raced down one narrow street and then another. *'Me dad's 'ome, Mr Tucker!'* he shouted at the top of his voice as he sprinted past Mr Tucker's shop. *'Me dad's 'ome an' e's 'ome fer good!'*

Round the corner and into Swan Row he raced, running,

running, running. Whenever his dad had come home on leave he'd always taken Bryce everywhere with him. 'You and me are mates, Bry,' his dad would say, his electric-blue eyes laughing down at him. 'Where shall we go today? Do you fancy the football? Millwall are playing at home. Or we could spend the day on the Thames, maybe take a steamer down to Southend. Or do you want me to teach you a bit of unarmed combat?'

Wherever it was they had gone, and whatever it was they had done, it had always been fun – the best fun in the world. And now his dad was going to be home for always and always and he was so happy he felt as if was going to burst.

'*Me dad's 'ome*!' he shouted as he careened past Gunter Nowakowska's house.

Next door, at number 20, Effie Craven again leaned out of her bedroom window. If Joe Reece was home she wanted a glimpse of him. Men in Swan Row were in short supply. Anton Nowakowska was tasty looking, but she couldn't quite bring herself to flirt with a bloke who didn't speak much English and only had one leg. Stan Wilkinson wasn't bad either, but where Stan was concerned the usual risqué jokes about milkmen didn't apply. Stan was a tediously faithful husband. Every woman she knew had tried it on with him at one time or another and the result had always been the same. Nix. Zilch. Nothing. Joe Reece didn't have a reputation as a philanderer, but that was probably only because he wasn't daft enough to get caught. He was certainly an accomplished flirt and, with his film star good looks and a physique hard-honed in the commandos, had no problem in getting plenty of practice.

'Tell your dad to come round for a cup of tea!' she shouted after Bryce. 'Tell 'im I've got something I want to give 'im!'

The coarse sexual innuendo was lost on Bryce. He pelted

31

past Ginger Briscoe's house and Victor's house, his heart pumping. Why wasn't his dad at the gate, looking for him? Why wasn't he out in the row where he could see him?

'*Dad*!' he shouted, as with wings on his heels he flew past the Parry's gateway. '*Welcome 'ome, Dad*!'

Catching hold of the gatepost he swung himself round and on to the short path leading to his front door. The door was open. The man in the narrow hallway beyond it was in army uniform and was wearing a commando's beret, but it wasn't his father. His mother was staring dazedly at the man, her face chalk white.

Bewildered, hardly able to breathe with disappointment, Bryce floundered to a halt. Neither the man nor his mother looked towards him.

'I'm so sorry, Mrs Reece,' the man was saying, every line of his body betraying desperate awkwardness. 'Joe didn't want you informed of his injuries – it was a stray bullet in the last week of the war and it wasn't obviously critical. He was confident he could be back on his feet in a few weeks without you being any the wiser. As it is . . .' He lifted broad shoulders, the gesture speaking volumes.

'Where's me dad, mister?' The blood was drumming in Bryce's ears and his voice had a strange cracked sound to it. 'Is 'e in the 'ospital? When is 'e coming 'ome?'

His mother was still staring in disbelief at the uniformed stranger, a hand pressed hard against her heart, her lips as bloodless as her face.

Wishing himself anywhere but here, the man turned and, his discomfiture now almost crippling, looked towards Bryce.

'I'm sorry, son,' he said inadequately, wishing he'd never taken it on himself to break the news personally; wishing to God someone had told him Reece had a nipper. 'It was pneumonia. Coming on top of the bullet wound to his chest there was nothing that could be done.'

Looking into eyes the same vivid blue Joe's had been, he

realised that he was going to have to be much more specific if he was going to be understood. 'Your dad's dead, son,' he said gently, cursing himself for not having had the foresight to ensure a neighbour was on hand. Strong cups of tea were obviously going to be needed all round.

'I don't believe you.' In his holey jumper and short shabby pants Bryce stood on the pathway, staring at the man in the doorway of his home; the man who was wearing the same distinctive uniform his dad wore; the man who was standing where his dad should have been. 'I don't believe you,' he said again, his face bone-white and pinched, the ground shelving at his feet, the world yawning into an abyss all around him. '*I don't believe you*!'

He launched himself at the man, pummelling him with his fists, kicking him, tears streaming down his face. '*I don't believe you*! *I don't believe you*! I DON'T BELIEVE YOU!'

# Chapter Two

## December 1945

'Sandra's dad ain't goin' to be 'ome fer Christmas,' Bryce said to his mother as she unenthusiastically dragged a dusty fake Christmas tree from the top shelf of their lumber cupboard. 'It's because there ain't enough ships to bring 'ome blokes still waitin' fer demob in India and Ceylon and Singapore an' Sandra's dad is in Singapore.' His voice was flat and queerly abrupt, just as it always was now.

Nell Reece stood the Christmas tree on the floor and then reached upwards once again, this time pulling a cardboard box of newspaper-wrapped Christmas decorations to the front of the shelf.

She already knew Len Parry was not going to be demobbed until the New Year and was sorry for Sheila and for Sandra – or as sorry for them as it was possible to be. Now that the war with Japan was over Len Parry would return home eventually. Her Joe never would. For her and Bryce there was nothing to look forward to.

She stood very still, her hands on the box, fighting for composure. For Bryce's sake she couldn't keep breaking down, sobbing uncontrollably. It wasn't fair to him. He was only nine years old and he had his own grief to cope with. She felt herself beginning to shake and her hands tightened on the box of decorations. She had to go through the motions of living even if she was frozen and dead inside. It would be Christmas in a few days' time. Bryce, she knew, didn't want to celebrate it any more than she did, but if they forced themselves to go through the family rituals – putting the tree up and going to the Sally Army carol service – perhaps they would, somehow, survive it.

Blinking back the tears that were burning her eyes, she finally lifted the box from the shelf. 'What d'you say we invite Sandra and her mum round here for Christmas dinner?' she asked, her heart twisting in her chest at the sight of his pale, tense face.

'If yer like.' He didn't care who came round. It wasn't going to be a proper Christmas dinner. How could it be, when his dad wouldn't be having it with them?

His mum still had the box of decorations in her arms and he couldn't bear the sight of it any longer. He didn't want a Christmas tree in the house. Christmas trees were for when everything was normal and happy and for when, if families weren't together, they were at least looking forward to the day when they would be.

'I don't want the bleedin' tree up,' he said fiercely, struggling hard not to cry. 'An' I don't want no bleedin' Christmas cards up neither!'

It was the first time he'd ever sworn when talking to his mum and he'd no intention of staying around to see her reaction. Turning on his heel so fast he stumbled, he ran from the room.

'Bryce! *Bryce!*'

Though he heard her throw the decoration box swiftly to one side he didn't pause. With his chest so tight he was fighting for air, he raced out of the house and into the street. It was a mild day for December. A weak sun glinted on the cobbles and a petrol slick, left by Stan Wilkinson's milk lorry, gleamed on them with rainbow iridescence. Ignoring it, and for once not armed with his bayonet, he raced blindly down the row, heading towards the Thames. He wasn't the only kid whose dad was dead but he felt as if he were.

35

Billy Dixon's dad had been dead since 1942 and it didn't seem to bother Billy at all, but Mr Dixon had never been Billy's best mate. He'd never taken him fishing nor played football with him nor taught him the tricks of unarmed combat. The dads of half a dozen of the kids in his class at school were also dead, but nothing they'd ever said had indicated that their dads had been even remotely as special as his had been.

What made it even worse to bear about his dad being dead was that the Cravens' dad and Victor's dad were back home. Even a good half dozen Briscoes were home. Not Ginger's dad, of course. Ginger's dad was in the nick and not likely to be set free this side of the next twenty years. Jimmy Briscoe's dad had come home, though, and so had two of Frankie's older brothers and his aunt's husband and a smattering of other Briscoes whose relationship to Frankie he'd never quite been able to work out.

'The row is being swamped with 'em,' he'd overheard Mrs Dixon saying disgustedly to his mum when he'd gone to the Dixon's corner shop with her. 'Chas Briscoe wasn't home a week before the police were round, battering on his door at five o'clock in the morning. God knows what he'd been up to. Thieving, I expect.'

Bryce had listened with interest. Big Chas was Jimmy Briscoe's dad and Frankie's uncle. A great bruiser of a man, whenever he walked down Swan Row's narrow pavement he seemed to fill it.

'And have you heard about the ruckus last night outside The Turk's Head?' she had continued, ticking items off Nell's shopping list and packing them into a cardboard box. 'Old Jug Ears must have made a flying visit home and the whole bleedin' family went out on a binge.'

'Jug Ears' was Frankie's dad's nickname. Bryce's interest sharpened.

'When they fell out of the pub at closing time they did

36

what they've always done when they've had a skinful,' Lilian Dixon had continued, wedging a tin of Spam in the box next to a can of sardines. 'They picked a fight with some poor bastards and when the police trolled along to break it up, Jug Ears did a runner over the Cravens' back fence.' She finished packing the box and pushed it across the counter towards Bryce, adding musingly as she handed Nell her ration-book back, 'I wonder how much longer Jug Ears Briscoe is going to be on the run from the army, now that the war is over.'

'I don't know, Lil,' his mother had said as he'd picked up the box of groceries in order to carry it home for her. 'It's a funny offence, desertion. Once you become a deserter, you're always a deserter – or you are unless you receive an amnesty from the King, and I can't see King George goin' out of his way to do that for Jug Ears, can you?'

Lilian Dixon had cackled with laughter and even his mum had given a ghost of a smile.

Bryce raced down the street that opened out on to the Thames and floundered breathlessly to a halt. He, too, didn't think it very likely that the King would give Frankie's dad an amnesty for running away instead of fighting the Germans and the Eyeties and the Japs like other blokes had done.

He sucked his teeth, looking out over the broad grey glitter of the Thames. Thinking about the Briscoes helped him to stop thinking about his dad. It was about time he and his gang had another major fight with them. With their older brothers and cousins now home, Frankie's gang was getting far too big for its boots and needed taking down a peg or two.

He mooched across to the embankment wall and leant against it, his arms resting on the cold stone as he stared down into deep tidal water. A major fight couldn't be undertaken without his gang being tooled up in one way or another. Since he'd so nearly had his private parts bayoneted, Frankie didn't go anywhere without his knuckleduster.

His eyes narrowed as he wondered how he could make a similar weapon. What he needed were several big steel nuts. If the threads could be filed down on the inside and then welded together, he'd have a knuckle-duster the equal of anything Frankie had. He'd have to find someone to do the welding for him, though.

A chill wind blew off the river but he didn't feel it. Since hearing the news that his dad was dead he didn't really feel anything anymore. Thoughts of his dad once again filled his head and he slammed down hard on them. He'd think about Frankie Briscoe's gang instead. He'd think about how he and his gang were going to put the Briscoe mob in their place.

'It was nice of you to go to such trouble for me and Sandra,' Sheila Parry said as she stood beside Nell at the sink in Nell's scullery, a tea towel in her hand. 'Especially under the circumstances.' She paused awkwardly as Nell plunged another lot of plates beneath water she had heated in a kettle. 'I mean . . . you can't have wanted to celebrate Christmas at all, not when . . . not seeing as how . . .'

'Not with my Joe dead,' Nell finished for her bleakly. With her hands still plunged deep in the hot water she arched her back, trying to relieve the constant ache she felt in it. 'You don't 'ave to be careful not to mention Joe's name, Sheila. And you don't 'ave to avoid talking about your Len coming 'ome in the New Year. I'm 'appy for you, girl. It wouldn't do if we were both war widows, would it?'

She turned to look her friend in the eye and to reassure her, but Sheila's eyes didn't meet hers. Instead she had dropped her head and was intently studying the frayed edge of the tea towel.

Nell chewed the corner of her lip, a slight frown furrowing her brow. There were times when she couldn't make her friend out at all. With her careful speech and excessive neatness Sheila stuck out like a sore thumb in Swan Row.

'Doesn't drink, doesn't smoke, doesn't swear. Doesn't ever give anyone the eye – not even the GIs that lodged fer a while at the Clarksons,' Effie Craven had been heard to say disparagingly. 'If that ain't bein' stuck up, I don't know what bleedin' is!'

Sheila still didn't raise her head and Nell resumed washing up the Christmas dinner pots and pans, her frown deepening. Unlike anyone else she knew, Sheila had been a grammar-school girl and that, of course, explained why she didn't speak with a South London accent. She hadn't stayed on at grammar school long enough to matriculate, though. Instead of going to a college or a university she had fallen in love with Len Parry and, only sixteen years old, had eloped with him.

Nell attacked the roasting tin she had cooked the black-market chicken in, scouring it fiercely. Sheila was only twenty-five years old now and, as she herself was thirty-four, she often felt almost maternal towards her. Partly this was due to Sheila's slight build and pale skin and fair hair. There were days – and this was one of them – when she looked as if a puff of wind would blow her over. It was a fragility emphasised by her quiet, diffident manner.

'D'yer think your Len will take to living in Bermondsey?' she asked, handing Sheila the roasting tin to dry and plunging the pan she'd cooked the spuds in under the few soapsuds remaining. 'He ain't never lived this side of the river, has he?'

Sheila shook her head and then, as Nell waited expectantly for a more expansive response, said in a voice curiously devoid of expression: 'No. Until Sandra and me were bombed out we'd only ever lived in Islington.'

As she was talking she was drying the roasting tin with such meticulous care Nell had to fight the urge to snatch it from her hands. Why couldn't Sheila talk properly about her hubby? Getting information from her about him was like getting blood out of a stone. 'What was Len's job before the war?' she had once asked, expecting her to say he'd been a craftsman of some sort, for Sheila definitely appeared used to a better standard of living than that found in Swan Row.

When Sheila had told her that Len had been a riveter for a while, and then a docker, Nell had hidden her surprise and then, when Sheila never mentioned her parents or other family members, had concluded it was because her new friend had married a bit beneath herself and her family weren't too happy about it.

Like her son, Nell didn't see the sense in pursuing a conversation if it was going nowhere. Pulling the plug and, as the water ran out, vigorously wiping the sink down with her washing-up cloth, she said, changing the subject: 'P'raps when your Len gets home he'll help me keep an eye on my Bryce. He's running wild at the moment, Sheil. I'm getting complaints about him from everywhere. Old Man Tucker says Bryce and his mates are nothing but hooligans and that it's Bryce who's the ringleader, and Hilda Clarkson says the next time he nicks anything from her washing line she's going to go to the cozzers about it.'

Sheila wiped the roast potato tin dry, a rare smile touching her mouth. 'The police aren't going to spend their time worrying about items missing from Mrs Clarkson's washing line, Nell, not when they have the Briscoes to contend with.' Her smile faded, her eyes darkening with anxiety. 'Have you heard the rumours about the guns that they have stashed away? Mr Roberts says they must have enough to arm a battalion by now. Why don't the police do something about it? Why don't they search all the Briscoe homes and confiscate the guns they've hidden away?'

'I 'spect they've tried and ain't found nothing.' Nell took a packet of Park Drive out of her apron pocket and lit one up. 'They won't 'ave 'em hidden anywhere obvious, Sheil. They're a crafty lot and always 'ave been. I remember years ago, in 1936 when a Briscoe robbed a Barclays Bank armed with a sawn-off shotgun. He got put away for it but the money weren't never found.' She folded her arms and exhaled a thin plume of smoke. 'Bein' able to scrounge weapons in Europe must seem like paradise on earth to 'em. Other London villains will be busy doin' the same thing. Gawd knows what the next few years are going to be like in the East End and around here, Sheil. Chicago in the twenties, I shouldn't wonder.'

It was an alarming thought and as Sheila followed Nell back into the living-room in order that they could listen to the King's Christmas Day speech on the wireless, her face was tense and drawn.

What if, in a few years' time, Sandra became friendly with any of the Briscoe boys? Bad lots they might be, but by the time they were sixteen and seventeen they might be very good-looking bad lots. Mr Tucker had called Bryce a hooligan, but he wasn't a hooligan of Briscoe proportions. The Briscoes were dishonest through and through and the thought of her daughter consorting with any of them gave her nightmares.

Bryce was a street scrapper and a regular young tearaway but considering how his childhood had been spent, being bombed and blitzed for months on end, it was only to be expected. She remembered the time a block of flats in Jamaica Road had received a direct hit. Bodies, and parts of bodies, were still being found the next day and Bryce and his mates had helped to remove them. It wasn't surprising that, accustomed to such gory spectacles and knowing nothing other than the violence of being at war, Bryce and his friends spent all their time play-acting their own mini wars and battles.

The main thing, however, was that Bryce's scrapes never involved thievery. Like his mum he didn't have a dishonest streak in him and she would be more than pleased if, when they grew older, Bryce and Sandra's friendship developed into something more romantic.

She sat down in one of the two shabby armchairs gracing the living-room, wishing she could confide her other worries to Nell; fretting, above all, about what was going to happen when Len came home; wondering how on earth she was going to cope; wondering, in a sudden, almost paralysing surge of panic, if she would even survive.


'First we're goin' to do a runner through the market, nicking what we can,' Frankie said to his brothers and his cousins as he sat on his doorstep, polishing his latest trophy, a bone-handled hunting knife. 'Then we'll either find Reece and 'is mob and give 'em a good thrashing, or we'll bunk into the flicks.'

Even though they were family, no one demurred. Just as Jimmy's dad, Big Chas, called all the shots where their dads and uncles were concerned, Frankie called the shots amongst their own junior family gang.

'Yer know Old Man Tucker?' Ginger said suddenly and rhetorically to Frankie. 'D'yer know 'e keeps a cash float in the till overnight?'

Frankie hadn't and, as always when his interest was aroused, the cast in his right eye became more pronounced.

'D'yer know that for a fact, Ginge? Yer not just pulling me plonker?'

'Nah. He's done 'is back in and 'e asked if I'd like to earn a couple of bob on an evening, sweepin' up fer 'im and everything. I noticed it then. When 'e locks up, 'e always leaves 'is float money in the till. It saves 'im buggering about when 'e opens in the morning.'

Frankie sniggered. 'Then we'd better give 'im a little surprise, 'adn't we? Leave the fanlight catch off when you're next sweeping up fer 'im, Ginge. Tommy's little enough to wriggle through it. We'll hoist 'im up and give 'im a shove. It'll be easy-peasy.'

'Shall we pretend it's a big job? A bank job?' Tommy asked, his ferret-like little face alight with anticipation. 'We could black our faces up like commandos do . . .'

'And wear gloves,' his older brother Jimmy interrupted practically. 'Dad says only stupid twats go on jobs without wearing something on their 'ands.'

'What about the rifle, Frankie?' It was Tommy again. Being the runt of the family he wasn't often given a starring role. This time he had been and he was determined to make the most of it. 'Can I take the rifle wiv me?'

The rifle was a Lee Enfield .303 that had been brought back from Dunkirk by one of Frankie's older brothers. Frankie was forever cocking it and firing it cold. It had great sights – far better than any of the other rifles in the Briscoe family collection. Even in untrained hands they calibrated for hundreds of yards.

'Nah,' Frankie said derisively. He took a swig from a bottle of Tizer and then passed the bottle on to Jimmy. 'Yer can't climb through a fanlight with a bleedin' great rifle, silly sod.'

The others laughed with him, but though Ginger was laughing there was a speculative look in his eyes. 'He'd never be able to climb in with it, Frankie, but it'd be good fun if we went tooled up, wouldn't it?' he said, knowing Frankie would never take the liberty of rubbishing his suggestions the way he did Tommy's. 'It'd make it just like a commando raid or a big bank job. We could wear our balaclavas and wool gloves an' if we went in the middle of the night, no one'd see us.'

43

He cocked his head to one side. 'What d'yer reckon, our Frank? If word gets out about it to the other gangs it'll do our reputation no end of good.' His snub-nosed face was as dirty as Newgate's Knocker but, as always with Ginger, it was beguilingly persuasive.

'It wouldn't do no harm, Frank,' said Ginger's brother, Terry. 'We ain't cut real loose fer yonks.'

It was true. Apart from Bryce Reece's gang, all the other gangs in the area now steered well clear of them and so they hadn't had a truly challenging fight for ages. Nor had they done any serious thieving. They rampaged through the local street market on an almost daily basis, but stuff nicked from markets was of absolutely no account. It was the green stuff that counted; a few of the old readies. With cash in their pockets they could barter for war souvenirs and, according to his dad, such negotiations had to be done now before the police cottoned on to just how big the trade had become and clamped down on it good and proper. Old Man Tucker's float wouldn't help much – he reckoned they'd be lucky if the take was even ten shillings – but pretending it was a major bank job they were pulling would liven things up no end.

'If we give the arsenal an airing, *I* carry the Lee Enfield,' Frankie said, aware now which way the wind was blowing and reckoning it was less trouble to go along with what the majority wanted than to exert his authority and put the mockers on it. 'We'll take a couple of air pistols and air rifles with us, as well as war souvenirs. If anyone sees us, we'll scare 'em shitless!'

'Do you know what really scares me, Bry?' Sandra said as on New Year's Day they sat hunched in coats and scarves on the low wall outside number 8, sharing a bag of coconut-ice. 'I'm scared that when my dad walks into Swan Row I won't know who he is!'

Tigger was lying on the freezing cold pavement, his

short legs pedalling the air as he indicated his desperation to have his tummy scratched.

Not laughing at Sandra's fear, Bryce popped another piece of coconut-ice into his mouth and leaned forward so that he could reach Tigger's tummy.

'If 'e comes 'ome still in uniform, like Victor's dad did, it won't be that 'ard to know who 'e is,' he said, envying her the problem so much he didn't want her to see into his eyes. 'There's no one else living in the row still to come 'ome, is there? The Cravens' dad is 'ome and so are all the Briscoes.'

*But not my dad*, he wanted to add and with great effort didn't. It wouldn't have been fair to Sand. It wasn't her fault her dad was coming home and his would never do so.

For once Sandra was unaware of the turn Bryce's thoughts had taken. 'But what if he doesn't?' she persisted, her face pathetically anxious. 'What if he's in civvies, Bry? What if he walks right past me and I don't know who he is? What if . . .'

Bryce could bear it no longer. Letting Tigger lick the coconut-ice crumbs from his fingers he said: 'I'm off dahn the market to see if I can find anyone who wants to swap a bloodstained army beret for some military badges. I'll see yer later, Sand. An' don't worry about not recognising yer dad – I don't suppose 'e'll recognise you straight off, either.'

Two weeks later Sandra's worries were proved groundless. Though she didn't recognise her dad when she first saw him, she instantly knew who he was.

She and her mum were walking up Swan Row after queuing for what seemed an age at Mr Tucker's for a few sausages and half a pound of mince.

'If the war's soddin' well over why are we still being soddin' rationed and why are there still all these soddin' shortages?' Mrs Craven, next but one to them in the queue, had complained long and loud. 'When are things goin' to get back to normal where food is concerned, that's what I want to know.'

'Did you read about the little girl who died after eating bananas?' Mrs Wilkinson had asked, speaking to everyone within hearing distance. 'She'd never seen one before and her mum bought some the first time they were back in the shops. Three she had and then she dropped down dead.'

There had been a lot of mutterings of 'Shame' and 'Poor little cow' and then it had been her mum's turn to be served. Afterwards, walking home, Sandra had resolved never to eat a banana again.

She was still wondering whether the little girl would have lived if she'd had only two bananas when her mother came to such a sudden halt that Sandra, holding on to her hand, stumbled against her.

There was a man swaggering down the row from the direction of Jamaica Road. He was a tall man, lean and fit looking. He was wearing an army greatcoat and had a kitbag slung over his shoulder.

'*Len*!' The word was a hoarse, harsh whisper, certainly not meant for the man in question to hear.

Sandra looked bewilderedly from the fast approaching man to her mother and then back again. Her dad's name was Len. Why, then, wasn't her mum rushing to meet him? Why was she looking so strange and sounding so odd?

Across the street, Hilda Clarkson, about to enter number 11 with two heavy bags of shopping, paused, and then, quite obviously wanting to see what was going to happen next, set her bags down on her immaculately white-stoned front step. Next door to her, Connie Briscoe stood in the open doorway of number 13, a half-smoked fag in her hand. In other houses, on both sides of the row, curtains were being twitched aside.

Sandra gripped her mum's hand hard. 'Is it dad, Mum? *Is it my dad?*'

'It's me, Sheila!' the man called out. 'Are yer blind, gel?'

'It *is* my dad!' Sandra let go of her mum's hand and began running. '*Daddy*! *Daddy*!' she shouted as she ran, her scrubbed face shining with happiness. 'It's me, Sandra!'

Stan Wilkinson, returning down Swan Row to the dairy depot, his lorry empty, slowed down in order to watch the emotional reunion. The Parry's weren't local people. Sheila Parry and her little girl had only moved into the row a couple of years ago after being bombed out of their Islington home. By then Len Parry was fighting the Japs in Burma, and so he wasn't known in the row at all.

Sandra was oblivious of Mr Wilkinson watching her from the cab of his lorry, and of Mrs Clarkson and Mrs Briscoe and all the other neighbours now taking a very great interest in what was going on.

'*Daddy*!' she gasped one last time as he slung his kitbag to the ground and she ran headlong into his arms.

With a rasping laugh he swung her round and round, off her feet, and then her mother was there and she was on her feet again as her dad's arm went round her mum's shoulders. 'So this is where we're livin' now, is it, Sheila?' he asked, hugging her close. 'South of the river wiv our feet nearly in the Thames?'

The way her dad spoke was the very first thing Sandra found strange about him. He spoke with a South London accent, just like everyone else in Swan Row. Everyone, that is, but her mother and herself – and the Clarksons.

Skipping along beside him, hugging his arm, Sandra decided that she liked the way her dad spoke. It meant that no one in Swan Row would think he was stuck up. It meant he would fit in.

'Christ, but it's brass monkey weather, gel,' her dad said

47

to her mum as the three of them stepped into number 8. 'That fire don't look too healthy. Bung some more coal on it before me whatsits turn to ice.'

Sandra's eyes widened. Didn't her dad know that coal was like gold-dust and that everyone had to be careful about how much they used? And what was a whatsit? And why hadn't he said please? Her mum was very fussy about pleases and thankyous.

'We have to be careful with the coal,' she began help-fully, but her mum cut her short, a big bright smile on her face.

'Not today we don't, Sandra. Today is a very special day, seeing as it's your dad's first day in Swan Row. I'll just put an extra shovel-full on the fire and you put the kettle on for some tea. There's a good girl.'

'I fink we'll 'ave the tea later, Sheila,' her dad was saying, his arm still around her mum's shoulders. 'I'll 'ave it afterwards, when I 'ave my ciggie.'

For some reason Sandra couldn't understand, her mother's cheeks flushed as if she'd suddenly become too hot.

'Christ, Sheila,' her dad said again, shrugging himself out of his army coat and throwing it over the back of the nearest chair. 'You ain't comin' over all bashful on me, are yer? I've bin away three bleedin' years!'

'No, of course not, Len.' Her mum was beginning to look desperately flustered. 'It's just that there's Sandra to think about and . . .'

Her dad sat down on the couch and began unlacing his boots. 'Tell her to clear off,' he said, not even looking towards her.

Her mum gave a little laugh as she picked up first one of his boots and then the other. 'It's the middle of winter, Len, love. I don't think that . . .'

Her dad's eyes met her mum's. Her mum's voice faltered and stopped and there was a pause. It was such a little pause and yet Sandra was to remember it until the day

48

she died, for during it her old, happy way of life came to an end and a new, terrifying one began.

'You!' her dad said suddenly, whipping his head round so that instead of looking at her mum he was looking at her. 'Hop it!'

Sandra blinked, the joy on her face draining to be replaced by an expression of utter bewilderment. What was happening? Why was her dad raising his voice to her? Why did he want her to 'hop it' when they were about to have cups of tea and, knowing her mum, slices of home-made cake?

She looked towards her mum for an explanation and reassurance.

'I think you'd better do as your daddy says, Sandra,' her mum said, still with a determinedly bright smile on her face. 'Go round to Bryce's for half-hour, there's a good girl.'

'But I want to stay here.' Sandra's bewilderment was total. 'I want to stay with dad and . . .'

'*Out!*'

Her dad was on his feet again, unbuckling his belt. Sandra backed away, able to draw only one conclusion from his action. The Briscoes and the Cravens were all regularly beaten with their dads' trouser belts. It wasn't something she'd ever imagined happening to her, though. Her mum never hit her; not with her hand, not with anything.

All joy was gone now and a strange sensation was bubbling up in her throat – a sensation of complete and utter panic. Somehow, somewhere, there had been a hideous mistake. This frightening man couldn't be her daddy. She didn't remember her daddy, but she knew he was like Bryce's dad. He was incredibly tall and strong and kind and he laughed a lot.

Still backing away she banged into the door. With perception far beyond her years she knew now why her mum had never talked to her about her dad – if this intimidating stranger *was* her dad – and why her very bright smile, when they had all first entered the house, hadn't reached her eyes. Her mum was frightened of him. Her mum didn't like him *and neither did she*.

The doorknob jarred into her back and she turned, fumbling for it with slippery palms, Tigger close against her legs. She didn't want her dad to be home; not if he was going to shout all the time and not want her in the house. She didn't want it to be *now*. She wanted it to be *then*. To be an hour ago when it was just her and her mum and she didn't have this horrid, hideous, whirling sensation in the pit of her tummy.

'An' when yer come back, don't bring that apology for a dog with yer!' her dad shouted after her as she stumbled out into the chill December air. 'A dog's place is outside the 'ouse, not in it!'

The door banged shut behind her. Blinded by burning tears she got as far as the low wall that separated their grave-sized patch of so-called garden from the street and then, her legs trembling violently, sat down on the freezing cold stone, hugging Tigger tightly.

Across the row, at number 7, Pearl Nowakowska paused in the act of taking down her nets for their annual New Year wash. Like several of the Parrys' neighbours she'd seen the lovely scene enacted fifteen minutes earlier when Sandra had run up the row into her dad's arms. Now Sandra and her little dog were sitting outside in the freezing cold and, unless she was very much mistaken, there were tears streaming down Sandra's face.

She chewed the corner of her lip, her eyes narrowing as she looked from the Parrys' downstairs windows to the upstairs. The bedroom curtains, drawn together so abruptly the cheap chintz material was still swaying, told their own story.

'Poor little cow,' she thought as Sandra continued to

hug Tigger so tightly it was a mercy he was still breathing; 'life ain't going to be the same now it ain't just 'er and 'er mum.' She scooped up her yellowed nets, hoping to God Len Parry was merely an insensitive sod and not, as so many other men in Swan Row were, violent into the bargain. Living as she did, sandwiched between two lots of Briscoes, she was in ear-shot of enough domestic violence without having to endure the knowledge that it was taking place in the house opposite too.

# Chapter Three

Nell opened her eyes and stared up at her pitch-dark bedroom ceiling, knowing a noise had wakened her. What had it been? A bike with squeaky wheels being cycled down the row? A scavenging fox? It came again and this time there was no mistaking it: a whine. A dog's whine. She looked across at the luminous hands of her bedside clock. Half-past two in the morning. The whining came again, insistent and pathetic.

Reluctantly she swung her legs from the bed and padded across the chill bedroom to the window, the linoleum breath-stoppingly cold beneath her bare feet. Pulling back the curtains she looked down into the street. There was no dog to be seen, but as she stood at the window in her old-fashioned nightie the whining continued. It was coming from the Parry's doorstep.

Concerned, she turned away from the window, slipping her feet into a pair of battered slippers and reaching for the old overcoat that served her as a dressing-gown. What on earth was Sheila thinking of, accidentally locking Tigger out on a night when the temperature was below freezing? Even more mystifyingly, why on earth hadn't they been woken by Tigger's whining, as she had been?

'What is it, Mum? What's the matter?' Bryce stood at his open bedroom door in a pair of pyjamas he had long since outgrown.

'Tigger's got locked out. God knows how.' Nell slipped goose-pimpled arms into the sleeves of the only overcoat Joe had possessed. 'I'm going down to let him in. He can sleep in the scullery. Get back to bed, lovey, or you'll catch your death.'

Bryce frowned, uncaring of the cold. 'Tigger won't like it in the scullery,' he said, worried. 'He always sleeps on Sandra's bed.'

'Then you'd think she'd have noticed he wasn't there.' Cross now, Nell went downstairs and unlatched her front door. No matter how enthralled Sandra was at having her dad home, there was no excuse for her being unaware of Tigger's whereabouts, especially on what was turning out to be the coldest night of the winter. He was only a little dog and his coat was typical Yorkshire terrier fur, silky-fine and thin. If he'd been outside since last evening he'd be half-perished.

Tigger *was* half-perished. Curled into a bedraggled and forlorn ball on the Parry's doorstep, he was so numb with cold that even when Nell opened her front door he couldn't make a move towards it. His tail moved feebly, rimed with frost.

Nell scooped him up, holding him close against Joe's overcoat. One thing was for certain. He'd never thaw out if she put him in her scullery.

'Thanks, Mum,' Bryce said, sitting up in bed as she handed Tigger over to him. 'Sandra's goin' to wonder where on earth 'e is when she wakes up in the morning. I bet it was 'er dad that let him out by accident, 'cos 'e won't be used to 'im, will 'e? She won't 'alf 'ave a surprise when I take 'im round there in the morning.'

When Bryce knocked on the Parry's door at half-past seven next morning, Tigger tucked beneath his arm, it was he who received the surprise.

'Sandra isn't going to school today, Bryce,' Sheila Parry said to him with an odd, over-bright smile.

Under the circumstances, and coming from anyone else, the statement would have been unremarkable. Certainly if it had been his dad who had just come home he wouldn't have gone to school and nor would his mum have expected him to. Mrs Parry wasn't his mum, though. She was very particular about Sandra's school attendance and he couldn't remember any other occasion when Sandra had been allowed to stay home, unless she had been ill with something infectious.

'Is Sandra worried about Tigger, Auntie Sheila?' he asked, aware that he and Tigger weren't receiving quite the reception he had expected. ''E got locked out last night and Mum let 'im into our 'ouse.'

The relief on Sheila Parry's face was vast, but there was another expression there, too; an expression Bryce couldn't for the life of him understand. Even more peculiarly, she was standing at the door in a way that meant he couldn't very well walk past her into the house. For as long as he could remember, he'd been going in and out of number 8 with the same freedom he went in and out of his own house and he found it all extremely odd.

He shrugged again. Sandra's mum had always been a bit peculiar and so it was only to be expected that on Mr Parry's first day home she wasn't behaving as she might have been expected to behave. 'Tigger was all right last night, Auntie Sheila,' he said reassuringly, setting Tigger down on the ground. 'He'd got so cold he was almost frozen stiff but Mum let him sleep on my bed and he soon thawed out.'

'That's ... that's nice to know, Bryce.' Before Tigger could hop over the doorstep into the house, Sheila grabbed hold of him. 'Will you tell your mum I'll be round to see her in a little while? She may be able to ...'

'*Shiel*!' a rasping male voice shouted from number 8's front bedroom, cutting across whatever it was she had been about to say. '*What the devil are yer doin' jawing on the doorstep when I ain't had my mornin' cuppa yet? Get a move on, gel, for Gawd's sake!*'

By Swan Row standards it was a reasonable enough question and a not unusual demand. Bryce's only surprise was at the realisation that Sandra's dad didn't talk posh like Sandra and her mum. Impatient to meet him, he knew he wasn't now going to be able to do so until much later in the day; until he called in at number 8 on his way home from school.

'See yer, Auntie Sheila,' he said, aware that his mum would, by now, have a steaming bowl of porridge waiting on the table for him. He was suddenly very hungry for the comfort of it. Sandra's dad being home was making him so conscious of the loss of his own dad that he could hardly bear it.

With freezing cold hands dug deep in the pockets of his short pants he shouldered open the door of number 6, knowing that his mates at school would be full of questions about Sandra's dad. They'd want to know if he'd met him yet and whether Mr Parry had brought any war souvenirs home with him from the jungle. Well, he didn't want to be questioned about someone else's dad; he wanted to think about his own dad. He stepped into the house, pushing the door shut behind him. He wasn't going to go to school today. Even though it was cold enough for snow, he was going to bunk off.

With his usual holey jumper and shabby short pants augmented by a thick jumper that had been his dad's, a coat that had once belonged to Victor Roberts, a mammoth scarf his mum had knitted out of wool oddments and wearing wellingtons that cut red weals into the backs of his legs, Bryce set off from home as if going to school. On reaching the top end of the row he changed direction, doubling back through a maze of side streets in the direction of the river.

What he was going to do when he reached the Thames, he didn't know. His favourite occupation when it was low tide, as now, was to walk the narrow ribbon of mud below the embankments in the hope of finding something of interest washed up there. Once, he and Victor had found an empty survival suit, and Curly Craven had found a German aeroplane tyre.

Today, though, it was a bit too cold to make trawling for flotsam and jetsam an appealing option. He began walking down-river, in the general direction of Greenwich, half wondering whether or not to hop a bus to Woolwich and spend the rest of the day on the ferry that trolled backwards and forwards across the Thames. The ferry was free and you could spend all day lounging against the deck rails and looking down into the spuming water or shouting greetings to the crews of the tugs and boats making their way towards the King George and Albert Dock entrances.

Still undecided, Bryce came to a halt and leaned over the cold embankment, staring moodily out over the slate-grey, oil-slicked water. If his dad were alive, wondering what to do wouldn't be a problem. He'd be doing whatever it was his dad wanted him to be doing – even if that meant going to school.

His eyes sharpened. Someone else from Swan Row was doing a bunk from school and – unusually for a Briscoe – was doing so solo.

With his wellies ankle-deep in the tidal mud, Frankie Briscoe was squelching along the water line, head down as he scanned the washed-up debris for anything of interest or, hopefully, of value.

'What's the matter, Frankie?' he jeered. 'Can't yer see properly for yer squint?'

Frankie spun round, his heels sinking further into mud rainbow-coloured from oil and chemicals and rubbish. 'Piss off!' he shouted back, furious at being spied on and at being caught with none of his cohorts in tow.

Bryce grinned, knowing he was safe from attack. Frankie's

style was to lead his brothers and cousins in violent gang brawls; one-to-one fights, even when he had a knuckle-duster stowed on his person, weren't his scene at all.

'What are yer lookin' for, Frankie? The brains you've lost?' he shouted back, beginning to enjoy himself. 'They'll be too small ter find without a magnifying glass!'

Even from a distance of fifteen yards or so, Bryce could see that Frankie was grinding his teeth in frustrated rage. He saw, too, that the tide was on the turn and that the mud was beginning to suck and quiver. The rule of the river – five hours' ebb, seven hours' flood – was one everyone living within sight and smell of it knew by heart. Once the water was on the up, it was on the up with a vengeance, swirling in fast and deep and taking no prisoners, especially not on this section of river, where there was a notorious back-flow of current against the tide.

'It's time yer called it a day, Frankie!' he yelled as water began slithering up and over the mud and the debris that had been entombed in it began to float. 'Unless you want to 'ave a swim!'

'Fuck off, clever arse.'

Instead of heading towards the narrow ribbon of shingle that lay directly beneath the embankment, an enraged Frankie stepped backwards. As he did so, the whole area around him wobbled and the foot carrying his weight went down into the mud with a gurgling sound that even Bryce could hear.

'For Christ's sake, Frankie!' Bryce was no longer having fun at Frankie's expense. That there were isolated pockets of quicksand along the Thames was well known – what wasn't well known was where exactly they were. 'Get out of there quick, Frankie!' He began running along the embankment to the nearest set of steps. '*Get out of there now*!'

The Thames was flooding fast. Water slopped up to

57

the rim of Frankie's wellingtons and over into them. As Frankie realised his predicament, his arms began to flail. He couldn't move his feet and the mud was closing cement-like round his ankles. Vainly he tried to heave his legs out of his wellingtons so that he could wade to the bank, but his ankles were trapped as if by iron bands. Worse – he was being sucked down.

Seeing what was happening, aware that Frankie had to be hauled free fast, Bryce sprinted helter-skelter down the steps on to damp, squelchy gravel.

'*I'm trapped*!' Frankie yelled at him, his face white with terror. '*I can't move me feet*!'

Bryce didn't need to be told what was happening; he could see for himself that Frankie was now almost knee-deep in the quicksand.

On his mad run to the steps he'd kept his eyes peeled for one of the many life-belts positioned along the embankment, but there were none in sight and he could see no one to shout to for help. He and Frankie were on their own – and he was going to have to somehow save Frankie or live with the memory of having watched the Thames lap up and over him.

'*Get me outta 'ere*!' Frankie was yelling hysterically, his every panic-stricken movement sucking him down deeper and deeper. '*For fuck's sake get me out*! *GET ME OUT*!'

Bryce had every intention of getting him out but didn't, as yet, know how. He couldn't just wade out to Frankie and haul and tug at him, not without sinking into the quicksand himself.

'*H-E-L-P*!' he shouted to the world at large, his hands cupped round his mouth. '*H-E-L-P*!'

How was it that, on the one of the busiest rivers in the world, there was no one near enough to realise that they weren't just kids messing about? There were plenty of boats and tugs plying up and down the central section of river, but, on such a raw day, all the crew members were below decks.

''*Elp me, Bryce! Fer Christ's sake, 'elp me!*''

Frankie was blubbering now and Bryce didn't blame him; not when he was being sucked deeper and deeper and the river was rising so fast the entire mud bank was beginning to slide beneath it.

Frantically he looked to left and right. What he needed if he was to reach Frankie without joining him in the quicksand was something he could throw out across it. He needed a rope or some stout wood, a long glorious plank of it.

Still shouting at the top of his lungs for help, Bryce began running over the now watery gravel. There was driftwood in plenty washed up beneath the embankment, but most of it was thin, insubstantial stuff. '*Don't leave me!*' Frankie shrieked after him. '*I'll drown if yer leave me!*'

Grimly aware that unless he found a suitable plank of wood fast Frankie was going to drown anyway, Bryce didn't waste his breath in shouting a response. Still running, still searching, still shouting for help, he frantically tried to assess how much time Frankie had left. At the rate the river was rising, and it would rise over thirty feet, it was probably only five minutes, six at the most.

A piece of decking had been propped against the embankment as if for just such an emergency. Panting for breath, the blood drumming in his ears, Bryce seized hold of it. Whether it would work or not he hadn't a clue, he only knew that unless he gave it his best shot Frankie was going to be a goner.

Hauling it behind him, he raced back to the fast dwindling mud flat.

'*GET . . . ME . . . OUT!*' Frankie hollered as the quicksand dragged him deeper and the black cold evil of the Thames rose higher.

Bryce scrambled out of his coat and jumper and kicked off his wellingtons. If his rescue attempt ended with him having to swim for his life he didn't want heavy clothing and waterlogged wellies dragging him down. His hand-knitted scarf, as strong and as long as a rope, was a different matter. Keeping it coiled around his neck, Bryce floundered out into the mud and water and then, when he judged himself to be on the brink of the quicksand, he crashed the plank through the rising water.

'*What yer goin' ter do? What yer going ter do?*' Frankie sobbed as the flood tide licked at his waist. '*I'm stuck fast! How yer goin to get me out?*'

'If yer stopped bleedin' panicking, it'd bleedin' 'elp!' The only safe purchase Bryce had for his feet was the planking and, as he inched out along it and the distance between himself and Frankie narrowed, he could feel it shuddering and settling. Within the next few seconds the quicksand would have the plank in its grip and unless the water was then deep enough for him to be able to keep his feet free by swimming, he'd be trapped just as Frankie was – the only difference being that, at the rate he was being sucked down, Frankie would by then be beneath the surface and long gone.

Bracing himself against the pull of the water, its icy temperature sending pain screaming through every cell of his body, he came to a rocky halt just out of reach of Frankie's hysterically thrashing arms.

'I'm goin' to throw one end of me scarf to yer!' he shouted through chattering teeth, wondering which was the greater danger: the quicksand, the rising water, or the crucifying cold. 'Loop it round yer, knot it under yer arms, an' then 'ang on to it while I try and pull you out.'

The instructions were simple enough but in rising panic Bryce knew that the searing, mind-numbing, heart-stopping temperature of the water was so disabling that even the simplest movement was fast becoming impossible, not only for Frankie but for himself as well.

'*Oh God,*' Frankie sobbed as Bryce threw the gaudily coloured scarf towards him. '*Oh Christ, oh shit!*' At the third attempt, his fingers mottled blue with cold, he finally managed to catch hold of it.

Bryce's relief was vast, but he couldn't enjoy it. He had too many other things to worry about. There was the strength and pull of the water, for one thing. The other was that the plank of wood was now lost and he was having to kick his legs like a frog to stay clear of the quicksand. It wasn't a position from which he could haul Frankie free. He needed something solid beneath his feet; preferably some good old-fashioned gravel.

'H-E-L-P!' he yelled again at the top of his lungs to the world at large. 'H-E-L-P!'

While Frankie, with ability born of desperation, looped the scarf round himself and tied it in a sodden knot, Bryce began thrusting his legs in the water, propelling himself backwards. Frankie was now chest-deep and with every passing second the chances of Bryce being able to pull him free were growing smaller and smaller.

Long before he had kicked himself backwards in the water to a point where he judged the quicksand gave way to normal mud, the scarf yanked like a live thing in his hand, fully stretched and taut.

His heart began beating high in his throat. This was it. This was the moment when he had to begin hauling on the scarf with every ounce of strength he possessed and, to do that, he had to have some solid purchase for his feet.

'*Pull me out, Bryce! Pull me out!*'

Frankie was screaming and frothing at the mouth with terror as the inky-dark Thames swirled round his armpits. Bryce didn't blame him one little bit. Knowing that the moment of truth couldn't be put off even half a second longer, he forced his painfully numb legs downwards.

As he made contact with the river-bottom, thick mud oozed vilely between his toes. In a moment which was to give him nightmares for years to come he felt himself beginning to sink. Convulsive panic gripped him and his knees jack-knifed. Gobbing oil-slicked water, aware now that he was on ordinary river mud and not quicksand, he dug his heels in deep and tugged on the scarf, struggling to inch backwards with it; struggling to heave Frankie free.

Feeling as if every blood vessel he possessed was going to burst, he was only dimly aware of distant shouting. The sodden wool scarf was stretched to breaking point and he could feel the water rapidly deepening around him. Unless he made it to the bank soon, the current would be so strong he would be helpless against it.

'*Come on, Frankie!*' he yelled, his arms nearly out of their sockets. '*Fer Christ's sake, come on!*'

Bryce was at the end of his strength. His limbs were so frozen they no longer seemed to be part of his body. He couldn't see clearly any more. Even Frankie's face was just a blur. Suddenly his heels were no longer in mud but on hard stones and knife-sharp debris, and as he heaved backwards, the water surging up and around his shoulders, his heels slithered from under him and the water closed over his head.

Afterwards, the one thing he remembered was that he never let go of the scarf – not even when the taut wool no longer had any kind of weight at the end of it. Struggling and kicking, his ears popping, his lungs bursting, he fought to regain the surface. His last thought, as a sinisterly strong force seized hold of him, was that his mum was never going to forgive him for leaving her on her own.

'Christ All-bleedin'-mighty,' someone was saying devoutly from above him as, flat out and face-down, he was fisted in the middle of his back. Thames water so foul it was a miracle it hadn't killed him outright streamed from his nose and throat. 'Run and tell his mother, Roy. Tell her he's going to need something hot to drink and a warm bed. And tell Frankie Briscoe's mum to get here fast as well.'

Bryce groaned, vomited, and, with a helping hand, rolled over on to his back.

'You're going to be all right, lad.' The speaker, who was saturated with river water himself, was putting something dry and heavy over him – something he later discovered to be an overcoat – and seemed vaguely familiar.

'Dad?' he said queryingly and then his vision cleared and he recognised Roy Clarkson's dad. He fought sweeping desolation and tried to heave himself into a sitting position. 'Where's Frankie? Is he drownded?' he asked, his voice a raw rasp, his throat and chest burning. There were lots of people standing nearby, some grouped around him, some grouped around someone, or something, further along the shore – he couldn't clearly see.

'No, lad, but he would have been if not for you.'

Bryce had never liked any of the Clarkson family – Roy was the only boy in the row that he and his gang had nothing to do with – but at that moment he warmed towards Mr Clarkson, knowing instinctively that he had been the strong force who had seized hold of him, saving him from a watery grave.

'Me and Roy were on our way back from the doctor's when we saw you,' Norman Clarkson was saying, vigorously pummelling Bryce in an effort to get his blood circulating again. 'Roy's asthma's been playing up, else we'd never have been down this way at this time of day. When we saw you, you'd hauled the Briscoe boy out of the current and to the shallows, but you were so whacked you were on the point of drowning yourself. What the devil were the two of you doing, mucking about in the Thames in the middle of winter?'

It was a reasonable question, but Bryce ignored it. 'Are yer sure Frankie ain't drownded?' he asked again, struggling to get a clear view of the near lifeless figure huddled on the ground a yard or so away.

'No, he hasn't drowned,' Norman Clarkson said again, beginning to help him to his feet.

'The silly young bugger should've been,' a spectator said grimly. 'The Thames ain't a river to mess around in, not even in the summer. I've known men and boys go in it when the water was gentle as a girl an' so still you could hear it whispering to itself, an' they've still come a grisly cropper.'

There were several murmurs of agreement and someone else added: 'What wiv all the oil and chemicals in the river, if they don't die o' drowning, they die o' poisoning.'

Now that Bryce was quite obviously not going to die at all, the crowd opened up a little and he was able to see Frankie clearly. Still prostrate and looking more dead than alive, Frankie turned his head and their eyes met.

'You all right, Frankie?' Shivering violently, Bryce tugged Norman Clarkson's overcoat closer around his shoulders.

'Yeah.' Frankie's voice was so hoarse it was barely audible. 'I reckon I owe yer one, eh, Bryce?'

Bryce nodded and then, as an ambulance squealed to a halt nearby, he coughed up another vile spume of river water and, as the ambulance-men began running towards him, felt his frozen facial muscles tugging into a grin.

When Frankie had got bogged down in the quicksand he'd had a squint in one eye. Now the poor sod had a squint in both eyes!

'So what can I do fer yer, Sheila?' Hoisting a string-bag full of groceries and a bulky carrier-bag on to the draining board – the only practical work surface her scullery possessed – Nell knew Sheila wouldn't be paying her a call so early in the day unless she was in need of a favour of some kind. ''Ave yer run out of sugar again?'

Still in her hat and coat and not bothering to unpack

her bulging shopping bags, she began filling her kettle at the tap. What she needed after an hour spent shopping for veg in the local street market was a cup of good, hot Rosie Lee.

'No, I'm all right for sugar . . .'

Nell glanced across at her friend, decided she was also in need of a cup of hot strong tea and put an extra caddy-spoon of tea leaves into her Coronation Day teapot.

'It's Tigger, actually.' Sheila stood at the scullery door, looking oddly uncomfortable. 'Len is . . . asthmatic. He can't be around dogs; they start him wheezing. I wondered if . . .'

'Christ, Sheil!' Deeply shocked, Nell spun to face her, the tea caddy still in her hand. 'Is that why the poor little bleeder was locked out last night?'

'I . . . it was a difficult situation,' Sheila said defensively, her eyes not meeting Nell's. 'Len had only just come home and . . . and it was difficult, Nell.'

Sensing the deep strain her friend was under, Nell's shock turned swiftly to concern. 'Well, if Tigger is makin' things that difficult for Len . . . and Len ain't able to breathe with Tigger around . . . then of course I'll take Tigger in. That is what you're askin', ain't it?'

Still unable to meet Nell's eyes, sure that if she did, Nell would realise she'd been lying when she'd said Len was asthmatic, Sheila nodded. 'Can I help you put your shopping away?' she asked, wanting to change the subject before awkward questions were asked. She looked curiously across at the carrier-bag. 'What have you been buying, Nell? Have you been using up your clothing coupons?'

'Nah. It's lost property. I fell over it outside Woolworths. I'm just goin' to 'ave a cuppa and then I'll pop over to the police station wiv it.'

More curious than ever, Sheila peeked inside the bag. It held one large parcel, wrapped in paper and neatly tied with string. 'I wonder what it is,' she said, temporarily forgetting all the grief that Len was giving her. 'You should open it, Nell. There's not much point in trailing to the police station with it, if it's nothing but rubbish.'

Nell poured steaming water into her warmed teapot. 'Yer can if yer like, Shiel. Don't make much odds though, does it? Whatever it is, it belongs to someone and that someone ain't me.'

Glad to be thinking of something other than the nightmare that was now her home life, Sheila lifted the parcel out of the carrier-bag, taking Nell's unflinching honesty for granted. That she was as straight as a die and as unlike their Briscoe neighbours as chalk was from cheese was one of the things that had first attracted her to Nell. 'It feels very odd,' she said, weighing the solid-looking parcel in both hands.

'Open it if yer want,' Nell said, pouring the tea. 'But try and do it neatly so it don't look too bad when I 'and it in to the coppers.'

Sheila was rummaging in Nell's cutlery drawer, looking for a pair of kitchen scissors, when running footsteps came clattering to a halt outside Nell's front door. The knocking that followed was loud and urgent and Nell swiftly put her teapot back on the draining board and hurried out of the scullery and across her living-room.

'What on earth . . .' Sheila heard her begin to say, and then she heard a boy's voice and the words 'accident' and 'river'. Alarmed, and with the scissors still in her hand, she stepped out of the scullery so that she could hear more clearly.

'Oh my God! Oh my dear God!' Nell was saying, and then she was shouting over her shoulder: 'My Bryce 'as 'ad an accident, Sheil!' The next thing she knew, Nell was running off down the row with Roy Clarkson.

Sheila stood at the open doorway for a few seconds, uncertain what to do. If Nell was going to have to go to the hospital with Bryce, she might not be back for hours and Len would soon be demanding his breakfast. Decisively she turned and walked back towards the scullery, intent on putting the scissors back in the drawer before going home.

The parcel lay enticingly on the draining board and, knowing that Nell wouldn't mind and telling herself that it would only take a minute, she snipped the string and undid the brown paper wrapping.

The next second she was tottering back against the sink. '*Christ Almighty*!' she whispered, her eyes the size of gobstoppers. It was money. Spankingly crisp, new money. Wads of pink ten-shilling notes. Wads of green pound notes. Even a wad of snowy-white five-pound notes.

'*Shiel*!' Len shouted from number 8's kitchen. 'Where the bleedin' 'ell are you?'

With her heart slamming and her hands shaking she hurriedly re-wrapped the money and shoved the parcel back into the carrier-bag. The sooner Nell got to the police station with it, the better. It looked very much as if it were bank money – and if that was the case, it was quite obviously stolen.

'*Shiel*!' Len hollered again. '*SHEIL*!'

Wishing to God the war with Japan had never come to an end, Sheila scurried out of number 6, slamming the door behind her.

It was much later when Nell arrived home from the hospital with Bryce and the last thing on her mind was the carrier bag she had found.

'You're going straight to bed,' she said forcefully, overriding all his protests, wanting to have him where she could keep an eye on him. A hospital doctor had checked him over very thoroughly and had said that he was none the worse for his dip in the Thames, but she wasn't convinced. How could he be none the worse? He'd come within a hair's breadth of drowning and he'd swallowed all kinds of river filth and oil and chemicals.

'I'll bring you up a mug of milky cocoa,' she said, stuffing the carrier-bag and its bulky parcel out of the way beneath the sink, wondering how on earth she would have coped if Bryce had drowned – especially if he had done so saving the life of a Briscoe.

'Well, thank God it didn't happen,' Sheila said days later when she was next in number 6. 'And thank God he wasn't poisoned by the water he swallowed.' She gave a ghost of a smile. 'I think Bryce must have been born under a lucky star, Nell.'

'I hope so, Shiel.' Nell's voice was fervent. Good luck was something everybody needed. It had run out for her Joe – and if the bruising around one of Sheila's eyes was anything to go by, she wasn't enjoying much good luck either, these days.

'What did the police say when you took the money in?' Sheila now asked, keeping the bruised side of her face slightly averted.

'Money?' Knowing that Sheila was doing her best to hide the fact that Len had given her a black eye, Nell began filling a kettle at the sink. 'What money? I don't know what you're talking about, Sheil.'

'Christ, Nell! The money in the carrier-bag!'

It was the first time Nell had ever heard her friend blaspheme and the shock was so great she swung around, the kettle still in her hand.

'You haven't seen it?' Sheila was uncaring now of her black eye. Facing Nell full on, her panic was so great it verged on hysteria. *Don't tell me the bag is still in the house, Nell*!'

'Yes ... somewhere ... under the sink, I think.' With growing alarm Nell put the kettle back on the hob and pushed aside the curtain that hid her sink shelves. Bending down on one knee, she dragged the forgotten carrier-bag from between a box of soap-powder and a packet of firelighters.

'But this isn't money, Shiel,' she said, standing upright, the bag in her arms. 'It's far too heavy for money.'

'No, it isn't!' With rare passion Sheila yanked the carrier-bag from her, spilling the parcel out on to the kitchen table. 'It's money, Nell! Lots of money!' She tore open the wrapping paper. 'Look at it, Nell! It's money that's been stolen! It *must* have been stolen – there are hundreds of pounds here! *Thousands* of pounds!'

Twenty minutes later a very breathless Nell hurried into the police station in Jamaica Road and with vast relief deposited her cargo on a counter in front of an officious-looking station sergeant.

'I found it a week ago,' she said, pushing the carrier-bag towards him. 'It was lying on the pavement outside Woolworths.' The smile she gave him was edged with nervousness. Up until now her only concern had been to deposit the carrier-bag and its contents into safekeeping. Now she had done so, she was acutely aware of her where-abouts. She had never been in a police station before and she was finding the experience intimidating. Why didn't the policeman smile back at her? Bobbies on the beat usually had a smile for respectable middle-aged women.

'I would have brought it in sooner,' she said apolo-getically, 'only my son nearly drowned in the Thames and it put all thought of it out of my head. He saved someone's life,' she added as he peered into the car-rier, prodding at the parcel with thick fingers. 'He's only nine and –'

'Name and address,' he interrupted leadenly, not bother-ing to look up at her and rudely indifferent to her account of Bryce's bravery. 'If the carrier isn't claimed within fourteen days . . .'

What would happen if the carrier remained unclaimed she was never to find out.

'*Fucking hell*!' The sergeant was staring down into the carrier-bag, his eyes nearly popping out of his head.

Nell's lips tightened. The unexpected sight of so much money was enough to make anyone forgetful of their language but a policeman, surely, should have had a little more self-control – especially when in the presence of a woman.

'My name is Mrs Reece and I live at 6 Swan Row, Bermondsey,' she said, eager to be back out on the pavement again. She'd promised Bryce she'd bake some scones for his tea and she was thinking of making some ginger cake as well.

'Swan Row?' At the mention of the address, the station sergeant made some very rapid assumptions and his voice was leaden no longer. Swan Row – Briscoes – armed robbery. He breathed in deeply, his nostrils whitening. The money was bank money, that was obvious from the newness of the notes and the unbroken wrappers securing each crisp, fat wad.

'Prescott!' he shouted to someone not in view as he lifted up a hinged flap in the counter-top, 'Take over for me!'

He strode through the gap towards Nell. 'I think you've some questions to answer, don't you?' he said grimly, taking hold of her by the arm as a young policeman hurried from the bowels of the station to take his place behind the counter. 'You may think handing in stolen money will get you off the hook of having received it, but it won't. Not when it's been in your possession for a week.'

'Pardon?' Nell was so startled that she couldn't, at first, take in what he was saying. 'Let go of me!'

He didn't do so. Instead, his grip on her upper arm tightened. 'I'm going to want a full statement,' he said, beginning to steer her towards an interview room. 'Dates. Names. The whole works.'

'I can't tell you anything else – I've told you everything I know!' Panic began bubbling in her throat as she was forcefully propelled down a linoleum-floored corridor and into a small, windowless room holding only a small desk and two hard chairs. 'I want to go home – I want to go home *now*. I have my son's tea to make. He'll be wondering where I am. He'll . . .'

'Full name,' the station sergeant demanded as the door clicked to.

It was the most ominous sound Nell had ever heard.

Wildly, she wondered if the man were mad. Why else would he be behaving in such an incomprehensible manner? 'Helen,' she said unsteadily, answering his question, fighting to keep her panic within manageable proportions. 'I found the money in the street, outside Woolworths . . .'

Four hours later, charged with the receiving of stolen goods, she was still frantically reiterating the same half-dozen sentences. 'But you *can't* charge me. I *found* the money. It was lying on the pavement outside Woolworths – though I didn't know it was money because it was all wrapped up! I thought it was someone's shopping. I didn't mean to keep it in my house for a week. If it hadn't been for my Bryce nearly drowning I wouldn't have forgotten about it. Truly I wouldn't.'

'Tell that to the magistrate when you come in front of him.' The station sergeant was spitting mad. He still hadn't got any names from her – though he was sure that Big Chas Briscoe was one of the names she was withholding – and a few minutes earlier his guv'nor had given orders that she was to be released on police bail.

'I can go?' The face she turned towards PC Prescott, who had delivered the order, was ashen with fatigue and stress.

Prescott nodded, wishing he had the balls to offer her a few kind words. 'See her out!' the reason he dared

71

not do so snapped, his fury at not having obtained the information he was after, obvious.

Unsteadily, Nell rose from her chair. PC Prescott stepped forward quickly, offering her his arm for support. It was an act of kindness too little, too late. Nell was barely aware of it as, almost insensible with distress, she stumbled from the room, unable to think of anything other than that she was going to appear before a magistrate on a criminal charge. Blindly she allowed PC Prescott to lead her down the corridor and into the station's tiny reception area. She would have to stand in a dock.

As she stepped out of the building into fresh air she felt as if her heart was about to fail her. What if there were newspaper reporters in the court? What if her name was in the papers?

Pressing the back of her hand to her mouth to stifle a sob she crossed the pavement to the kerb. Dear God in heaven, what if she were found guilty and sent to prison? What would happen to her Bryce? Who would look after him?

It was late afternoon and the traffic thundering up and down Jamaica Road was heavy. Nell was oblivious to it. Bryce would be home from school by now and he would be wondering where she was. How was she going to explain to him about her having to go to court? Even worse, how was she going to explain what might happen to her?

Deep in nightmare, not giving the oncoming traffic even the briefest thought, she stepped out into the road.

The bus bearing down on her swerved, but did so too late.

In the split second before it slammed into her, causing almost instantaneous death, she remembered the scones and the ginger cake she had been going to bake for Bryce's tea.

And then there was nothing.

Not even pain.

# Chapter Four

It was a Saturday afternoon and Bryce was lounging against the wall of Tucker's shop, his feet crossed at the ankles, his thumbs hooked into his trouser pockets, his nonchalant stance a perfect foil for his long, loose, midnight-blue jacket, his thick crêpe-soled shoes and the Brylcreamed 'elephant-trunk' roll of hair that fell low over his forehead.

He had become a teddy boy before most of his mates in Swan Row had even heard the expression. Now they were all Teds, the only exception being Roy Clarkson, who had never been a mate of his anyway, and who still dressed the way his mother wanted him to dress.

He didn't see Gunter Nowakowska's dad wave to him from across the street and so didn't acknowledge the gesture. He was, as often happened, deep in thoughts of the past.

His mouth tightened into a hard line. Christ, but he missed his mother. Just as Sandra always thought of her life in two distinct sections – before her dad came home and after – so the day his mother was killed was the dividing line in his own life. Before that day, even though his dad had only been home irregularly and for short periods, his life had been heedless and happy. After it . . . His mouth tightened even further. After it, life had become the absolute pits.

He unhooked his thumb from the pocket of his drainpipes and shot back his sleeve to see the face of his watch, his ostentatiously initialled signet ring glinting in the afternoon light. Two fifteen. Sandra was late. But was she late because she was still doing her hair and make-up, or was she late because her dad was laying into her again?

He chewed the corner of his lip. After the last vicious confrontation between himself and Len Parry, Parry had been minding his manners – or at least he'd been minding them where Sandra was concerned. There was no sense in hammering on the Parrys' door and causing a ruckus if all that was happening was that Sandra was trying to put on as much mascara as Sheila would let her get away with.

Hooking his thumb back into his trouser pocket he decided to wait until two thirty before storming up to number 8 to sort out whatever it was that might be going on there.

''Lo there, Bryce.' The speaker was Joan Wilkinson, heavily weighed down by a shopping bag bulging with fruit and veg.

''Lo, Mrs Wilkinson.' Bryce had a soft spot for the Wilkinsons' mum. Unlike many of the women in the row she was honest and decent and caring – just as his mum had been.

His eyes hardened with pain. It was his mum's honesty and decency that had led to her death – that and the scumbag behaviour of the police.

When the news had first been broken to him that his mother had been run over and killed by a bus in Jamaica Road, his Auntie Sheila had told him why his mum had been on the far side of the busy main road – and how large the parcel of money was that she'd been handing in.

His grief over his mother's death was so intense he hadn't given the money a thought, not even when Sheila had said that there was bound to be a reward and that, as his mum was dead, the money would be paid into her estate and become his.

74

He hadn't understood what words like 'estate' and 'internment' and 'beneficiary' meant. All he had understood was that he had lost both his mum and his dad – and that he was losing his home, too.

'Hasn't the child any blood relations who can care for him?' he dimly remembered a silver-haired man in an intimidating-looking office asking his Auntie Sheila.

There weren't. He'd known that, of course, and he hadn't been very bothered about it. If he couldn't have his mum looking after him, he didn't want anyone. He was nine years old and quite capable of looking after himself. Other people didn't seem to think so, though. Worse, to his thunderstruck amazement, he'd discovered he couldn't remain living at number 6. The house was rented – all the houses in Swan Row were – and within days of his mum's death the landlord had re-let it to another tenant.

'He either moves in with you, Mrs Parry – that is, if you and your husband become his legal guardians – or he spends the next seven years in an orphanage,' the silver-haired man had said. 'Now, what is to be?'

Auntie Sheila had collapsed in a flood of tears and he'd been bewildered by her apparent reluctance to take him in. It had been at this time, when he hadn't know what was going to happen to him, that the letter had come for his mum, detailing the charge for receiving that had been made against her, and giving the date she was to appear at Southwark Magistrates Court.

It was a letter that was to change him, and his life, irrevocably. His mum hadn't stepped in front of the oncoming bus in a moment of innocent carelessness. She had been heedless of the traffic because she had been out of her mind with shock and distress. She had handed into the police hundreds – perhaps thousands – of pounds, and instead of being thanked and given the respect that was her due, she had been treated as a criminal.

Young as he was, he knew what would have happened

if she had lived to attend court on the date given. Her name would have been in the papers. Gossip about her would have been rife. She might even have gone to prison.

The enormous wickedness of the police action had filled him with such rage and pain that there were times, alone in his bed in the dark, when he didn't think he was going to be able to live through it.

It wasn't the bus driver who was responsible for his mum's death. It was the police. If she hadn't been so shocked and distressed at the scumbag way they had treated her, she would never have stepped so blindly off the pavement and into the path of the bus.

'I told yer they was all pigs,' Frankie had said to him, happy in the knowledge that, for once, Bryce wasn't likely to disagree with him.

Bryce hadn't disagreed. The police had treated his mum as a criminal, and hatred and contempt for them burned in his gut like a physical pain.

In those early days it had been Frankie who had helped him the most. Ever since he had saved Frankie from drowning, his old enemy had taken it upon himself to cease all hostilities between their gangs and had begun treating him as a mate. Frankie's stories against the police, of how they were always stitching people up for things they hadn't done, or taking bribes and back-handers, had been the kind of thing, true or untrue, he had wanted – and needed – to hear.

He looked down at his watch. It was now half past two and still there was no sign of Sandra. Easing himself away from Tucker's wall, Bryce began walking in the direction of the row, brooding on the malignancy that was Len Parry, wondering how he could settle the bastard for good and all.

Once, for an infinitesimally short period of time, he had thought Len Parry the bees' knees. That had been in the first few days of his moving into number 8. Len had been jovial and welcoming, sauntering about the small terrace house bare-chested, a long-bladed knife in his waistband. 'Tell us about Burma, Mr Parry,' Bryce had urged in round-eyed fascination. 'Tell us about 'ow yer killed Japs in the jungle.'

Sandra always slid away whenever her dad began talking about how he and his company had fought their way down through the country to Rangoon. Still in deep shock over his mother's death, Bryce had never registered her behaviour as odd, hadn't noticed that she'd become quiet to the point of being mute. It had been the incident with Tigger that had opened his eyes.

'I thought I'd told yer to give that bloody dog away,' Len had said to Sheila one morning when they were getting ready for school. 'Why the bleedin' 'ell is it still in the 'ouse?'

'You know why, Len,' his Auntie Sheila had said, her hand trembling slightly as she put a plate of bacon and eggs in front of him. 'It was Nell that was going to have him and . . . and so he's still here,' she had finished with a quick, nervous smile.

'Well I don't bleedin' want 'im 'ere!'

Bryce had crammed a last mouthful of bread and salted beef dripping into his mouth and stared at Len. Why was he suddenly so angry? And had his mum really been going to take Tigger in? She hadn't said anything to him about it, though now he thought of it, Tigger had been round their house a lot in the days before she'd been run over.

'I'll just put Tigger outside for a little while, Mum,' Sandra had said, her voice almost as nervous as her mother's.

As she spoke, Tigger darted eagerly towards her and, in doing so, brushed past her father's legs.

Len had erupted to his feet, his chair toppling backwards. *That's it – I'll put the little bleeder outside fer good*!' he had shouted, spittle forming at the corners of his mouth.

Startled, Bryce stood by, wondering what on earth was happening, as Sandra rushed to snatch Tigger out of harm's way. Len's booted foot, kicking with full force, had reached him first.

Only a little dog, weighing almost nothing, Tigger was sent flying across the kitchen to slam into the wall, screeching in agony.

As his Auntie Sheila cried out and Sandra screamed, Bryce hadn't hesitated. White-faced with fury he had launched himself at Len, pounding at him with his fists and feet.

'*See 'ow you like bein' kicked*!' he'd shouted in the brief moment before Len had retaliated. 'I 'ope you go to 'ell and burn forever!'

Len hadn't messed about. He'd fisted him with such force that Bryce had been sent rocketing in Tigger's wake, semiconscious. Even then, that hadn't been the end of it. Len had come at him again, this time with his belt.

There been no school for him that day, or the next few days – not until his bruises had begun to fade.

'If anyone asks, say you were in a street fight,' Auntie Sheila had said to him, tears streaming down her face. 'Please, Bryce. For my sake and Sandra's. Otherwise . . .'

It was a sentence she hadn't finished and hadn't needed to finish. Bryce understood now why she'd been reluctant to take him in and why Sandra was so reticent about her dad. She was scared of him, just as Auntie Sheila was.

He turned the corner into the row, his light-coloured eyes hard as granite as he continued to remember. Tigger had been taken in by Gunter Nowakowska's mum and dad, but he hadn't lived for long.

'He kept whimpering, and he was bleeding from his back passage,' Gunter's mum had said to him and Sandra. 'I reckon some bad bastard laid into him, don't you?'

Neither he nor Sandra had said anything; Bryce had had the feeling they didn't need to. The expression in Mrs Nowakowska's eyes told him that she knew very well a bad bastard had laid into little Tigger – and exactly who the bad bastard had been.

After the incident with Tigger there had been no more pretence of Happy Families at number 8. Every time Len knocked Sheila or Sandra about, Bryce had pitched into him, never to any good purpose and always with the same result – a bloody beating that ensured he wasn't allowed out of the house for days.

'Move into our 'ouse,' Frankie had said to him, time and time again.

He had appreciated the invitation, but, aware that the Parry's were his legal guardians and that Sandra depended on his presence in the house in order to make her life even partially bearable, he hadn't taken Frankie up on it. Only when he was twelve years old and Len threw him out of the house, shouting that he was never to step back into it, did he leave number 8 for good.

Victor Roberts was still his best mate and Mrs Roberts had been appalled at Len Parry's behaviour. ''E needs reportin',' she had said as his nose dripped blood over her kitchen sink. 'Every night we 'ear Sandra cryin'. She started when that little dog of 'ers died, and she don't seem to 'ave stopped since. The best thing you can do, Bryce, love, is to move in 'ere for a while – at least until we see what's what.'

Bryce already knew what was what. Len Parry was a thug and, though he hated being separated from Sandra, he was never going to live beneath his roof again. He wasn't going to live with the Roberts either. Victor might be his best mate, and Victor's mum might put ace dinners on the table, but Mr Roberts was a night-watchman – and in Bryce's eyes, a night-watchman was only a step away from being a policeman.

'Yer mean you'd rather live with the Briscoes than wiv me and me Mum and Dad?' Victor had said, gazing at him goggle-eyed. 'Yer can't mean it, Bryce. They're as rough as a monkey's arse.'

Bryce had shrugged. The Briscoes *were* rough, but at least he knew where he was with them. Victor's mum had said Len Parry needed reporting for his treatment of him, and the way he knocked Sheila and Sandra around, but she hadn't done anything about it and he knew that she wouldn't – not as long as Len Parry lived next door to her.

The Briscoes were different. If one of the Briscoes said they would sort someone, then they sorted them, no messing. The fact that they were always sorting each other out as well – especially when they were drunk and it was closing time – was, to him, neither here nor there. With his new hard attitude to life he'd known he would fit in far better at the rough-and-ready Briscoes than he would with Victor's mum and dad.

It wasn't an arrangement that caused any legal difficulties; the last thing Len Parry wanted was for anyone in authority to be informed and for questions to be asked. As far as his teachers and his doctor were concerned, he was still with the Parrys. In reality he lived with Frankie's family. Though it didn't cause problems elsewhere, it caused major ructions within his gang.

'My mum ain't half giving me grief fer hanging around wiv yer, now you're living with Frankie,' snub-nosed Billy Dixon had said to him. 'She says if yer living with 'em, yer must be like 'em.'

'And yer can't 'ave a gang of yer own – which is us lot,' Robert Wilkinson had pointed out, reasonably if not very grammatically, 'not if yer runnin' wiv Frankie's gang. And me and Richard and Jack ain't goin' to start runnin' with the Briscoes. Our dad'll stand fer a lot, but 'e won't stand fer that.'

80

As his mates had divided into two camps, those who drew the line at having anything to do with the Briscoes and those who didn't, he had become exasperated almost beyond endurance. The Cravens never gave him any grief about his friendship with Frankie – though that wasn't surprising, seeing how friendly their mum had always been with Ginger Briscoe's mum. Gunter Nowakowska, too, was easy about it. Robert and Richard and Jack Wilkinson were a pain in the neck, though, as was Billy Dixon.

'If yer scared of 'anging round wiv me now I live with Frankie, why don't yer start 'anging round with Mummy's Boy Clarkson?' he had jeered at them. 'If yer want a bit of real excitement, yer could go with 'im to the Boys' Brigade.'

The prospect had been so terrible there had been no more whingeing about the kind of trouble they were going to get into at home if they continued hanging around with him. As a gang they had continued to survive, though the Wilkinsons and Victor and Billy steered pretty well clear of any involvement with Frankie's mob.

Bryce's eyes narrowed as he neared number 8. A young married couple had moved into number 6 only days after he had been forced to go and live with the Parrys, and their eldest kiddie was now the same age he had been the summer his mum had died.

Pain knifed through him, as raw now as it had been all those years ago. If the police hadn't been so brain-dead as to have believed his mum was connected with the theft of the money she had handed in – that she had been looking after it for whoever had stolen it and had then been panicked into 'honestly' off-loading it – she would still be alive.

He averted his eyes from the peeling, green painted door, unable to bear the thought of all the ifs and might-have-beens crowding his brain.

The door of number 8 was ajar, which was a good sign. It meant Parry wasn't ranting and raving, for the first thing Sheila did when he got started was to slam all the doors and windows shut in the vain hope that none of her neighbours would hear.

There was a tap from the front bedroom window and he looked up to see Sandra waving down at him, mouthing that she was sorry she was late and would only be another couple of minutes.

Not knowing whether he was relieved or disappointed at avoiding another set-to with Parry, he turned his back on the house and lit a cigarette. Across the row, a little further up at number 11, Roy Clarkson was leaning against the doorjamb watching him. Or was he watching number 8? Bryce's mouth tightened as a thought occurred to him. Had Clarkson been watching the front bedroom window of number 8?

Even though it would be almost another year before he received his national service call-up papers, Clarkson's hair was army short and neatly parted. His trousers – grey flannels – looked positively pre-war and he was wearing a Fair Isle sleeveless pullover over his shirt.

Bryce's lip curled contemptuously. The pullover would have been knitted for him by his mother. It had always been the same. An only child, Roy had always been as namby-pamby as they come and Bryce had never known whether to feel contempt for him or pity. When they'd been small kids he'd made the occasional attempt to be friends, but it had always been a complete waste of time. All Roy had been interested in was playing with his train-set – a Hornby that took up nearly all the floor area of his bedroom. Unlike anyone else in the row, except sometimes Victor, Roy had always done his homework and had passed his eleven-plus and gone to a grammar school, making the division between himself and the rest of them deeper than ever.

'Hi ya,' Sandra said bouncily, bursting out of the house behind him, her fair hair swinging in a ponytail. 'Sorry I'm late. I had a whole pile of Saturday jobs to do for Mum and they took ages.'

Dressed in pink cut-off jeans, a grey cropped mandarin-necked jacket and with black ballerina pumps on her feet, she slipped her arm through his. If her dad was watching, it was just too bad. There wasn't much he could do about her and Bryce any more – and hadn't been since Bryce had turned seventeen and, tough and fit from long hours spent in the boxing gym, had given him the thrashing of his life.

'Does Wonder Boy make a habit of watching your house?' Bryce asked as they began to walk up the row in the direction of Jamaica Road.

Sandra took a swift look over her shoulder to where Roy Clarkson was standing, still watching her. 'Sometimes.' She shrugged, trying to make light of it. After five years of living with Frankie Briscoe's family, Bryce, like them, didn't allow anyone to take liberties with him or his. 'He's harmless, Bry,' she said, not wanting the hapless Roy to be beaten to pulp on her behalf. 'Bloody pathetic, really.'

It was so patently true that Bryce merely grunted and thought no more about it. Sandra did, though. Roy Clarkson fancied her – had fancied her for ages – and he was beginning to be a nuisance.

'You should encourage Roy Clarkson,' her mother was always saying to her. 'I know he's only working as a furniture salesman at the moment, but he's just filling in time until he does his national service. Once he's got that over with he's going to go to teacher-training college.'

Sandra didn't care if Roy Clarkson was going to be the next Prime Minister. There was something odd about him and there always had been. 'I'm going to marry Bryce,' she had said, being utterly, certainly sure of it. 'Just as soon as I'm sixteen we're going to elope to Gretna Green, and

I'll never have to live with my dad again – and nor will you, Mum. When me and Bryce have a place of our own, you'll live with us.'

At the mere thought of such salvation, relief had swamped her mother's weary, gaunt face. Another emotion, conflicting with the relief, had followed fast and Sandra had been well aware of what it had been: disappointment.

Long ago, when Bryce and his mum had lived next door to them, her mother had had fond daydreams of her and Bryce marrying. Those days, however, were long gone. Bryce was no longer what her mother termed 'nice and respectable'. Unlike Roy Clarkson he didn't dress 'nicely', instead he preferred draped jackets, lurid-coloured shirts, string ties, drainpipe trousers and thick crêpe-soled shoes. He didn't have a 'nice' and 'respectable' job either. Whereas Roy Clarkson went to work dressed in a smart suit, Bryce earned his living in jeans and a donkey-jacket, helping Big Chas Briscoe run the family scrap-metal business.

She tightened her hold on his arm, convinced that it wouldn't always be like that. Once they were married with a place of their own, Bryce would have less and less to do with Frankie and the Briscoe family.

'Do you fancy goin' north of the river tonight?' Bryce asked, breaking in on her thoughts as he walked her out of the row with a swagger indicating he owned it. 'The Cravens and Robert Wilkinson went to a dance hall at Tottenham last Saturday: the Royal. They said the place was heaving.'

Sandra nodded. 'If that's what you want to do, Bry,' she said, happy to do whatever he wanted, just as she had when they'd been kids.

From his near six-foot height he shot her a swift, down-slanting smile. 'I love you, Sand,' he said, knowing he must do or why else did he drive himself crackers, respecting her virginity? He certainly wasn't such a gent where other girls were concerned – but then, he wasn't going to marry any of the other girls who, when Sand wasn't about, swarmed around him like bees around a honey-pot.

Carelessly happy, mercifully oblivious of what the immediate future held, he steered her into the noisy coffee-bar his gang habitually hung out in.


Roy Clarkson stared moodily up the now empty row. There was no one about, not even a poxy Briscoe. He wondered if the rumours he had heard were true and Big Chas Briscoe really did have a mansion somewhere out on the Kent borders. It wouldn't surprise him. Big Chas must have thieved enough money in his time to be able to fund a whole string of mansions.

He stopped thinking about the Briscoes and began once more thinking about Sandra Parry. His prick stirred, so swollen and heavy it hurt. For as long as he could remember, he'd wanted Sandra to take some notice of him and she never had done. Instead, she followed Bryce bloody Reece around like a little puppy-dog.

He didn't understand it. Reece was as near to being a dog-rough Briscoe as made no damn difference. For years, whenever his mother went into Dixon's corner shop, she and Lilian Dixon had grimly predicted that both Bryce Reece and Frankie Briscoe would finish up on the end of a rope. It was a fate that couldn't come quick enough for them as far as he was concerned.

He plunged a hand deeper in his trouser pocket in an effort to ease the insistent throbbing of his prick, his thoughts once again reverting to Sandra Parry. She obviously let Bryce Reece go all the way with her, because good-looking, swaggering louts like Reece always went all the way with the tarts they went out with. He wondered where they did it. Not in Sandra's bedroom, that was for sure. Len Parry hadn't allowed Reece over number 8's threshold for years. At the Briscoes', then? Or at night, in the local recreation ground; or perhaps standing up in a dark shop doorway?

Sharply he stepped back off the doorstep, into the house, slamming the door shut. His mother and father were on a Methodist church outing to Bognor. It was that rare occasion; a Saturday when he was home from work and had the house to himself. He could get his girlie magazines out from their hiding place beneath the floorboards of his room and drool over them with no fear of being disturbed. And he'd think of Sandra Parry whilst doing so. He had quite a repertoire of fantasies, but fucking Sandra was his favourite.

Sandra tied a pink chiffon scarf jauntily around her throat and looked at herself in the mirror, her head tilted slightly to one side. Would she do? Never having been to the Royal before, she had no idea how the girls who went there dressed. She had as many stiff net petticoats beneath her azure-blue felt skirt as she could cram and her waist was cinched to a handspan by a black elastic waspie belt. She flicked up the collar of her white shirt blouse and then leant towards the mirror and spat on her mascara block. One more coating on her eyelashes and she would be ready.

She liked Saturdays. The afternoons were nearly always spent, as this afternoon had been, in the coffee-bar on Jamaica Road, playing the jukebox, drinking Coke and listening to Bryce's gang's daftness. Billy Dixon had just become a gravedigger for the local council and the stories he told were creepily hilarious. Robert Wilkinson was a milkman, like his dad, but unlike his dad he was the kind of milkman risqué jokes were told about and his stories about some of the married women on his round had to be heard to be believed.

Richard Wilkinson, at sixteen a year younger than Robert and Victor and Bryce, had managed to get himself a job in the print. It was generally agreed that, job-wise, he was set for life. Only Victor envied him.

'Who the 'ell wants to know what job they'll be doing this time next year or this time in ten years?' Richard's kid brother, Jack, had asked scoffingly. ''Ow bleedin' boring can yer get? Yer might as well be dead.'

'At least I'll always know where my next pay packet's coming from,' Richard had said, flushing scarlet.

It was a statement that had been greeted by howls of laughter. Copping hold of a pay packet was no problem whatsoever. Gunter was in the scaffolding business and when he wasn't showing off to girls in the street, teetering bare-chested along steel girders seventy and eighty feet from the ground, he was arranging with Jimmy Briscoe, and Jimmy's cousins Ginger and Terry, to go back at night and dismantle whatever it was he had been helping to erect. The four of them would then hoist the girders on to the back of a lorry and fifteen minutes later the lorryload would be safely in the Briscoes' scrap-yard and Big Chas would be handing them a wad of cash, no questions asked.

The Cravens, too, weren't averse to a bit of shady ducking and diving, but it was young Jack Wilkinson who had become the real tearaway of the gang. Only fifteen and so good-looking he was already stealing girlfriends from his older brothers, he was as thick as thieves with Ginger and Terry Briscoe and so recklessly daring even Frankie admired him.

The conversation for much of the afternoon had centred on the subject of John Christie, who had been hung some months previously after the bodies of four women, one of them his wife, had been found strangled and walled up in his house.

'And four years ago 'is lodger was hung for murdering 'is wife,' Victor had said with keen interest. 'Two murderers livin' together in one house is too much to believe, ain't it?'

The general consensus of opinion was that Christie had obviously done for his lodger's wife and then let his lodger be hung for it.

The subject had been so grisly that, remembering it, Sandra shuddered as she surveyed her spikily coated eyelashes. Satisfied with them, she walked swiftly out of the room, her many-layered net underskirt rustling. Her dad hadn't knocked her about for ages now – not since he'd become wary of Bryce – but she still didn't want to come to his attention, for if she did, she knew she'd be on the receiving end of a whole torrent of verbal abuse.

Quietly, under cover of the noise of the television, she let herself out of the house. She was a few minutes late – as usual – and Bryce would already be outside Tucker's, waiting for her. Walking as quickly as her stiletto-heeled shoes allowed, she'd barely gone half a dozen yards when she heard someone hurrying across the road behind her.

'Sandra!' There was no mistaking the voice and her heart sank. 'Sandra, have you got a minute?'

Reluctantly she came to a halt and turned to face Roy Clarkson. Further up the row, on the other side of the road, the door of number 11 was wide open, as if he'd left home in a rush.

'What is it, Roy?' she said pleasantly, polite as always. 'I'm in a hurry.'

'It's . . . there's a problem at home.'

Even though she didn't want to look at him, she couldn't help it, not when his Adam's apple was bobbing up and down as if it had a life of its own.

'There's a stray cat in the house,' he said, obviously agitated. 'It's jumped on top of a wardrobe and I can't get it to come down.'

'And?' Looking at him, his Boys' Brigade-short hair looking oddly ruffled, as if he'd just got out of bed, Sandra didn't know whether to feel irritation or compassion. He

88

was nearly eighteen, for pity's sake! Surely he could sort out a cat?

'And . . . and I think it's hurt,' he said, picking nervously at a spot as she made no sign of offering to come across to the house.

It was a masterstroke. Late as she now was in meeting Bryce, there was no way Sandra could turn her back on an injured animal.

'Couldn't your mother help you with it?' she asked, her heels tip-tapping on the cobbles as she began to cross the road in the direction of number 11.

As awkward physically as he was socially, Roy half-walked and half-loped at her side. Not for the first time, she noticed how large his hands were; far too big for his narrow, bony wrists.

'She's on a church outing,' he said, reaching number 11's open front door before her and standing with his back against it so that she had to brush past him to enter the house. 'She doesn't like cats. They give her asthma. That's why I have to get it out of the house.'

Sandra mentally called Hilda Clarkson a rude word. A foray into number 11 was not her idea of a good way to start off a Saturday night. The house was like a tomb, for one thing. Where most people in the row, even the Briscoes, had moved with the times, decorating their living-rooms 'contemporary' so that the walls were covered in two differently patterned and colourful wall-papers, the Clarksons had kept to pre-war treacle-brown paint and muddy cream paper. There was no cheerfully bright linoleum on the floor, either. Instead it was a dingy green, reminding Sandra of a hospital ward.

'Which bedroom is the cat in?' she asked, eager to get her mission of mercy over and done with as quickly as possible. 'The front or the back?'

'The . . . the back.' Roy could scarcely believe his luck. She was in the house. They were on their own together.

Now all he had to do was to make a pass at her. 'Would you like a cup of tea?'

Standing at the bottom of the stairs, her hand already on the dull wood of the banisters, Sandra stared at him as if he'd taken leave of his senses. 'I'm here to help you with a stray cat, Roy,' she said, aware of Bryce waiting for her outside Tucker's and holding on to her temper only with difficulty. 'Now, are we going to get on with things or not?'

'Yes ... only ... perhaps if we have a cup of tea first the cat will fall asleep. Then it will be easier to catch, won't it?'

Sandra lifted her eyes to heaven. How could anyone be so dozy? At the thought of what Bryce would say when she told him of why she was so late, giggles rose in her throat.

Roy registered her reaction and his nails dug deep into his palms. She was laughing at him. She thought he was weedy and inept. He shouldn't have offered her tea. He should have bought in something alcoholic. Babycham, perhaps.

She was standing on the first tread of the stairs and her breasts were almost level with his eyes. Beneath the white cotton of her blouse he could see the faint outline of a white lace-edged bra. For a fifteen-year-old girl her breasts were full and lush, just like the breasts of the girls in the magazines he had been poring over all afternoon. Some of the girls had had erect nipples. He wondered what Sandra's nipples would look like when they were erect. He wondered what shade they would be. Would they be a dark glossy red or would they be a pale satiny pink?

His prick was burning and throbbing so hard he felt giddy. 'Are we going upstairs then, or not?' she was saying impatiently.

He cleared his throat, trying to think of what was the best thing to do. Once she went upstairs and found there was no cat, she'd be out of the house in a flash. He'd imagined them sitting in the kitchen drinking tea together. He'd imagined asking her if she fancied going to the cinema. He'd imagined her saying things such as how strange it was that they'd never spent time together before. None of that would happen if she went upstairs. When she saw there was no cat on top of the wardrobe she might cotton on to the fact that there'd never been a cat in the house at all, and then what would happen? Would she be angry or would she laugh at him? And when she was next with Bryce Reece, would they laugh at him together?

'I haven't got all day, Roy.' She turned away from him and began to run lightly up the stairs. From where he was standing he could see the swirling ruffles of her underskirt; he could see high up her legs, too. She was wearing stockings and though he couldn't see her suspenders, he wanted to. 'And if you don't mind me saying so,' she added as she neared the top step, 'I've got much better things to do with my time than waste it here with you.'

Roy did mind her saying so. He minded so much that the churning emotions he had sat tight on for so long could be controlled no longer. Anger at the unfairness of life, fraught sexual frustration, the knowledge of his own pitiful inadequacies – all erupted into a God Almighty explosion.

'Cunt!' he shouted, his voice breaking on a sob. 'Slag!'

Sandra was so stunned that she missed her footing on the top step. She fell down hard on the minuscule landing, breaking her fall with splayed hands, her knees hitting threadbare carpet.

If she'd fallen down willingly for him, Roy's reaction couldn't have been any swifter. Blood was pounding in his cock and behind his eyes; he was off the leash and out of control, determined that for once he was going to

91

do what *he* wanted to do – he was going to do to Sandra Parry what Bryce Reece did to her.

Before she could struggle to her feet, he seized hold of her by the ankles, dragging her knees from under her, filled with the raging desire to do more than simply fuck her. He wanted to hurt her. He wanted to make her *pay*. To pay for having always ignored him; for having preferred Bryce Reece's company to his; for making him feel stupid and inadequate; above all, for *laughing* at him!

'Roy! *Roy!*' One of his hands was in her ponytail and he was using it to wrench her on to her back. '*Stop it! Stop it! STOP IT!*'

He wasn't listening. He couldn't even hear her. All he was aware of was the sound of his own voice shouting over and over again, '*Bitch! Bitch! Bitch!*'

Sandra clawed and kicked and struggled, terrified at the discovery that weedy Roy Clarkson was too strong for her; still unable to believe what was happening. He was on top of her now and she could smell his sweat and feel his spittle on her face. Desperately she bucked in an effort to be free of him and her head slammed into the wall.

She was crying now, no longer disbelieving. He had her wrists pinioned above her head and his free hand – his big, ugly, over-large hand – was up her skirt, in her knickers.

'*Please stop! Oh, please stop!*' She was no longer shouting. She was pleading, tears streaming down her face.

Roy liked hearing her plead. No one had ever pleaded with him over anything before. Handicapped by having to keep her hands pinioned; by the violent struggles she was still making; by never having done before what he was now attempting to do, he rammed blindly at her fanny with his swollen prick.

'*Oh God!*' she sobbed, tightening her body against him, pain and fear and revulsion engulfing her. '*No! Oh Christ, NO!*'

Roy's throbbing member found what it was looking

for and, terrified that success would elude him at the last possible moment, with eyes tight shut he rammed himself home.

Bryce had nearly reached number 8 when he heard Sandra's muffled scream. He'd waited at Tucker's until quarter to eight, and then, when there was still no sign of her, had headed back into the row to see what was keeping her. He was pretty annoyed with her, for it wasn't as if they were going to go over to the Royal ballroom by themselves. The entire gang was going, with both Curly and Gunter taking girls with them.

Bearing in mind that they'd be way off their own patch and that dance halls were territorial places where scuffles over girls often developed into full-scale fights, he had his flick-knife on him. Years of going to the Thomas à Becket boxing gym in the Old Kent Road had made him so expert with his fists that he was contemptuous of knives, but he knew that the tough North London gangs who frequented the Royal would be tooled-up and, in the foreign territory of Tottenham – and with Sandra with him – he wanted to be safe rather than sorry.

With his hair in an immaculate teddy boy roll and wearing a maroon drape jacket and a brand new pair of drainpipes, he was just about to hammer hard on number 8's door when Sandra screamed.

He didn't know it was Sandra, of course, not at first. He simply turned round to check the street, mildly curious. Then there was another scream, and this time there was no mistaking the nature of it, or the direction from which it was coming. It was coming from inside number 11.

He knew then. He knew by instinct, instantly and without the slightest shadow of a doubt. He streaked across the road, bursting into the house with such force that the door rocked on its hinges, slamming shut after him as he went flying headlong into the narrow hallway.

He wasn't off balance for more than a second. At the top of the stairs Roy Clarkson was sprawled post-orgasmically on top of Sandra, his pants down, his bare arse sickly white. Sandra was no longer screaming. With her hair tugged out of its ponytail, her skirt rucked to her waist, one shoe half-on, the other missing completely, she was sobbing as she struggled to push herself free of Roy Clarkson's slumped body.

It wasn't slumped for long. In the same moment that Bryce catapulted into the hallway, his eyes on the scene taking place at the top of the stairs, Roy began scrambling free of Sandra, dementedly trying to distance himself from what had happened, and from Bryce. '*Get out*! *Get out*!' he shouted in high-pitched near hysteria. '*This is my house, Bryce Reece*! *I haven't done anything wrong*! *She came round here begging for it . . . asking for it*!' He was stumbling to his feet, grabbing at his trousers, the knob of his rapidly deflating prick glistening with spunk and a gleam of blood. '*Don't hit me*! *Oh Christ*! *Oh shit*!'

Bryce was leaping up the stairs, taking them two and three at a time. Vainly Roy staggered backwards, trying to gain the bathroom; knowing his only chance of escaping being hurt was to be on the far side of a locked door.

Sandra, still sobbing, was using her heels to push herself frantically backwards on her bottom, out of the way.

Bryce registered her total dishevelment; her torn stocking-tops, her ripped knickers, her scratched inner thighs, and with a roar of primeval rage he leapt the top step and dived on Roy.

It could never have been a fair fight. Bryce had spent too many years being a gang leader and running wild with the Briscoes for Roy to stand a chance against him. Luck, however, was on Roy's side. As Bryce's fist connected with his jaw, sending him slamming into the wall beside the bathroom door, Bryce slipped on the thin carpeting. Driven on by the momentum of the punch he had just thrown he fell heavily against the newel post.

With his back against the wall in far more ways than one, Roy launched himself into the kind of action he would never have believed himself capable of. He sprang on to Bryce's back, one arm tightening round his throat, the other gouging at his eyes.

Bryce could feel himself teetering on the edge of the top step. The ignominy of his position, Roy Clarkson having gained an advantage over him, was beyond belief. He could hear Sandra screaming. He remembered her torn underwear; the deep scratch marks on her inner thighs made by Clarkson's fingernails; the smear of blood on Clarkson's prick.

'*Bastard*!' he shouted and, struggling to prevent himself from falling, he reached for the flick-knife. The movement he made with it, behind him and upwards, was totally blind. It wasn't a purposeful lunge to Roy's heart, but it may as well have been.

There was a moment when everything seemed to pause; everything except Sandra's hysterical screaming, and then Bryce twisted from beneath Roy's weight and it was Roy, not Bryce, who, with a long sucking sound, toppled headlong down the stairs.

'*Oh God! Oh Jesus!*' Sandra was on her feet, grasping hold of the newel post, shaking convulsively. '*You've killed him, Bryce! He isn't moving! He isn't even groaning!*'

'The bastard's unconscious, that's all.' Bryce pushed his teddy boy roll of hair away from his forehead, his eyes meeting hers. 'You all right, Sand?' His voice was choked. He didn't give a stuff about Clarkson's prone body lying in a crumpled heap at the foot of the stairs. All he cared about was Sandra.

'Yes . . .' She nodded, far from being all right. She was terrified now, not for herself but for Bryce. 'Look,

Bry, Roy's huddled up all funny! He's dead, I know he is!'

Bryce looked down the stairs. Sandra was right. There was something creepily sinister about the way Clarkson was lying ... and the flick-knife was no longer in his hand but embedded somewhere in Clarkson's miserable rotten body.

'Take a look at him, Bry.' Sandra couldn't stop shaking; without the newel post to hold on to she wouldn't have even been able to stand.

With great reluctance Bryce began to walk down the stairs. He'd wanted Roy to be dead. When he'd charged up the stairs towards him, his one intention had been to beat the scumbag senseless ... and then some. Roy had cheated him of that satisfaction. He'd only punched him the once before he'd slipped on the carpet and Roy had leapt on to his back.

He reached the bottom step suddenly aware of how very, very quiet it was. Roy lay utterly lifeless and, though Bryce couldn't see the knife in his chest without moving the body – and the last thing he wanted to do was to touch Roy Clarkson at all – he knew now where it was embedded. And he knew that Roy was dead.

'Christ ...' He whispered beneath his breath. 'Jesus fucking Christ.'

'Bryce?' The newel post was no longer enough support for Sandra. She slid down it on to her knees. 'What are we going to do, Bryce? What are we –'

It was a sentence she never finished, for suddenly it was no longer quiet. Footsteps could be heard coming down the row. And voices.

'I hope to goodness our Roy has got the kettle on,' Hilda Clarkson could be heard saying as the footsteps came to a halt outside number 11's front door. 'I could murder a cup of tea.'

Bryce felt his bowels turning to water. There was going

to be no getting out of this one. He remembered how Norman Clarkson had hauled him from the Thames the day the quicksand had so nearly done for Frankie. He owed Norman Clarkson, and for that reason if for no other, he wished to God he hadn't had his knife on him when he'd stormed into the house.

'What the devil . . . ?' Mr Clarkson began as he pushed the door open and, about to step over the threshold, stopped short, stunned at the sight of Bryce Reece in his hallway.

'What's the matter?' Hilda pushed belligerently past him and then, on seeing Bryce, stopped short just as he had done. '*What are you doing here*?' she demanded in high-pitched indignation. '*What* . . .' And then she saw her son's body on the floor and there were no more words, only screams.

Her screams went on and on, resounding in Bryce's brain as first the ambulance arrived, and then the police. 'He was raping Sandra!' he shouted over and over again, Sandra hysterically confirming every word. 'I didn't mean to kill him, but he shouldn't have touched Sandra!'

It was useless. No one was listening to him and he could hardly hear his words himself. Sheila had run across the narrow road from number 8 and, clutching and hugging Sandra, was giving vent to hysterics even noisier than Sandra's.

Len was there, too, putting in his twopenny-worth about how he'd always known Bryce Reece was a bad lot. By the time Bryce felt handcuffs snapping on his wrists there was quite a crowd for Len to spout off to. Victor Roberts' mum had run across the road, leaving her front door wide open behind her. Effie Craven had barrelled up the row, her head bristling hedgehog-like with pink plastic curlers. He was aware of the horrified expression on Pearl Nowakowska's face and the disbelieving one on Joan Wilkinson's.

'He was raping Sandra!' he shouted again as he was manhandled towards a police car. 'It wouldn't have happened if he hadn't raped Sandra!'

'*Liar!*' The screeched epithet was hurled by Hilda Clarkson as she struggled against the restraining hold of her husband and a policewoman. '*You were burgling my house and having it off on my floor with your tart of a girlfriend and my Roy walked in on the pair of you! I know how it was, Bryce Reece!*'

Even as he was bundled into the back of the car, Sandra still screaming his name, Hilda Clarkson's voice resounded after him. '*And the judge will know as well!*' She was free of restraining handholds now, running towards the police car, battering on the rear window, spittle foaming at the corners of her mouth. '*You'll hang for murdering my Roy!*' she sobbed as it pulled away from the kerb. '*You'll swing by the neck, Bryce Reece! You'll swing until you're dead!*'

# Chapter Five

'Bryce! *Bryce*!' Sandra screamed his name as, accompanied by her mother and a policewoman, she too was bundled into a police car. 'It was an *accident*!' she sobbed as the car sped out of the row. 'Bryce wasn't robbing the Clarksons! Roy raped me, Mum! He *raped* me!'

Hugging herself desperately, she rocked backwards and forwards, terrifyingly aware that the world had gone mad. No one believed her. She could tell that no one believed her. Her mother was patting her arm and making crooning, comforting noises, but she didn't believe her; she wasn't saying loud and clear that Bryce would never in a million years have entered the Clarkson house in order to rob it; that he and she would never, *never* have made love beneath Hilda's horrid, hateful roof.

Hiccuping, gasping for breath between sobs, she knew *why* her mother didn't believe her. It was because Roy Clarkson was such an unlikely rapist. If it had been anyone else – Frankie Briscoe, Jimmy Briscoe, even one of the Cravens – then her mother would have believed her, but she wasn't going to believe that studious, wimpish, too-good-to-be-true Roy was capable of rape. And if her mother didn't believe it, then no one would.

The utter horror of it, the poleaxing terror as she realised that Hilda's crazy allegations would be believed, was suffocating in its intensity. '*I want Bryce*!' she screamed as the car swept through the gates of the police station's parking area. '*I want to see Bryce*!'

'My dad says Sandra isn't going to be allowed to see Bryce,'

Victor said, as, four weeks after Roy Clarkson's death, he and the rest of Bryce's gang met with Frankie to glumly mull things over.

'That ain't surprising.' Frankie chewed the corner of his lip. 'What is surprising, though, is that the cozzers seriously believe Bryce was robbin' the Clarksons' gaff.' Perplexity made his squint more pronounced than ever. 'I mean, Bryce might live at our place but, 'e ain't got no form – 'e's never been done for nuffink. Not ever.'

'It was that bloody cow, Hilda, who put the idea in everyone's heads,' Victor said flatly, knowing no one was going to disagree with him. No one did. Instead they pondered the unbelievable outcome of Hilda's demented accusation.

The fact that Roy had been found with his trousers at half-mast and spunk glistening on his prick had been explained away by the girlie magazines found in his bedroom. Roy, the police contended, had been upstairs masturbating when Bryce and Sandra had broken into what they believed to be an empty house. They had then fornicated on the landing at the top of the stairs and Roy, hearing them, had been too frightened to disclose his presence. Only when Bryce had begun a troll of the bedrooms for jewellery had the confrontation taken place, resulting in Roy being stabbed in the chest, the knife puncturing his heart and causing instantaneous death.

That was one police version of what had taken place. The other was so sick even Frankie had been dumbstruck by it. It was that the confrontation had taken place *before* Bryce and Sandra had indulged in sexual relations; that they had done so as Roy had lain dying at the foot of the stairs.

'If the jury believe that one,' Victor had said grimly, 'they'll sentence Bryce to death whether he's under-age or not.'

That having been charged with Roy's murder, Bryce would face the ultimate penalty, was a terror that was traumatising all his friends. Bryce's eighteenth birthday had taken place only a couple of weeks after Roy's death. Technically, as he was under-age when the crime was committed, the death penalty should not have been an issue, but Bryce was eighteen now and, in Jug Ears' much-voiced opinion, the judiciary would, if they could, stitch things so that Bryce swung.

Even thinking about it brought Victor out in a cold sweat. Until the horror over Roy Clarkson's death had begun he'd always skirted shy of involvement with Frankie and the Briscoes. Now, however, his conversations with Frankie's uncle, Big Chas, were long and intense and on a daily basis.

'How long will Bryce be held on remand?' he had asked him only a few hours earlier, waylaying Big Chas as he left his office in the scrap-metal yard. 'My dad says it could be months before his case comes to trial. Maybe not even until next year.'

'Depends a lot on whether his case goes to Sessions or the Old Bailey,' Chas had said, dropping a cigarette to the pavement and grinding it to ashes beneath the heel of a highly polished shoe. 'With the committal proceedings already under way it'd probably be quickest if it went to Sessions.'

'And then what?' He hadn't been able to put into words the nightmare dogging him night and day: that Bryce would be hanged as, a couple of years ago, nineteen-year-old Derek Bentley had been.

Big Chas had rocked back on his heels, scarlet braces straining over a hard-muscled paunch. 'Because of his age, he'll be detained during the Queen's pleasure,' he'd said knowledgeably. 'For how long is anyone's guess. If he's lucky, maybe seven years and out in five.'

'Thanks, Chas,' he'd said, thankful that someone who knew what they were about had Bryce's interests at heart.

It was Big Chas who, in the aftermath of Bryce's arrest,

had swiftly established himself as being, as near to dammit, Bryce's kith and kin and had gained visiting access to him. He had also announced he was engaging a top-class lawyer for Bryce's defence.

Though Big Chas's scrap-yard was within spitting distance of Swan Row, and though his family connections ensured most of his time was spent in the row, Big Chas was moneyed. Rumour was that most of the money that had bought his mansion out in Kent, near Eynsford, had been stolen from Barclays Bank. Big Chas said it had been paid for from the profits from his very profitable scrap-metal business.

Whatever the truth of it, as well as being a hardened villain he was a shrewd businessman and, wearing his businessman's hat, he had long regarded Bryce as his protégé.

It was Bryce's pluck and nerve in saving Frankie from the Thames that had first brought him to Chas's attention. Pluck and nerve were qualities he deeply admired – and Bryce had proved he possessed both qualities in spadefuls.

Over the years Bryce had proved ace at helping him run the scrap-yard. It had been Bryce who had suggested to Gunter Nowakowska that the scaffolding he and his mates erected through the day could be criminally dismantled, finding its way to the Briscoe yard by night. Whatever the circumstance Bryce had never let him down and he had no intention of letting Bryce down.

Sandra, charged as a minor with breaking and entering, had no such strong character batting in her corner. Len declared loud and long, to both the police and neighbours, that Bryce Reece was a bad lot through and through and ought to hang, and that his daughter, involved with Reece against all his parental advice, deserved whatever sentence she got.

'It's a bit of a rum do, ain't it?' Effie Craven had said to Pearl Nowakowska as they walked down the row to

Tucker's. 'I can believe a lot of things of Bryce Reece, but I can't believe 'e'd stab that silly sod Roy in the chest. It just ain't 'is style.'

'No, it ain't.' Pearl's finely plucked eyebrows had pulled into an unhappy frown. 'But 'e did 'ave a knife on 'im, Effie. What if your boys and my Gunter carry knives as well? They're all mates. What one of 'em does, the others do, 'specially since they've all been in this teddy boy lark together.'

Effie, who knew her boys carried flick-knives and who was sure Gunter Nowakowska did, too, had ignored the question and, concentrating on the aspect of events at the Clarkson house that mystified her the most had said, 'And what about Sandra supposedly 'aving it off with Bryce on Hilda Clarkson's carpet? I don't believe it in a million years. Sandra's too much like her mum. She's very fastidious about her person. Shiny-clean hair, clean fingernails, clean shoes. Shagging on Hilda's best bit of Sisal just ain't in keeping with all that, is it?'

'No, it ain't,' Pearl had said again, her frown deepening. 'Trouble is, Effie, the alternative – that Roy was raping Sandra and that that was why Bryce barged into the house – ain't any easier to believe. The magistrate she came up in front of didn't believe it, did he? And if he didn't, why should the judge when Bryce comes to trial?'

Sandra had been deemed to have played no role in the attempted burglary or in Roy's death. Her version of events, that she had been raped and that the knifing of Roy had been near accidental, a blind thrust by Bryce as, with Roy gouging at his eyes, he had teetered on the top step of the stairs, had been discounted as a fabrication to aid Bryce's defence.

Charged with breaking and entering, her appearance before the magistrate had been brief. Her solicitor put forward the case that Bryce had entered the Clarkson house first and then opened the door to her as if he were there at Roy's invitation, and that she had entered the house unaware of his illegal intentions. Distraught to the point of being near out of her mind, she had looked far younger than fifteen. The sentence she had received, two years probation, had been unbelievably light.

Sandra hadn't regarded it as being light, though, not when she realised the full implications of her defence statement. It had been one her lawyer had insisted was necessary if she were to avoid one or two, or perhaps three years in an approved school. Only afterwards did she realise the pit she had dug for herself. She couldn't now assist Bryce's defence by testifying at his trial as to what had really happened; not when she had sworn to an entirely different version of events before a magistrate.

What she had done, out of fear and distress and ignorance, was to collude with Hilda Clarkson's version of events – a version the police seemed to regard as being gospel. She had let Bryce down in the most terrible way possible and she knew no way of making amends.

'Why won't people believe what Bryce keeps telling them?' she had sobbed to Victor as the horror had gone on and on; first her own appearance at court and then the long months of remand for Bryce, his court date set for sometime in January. 'How is it no one in the row saw Roy and me walking into his house together? How is it no one, apart from Bryce, heard me screaming my head off five minutes later? *Someone* must have seen something that would prove Bryce wasn't in there to burgle the place. Why is everyone so eager to believe the worst of Bryce, Victor? Why will no one believe the truth when they hear it?'

Victor had been unable to come up with an answer. Any number of Briscoes were quite prepared to go in the witness-box and swear they had seen Roy and Sandra entering number 11 together a good five minutes before Bryce raced across to the house, but Big Chas's QC had advised against their doing so. With their reputations, and knowing they would be lying, such testimony could do more harm than good.

'I haff seen Sandra come out of her house and walking down the row, in the opposite direction to number 11, about ten minutes before the time the police say that Roy was killed,' Gunter's father, Anton Nowakowska said to Victor when asked if he'd seen or heard anything which could possibly help Bryce. 'That must haff been just after seven thirty and she was by herself then. Bryce wasn't with her.'

Victor's heart had felt as if it was going to stop. 'And did you see Roy run after her, Mr Nowakowska? Did you see him talking to her, spinning her the line about the cat? Did you see her turn round and walk back up the row to number 11 with him?'

The silence that followed was so long Victor lost nearly all hope. Mr Nowakowska was an East European Roman Catholic and Victor knew, from Gunter, that his religion was very important to him. Mr Nowakowska wouldn't lie on oath; it would be too great a sin. On the other hand, for Bryce to receive a heavy sentence for a crime that had been accidental, not intentional, was also a sin.

'Bryce didn't mean to kill Roy, Mr Nowakowska,' he said fiercely. 'It was an accident. And Roy *did* run after Sandra in the street. He *did* ask her to go into the house with him. If only someone saw him go up to Sandra, saw them walk into the house together, then the judge would know that Bryce didn't enter the house with Sandra in order to burgle it. It's very important, Mr Nowakowska. It would be a *sin* if, instead of believing the truth, the court believed lies!'

Their eyes held, Victor's burning with passion, Anton Nowakowska's troubled and then, after what seemed an eternity, decisive.

'I haff seen them,' he said, using the words he knew he would have to use to policemen or a solicitor. 'I haff seen

105

them out of the corner of my eye as I turned away from the window. Iff there is the chance that Bryce vill hang for vhat it is they say he has done, then I think that I did definitely see Sandra and Roy together.'

Victor had been euphoric. That he hadn't been able to find anyone who had seen Bryce waiting for Sandra outside Tucker's wasn't going to matter too much now. Not with a statement from a man like Mr Nowakowska – a war hero of irreproachable reputation. It was a statement any jury would have to take seriously. First he relayed the news to Big Chas, then he knocked on the door of number 8 to tell Sandra.

Sandra heard the knocking on the door but, lobster-red in a scalding-hot bath, an empty brown bottle lying beside the taps, her face blotched and bloated from crying, she made no attempt to answer it.

She was pregnant. She just knew she was pregnant. She hadn't had a period for three months, her nipples had got bigger and darker and her skirts would no longer zip up. She was pregnant with Roy Clarkson's baby and she had to get rid of it – and she had no idea how.

She'd told the man in the herbalist's that she thought she must be anaemic as she'd stopped having periods and needed something to bring them on. She could tell he knew that she really wanted something to end a pregnancy, but he'd gone along with the pretence of her 'anaemia', and had sold her a concoction that would, he said, put matters right if she drank it all at one go whilst sitting in the hottest bath she could bear. This she was now doing, but nothing was happening and she had a terrible feeling that nothing was going to happen.

'*Sandra*!' Victor wouldn't have yelled through the letter-box if there'd been the slightest chance her mum and dad were in the house – especially her dad – but he'd passed Mr and Mrs Parry leaving the row as he entered it. '*Can yer hear me, Sandra?*' he shouted persistently. '*I've got some good news – don't yer want to hear it?*'

Five minutes later, huddled in a dressing-gown and with tears still coursing down her scarlet-flushed cheeks, Sandra opened the door to him.

'Christ, Sand! What've yer bin doing?' he said, startled. 'Yer look as though yer've bin tryin' to boil yerself alive!'

His sympathetic presence was more than she could cope with. 'I'm p-p-pregnant, Victor!' she howled, throwing herself against his chest. 'I'm p-p-pregnant with Roy Cl-Cl-Clarkson's baby!'

'Christ All-bleedin'-Mighty!' Before any nosey-parker should see them or overhear, Victor hustled her off the doorstep and into the house. 'You're *what*?' he said incredulously, once he had slammed the front door shut. 'Are you *sure*, Sand? Are yer sure it ain't Bryce's . . . ?'

Sandra's open palm cracked hard across his face. '*Me an' Bryce never, not ever . . .*' She was in hysterics, near incoherent. '*I was saving myself for my wedding night, Victor Roberts! I was a virgin when that . . . that pervert raped me!*' She was sobbing so hard he was terrified that if he let go of her she'd fall to her knees. '*How am I going to get rid of it, Victor? How am I going to get rid of it?*'

Victor didn't have a clue. Why should he? Getting rid of babies was something girls knew about. When Curly Craven's girlfriend had found herself in the family way she'd sorted it out herself. Curly hadn't been involved. All Curly had done was drink himself silly with relief when she'd told him everything was tickety-boo again.

'I can't tell Mum.' Sandra wiped her dripping nose with the back of her hand. 'If I tell Mum, Dad will find out and he'll kill me. No messing, Victor. He'll kill me, I swear he will.'

Victor knew enough about Len Parry to realise that her fear was justified. 'I came to tell yer that Gunter's dad is willing to swear 'e saw you walkin' down the row and Roy Clarkson runnin' after you and then the two of you walkin' back towards number 11,' he said inadequately, stalling for time, frantically trying to think of what it was she should be doing. Drinking gin, surely? And drinking it in a hot bath. He remembered how lobster-red she'd been when she'd opened the door to him. She'd probably been doing that already. 'Coming from a war 'ero like Gunter's dad, it should be enough to swing things in Bryce's favour,' he added, remembering something he'd once heard about knitting needles.

Sandra gave a choking hiccup, her relief vast. 'That's smashing news.' Her voice cracked and broke. 'But what about me, Victor? I can't have this . . . this . . . *thing* of Roy's growing and growing inside of me! The thought of it is sending me mental. I have to get rid of it! If I don't, I swear to God I'll kill myself!'

She clutched hold of his arm, tears once more streaming down her face. 'There are women . . . women who know what to do and who will do it if they're paid. You've got to find me one, Victor!'

'I can give you an address, but it'll cost you a tenner,' the herbalist said when Victor asked him for the name of an abortionist. 'The lady in question don't come cheap. She'll charge fifty quid at least.'

Fifty whacks was money Victor didn't have and he knew, without even asking, that Sandra wouldn't be able to lay her hands on fifty pounds.

With the address safely in his pocket he wondered who to go to for the necessary. Big Chas was the most obvious person – but despite the fact that Big Chas was doing all he could to help Bryce, Victor flinched from the thought of asking him for help on Sandra's behalf.

Sandra was utterly straight. Though she wouldn't care about being beholden to Big Chas now, she would care later. Gunter, then? As a scaffolder, Gunter earned good money. It was, however, good money incremented by hookey money.

Victor paused on the pavement outside the herbalist's, considering. If Gunter's money was a little dodgy, Richard Wilkinson's certainly wasn't. Being in the print, Richard received an enviable weekly wage. He'd borrow the necessary off Richard – and he'd pray to God that when he handed Sandra the address he'd been given, she wouldn't insist on his accompanying her when she visited it.

'You'll come with me Victor, won't you? I can't go by myself.'

Standing on the corner of Swan Row with her, Victor rolled his eyes, wishing himself on another planet. The old girl she was going to visit would think the baby was his. There'd probably be blood – and he hated the sight of blood.

'Okey-doke,' he said reluctantly, knowing he'd very little option. The poor cow had no one else she could ask to go with her. As far as the baby was concerned, he was the only one in the know. 'We'd better go as soon as poss. I've got the necessary.'

'How much?' Sandra's voice was hoarse. However much it was, she'd never be able to pay it back.

'I've got fifty – though it may not come to that much.'

'Let's go tonight, Victor.' Her voice was now a whisper. She was scared of so many things, she didn't know which fear was uppermost. Her fear of being hurt at the abortionist's; her fear that the abortionist wouldn't hurt her enough and that she wouldn't lose the baby; her fear that a politician would announce that the law had been changed and, as Bryce was now eighteen, he could he hanged for a murder committed when he was seventeen; her fear that even if he weren't hanged he'd be sent to prison for so long that she'd never see him again.

She hugged herself tightly, wishing Roy Clarkson had never been born; wishing that Hilda had never been born; wholly determined that Hilda's grandchild never would be born.

Their evening expedition was far worse than anything Victor had even remotely imagined. It was so bad it almost ranked with the nightmare of Bryce being charged with murder.

He'd always thought of the old girls who did abortions – if he'd thought of them at all – as being grandmotherly figures performing a social service.

The woman at the address the herbalist had given him wasn't grandmotherly – she was hard-faced, tarty and fortyish.

'Let's be seein' the colour of your money,' she said before they'd even got over the threshold, a ciggie in the corner of her mouth. 'Have you brought your own towels with you? I charge extra for towels.'

'I . . . I didn't know about the towels,' Victor said, aware that Sandra was so scared and nervous she was beyond speech. 'I 'ave money for them, of course. It's all right.' The woman held out her hand and he crashed the entire fifty into it.

The woman counted it, stuffed it into the pocket of the off-colour pinny she was wearing and said, 'Take her through into the kitchen. I need her on the table with her knickers off and a hanky stuffed in her mouth.'

Sweat broke out on Victor's forehead. The woman was talking to him about Sandra as if she had ceased to exist as a person, as if she was just an object. Even worse, she was talking to him as if he was going to help with whatever it was that needed to be done.

'I've . . . er . . . got to be on my way,' he said, backing down the hallway. 'I'll be back to take Sandra 'ome, of course, but just for now I 'ave to be off.'

'NO!' Sandra, who had been zombie-like ever since they

110

had left Swan Row, screamed into life. *'Don't leave me, Victor! You can't leave me! I won't stay if you leave me!'*

'He won't be leaving, darlin',' the woman said, shooting Victor a look that had him nearly crapping his pants. 'Now, into the kitchen with you. Get yourself up on the table. I haven't got all evening to waste.'

For ever afterwards Victor was to remember the woman with the deepest, most passionate loathing possible – not just for the agony she put Sandra through, but because from then on heterosexual sex was, for him, an impossibility. How could it be otherwise when he'd seen how hideous the outcome could be? And the worst of it was that, for Sandra, it was all for nothing.

She had bled like a stuck pig when the woman had finished prodding a hooked instrument up her fanny to scrape the neck of her womb, but no foetus had slithered out into the bowl rammed between her sweat-sheened, splayed knees.

'She'll lose it down the lavvie when she gets home,' the woman had said, unconcerned.

Victor hadn't been unconcerned. He'd been appalled. How could Sandra lose the baby at home with her mum and dad in the house?

Somehow he'd got her into a taxi-cab. Somehow he'd got her home and somehow Sandra had crawled up to bed without her mum or her dad seeing her.

It was by overhearing a conversation between Mrs Wilkinson and his mother, three days later, that Victor learned what had happened afterwards.

'She was in agony,' Joan Wilkinson said, transferring a shopping basket full of groceries from one hand to the other. 'Sheila called an ambulance and it was at the hospital that she found out Sandra was in the family way. She'd been trying to lose it, of course, and perhaps if Sheila hadn't been so quick off the mark calling the ambulance, she would have done.'

His mother's eyes had widened to the size of gobstoppers. 'Dear God in heaven!' she'd said devoutly. 'And Bryce on a murder charge! What will the poor girl do now?'

'God only knows.' Joan Wilkinson's plump, kindly face was harrowed. 'The Parrys have arranged for her to go to one of those Salvation Army homes for girls in trouble. She'll have the baby there and have it adopted, I 'spect.'

Victor had been unable to contain himself a second longer. Abruptly he stepped from behind the open front door where he'd been loitering and listening, and stumbled past the two women. He could have wept: fifty quid, and all for nothing. Even worse, all the blood, snot, screams and sobs had been for nothing, as well. And he wasn't going to be able to see Sandra and talk to her, not if she was going to be whisked away into a Sally Army home. Bryce would have to know. The mere thought had Victor's bowels turning to water. He would have to tell Big Chas all about Sandra being pregnant with Roy Clarkson's baby and Big Chas would have to tell Bryce. Christ Almighty, but it was the biggest, stinkiest mess possible.

It was a mess that turned out to be one with a silver lining. Bryce's QC told Big Chas he would be able to make much of the fact that Sandra had tried to abort the baby she was carrying.

'She'd hardly have done so if Reece was the father,' he had said to Big Chas in his chamber, through a haze of cigar smoke. 'She's in love with Reece and was planning to elope with him. Her behaviour does, however, lend credence to her statement that Clarkson raped her. The weeks of pregnancy tie in very neatly, and it is certainly a pregnancy she would wish to terminate.'

The brief had pushed his plush leather swivel chair away from his mahogany desk. 'All in all, taken together with

Mr Nowakowska's statement, I think it's safe to say the charge will be dropped to one of manslaughter. How's your brother doing these days, Chas? He must be pretty relieved at the general amnesty being given to all army deserters by the Queen. Be seeing a bit more of him now, will you?'

The autumn and early winter seemed, to Victor, as long as eternity. The Salvation Army home for unmarried mothers in which Sandra was incarcerated was in the north of England. Even if he'd made the journey, he knew he stood little chance of being allowed to see her; not being a blood relation, it would be assumed he was the errant father.

He had written to her, though, and she had written back, telling him that all mail addressed care of the home was opened and read before being ultimately delivered, and that all letters out were similarly scrutinised.

Victor had blown a gasket over it. 'Sand might as well be in a bleedin' prison!' he had stormed to Billy Dixon and Robert and Richard Wilkinson. 'And what's going to 'appen when the baby is born? If she's left on 'er own with it, she'll probably strangle it!'

The baby was due in February; approximately four weeks after the date set for Bryce's trial, and the closer that date came the more Victor was aware of the profound change in his attitude and outlook on life – and of the attitude and outlook of some of his mates, also.

He, Billy, Robert and Richard had all stopped dressing as teds. Teddy boys were getting an increasingly bad press and, without Bryce's confident leadership, being teds seemed simply to be asking for trouble. Unlike Jack – who had always been almost suicidally reckless – and the Briscoes, Cravens and Gunter, they ceased their visits north of the River, giving all dance-hall gang fights a very wide berth.

To Victor, it was simple common sense. They were all known associates of Bryce's and if they attracted the attention of the police there was a very real risk that they would be stitched up. The result of that would mean they'd be looking at a prison sentence or, at the very least, borstal.

His new attitude towards the police was one he found deeply unsettling. Though he'd run wild with Bryce since being a kid, he'd never been seriously lawless. His dad was a security guard and he'd been brought up to respect authority. Though he'd often flouted it for fun, he'd never done so in a major way – but then, neither had Bryce.

Whenever he thought of the ghastly predicament Bryce was now in, he felt giddy and sick. It was so obvious that Bryce had told the truth about what had happened in the Clarkson house; so obvious that Bryce hadn't meant to kill Roy – and certainly hadn't *planned* to kill him. Yet the police hadn't even attempted to give him a fair hearing.

The injustice of it baffled him. Even more baffling had been the way so many people he thought would have been leaping to Bryce's defence – his own parents among them – weren't doing so. Or at least weren't doing so in any way that really counted. The only person doing that was Big Chas Briscoe.

It made the way he now felt toward the Briscoe clan complicated.

In October Jimmy, the most personable of all the Briscoe boys, was banged up in a detention centre after being found guilty on charges of house-breaking, shop-breaking, aiding and abetting dangerous driving and causing actual bodily harm.

When Jimmy's little brother Tommy had said to anyone who would listen, 'It weren't 'is fault the car 'e'd nicked spun out of control. It wouldn't 'ave 'appened if the cozzers 'adn't bin chasing 'im. Over eighty miles an 'our they were doin'. Me dad says their behaviour was bloody criminal!' Victor had found himself agreeing.

The following month, though, when Ginger and Terry were sentenced to six months each for causing an affray after setting on a group of youths with starting-handles, he was appalled by their violence and when, in December, their dad was released after serving seven years of a nine-year sentence, Victor didn't go to the celebratory booze-up, despite being invited to it by Chas.

It was as if he was sitting on a fence and didn't know which way to fall. He no longer believed in appearances. Too many people whom he had assumed to be decent and honourable had proved themselves not to be – not when it came to the crunch – whereas a rogue like Big Chas had turned out to be a diamond.

In January the agony of waiting came to an end as Bryce's case finally came to court. Seated in the public gallery, squashed between his mother and Len Parry, Victor could have whooped with admiration at Bryce's air of cool, suave, almost negligent self-possession. Despite his long months on remand in an adult prison, and despite his neatly shorn hair and white shirt and sober grey jacket, there was nothing cowed or browbeaten about him. He didn't adopt a provocatively arrogant stance in the dock, but neither did he look guiltily uncomfortable or fearful. Whatever the experiences he had undergone whilst on remand he quite clearly hadn't allowed anyone to get to him.

'*Good for you, Bryce*!' he whispered fiercely beneath his breath. '*Good for you*!'

His biggest shock, one that had him practically struggling for breath, was the sight of Sandra when she took the stand as a witness for the defence. If her name hadn't been called out beforehand he would never have recognised her. Apart from the unspeakable obscenity of her swollen belly, she was thin to the point of emaciation. Her fair hair hung to her shoulders, dull and lifeless, and her face was as pale as death.

'Sandra!' Bryce shouted, and for a heart-stopping moment Victor thought he was going to vault from the dock and sprint to her side.

The commotion was instant. Two policemen leapt to contain Bryce; the judge pounded his gavel and roared for order; the public gallery was in uproar.

Sandra collapsed in sobs and a chair was brought for her. 'That child must have cried a river in the years I've known her,' his mother said over the din, glaring across towards Len Parry. 'And the sin and the shame of it is, she's always done so with good reason!'

Despite laying herself open to charges of perjury, Sandra insisted on giving as evidence the true version of events. Regardless of what she had said on oath at her own court appearance, she was adamant that Bryce had not been in the Clarkson house before her and had not opened the door to her.

'Then why, Miss Parry,' the judge asked, 'did you commit the grave offence of swearing on oath, in your own defence, that the defendant in the dock today had done so?'

'Because the mister who was my solicitor told me to!' Sandra wailed, looking pathetically more like a grossly pregnant thirteen-year-old than the sixteen-year-old she now was. 'Roy Clarkson told me there was a frightened cat in his house. I wouldn't have gone into it otherwise! And then he *raped* me and this . . . this . . .' – frenziedly she jabbed at the swollen mound of her stomach – 'thing is *his* and I can't bear it! I can't! I can't!'

All through her hysterical outburst the judge had been calling for order and a female court usher had been attempting to thrust a glass of water into Sandra's hand.

'Order!' the judge thundered for the last time. 'These proceedings will be adjourned!'

'He believed her, though,' Victor said three days later to Robert and Richard and Billy as they met up in the coffee bar on Jamaica Road. 'She's not goin' to have to go to prison or anythin' because of lying to the magistrate, not seein' as how they now reckon Roy did rape her because apparently rape sends women doo-lally-tap – and also not taking into account how far gone she is with the baby.'

'And the baby is Clarkson's?' Billy asked, goggle-eyed. 'How is Hilda Clarkson goin' to take that, d'you think?'

'Christ only knows.' Victor shuddered, not wanting to think about the repercussions with Hilda. 'She was removed from the public gallery screaming her head off when Sandra gave her testimony. The main thing is, even though Bryce was found guilty of unlawfully killing Roy, there was enough doubt about the actual circumstances that he didn't cop a life sentence with a recommendation of time to serve. According to Big Chas, he'll probably be out in six years, maybe even in five.'

'It's still a bleedin' long time,' Robert Wilkinson said tightly. 'I wouldn't want to have to do it, would you? Specially as he's not going to be serving it in a borstal. Prison could mean any prison, couldn't it? He might even be sent to somewhere high security like Parkhurst.'

It was a grim thought, but at least there he'd be spared the nightmares of nooses and black hoods and trap-doors.

'That's it then,' Richard said as Jack swung through the coffee bar's doors, heading towards their table. 'Apart from Bryce serving his sentence, it's all over and done with.'

'No, it ain't.' Jack, all straw-gold hair and honey-brown eyes, slid on to the chair next to Victor. 'Your mum's just called on our mum to tell her that Sandra gave birth to Roy Clarkson's kid at seven thirty last night. It's a girl and three weeks premature. I'm getting a frothy coffee in.' He rattled the silver in his hip-length, draped maroon jacket. 'Anyone else want one?'

117

# Chapter Six

## March 1955

'I can't go in, Victor! If I go in I'll know it's real – I'll know that Bryce really is locked up in there and I don't want it to be real. I don't want any of it to be real!'

Sandra and Victor stood in a drizzle of rain outside Hull Prison. A trickle of fellow prison visitors by-passed them. Many of the women shot Sandra sympathetic glances; others, prison-visit-weary, simply trudged on towards the massive gates where prison officers would go through all their gear, searching unnecessarily in things it would be impossible to smuggle anything in.

'We have to go in, Sand.' There was desperation in Victor's voice. They had travelled over two hundred miles for this visit and, though he too was finding it agonisingly difficult, he had no intention of turning back. Bryce was expecting them and he would walk to hell and back rather than let him down.

'But how am I going to tell him what Hilda has done now?' Sandra's voice was thick with barely suppressed hysteria. 'What if he thinks I could have stopped it all? What if . . .'

'If you're visiting, pass through the gates,' an authoritative voice bellowed at them from where the searches were taking place, 'If you're not, make way for people who are!'

'Come on, Sandra.' Victor took hold of her arm. 'You're going to have to get used to the hell of prison visiting. Both of us are.' He began walking her towards the dreadful-looking gates. 'And the sooner you see Bryce and tell him about Hilda and the baby, the better. You don't want it to be Frankie who breaks the news to him, do you?'

Sandra shook her head and, pale-faced, her hair damp with rain, allowed him to propel her towards the prison visitors' entrance.

All through the nightmare months of her pregnancy she had lived only for the day when her body would be rid of the result of Roy Clarkson's rape. The birth had been long and complicated and monstrously painful – and she hadn't cared; she hadn't cared about anything but being free of her loathsome burden.

It was mandatory at the Sally Army home that babies being offered for adoption were cared for, during their first few days, by their mothers. It was a policy that often resulted in a change of decision. It hadn't done so in Sandra's case. She had bathed and fed Roy Clarkson's daughter – never, ever, would she think of the baby as hers – with gritted teeth and revulsion that was bone-deep. And then, hours after she had signed the papers giving permission for it to be offered for adoption, had come the bombshell.

'Hilda wants to see the baby,' her mother had said to her, her face chalk-white. 'She's in the office now with Matron. I'm sorry, Sandra. I couldn't stop her. Nothing would stop her.'

She was speaking God's honest truth. When Hilda Clarkson had heard on the Swan Row grapevine that Sandra had given birth she hadn't hesitated to destructively steam into the situation, making an already bad scenario far worse.

'I want to see the baby!' she had ranted, standing on the doorstep of number 8, her hands on her hips. 'I don't believe for one minute that my lovely boy was guilty of what your slag of a daughter accused him of, but I wouldn't put it past her to have lured him on, and if she did . . . if that baby is our Roy's . . . then I'll know the instant I see it and I have

119

a right to see it, Sheila Parry! I've been to my solicitor and I have a right!'

Numbly, Sandra waited for a prison officer to finish his search of her handbag. Hilda Clarkson's rights had been respected. Matron had allowed her to see the baby and now the Clarksons were in the process of adopting it.

'I feel as if I'm in a tomb,' she said in a low voice as, the search completed, she and Victor were shepherded down long corridors deep within the prison complex.

Victor made no response; his throat so tight speech was beyond him. Despite light paintwork and blue linoleumed floors the sense of confinement was tangible. Even after only a few minutes he felt as if he was suffocating beneath a lead weight. How did men survive such claustrophobia for years and years on end? How was Bryce going to survive it?

As they stepped into the shabby, noisy, communal visiting-room Sandra's hand tightened in his. This was the moment that for months she had been both yearning for and dreading. Feverishly her eyes scanned the crowded room – and then she registered the grubby glass partitions. She wasn't going to be able to touch him; to hold him. The disappointment sent the blood ringing in her ears.

'There he is – over there, down to the left.' Victor said.

Fighting for breath she looked, saw him, and, in her haste to cross the space dividing them, stumbled. Only Victor's arm saved her from falling and then they were at the glass partition and Bryce was saying fiercely, his electric-blue eyes near black with concern: 'How are you doing, sweetheart? Was the journey OK? Are you OK?'

She put her fingers up to the glass, knowing that for his sake she should lie, but knowing that she couldn't. 'The Clarksons are going to adopt the baby,' she blurted, unable to contain the monstrous news even for a second. Her brimming eyes burned his. 'I don't know how I'm going to bear it, Bryce! I'll never be able to go back to

Swan Row to visit my mum. How can I, if . . . if *it* is living in the row?'

Despite her fierce determination that she wasn't going to cry, tears began spilling down her face. 'I knew exactly what I was going to do when the baby was adopted, Bry. I was going to get a job and get on with life until the day you came out of prison and we could get on with our lives together. I was going to forget all about Roy Clarkson's baby – and now, thanks to Hilda, I won't be able to!'

'Keep the noise down, young lady,' a prison officer patrolling nearby said brusquely. 'Otherwise you'll have to leave.'

Victor saw Bryce's eyes blaze; saw his jaw clench and his hands bunch into fists. For a brief, terrifying moment he thought his friend was going to be unable to control his anger. Knowing that if there was any sort of a fracas Bryce would be dragged away and the visit would be over even before it had properly begun, he said swiftly: 'You realise what the Clarksons adopting the baby means, Bryce, don't you? They *know* the baby is Roy's – which means Roy must have had sex with Sandra, so she wasn't lying about what happened in the Clarkson house. That being the case, your knifing of Roy has to be seen in a different light. It must be grounds for an appeal, surely? It *has* to be!'

As she saw the expression on Bryce's face, Sandra sucked in her breath. What Victor was saying had never occurred to her, but if it was true then it meant Bryce might not be inside for years and years and years. It meant his sentence might be reconsidered – that perhaps he might even be released.

Hope burgeoned into life, spiralling sky-high. Perhaps in only a few months' time they would be together again, living somewhere far away from Swan Row. Perhaps her mother would be living with them, just as they had always planned. She might even get pregnant again – this time with a baby she would really, really want.

'It's going to be all right, Bryce,' she said fiercely as hope blazed on his face too. 'All you have to do is to tell your solicitor about the Clarksons adopting the baby. Oh, but I love you, Bryce! I love you so!'

It hadn't been all right. For nearly a year all three of them had lived with such hope and optimism it had been almost unbearable and then, incredibly, Bryce's silk's request for an appeal was dismissed.

'And is that it? Is that the end of it all?' It was New Year 1956 and Sandra's disbelief was total. 'But how *can* it be, Bry?' There was rising panic in her voice. 'How can it be that the only result of the Clarksons adopting the baby is that I can't ever forget it was born!'

'I don't know, sweetheart,' he said wearily, for once almost as crushed as she was. He ran a hand over his brutally short prison haircut, knowing how difficult life now was for her. If she visited Swan Row she ran the risk of seeing Hilda or the baby – and so, despite her desperate need to keep in touch with her mum, she couldn't do so.

Sheila's predicament, living nearly opposite the house where the child was growing up, was even worse. 'Sheila Parry has aged twenty years,' Victor had said on his last visit. 'She desperately wants to move, but my mum says that bastard Len Parry won't even consider it.'

'Tell me about the nursing training you're about to begin,' Bryce said now to Sandra, consumed by concern for her. 'You're only seventeen, sweetheart. You have to be eighteen to be a nurse.'

'Not to be an orthopaedic nurse.' Her voice was flat and bleak. 'It's two years' training and you can start it at sixteen. Then, when you get your orthopaedic certificate, you go straight on to train as a State Registered Nurse. I'll have a small wage and I'll live in a nurses' home . . .'

Her voice cracked and broke. Never having had the slightest ambition to become a nurse, the prospect of being

122

able to live in a nurses' home was the only reason she had applied for the training. A nurses' home would be clean and orderly, and cleanliness and orderliness had always mattered to her. Even thinking about the grubbiness of her present hostel accommodation made her feel ill.

'I just want you to be released, Bry,' she said passionately, hating the glass between them so much it was a physical pain. 'I just wish you hadn't been so ... so *respectful* of me and that I hadn't wanted to save myself for our wedding night.'

To Bryce's vast relief the prison officer standing nearby moved discreetly away, out of earshot.

'I just wish the baby had been yours, Bry,' she sobbed as the bell rang, indicating that the brief twenty-minute visit was at an end. 'I wouldn't have minded anything then.'

Many prison visits were nightmares, but that particular one had been a lulu and, for hours afterwards, he had lain on his bed, tortured by feelings of frustration and impotence.

Ever since they had been children, Sandra had needed him – and that need had fulfilled deep needs of his own, making him feel important and necessary. As a child he had taken her to and from school safely, protected her from playground bullies, comforted her when Hitler's rockets had terrified the wits out of her and, later, he had protected her from her father's brutal temper.

He had never minded any of it. The responsibility for protecting and caring for Sandra had been given him by his mother when he'd been in short, ragged-arse pants and, knowing how proud it made her of him, was one he'd been happy to shoulder.

With a nerve still throbbing tensely at the corner of his jaw he had stared at the two photographs on his cell wall, one a faded wedding photograph of his mum and dad, the other a photograph of himself and Sandra, taken when they'd gone with Curly Craven and his girlfriend on a day trip to Brighton.

In a way he couldn't define it was as if, so long as Sandra was in his life, his mother was still in his life also – and that made his not being able to be with her, when she so needed him, a torture that was doubly agonising.

'Hi there, lover boy. Feeling friendly yet?'

It was a week or so after Sandra's visit and Bryce was on the landing outside his cell, about to go down to the exercise yard. The three bruisers blocking his way were cons determined on having as much sex in prison as they had had out of it. He'd already had a violent run-in with one of them in the shower-room, but from the way they were coming on to him now, it hadn't been serious enough to have taught any lessons.

'Nope, and I never will,' he said, forcing his voice to be ice-cool, aware that activity on the landing had come to a sudden halt and that he was the centre of a lot of very taut attention. He was also aware that, conveniently, there wasn't a screw to be seen.

'Whooee!' the biggest of the predators said, incongruously fluttering his eyelashes. 'But I do like a bit of reluctant resistance, don't you, boys?'

Bryce eyed him with contempt. There were plenty of genuine poofters among his fellow cons, but they didn't generally hassle anyone who didn't want to be. The men he was confronting, and a couple of others like them, were different. Outside of the nick, they fucked women. Inside, they enjoyed the sport of fucking anyone they could get their hands on – and because the humiliation they caused was all part of their power trip, they preferred getting their hands on straight goers rather than someone who might have been appreciative.

'Back down, you mongrel bastard,' Bryce said, his eyes narrow, his lips thin against his teeth, 'or you're going to

124

meet with real resistance – and I promise you won't like it.'

Something changed in their eyes, but it wasn't enjoyment turning to trepidation. It was more like anticipated pleasure deepening. Bryce was only eighteen. However well built he was, he was still only a kid. One of the men, his hands and face heavily tattooed, ran his tongue over his lower lip.

'Ain't he a pretty baby, then?' he said leeringly. 'Won't he make a lovely little wifey?'

Despite his outward cool, Bryce's heart was slamming with sickening force against his ribcage. For all he knew, the bastards taunting him were tooled-up. In the short time he'd been in Hull, he'd seen more than one smuggled-in knife. The recent brawl in the showers had been a fairly straightforward one. He hadn't pulled any of the stunts he'd learned from his dad's commando training manual – a manual which, when he'd found it, he'd studied hard.

He breathed in deeply, aware that brawling straight-forwardly hadn't got him anywhere. Despite the fact that Big Chas had passed the word in that the two of them were connected, he was still regarded as easy meat. He was quite alone – and he knew it.

'Who's goin' to 'ave 'im first?' the ringleader asked, flexing his biceps. 'An' where shall we do it? In 'is cell or down in the gym, where there's a bit of equipment?'

In the weeks he'd been inside, every fight Bryce had witnessed had been one on one. He didn't know if this was a cardinal rule, but as he sprang at the brick shit-house in front of him, taking him completely by surprise, he hoped to God it was.

With a violent right-arm jab he slammed the flat of his palm upwards beneath his opponent's nose, smashing it high between his eyes and into the back of his head.

Even above the bedlam that broke out, the sound of splintering bone was clearly audible. He literally felt the nose crumble against his palm; felt blood splatter hotly over the front of his denim shirt; heard the pounding of feet running towards him. As his opponent slumped, screaming, to his knees, Bryce knew with sick relief that the violent hands laying hold of him weren't those of the man's mates, but official ones, dragging him off towards a punishment cell.

He was deprived of visits for two months and, when they were resumed, he found them just as agonising as before.

'How's the nursing, sweetheart?' he asked, appalled by how much weight Sandra had lost since he'd last seen her.

When she told him everything was fine, flashing him a bright, quick smile, he had known she was lying.

'The trouble is,' Victor said to him in August, looking almost a different bloke in his national service uniform, 'Sandra's neat and tidy fastidiousness just isn't suited to being on a men's ward, clearing up sick, emptying bedpans and rubbing hairy backsides to prevent bedsores. I'm not surprised she doesn't like it too much. I don't think I'd like it either.'

In September it was Frankie's turn to visit. 'Our Ginger and Terry are making the old man really proud of them,' he said, biting into one of the apples he had brought with him. 'They've been deserters almost from the first day they were called up. Deserting is sort of like a family tradition now for Briscoes, ain't it?'

'If Frankie wasn't exempt from national service because of his flat feet, he'd 'ave been on the run as well,' Victor said, eyeing the visiting-room's Christmas decorations glumly. 'Has Sandra told you Billy Dixon's got engaged? She's a fast little piece, so Billy's got his work cut out. He reckons she's going to look after the shop for him, but I think he's in for a let-down.'

\* \* \*

'Big Chas has been to see me.' It was almost a year to the day since he'd been sentenced and Sandra's voice was fraught with tension. 'He came to the nurses' home, Bry. I couldn't believe it. He said he just wanted to make sure that I was all right. He said that if I had any problems I was to get in touch with him – but I don't want to, Bry. I don't *like* the Briscoes. They're all criminals – real criminals – and they look it, too. I'm sure the other girls at the home could tell that Big Chas was a villain, and I think they thought that he was family!'

'Where I'm concerned, he is,' Bryce said gently, not wanting to distress her further. It had been a sticky moment. It was as if both of them were on opposite sides of a divide, with Sandra appalled at the thought of future contact with Chas, whilst he regarded him as a diamond of a bloke.

'Wotcha mate,' Gunter said, sliding his long, khaki-clothed body on to a visitor's chair. 'How are you doing? Has Jack been giving you all the gen?'

'If you mean about Ginger and Terry throwing their weight about as a couple of heavies, yep. Jack says they spend a lot of time Peckham way, now. He reckons they and the mates they're running with are sewing south-east London up as tight as a teddy-bear's arse.'

'Yeah, well . . . Jack ain't wrong.' Gunter gave a wolfish grin and Bryce grinned back, happy to be talking to a mate who never even pretended to be anything other than a full-blown rascal.

'I don't think I can keep coming to visit you, Bry.' It was Easter 1957 and Sandra's voice was dangerously unsteady. 'Each time visiting day comes round I get so frightened . . . it's as if I can forget you're in prison for the rest of the month . . . sometimes I pretend you're away on a ship in the navy and sometimes I pretend that you're away in hospital . . . but when I get on the train to Hull I know none of that is true. I *know* you're in prison . . . and I can't bear it, Bry! I can't live with it, truly I can't!'

She had begun crying and couldn't stop. As a prison officer escorted her from the room, Bryce had been so demented with anxiety and concern and fear he'd thought he was going to lose his mind.

His fear of how he would survive if she stopped visiting him proved to be groundless. A month later she was in the visiting-room as usual, pale and wan and deeply apologetic.

'I'm sorry, Bry. Truly I am. I love you so much and I don't mean to make things harder for you to bear. It's just that sometimes . . . sometimes I can't see the end.'

She pushed a fall of shoulder-length hair away from her face and it was so dull and lifeless he felt as if a knife was twisting in his heart.

'What I really want is to be able to live somewhere Mum will be able to live with me. Len won't let her out of the house to meet me anywhere and she isn't well, Bry. Mrs Roberts thinks Mum is ill with something really serious.'

The year had limped on. If Sandra's situation was becoming no easier, his was. He'd got a handle on prison life now and knew how to hack things. One way had been by moving in on the prison's gambling scene. Football betting, horse betting, card-playing; over the last few months, with the innate business acumen Big Chas had been long aware of, Bryce had muscled in on it all. It was a way of enduring the mind-numbing monotony – and a way of establishing identity and gaining respect.

'All I want, Bry,' Sandra had said emotionally on her Christmas visit, shortly after he'd been moved from Hull to Gartree, 'is a home of my own. Somewhere cosy and safe like your home was before your mum was killed, and like my home was before my dad came home from the war. And I want a baby, Bry. I want *our* baby.'

Everything she wanted, he wanted too. The only difference was that when he thought of their future together, he also thought of the money they would need and of how he would get it – and the answer was always the same. Initially, he would work for Chas.

'My Jimmy ain't interested in the scrap business and Tommy's bleedin' useless,' Chas had said on one of his rare but influential visits. 'As I've got other irons in the fire, I reckon the scrap metal's goin' to be your department. You ain't got no problems with that, Bryce, have yer?'

He hadn't. He'd been near running the yard for Chas before the Clarkson nightmare anyway. Its mix of straight business and dodgy business had suited him then and it would suit him when he shook the prison dust from his heels. Sandra wouldn't like it, of course, but as he had every intention of keeping his working life and his home life in two very distinct compartments, she wouldn't need to worry about it.

In the New Year Victor came to see him. 'I've something to tell you,' he said, looking deeply uncomfortable. 'I've got myself a job. A proper job. More like a career, really.'

'Oh yes?' Bryce did his best to look interested, but it was hard. Anything Victor intended doing was bound to be tediously straight and chronically boring. 'What are you going to do? Go into the print, like Richard?'

'No.' Victor shook his head, looking as if he wished he were a million miles away.

'You ain't thinking of helping Billy run that shop of his, are you?' It wasn't a serious query. Victor might be Mr Nice and Sensible and Boring, but he wasn't a complete tosser.

Victor gave a dismissive laugh. 'No!' He leaned forward

on his hard chair, his hands loosely clasped between his knees. 'This is something that will set me up for life, Bryce. Sick pay, holiday pay, job security, pension – you name it and I'll have it.'

'Christ, Victor! Why would you want it? You're talking like bloody Richard! You're twenty-two, for Christ's sake! What's all this crap about job security? It ain't the 1930s!' Bryce ran a hand over his prison haircut, irritated beyond belief. He and Victor had been thick as thieves since they'd been toddlers, but exactly *why* they'd always been such good mates was often a mystery to him. There were times, and this was one of them, when talking to Victor was like talking to a bloke from a different planet.

'I know how you've always felt about the police, of course,' Victor said, 'and after everything that's happened to you, I can't say I blame you. Coming to terms with how many bad-apple coppers there are in the force has been a problem for me, too, but I know, now, what the solution is, Bryce. It's for there to be more *good* coppers . . .'

Bryce tuned out. Where Victor was concerned, he could put up with a lot, but this was just too much. He wondered if Victor knew how Sheila Parry was. According to Frankie, she wasn't doing too well.

'Anyway, I applied a couple of months ago and I've been accepted,' he heard Victor say in what sounded like a rush of relief. 'I start my training at Hendon next month . . .'

'Hendon?' He forced his attention back to Victor's ramblings. 'What the hell will you be doing at Hendon? The only thing at Hendon is the Police Training College.'

The expected derisive laugh from Victor didn't come. Instead there was a long, pregnant pause.

'W-e-ll, if you'd been listening to me, Bryce,' Victor said at last, clasping and unclasping his hands, 'you'd have realised that . . .'

The blood drummed in Bryce's ears.

'You've joined the cozzers?' His voice was almost normal, but that was only because his brain was still registering information too incredible for belief. Then he saw the expression in Victor's eyes and he felt, quite literally, as if the sun had turned black.

'*You're goin' to be a copper?*' The breath was so tight in his chest he thought he was going to explode. Victor couldn't be a copper. They were best mates. Even after he'd gone to live with Frankie's family, he and Victor had always been best mates. How could he be best mates with a copper? He couldn't. It just wasn't possible. Victor being straight was one thing; he could have lived with that quite happily. But Victor signing up as an active member of the enemy?

'*You stupid fucker!*' he bellowed, erupting to his feet so fast his chair toppled backwards, crashing to the floor. '*How can we go on being mates if you're on the other bleedin' side! Don't you remember what the fuckers did to my mum? What they've done to me?*'

Warders rushed towards him from every direction. All across the large visiting-room the wives and girlfriends of fellow cons stopped talking, looking towards him.

'Enough of that bloody racket, Reece!' the first screw to reach him shouted, seizing hold of his arm.

He wrested himself from the screw's grasp, lunging towards Victor, intent on hammering sense into him.

Victor shot his chair back at the speed of light, half falling off it in his haste to spring to his feet.

'What's the matter, Bryce?' some joker enjoying the show called out. 'Your mate been shafting your girlfriend, has he?'

For one brief second he had hold of Victor and then half a dozen screws leapt on him and they were inches, and then feet, and then yards apart.

'*Go to Hendon and you'll cut yourself off from everyone!*' he yelled as he was dragged with great force from

131

the room. *'Even Billy'll be embarrassed to be seen with you!'*

For days afterwards he'd believed he'd hit an all-time low and then, a week later, he received a letter from Sandra telling him that her mother had died.

He moved heaven and earth to get permission to attend the funeral, but, despite the fact that the Parrys had once been his guardians, permission was denied. His reaction was to raise such murder he was accused of trying to start a riot and for three weeks he was locked up in the chokey, unable to rage against anyone other than himself.

When he was back on his own landing again and his visiting rights had been reinstated, the final crushing blow fell.

Sandra didn't show.

'You have to find her,' he said urgently to Jack when he next visited, slickly suited and booted as always. 'I can understand Sandra taking her mum's death badly, but she can't go into such a depression that she stops visiting me. Hell, even with maximum parole I've got another two years to go yet! We can't not see each other for another two bloody years!'

'I haven't been able to trace her, mate,' Jack reported a month later. 'She's moved out of the nurses' home, but where to, no one knows. It's a bit of a facer, Bry, but I wouldn't worry about it too much. Lots of women can't hack prison visiting. It does their heads in, know what I mean? She'll turn up again eventually, when she's got herself sorted.'

Bryce's anxiety hadn't eased. Unlike Jack, he knew how deeply the events of the last couple of years had traumatised Sandra. The rape had been bad enough, but what had followed had been even worse. There had been her pregnancy

132

and, at the same time, she had also had to endure the long wait for his case to come to court and then the terrible tension of awaiting its outcome.

All that she would have been able to cope with – just. What she hadn't been able to cope with was the adoption of the baby by the Clarksons. It had made visiting Swan Row, let alone living in it, impossible – and then her father had prevented her mum from leaving the row so that they could meet elsewhere.

That last bit of sadism – being robbed of her mum's loving comfort when she had needed it most – had, he knew, been more than she could bear. And now Sheila was dead. What this last blow would have done to her, he didn't know – but he knew what he feared, and his fears were horrendous.

'I've got a lead on her, but I ain't been able to follow it up yet, so don't get too charged up about it,' Jack said, sitting down at the visiting table.

With his corn-gold hair, black turtleneck sweater, doe-soft black leather jacket and black jeans, Jack looked like someone out of a Hollywood gangster movie.

'I've spoken to one of the girls living at the nurses' home and she says that Sandra is working as a waitress Waltham Cross way. She didn't know where, so I'll have to do some checking round.' He flashed Bryce a wicked grin. 'I never realised how sexy nurses are – it's the uniform, I suppose, and knowing they'll be good with their hands!'

'Christ, mate! Jack's lookin' for her, the Cravens are lookin' for her, I'm lookin' for her! What more do you bleedin' want?' It was another six weeks down the line and Frankie was fed up of being asked about Sandra. 'I even went to the nurses' 'ome like Jack did. The girl I spoke to said Sandra jacked the nursing in 'cos she was never any good at it. She

133

said she was always crying. Well, that's Sandra, ain't it? I've never known her do anyfink else.'

Nothing had come of Jack's enquiries around Waltham Cross. With anxiety at explosion point, Bryce had thrown pride out of the window and asked Jack to have a word with Victor. Victor was a copper. He had access to resources.

'She worked at a pub-cum-restaurant in Waltham Cross called The Woodman for a while,' Victor said when, despite the ugly rift between them, he reported back with admirable speed. 'It was a live-in job. When she left it, she was vague about where she was moving. I've made enquiries everywhere in the area, but I haven't come up with anything.'

'You have to come up with something, Victor!' The skin was taut over Bryce's cheekbones and there was naked panic in his voice. 'You know what Sandra's been through – and you know what it is I'm terrified of.' He couldn't bring himself to say the word 'suicide' but as he saw Victor's eyes widen in shocked understanding he knew he didn't have to.

Victor continued to search, as did Jack and Frankie.

The result was nix. Zilch. Zero.

In black despair, Bryce scraped the bottom of his private barrel. 'Speak to Parry,' he instructed Jack, hardly able to believe the situation was so bad he was prepared to accept Len Parry's help.

'I have, Bryce. It was a complete waste of time.' Considering his surroundings, Jack, wearing a white jacket and black shirt and black pants, was remarkably relaxed. 'Parry's a shit,' he said unnecessarily. 'He's moved some little tart into number 8 and the place is a shambles. When I asked about Sandra, he said he didn't know where she was and he didn't care. Then the fucker put his life at risk by telling me to bugger off!'

\* \* \*

'Whatever your problems on release, money ain't going to be one of them,' Big Chas said with a wink, after letting him know the state of play on the gambling debts he had collected for him.

The amount was substantial. With tobacco the only currency inside prison, many cons laid bets with cash held for them by wives and girlfriends. Friends on the outside did the collecting and paying-out and, in Bryce's case, money due to him was garnered by Chas. The amount wasn't small beer either – not when some bets ran into thousands of pounds.

'The brothers Ginger and Terry are acting as heavies to – the Richardsons – are carving themselves quite a reputation.' Big Chas had continued, filling him in on all the latest gossip. 'They're high-fliers in the scrap-metal business, so our paths cross. Frankie don't have anything to do with 'em. He spends most of his time north of the river.'

All gossip was welcome – it helped to ease the tedium – but the only info he was desperate for was news of Sandra.

'I thought I'd traced her,' Victor said on one of his impossibly tense and strained visits. 'When she left Waltham Cross she went to the Epping area and a girl answering her description worked for a while at The White Bear, Theydon Bois. It wasn't Sandra, though; the girl in question was engaged to a policeman and left when she got married.'

Not knowing where Sandra was, was a nightmare without end. His only hope had been Big Chas's conviction that Sandra would show of her own volition once his parole date swam into sight.

'I've known lots of women behave the same way,' Chas said as 1958 gave way to 1959. 'She'll be at the gates when you walk through 'em. They always bloody are.'

By the time it was 1960, and he was in HMP Exeter, he'd

come to believe in Big Chas's prediction. Sandra could add up. She'd know when his parole was due. She would telephone to find out the exact date and, when he walked through the gates, she'd be there to meet him.

'The main bit of adjusting is going to be where your old gang are concerned,' Big Chas said at the end of April, giving him all the latest gen. 'It ain't there any more, Bryce, if yer take my meaning. Gunter's OK. He's quite useful to me. Same goes for Jack. The other two Wilkinsons are no-go zones. Robert's a milkie, like his dad, and married with a couple of kids. Richard is living in Greenwich and keeping his nose clean. Billy Dixon's still in the shop and the riskiest thing he does is to give credit to Effie Craven. Christ, but that woman's a slag. As for the Craven boys, they're okey-doke. Where family are concerned, though, it's a bit trickier.'

He rolled a cigar from one corner of his mouth to the other. 'Ginger and Terry are still making themselves useful to the Richardsons, and Frankie's north of the river, running with the Twins. It don't bode too well, long term. The two set-ups 'ave too much in common. They're bound to step on each other's toes eventually, know what I mean?'

Bryce had a pretty good idea. The twins were Ronnie and Reggie Kray. The Royal, Tottenham, had once been their hangout and it was there that Frankie had first hooked up with them. It was also the ballroom he'd been all set to visit the night Clarkson raped Sandra, and he couldn't help wondering how things would have turned out if he'd actually got to the Royal that night.

'Uncle Chas is growing into a right old woman,' Frankie had said disparagingly when he'd visited just a week before his parole date. 'The Twins are OK. Anyway, I ain't runnin' hard with 'em.' He lowered his voice so as not to be

136

overheard by any of the screws patrolling the visiting-room. 'Ain't no point, 'cos there's no money in it. They never pay proper wages. It's all a matter of nipping a bit here and a bit there. They have a reputation, though. They command a lot of respect. If people know you're in with them, they mind their manners. I'll slide away from them after you're out. You, me and Jimmy. We'll be able to pull proper stunts together.'

'And Gunter, Jack and the Cravens,' Bryce said, having no intention of letting the core of his old gang lapse into extinction. 'And do you know what we're going to go into? Gambling. If I can organise it here, I can organise it anywhere.'

He hadn't added the other reason why he knew big-time gambling was the way they should go. In-depth pros and cons would have been of no interest to Frankie. Unlike himself, Frankie never read a serious newspaper and so would be unaware that Parliament was legalising gambling, the political reasoning being that it would rob criminals of their massive profits from illegal gambling.

Which was all a load of tosh.

Legalised casinos would simply mean sky-high profits for everyone involved in the running of them – if they knew what they were about. Thanks to the education he had received during his years of imprisonment, Bryce did know what he was about. He had the nous, he had the contacts, and he had the bottle.

A boy when he'd entered the prison system, he was a boy no longer. He'd had to hack it amongst some of the most hardened villains in the country – and he had the scars to prove what a tough rite of passage it had been. Big Chas's name had carried enough clout to ease his way some of the time, but Big Chas was on the outside and he was on the inside. When push had come to shove, he'd been on his own and he'd had to sort things on his own.

A grim smile touched his mouth. Without prison, he'd

never have been more than a young hooligan, easy in the company of crims. Now, thanks to his college education in crime and with his original contempt for the police maximised a hundred times over, he was a full-blown rascal just waiting to hit the streets.

Visiting-time over, he sauntered back to his landing, still deep in thought. With the core of his old gang and Frankie, and Frankie's brothers and cousins, he was going to hit London's clubland big-time. He'd be the boss, of course, just as he'd always been. Anticipating Frankie's opinion of such an arrangement, his smile deepened. He could handle Frankie Briscoe. Frankie owed him. Once on the outside, reunited with Sandra, he could handle anything.

Sandra.

Tension roared through him. Would she be at the gates when he was released? He entered his cell, his hands clenched so hard the knuckles were white. If she wasn't there, he would find her. Victor, Jack and Frankie may have failed to do so, but he wouldn't. He would find her if it were the very last thing he ever did.

He looked across at the two photographs on the wall, his tension ebbing, hard certainty replacing it. He and Sandra were going to be a couple just as his mum and dad had been, needing no one apart from each other. There'd be no more shit and grief. Life was going to be sweet for them – sweet as a nut. Anything else was utterly unthinkable.

# Chapter Seven

In a mohair suit Victor had had sent into him – and that wasn't tailored sharply enough for him to feel even comfortable in – Bryce stepped through Exeter Prison's gates at ten o'clock in the morning on 1 June 1960.

Two people were waiting for him. Sandra wasn't one of them. His disappointment was so intense he felt as if an iron band had tightened around his chest.

'Wotcha, Bryce,' Frankie said, striding towards him. 'Do you like the motor? I hired it special.'

The motor in question was a splendidly vulgar white Rolls Royce and, standing beside it, obviously intensely embarrassed by the whole business, was Victor. As Frankie hugged him hard, Bryce grinned. Under normal circumstances, Victor now avoided being seen with Frankie. An ambitious young policeman with his sights set on the CID didn't need rumours circulating about unsuitable friendships. His accompanying Frankie in such a flamboyantly ostentatious car must have cost him dear.

'Hi, Victor,' he said, walking towards him as Frankie began retrieving celebratory cigars from the inside pocket of an immaculately tailored suit jacket. 'Nice of yer to be 'ere.'

It was Victor's turn to grin. Ever since he had broken the news to Bryce that he intended joining the Met, their relationship had been tense and strained. Today, though, it was just like old times. 'Where else would I be?' he said, giving him the same kind of hug and slap on the back that Frankie had given him. 'I just hope no one's taking photos of the three of us!'

Cracking up with laughter, they had taken the cigars Frankie was proffering and piled into the Rolls.

As Frankie slid it into gear, Bryce twisted round in the front passenger seat to face Victor. 'Sandra . . .' he said, 'tell me again about the pub you traced her to and why you weren't able to follow up on it. She must be somewhere, Victor. And someone must know where.'

Victor's laughter died. For a few minutes, swept up in the camaraderie of reunion, he had almost forgotten he was a policeman. Bryce's question reminded him sharply of the divide that now existed between himself and Frankie and Bryce.

'The pub was The Woodman at Waltham Cross,' he said, leaning forward on the plush white leather of the rear seat, his hands clasped loosely between his knees. 'The landlord thought she'd gone off to The White Bear at Theydon Bois, but I checked it out and she wasn't there . . .'

'For fuck's sake! She must have left a forwarding address with someone!' Bryce ran a hand over his hideously short prison haircut. 'And what about references? She'd need references for whatever job it was she left to go to. Did you ask if she was given a reference and who the reference was addressed to? Jesus Christ, Victor! What sort of soddin' policeman are you if you can't even track Sand down?'

Frankie, with his foot now hard on the accelerator, snorted with laughter. Victor didn't laugh. Instead he clasped his hands together even tighter, determined he wasn't going to tell Bryce what he had learned when he'd made enquiries at The White Bear.

If Sandra had fallen in with a police cadet whilst working there, then the landlady of The White Bear could be the one to tell Bryce. As to the landlady's claim that Sandra had become engaged to the police cadet in question and had left her employ when he had joined the police force proper and they had married . . .

140

He blanched. If it were true, it didn't bear thinking about. At least it didn't as far as Bryce was concerned. Things were different for Sandra – to his way of thinking, at least. Bryce wasn't going to live his life straight. He'd made that obvious when he'd announced his decision to work for, and with, Chas Briscoe. Sandra deserved better than to live her life married to a professional criminal – and every instinct Victor possessed told him that this was the route his lifelong mate was heading. A copper, though, would be good husband material for a quiet, conventional, emotionally scarred girl like Sandra. He'd be able to offer her stability and security. If he'd had the bloke's surname, Victor would have tracked him down simply to satisfy his own peace of mind. But the landlady at The White Bear hadn't known it, and he couldn't trawl through the last two-year intake of the Met, asking every married copper if his wife's name was Sandra!

'I've done my best, Bryce,' he said truthfully as Bryce continued to wait for some sort of answer from him. 'When you start looking for Sandra yourself, you'll real-ise that.'

Aware he was probably being unfair to Victor, Bryce transferred his attention to Frankie.

'Where are we going, Frankie? What's the agenda? Can we go straight to Waltham Cross?'

'Nah, we bleedin' well can't!' There was alarm in Frankie's voice. He hadn't spent a couple of score hiring the Roller in order to trundle it around the backwoods of Middlesex. 'The boys are waitin' for us at The Spinners in the Old Kent Road. Curly is the landlord. It makes a nice meeting place, know what I mean?'

Suppressing his impatience with difficulty, Bryce gave an acknowledging grunt. He didn't particularly want to start his search for Sandra with Frankie and Victor in tow. The customary returnees' drink awaiting him at The Spinners would simply have to be endured with good grace. When

141

it was all over, he'd pick up a motor and drive out to Waltham Cross. After all the waiting he'd done so far, another few hours wouldn't make much difference.

The minute he stepped into The Spinners, Bryce was greeted by shouts of welcome from all sides. 'Whoa there, Brycie!' Ginger Briscoe called out, raising the glass he was drinking from high in his direction. 'Nice ter see yer!'

'Did yer nick the Roller on the way down?' his younger brother Terry shouted good-humouredly.

'What yer 'avin'?' It was Georgie Craven doing the asking.

'Have a double Remy on me!' Gunter Nowakowska yelled.

'Welcome home!' 'Good to see yer mate!' 'Great to 'ave yer back!' came loudly from a host of other familiar voices and faces. All three Wilkinsons were there, Robert and Richard sticking out amongst the criminal contingent like two sore thumbs, Jack looking unnervingly at ease. Billy Dixon was there, too, trying to look as if a pub with such a dicey reputation was his usual watering-hole.

Eddie Briscoe, Ginger and Terry's dad, was propping up the bar, as scruffily dressed as ever. Bryce remembered that Eddie, too, had served time for manslaughter and he grinned, knowing that Eddie would think this bonded them in some way. Old Jug Ears was clearly in evidence, as were a good dozen mates he had met in the nick and who had been released before him.

His quick scan of the oak-beamed, raftered bar showed him there were other faces there, too. Faces he didn't know though the majority of those present clearly did. Faces that were quite obviously 'well connected'.

His grin deepened. Big Chas had done him proud. Even a hardened crim with a lifetime of major bank and bullion jobs behind him couldn't have come out to a better reception.

The man in question, immaculately suited and booted and with scarlet braces straining over a paunch clad in a white hand-stitched shirt, eased himself away from the bar and strolled towards him.

Lesser mortals in the throng – especially two of the Wilkinsons and Billy – stepped hastily backwards, making a passageway for him, and Bryce was reminded of the Red Sea parting before Moses.

'Welcome home, Bryce,' Big Chas said, sliding an arm round his shoulder and speaking in a way that took in everyone present. 'We've waited a long time for today, haven't we, boys?' There was loud assent. 'Now it's time to get on with life,' Big Chas continued expansively, a fat cigar in his free hand, 'and you can't do that without a wad in your pocket, a full glass in your hand, a bird on your arm and a motor at the ready – ain't that right, boys?'

There was noisy laughter, ribald agreement and shouts that it was time to get another round in.

Bryce turned to say a word to Victor, but Victor was no longer beside him. Twisting further round so that he was looking back at the open door he had just entered the pub by, he saw that Victor was standing on the pavement, his hands pushed deep in his trouser pockets. As their eyes met, Victor lifted his shoulders in a wry shrug.

Bryce's stomach muscles tightened. No words were needed; the shrug said it all. As a straight copper, Victor could only maintain social contact with him in certain situations – and fraternising in a pub heaving with known villains was not one of them.

It was a moment of choice and Bryce knew it. He could make his excuses to Big Chas and walk out of the pub, turning his back not only on all the geezers who had crowded there to celebrate his release, but also on their way of life. Or he could give Victor a rueful, answering shrug, and walk with Big Chas towards the bar. Even taking Sandra into account – and he knew that Sandra was as straight as a die – his hesitation was minimal.

With his eyes still on Victor's, he lifted his shoulders in a gesture of regret and, turning, stepped deeper into the throng of villains he now felt most at home with.

Victor chewed the corner of his lip for a second and then, tension in every line of his body, turned on his heel and began striding away in the direction of the nearest bus stop. Bryce's life was his own. He couldn't live it for him, just as Bryce couldn't live his for him. They'd both been faced with choices and they'd made totally opposing decisions and no amount of brooding would make things any different.

It was a glorious day, but as he mooched down the Old Kent Road he was sunk in gloom. Bryce had a wild side to him – even as a kid when his mum and dad had still been alive, he'd been a tearaway – but he didn't have a criminal nature the way that many of those now drinking with him in The Spinners had.

Or at least, he corrected himself as he came to a bus stop and lounged despondently against it, he hadn't six and a half years ago, before he'd done time. He wondered if it was possible for anyone to do six and a half years in some of the hardest prisons in the country without the experience changing them for the worse; though as a copper he felt he should think differently, Victor doubted it.

It was all very depressing. Equally depressing was the knowledge that, as a jailbird, Bryce was going to find it near impossible to get a decent job – assuming, of course, that he troubled to look for one.

A 53 bus trundled to a stop and, as he boarded it, remembering Bryce's immediate intentions, his gloom deepened. No good could possibly come out of Bryce running Big Chas's so-called legit business affairs. For one thing, nothing Chas did was totally legitimate. Legitimacy simply wasn't in the Briscoe vocabulary. If Bryce believed he could operate on the edges of Chas Briscoe's world without being sucked into it completely, as Gunter had been, he was fooling himself big-time.

More miserable than he'd ever been in his life, he lit a cigarette, realised he was seated on the lower deck and dropped it to the floor, stubbing it out beneath the toe of his shoe.

Bryce hadn't served six and a half years because he was a criminal. He'd served them because of a set of disastrous circumstances – circumstances that could quite well have happened to him. As a teddy boy, he too had carried a flick-knife. Nearly every teddy boy he'd ever known had done so – and the number who had come to grief because of it had been minimal. Bryce would never have used the knife in a run-of-the-mill gang fight, any more than Victor would. Knife-fighting simply hadn't been their style.

'Trafalgar Square,' he said, becoming aware that the conductor was waiting for his fare.

If Victor had been togged up in his teddy boy gear and had heard the screams coming from the Clarkson house, then everything that had happened to Bryce could quite well have happened to him. The 'there but for the Grace of God, go I' sensation was one he had lived with from Bryce's arrest right up until the moment twenty minutes or so ago when, instead of walking away from The Spinners with him, Bryce had chosen to remain with Big Chas and his shady friends.

It was not a choice he would ever have made. For him, Bryce came first and always had.

As he thought of the possible consequences of Bryce's choice, his misery plumbed new depths. Bryce might not have entered prison a criminal, but he was obviously now happiest in their company – and the next step from that was to become like them.

White lines of tension etched his mouth. What would happen then? He was a straight career copper. If Bryce became an out-and-out rascal, how could he possibly maintain their friendship without fouling up his career?

'Elephant and Castle!' the conductor called out to anyone who was interested.

Victor stared bleakly out of the window, his loneliness as palpable as a physical weight. Without Bryce as a friend, what friendships did he have? Though he was still on terms with Jack, Gunter and the Cravens, they weren't friends any longer. How could they be, when they saw him as a member of the 'enemy' and he was always terrified he might one day be called upon to arrest one of them, or, God forbid, all of them?

Billy and the Wilkinsons were nearly as bad. Even though they were irreproachably law-abiding he could tell that they didn't like being in the company of an off-duty copper; there was always an edge of tension, an underlying nervousness. It was the same with nearly everyone he met. As a copper, he was set apart. His colleagues overcame the inconvenience by socialising almost exclusively with other policemen.

He had never done so.

There probably were careers where homosexuality was tolerated; though apart from the theatre he couldn't think of one. One thing he did know. It wasn't tolerated within the Metropolitan Police Force. How could it be, when it was a criminal offence, carrying a heavy prison sentence? And so he kept his distance, not allowing anyone to get to know him too well. Most of the time, he lived in lonely celibacy. He had to. To live any other way carried too great a risk.

Time and again he'd wondered what Bryce's reaction would be if he were to unburden himself and reveal his secret. No opportunity – at least, one that felt right – had ever arisen. He certainly couldn't have told him in a prison visiting-room, and nor could he tell him when anyone else was within earshot.

As the bus creaked towards Westminster Bridge and he remembered the boisterous reception that had greeted Bryce in The Spinners, he knew that occasions when the two of them would find themselves alone were going to be few and far between. Unlike himself, Bryce had never had the slightest difficulty in making friends. Both as a child and as a teenager, Bryce had been the pivot around which he, Gunter, Billy, the Cravens and the Wilkinsons had revolved. And within a couple of hours of being released from prison things were no different. Once again he was the centre of a tight-knit clique – only this time the clique and the camaraderie were criminal.

As the bus careened into Trafalgar Square he experienced an alien sensation that he knew, with despair, was envy. He, too, needed the sense of belonging that Bryce carried effortlessly with him. He even longed to be in The Spinners, sharing the sense of unity everyone there was so obviously enjoying. Not many criminals were lonely. The freemasonry of the crooked saw to that. It was all inter-marriage and bush telegraph, with everybody knowing everybody and always being someone's cousin.

Heavily he rose to his feet, well aware of the impossibility of it all. He never was going to be part of a group – any group. All he would ever be was an outsider; an outsider existing on the periphery of the life of the man his world revolved around.

With a pint tankard stuffed with five-pound notes serving as a kitty, and everyone stuffing fresh fivers into it whenever it showed signs of depletion, the party at The Spinners was both long and rowdy. Holding his impatience in check with difficulty, Bryce gave up all thought of borrowing a car and driving out to Waltham Cross. It just wasn't possible. He couldn't walk out of this particular party. Not if he wanted to live to tell the tale.

'And don't worry about a motor,' Big Chas said, an arm still draped around his shoulders. 'There's one all sorted, a Jag. It'll be outside number 5 for you, in the morning.'

Bryce wasn't remotely surprised that Chas had arranged a car for him, but he was taken aback by the assumption that he'd be moving back into Swan Row again. Frankie didn't live at number 5 any longer. Now he had money in his pocket, he had moved out of the family home and into a flat near London Bridge. Whether Jimmy and Ginger and Terry still lived in the row, he'd never thought to ask. Big Chas certainly didn't, but then, Chas had moved out of Bermondsey and into the grandeur of a mansion in Kent years and years ago.

'I'll be bunking up at number 5 myself tonight,' Big Chas said, as if reading his mind. 'So will Frankie. Jimmy's never moved out of number 13. He loves his mum's home cooking too much.'

'And Ginger and Terry?' Bryce asked, already fairly sure of the answer. 'Are they still at number 18?'

'Yeah. Leastways, they are when they're not doin' a bit of business up north. Quite entrepreneurial those two are. Birmingham, Manchester, Glasgow – they put themselves about quite a bit these days.'

Since Bryce had last seen him, Big Chas had grown a trim, grey-flecked moustache. He stroked it now with a well-manicured stubby forefinger. 'The rest of the row's much the same. Billy's got a drinks licence so the corner shop is now an offie. It's very useful for Frankie's mum. God, how that sister-in-law of mine can put sherry away – but then you don't need me to tell you that. You lived under her roof for long enough.'

Bryce gave a wry smile. He had, and it looked as if he was going to be living there again, at least for the next few days. The Briscoes' tribal tendencies amused him. Even though some of them – Jimmy, for instance – were now pulling major heists and sauntering the streets, back pockets stuffed with dosh, they still all congregated together in the cramped terraced houses they'd been born in.

As for moving out of Bermondsey completely . . . the only Briscoe who had ever done so was Big Chas and, as far as Bryce could make out, Chas's mansion in Kent was mainly for the benefit of his two extremely pretty wives, both of whom were cheerfully in residence. One of them, his ex-wife, was the woman he had left his first wife for, and his other wife, the current Mrs Chas Briscoe, was several years younger than his youngest son.

'Ta, mate,' he said, genuinely grateful to Big Chas for all he had done and wondering just what the pay-off line would one day be. 'Is that my Remy standing on the bar, or is it yours?'

There had been hooch in prison and quite a bit of marijuana, but Whitbread's Best Bitter and Remy chasers had been in short supply and he woke next morning with a hangover.

'Hair of the dog, Bryce. That's what you need,' Frankie said blearily from a nearby twin bed. 'What say we stay in bed till eleven and then go down to The Spinners? This afternoon we could go to a drinking club that owes me a few favours, pick up a couple of birds, and then this evening we could . . .'

With great effort Bryce sat up and swung his legs over the edge of the sagging bed. 'Whoa,' he said, putting a hand to his throbbing head. 'I've things to do today, Frankie. Until I find Sandra, everything else is on ice. Understand?'

'I understand you're frigging barmy.' Frankie reached out for the cigarettes and lighter lying on the floor by the side of his bed. 'She's done a frigging bunk, Bryce. She'll be shacked up with someone else by now and . . .'

'Bollocks.' Frankie's remark was so ridiculous he wasn't even angry with him, just pissed off. It was at times like this that he missed Victor. Victor could be irritating, but he was never out-and-out stupid. Forcing his legs into action, he walked across to the window and lifted the curtain. A white Jaguar was parked at the kerb.

'Nice one, Chas,' he said beneath his breath and then, his stomach muscles tensing, he looked across the cobbled street at number 6. Had he and his mum and dad ever, ever lived there? Sometimes it just seemed impossible to believe. The house looked so different now. It had a new modern door and the sash windows had made way for more convenient picture ones. In a way he was glad. If the house had looked just the same as when he had lived there, the pain he felt, remembering the past, would have been so intense as to be unbearable.

With far different emotions he turned his attention to number 8. Richard had been right. Sheila Parry's once pristine home now looked shabby and uncared for. The paintwork was scarred and peeling, there were unwashed milk bottles on the step and dingy curtains at the windows. Bryce wondered what Len Parry's reaction would be on finding out that he was out of prison and living opposite once more. Whatever Len felt, he wouldn't give a flying fuck. One wrong word from Parry and he'd knock him into the middle of next week.

'Close the bleedin' curtain,' Frankie said grumpily, lying flat on his back, a lit ciggie in his hand. 'If it ain't eleven o'clock, it's too early for daylight.'

Bryce glanced across at Frankie's bedside clock. It wasn't yet nine. By the time it was eleven he had every intention of being in Waltham Cross. 'Okey-doke,' he said, wondering if, after all his years of enforced early rising in the nick, he'd ever be able to get back into the habit of sleeping late. He was just about to let the curtain fall and to wash, shave and dress, when he heard the sound of a front door closing just along the row.

Curious, he waited to see who it was. The Wilkinsons lived only two doors further up and he'd always had a soft spot for Mrs Wilkinson. Every Christmas, all the time he'd been banged up, she'd sent him a Christmas card and a box of chocolates.

It wasn't Joan Wilkinson. His lips tightened against his teeth. It was Hilda Clarkson. If he had cause to hate anyone, he had cause to hate Hilda. Without her impassioned accusation that he'd been burglarising her home when he'd stabbed Roy to death, the police might never have taken the line with him that they consequently did.

There was a child trotting along at her side, a little girl about five or six years old dressed in a red gingham dress with a white Peter Pan collar and, over it, a red cardigan, obviously hand-knitted. For a second he was puzzled, wondering who the child could be, and then realisation hit.

'Christ Almighty,' he whispered, his pupils dilating. Why had he never realised before that, in returning to Swan Row, he'd be bound to run into Sandra's kiddie? Somehow, he'd never really believed in the kid's existence. In the years before Sandra had stopped visiting him the subject had never been one they had talked about, other than right at the very beginning, of course, when Sandra had told him that Hilda had adopted the baby.

Now, in sick fascination, he stared hard at Clarkson's daughter, expecting to feel nothing but repugnance. The repugnance didn't come. It couldn't, for the little girl didn't look like Clarkson; she looked like Sandra. Her hair was fair and short and straight, just as Sandra's had been when she was six. He remembered taking Sandra to and from school – which was probably what Hilda was doing with Sandra's daughter now.

'Frankie?'

Frankie grunted in response, his eyes closed against the offensive daylight Bryce was still allowing into the room.

'What name did Sandra give the kiddie she had?'

'The kid the Clarksons adopted?' Frankie opened his eyes, the cast in his right eye alarmingly evident. 'I dunno. Hilda calls her Debbie, but whether that's the name Sandra give her, I ain't sure.'

Hilda and Debbie were now walking directly past number 5 and he let the curtain fall sharpish before Hilda should sense she was being watched and look up and see him. There'd be time enough for that situation – and a proper encounter with Sandra's daughter – another day.

'Tell Chas I'll be back this evening to talk to him about the scrap-yard,' he said, reaching for the none too stylish trousers Victor had seen fit to buy him and determining to buy some decent Levi's and a new suit at the very first opportunity. He groped in the zip-up holdall that held all his worldly goods, retrieving his toilet-bag. He'd be washed and shaved and out of the house in ten minutes flat. 'I'm off,' he said to Frankie, elated at the prospect of his first real day of freedom in six years; taut with excitement at the prospect of being reunited with Sandra. 'See yer.'

He was driving against the traffic for most of the way and so it was a much quicker journey than he had anticipated. The car was a joy to handle and as he sliced through London's northern suburbs he wondered wryly if Big Chas had realised how little practise at driving he'd had before he'd been imprisoned. He smiled, secure in the knowledge that what Big Chas didn't know couldn't hurt him, grateful for the number of cars he'd nicked for joyrides when he'd been sixteen and seventeen.

As he neared Waltham Cross he passed a signpost for Hendon. To him, Hendon meant the Police Training

College and automatically his thoughts turned to Victor. Why the fuck Victor had become a cozzer – especially a straight cozzer – he would never, never know. It had the potential for making things very difficult between them. Not that he was going to emulate Tommy and become a thief, or make a threesome with Ginger and Terry in the protection racket. What he was going to do, though, was to go into the gaming business, backed by whatever money Big Chas's scrap-metal business brought him – and gaming and the law were not compatible professions. Neither, come to that, were the scrap-metal business and the law. Eventually he and Victor were bound to come to grief – and the day they did wasn't a day he was looking forward to.

He sped on into Waltham Cross, trying to imagine Sandra living there, and failing. He could only imagine Sandra in Swan Row. He clenched his jaw hard. If it hadn't been for Hilda adopting the baby and Len Parry being the unpleasant fucker he'd always been, Sandra would never have moved out of the row and he wouldn't now be chasing all over the Home Counties looking for her.

That he would find her, even though Victor and Frankie and Richard had failed, he didn't have a second's doubt, and nor did he doubt that she would want him to find her.

Unlike Frankie, who simply assumed that Sandra had grown bored with visiting him in prison and had shacked up with someone else, he knew Sandra. She'd stopped visiting him just before her mother had died and he was certain it was because life had become more painful for her than she could bear. Not seeing him at all, in her new set of circumstances, was, for her, preferable to seeing him under prison visiting conditions and having to endure the agony of tortured goodbyes.

He swung off the main road, following the directions he'd been given for The Woodman. He was well aware that some of his old Swan Row mates, Frankie in particular, didn't rate Sandra very highly. As far as they were concerned, she was nearly always in tears and they couldn't understand what it was he saw in her.

He slewed to a halt outside a large ivy-covered pub-cum-restaurant. What he saw in her was, quite simply, the other part of himself. As children, their shared history had made them as close as brother and sister and, as teenagers, it had always seemed to him the most natural thing in the world that their relationship should deepen into a sexual one.

He parked the Jaguar and strolled into the pub. It wasn't yet opening time and a charlady was at work, polishing tables. 'Is the landlord about?' he asked as he walked towards the bar.

'We don't start serving until eleven o'clock.' The woman's voice was prim and, as he looked towards her, he saw from the expression in her eyes that she didn't like the look of him. Remembering his still fiercely short prison haircut, he didn't blame her.

'I don't want to be served, I want to ask him if he knows where a barmaid of his has moved off to.'

The woman straightened up from the table she'd been cleaning. 'Well, if the barmaid in question is Sandra Parry – and as you aren't the first to come here asking about her, I assume it is Sandra – you don't need to speak to the landlord because I can tell you. She went to Theydon Bois, to The White Bear.'

Bryce frowned. Theydon Bois rang a bell, but he couldn't remember why. His frown deepened. 'If I spoke to the landlord, would he tell me the same thing?' he asked, wondering why the hell Victor hadn't managed to glean such easily available information.

The woman shrugged. 'He might, or he might not. I can't say I'd want him giving information about me to any Tom, Dick or Harry who came in asking.'

Bryce reached into his back trouser pocket for the wad

of notes that had been collected for him in the whip-round at The Spinners. 'Ta,' he said, peeling off a quid and placing it on the bar. 'Buy yourself a drink.'

She nodded appreciation, her eyes still unfriendly.

'As a matter of idle curiosity,' he said as he walked past her, heading towards the door, 'if you wouldn't want anyone giving information out about yourself, why have you given me information about Sandra?'

A malicious gleam lightened the woman's eyes. 'Because I didn't like her. She was lousy at her job. She didn't have a clue about being bright and cheerful. That's why she got the sack. Why she moved off into another large pub and restaurant I'll never know. Working in a morgue would suit her better.'

Regretting the pound tip he'd left, Bryce strode out of the pub and across the sunlit pavement to his car. He knew why Sandra had gone to work in another large pub-cum-restaurant. It was because it was the only kind of employment she was capable of where live-in accommodation was provided.

His face was grim as he slid behind the Jaguar's wheel and reached for the *AA Book of the Road* lying on the passenger-seat beside him. He also knew why Sandra didn't have a clue about being bright and cheerful. It was because she was so desperately unhappy.

A cursory glance at the map told him all he needed to know about driving from Waltham Cross to Theydon Bois and he gunned the engine into life. He'd be there in half an hour or less, and once Sandra saw him striding towards her, their long years of unhappiness would be at an end.

'She did work here,' the landlady of The White Bear said, eyeing him speculatively. 'Only she left when she got married.'

'I don't think we're talking about the same person.' Bryce took a photograph out of his inner jacket pocket.

It had been taken when he and Sandra, and Curly Craven and his girlfriend, had gone to Brighton for the day in the summer before he'd been imprisoned. 'This is the girl I'm looking for. Before coming here, her last place of employment was The Woodman at Waltham Cross and . . .'

'And she left here to get married,' the landlady finished for him, looking at the much-handled photograph. 'Not that that's a good likeness. It's years old, isn't it? She only looks a kid. You look pretty different, too, if you don't mind me saying so. Quite a teddy boy then, weren't you? What happened?' Her eyes flicked to his hair. 'Did you go in the army?'

'In a manner of speaking.' Bryce had no intention of telling her he'd been in the nick. He'd never get any information out of her if she knew he was an ex-con. 'This girl isn't married. She came here two years or so ago. If she isn't working for you any longer, I'd appreciate it if you could tell me where she moved on to.' He drew out the wad of notes from his back pocket and this time the note he rolled off was a fiver. 'I've been away for a few years and lost track of her . . .'

'You're very deaf, aren't you?' She leaned on the bar, her arms crossed, gold bracelets gleaming. 'Sandra Parry came here after leaving The Woodman. She was with me seven months or so and then she married her fiancé, who she'd met whilst working at The Woodman, and they set up home in Romford.' She cocked her head slightly to one side. 'I told all this to the other fellow who came asking after her. Friend of yours, is he?'

Bryce didn't answer her. For once in his life the breath had been knocked completely out of him. Victor had been told exactly what he had just been told and the stupid fucker, believing every word, hadn't passed the info on.

'Do you have an address for her in Romford?' he said tersely, ignoring his still untouched pint of light and bitter.

'I do, as a matter of fact, but Sandra didn't leave me it. Her fiancé did. It was about Christmas time and he wanted to make sure any Christmas cards that arrived for her would be sent on. Not that there were any – and there were never any letters for her, either.'

Bryce put the fiver on the bar-top. 'I'd appreciate the address,' he said tersely.

'I'd appreciate you calling back some time,' the landlady said, not concealing that, though a decade his senior, she found him a very tasty item. Turning away from him, she walked down the bar a little way to where there was a wall telephone. On the shelf below it was a phone book stuffed with scraps of paper and cards. 'Here you are,' she said, retrieving a piece of paper from the back of the book. 'It's a miracle I still have it because I'll never need it . . .'

'Ta.' Bryce tweaked the label from between her fingers and turned on his heel.

He had a very nice bum and a sexy, swaggering walk and the landlady's eyes followed him every step of the way to the door and then, from a window, every step of the way to his car.

Bryce yanked the driver's door open and slid impatiently behind the wheel. Why Sandra had found it necessary to say she was leaving The White Bear in order to get married, he hadn't a clue. Perhaps the landlady's husband, or a customer, had been hassling her. He slammed the piece of paper on the dashboard and stared at it hard as he turned the key in the ignition and engaged the clutch. Sandra Hurst, 2 Dovedale Avenue, Romford. Where on earth had she got the name Hurst? If she'd had to lie about getting married, why hadn't she called herself Sandra Reece?

In a very different frame of mind from the one he had driven out of London in, he began to make his way south-east in the direction of Romford. That Victor had believed Sandra to be married and had not told him was so out of line he couldn't even begin to think how he was going to handle it. He couldn't very well thump him – though that was what he most felt like doing. And their friendship meant too much for him to simply cut Victor dead.

He overtook a lorry, increasing his speed from fifty miles an hour to sixty. Presumably Frankie and Richard hadn't traced Sandra as far as The White Bear. Frankie, certainly, would never have kept quiet about it if he had been told that Sandra had married.

Because the only halfway-decent clothing he had was the suit Victor had bought him, he was wearing a shirt and tie. Keeping the wheel steady with one hand, he loosened his tie with the other, and unbuttoned his shirt at the neck. Sandra. Why on earth was she behaving so bizarrely? Had she suffered a nervous breakdown of some kind when her mother had died? It wouldn't be too surprising if she had, considering the trauma she had suffered giving birth to Roy Clarkson's kiddie and the ongoing mental agony of knowing that he, Bryce, still had years to do before being released. If she'd had a breakdown, it would explain a lot.

He turned off the A13 on to the A12, no longer getting a thrill out of the novelty of driving. Number 2 Dovedale Avenue sounded very much as if it was going to turn out to be a private address. If Sandra had been as unhappy in the pub and restaurant business as she had been when nursing, she may well have opted to try a different kind of employment, office-work perhaps, and moved into a rented house, sharing with a group of other girls.

He turned left when he reached the T-junction with the A12. Romford seemed an odd choice if she were now doing office-work. He could well understand her not returning to Swan Row – she couldn't very well move back into number 8 with her dad and his girlfriend – but he would have expected her to gravitate back to the area. If not Bermondsey itself, to Deptford or New Cross or Greenwich.

Now in Romford, he drew up at the kerb and, leaning across to the passenger-seat window, rolled it down. 'Dovedale Ave, mate!' he called to a nearby pedestrian. 'Can you give me directions?'

The middle-aged man he had accosted walked over towards the car, a small dog trotting on a lead beside him.

'Dovedale? You're nearly on top of it, young man,' he said helpfully. 'Go to the end of this road and turn left, then continue until the second row of shops, turn left again, then right. That'll bring you to Dovedale.'

'Ta.' Bryce wasn't looking at him. He was looking at the dog. It was a Yorkshire terrier and the years rolled back. It was as if he was eight years old again and looking down at Tigger.

'He's not my idea of a dog either,' the man said wryly, imagining he was reading Bryce's thoughts. 'He's the wife's dog. Women like silly little dogs, don't they?'

The Yorkie was looking up at Bryce out of bright brown eyes, his ears pricked, his tail going ten to the dozen.

'He's a smashing little dog,' Bryce said tersely, appalled at the lump that was forming in his throat. 'Yorkies are the best breed in the world.'

Leaving the man looking after him with a rather startled expression on his face, Bryce pulled away from the curb fast. Christ Almighty, he'd served six years in some of the hardest nicks in the country without showing the slightest emotion and now here he was, near blubbing over a dog!

He zoomed down to the end of the busy road and turned left. When he reached the second row of shops he slowed down. He'd been so busy holding eye contact with Tigger's double that he hadn't paid proper attention to the instructions he'd been given. Was it left at the next junction, or right?

'Excuse me –' he came to a halt outside a greengrocer's – 'is it next right, or left, for Dovedale Avenue?'

The young woman he was speaking to was pushing a pram. She slipped the brake on and gave him a sunny smile. 'It's next left and then right.'

Bryce flashed her a grin of gratitude, and her tummy did somersaults. He was astonishingly handsome; as handsome as the young American presidential candidate, John F. Kennedy.

'Are you a policeman, then?' she asked, wanting to engage him in conversation for a few moments longer.

Bryce was already easing the Jaguar away from the curb. He took his foot off the accelerator smartly, swinging his head once more towards her. 'No,' he said, his eyes narrowing. 'Why?'

The girl looked flustered. There was something about his manner that was extremely disconcerting. 'Oh, I just wondered.' She gave him another smile, this time uncertainly. 'There's only four houses in Dovedale and, as they're all police houses . . .'

At the expression that flooded his eyes, her smile vanished completely.

'Jesus!' she heard him say viciously beneath his breath and then the Jaguar was roaring away from her, slewing round the first left turn with all the speed of a racing car.

He didn't round the right-hand corner into Dovedale Avenue at the same breakneck speed. Instead he parked at the corner of it, his hands tight on the wheel. She was walking down the avenue from its opposite end. Her hair, which had been skimming her shoulders the last time she had visited him, was now pulled severely back from her face and knotted in the nape of her neck. She was wearing a white blouse, a red circular skirt with an uneven hemline, and low-heeled sandals. Despite the vividness of her skirt, she looked almost matronly.

The reason was the two heavy bags of groceries she

was carrying, and the way she was looking down at the ground, taking no interest in anything going on around her. She certainly hadn't registered his parked car.

As she drew closer, Bryce's heart began slamming somewhere up in his throat. This wasn't how it was meant to be. He had imagined their reunion millions of times and not once had it been anything like this.

As she turned in at the gateway of number 2 he opened the car door. 'Sandra!' he called out, aware of a feeling almost akin to terror. Things couldn't be how they looked; she couldn't be a married woman returning home with the groceries – especially not when the house she was about to enter was a police house.

She span round so fast he thought she was going to fall.

'Sandra!' He began running towards her and she dropped both shopping bags, joy and fear so inter-mixed on her face he didn't know which was uppermost. What he did know, though, was that fear had never played any part in the reunions he had imagined for so long and so often.

'Bryce!' She took a step towards him and then came to an abrupt halt. 'Bryce!' she said again, her voice choked. 'I'm so glad you're out of prison! So, very, very glad.'

As he swung through the gateway towards her, she began crying. Incredibly, as the distance between them vanished to almost nothing, he felt a flash of irritation. Frankie was right. Sandra *was* always crying. He opened his arms to her, and in that moment he saw the gleam of gold on the fourth finger of her left hand.

He froze, his heart hammering, the blood singing in his ears.

'I'm sorry!' Far too late, Sandra clumsily covered her left hand with her right. 'I'm sorry, Bryce! Truly!' She was crying as she'd cried as a child, tears streaming down her face and dripping on to her hands. 'I just wanted to be *safe*, Bry! Big Chas said that when you came out of

161

prison you would be working for him – and I knew what that meant.' Her eyes pleaded for understanding. 'I don't like the Briscoes, Bryce. I don't like criminals. I didn't like visiting you and seeing you with criminals . . .' She began crying harder than ever. 'I just had to do what was best for myself, Bryce. Please try and understand. I wanted a home of my own and . . .'

'You ran out on me without even telling me.' His voice was hard, strangely abrupt. 'You ran out on me and you married a *copper*.'

'Oh God!' she pressed a hand to her mouth, her eyes desperate. 'Oh Christ!'

'For six years I believed you'd be waiting for me when I got out, Sand. Frankie told me you'd have shacked up with someone else, but I didn't believe him. And even Frankie would never believe that you'd shack up with a cozzer!'

'Oh, please don't, Bryce. Please don't . . .'

She was breathing so fast and shallowly now that she seemed to be on the point of collapsing. He was uncaring. His arms, which a few brief moments ago had been open to hug her tight, were open no longer. Instead his hands were clenched, the knuckles white.

'You left me just like you left the kiddie you had. If I hadn't tracked you down, you would never have got in touch with me to explain, would you?' He, too, felt as if he was hyperventilating. 'I'm back in Swan Row, Sand, living at number 5, and I've seen the kiddie you had. She doesn't look the remotest bit like Clarkson. She looks like you.'

'I don't *care*!' Sandra wasn't pleading with him now, she was shouting, her eyes wild. 'I never wanted to have her and I hate her! If it wasn't for . . . for . . .' Even after six years she still couldn't say the word 'rape'. 'If it wasn't for what Roy Clarkson did to me, you'd never have gone to prison. We'd be married now and –'

'Sandra!'

The voice was one Bryce had never heard before. It was

querying, authoritative, male, and, from the sound of it, its owner was approaching the gateway of number 2 fast.

Sandra gave a scream, her eyes dilating until her pupils were black. Bryce turned his head and sucked in his breath.

A uniformed policeman was striding towards the gateway. A young policeman whose face was taut with anger.

Bryce didn't have to ask who he was. He swung his head round to face Sandra again. Time was fast running out on them and he had to know one thing. Did she regret what she had done and did she want him to give her a second chance?

'Sandra . . .' he began as her husband bore down on them, and then stopped.

Even if she did want a second chance, even if she was prepared to leave her copper husband then and there, he knew that it wouldn't work.

Ever since she'd been a child, Sandra had yearned for stability and security and, for the person he had become, stability and security were an anathema.

She wouldn't be happy about him running things for Chas; mixing with the Briscoes; never quite knowing where he was or who he was with. This – a neat and tidy, box-like home in stultifying, boring suburbia, with a husband who was salaried and had a good pension to look forward to, was what Sandra needed. And, just as he was incapable of making her happy by giving her what she most needed, so she was incapable of being the person he needed.

With sudden clarity he realised how unfair to her his prison fantasies had been. He'd idealised her, believing her to be a carbon-copy of his mother, yet the real Sandra wasn't remotely like his mum. Nell Reece had been strong and stoical and had endured faithfully through long periods of separation. Those qualities weren't Sandra's – and nor was there any reason why they should be. Sandra was Sandra. She was uniquely herself and, though he

163

now knew he didn't love her as she needed to be loved, his affection for her was bone-deep and would, he knew, last life-long.

'Look after yourself, Sand,' he said, knowing there was nothing more to say; knowing that yet another wodge of his life had come to an end. 'Be happy.' Then, as Sandra's husband stormed with long-legged strides down the path towards them, demanding officiously, 'What's going on here? Why are you annoying my wife?' he turned to face him and slammed a perfect right-hander into his jaw.

It was a punch with the force of a pile-driver. Taken totally by surprise, Malcolm Hurst went rocketing back against the fence that separated his garden from the neighbours'. As he slithered dazedly down against the palings, his helmet was knocked askew and, striding over and away from him, Bryce registered with wry satisfaction that his victim looked ridiculous.

Unhurriedly he walked back to the Jaguar and slid behind the wheel, knowing that if the incident were reported he'd be re-arrested and back in the nick within hours. For that to happen, though, Sandra's husband would have to know his identity – and somehow he didn't think that Sandra would reveal it.

He turned the key in the ignition. With luck, he'd be back in Bermondsey in time to take Frankie up on his offer of an afternoon drinking session at one of the many clubs Frankie favoured. And he'd pull himself a bird. Where sex was concerned, he'd been without for far too long.

# Chapter Eight

Betty Dracup stepped out on to The Centurion's small stage, neither grateful for, nor annoyed by, the bright spotlights that made it near impossible for her to see her rowdily appreciative audience.

She'd been a stripper for three years now and was indifferent as to whether or not she could see the punters' faces. Some nights – and tonight was one – she even got a buzz out of seeing the expression in their eyes.

She shimmied her crotch-short black leather skirt down over her hips to the usual storm of lewd encouragement. The Briscoe mob was in again. She'd heard enough rumours about Ginger and Terry Briscoe's activities to be very chary of them. In her book, no matter how thick the wads they were carrying, blokes in the habit of removing parts of other bloke's faces were blokes to avoid.

She stepped out of the skirt, kicked it with the toe of a red-spangled stiletto-heeled shoe on to one of the front tables and, turning her back on her all-male audience, bent over so that her torrent of flame-red hair skimmed the stage as she began lasciviously rotating black-suspendered hips.

Frankie Briscoe was with Ginger and Terry. Even with the spotlights full in her face, she'd been able to distinguish his spectacularly ugly features. Frankie's persistent attentions were a nuisance she could well do without. He'd even brought one of the Twins in to see her when she'd stripped at the Lapis Lazuli. With her head still somewhere near the floor, her hands on her hips and her hips still doing their stuff, she rolled her eyes in exasperation. At least Frankie's guest had been Reggie Kray, not Ronnie. Giggles fizzed in her throat. It would take more than Frankie to get Ronnie Kray into a female strip-club.

'*Come on, darlin', let's have a bit of fanny in our face!*' someone, probably a Briscoe, called out over and above all the other choice suggestions being made.

As the music she habitually stripped to blasted the room, Rusty continued with her well-honed routine. Still not removing her feathered G-string, she sashayed forward to the very edge of the stage, so that she was almost within touching distance of the punters at the front tables, and began provocatively wriggling out of her black-sequinned, midriff-skimming bolero.

There was a new face with the Briscoes. She'd noticed him when she'd inconspicuously entered the club by its service door twenty minutes ago. She always liked to take the measure of the audience, unseen by them, before going backstage to change. If they proved to be the dirty-mac pervert brigade, she never put her heart and soul into things. Not that the dirty-mac perv brigade were in the habit of frequenting The Centurion. It was a villains' club, and villains and nonces didn't mix.

With her arms high, the tassels on the nipples of her awesomely full breasts dancing and swinging, she looked towards the table the Briscoe mob was congregated around. There were times, and this was one of them, when she got a real buzz out of her job. She let the throaty giggles she'd been suppressing at the thought of Ronnie Kray in a female strip-club, fizz into life. God, but this was better than standing at a conveyor belt, folding dry-cleaned work-overalls, which was what her last job had been.

That had been before she'd had Tricia; before she'd had to earn real money in order to keep her.

As she hooked a thumb over the tie of her G-string, pulling it low to expose her spicy red bush, she reflected that not many women who'd had a baby could boast a body as gogglingly incredible as her own. It was the dramatic difference between her breast and waist size that set her apart. Like Jayne Mansfield, her breasts were large and lush and her waist was a handspan.

She had good bone structure, too – something she had inherited from her mother. When her mother had died aged forty-six, eight years ago, she'd still had the looks of a woman barely thirty.

To a cacophony of shouts and whistles and drumming feet she finally gave her customers what they had been waiting for.

Life had been fucking miserable after her mother had died. She'd been twelve, just the wrong age to be left with a man with her stepfather's tendencies. She blotted the thought of his 'You've got to be nice to Daddy, Betty . . .' 'You've got to take the place of Mummy and keep Daddy's tummy-stick happy' from her mind. God, what a tosser that man had been. It was because she couldn't bear the memory of her name on his lips that she'd changed it – that and the fact that Betty Dracup was no name for a stripper.

She was Rusty now. Rusty Daniels. She wondered what the bloke seated with the Briscoes was called. His face was hard-boned, but in a handsome way, and he was dressed as if he had money. A dark blue suit, white shirt, tightly knotted tie, heavy gold signet-ring, gold bracelet watch.

There was a look of intense virility and sophistication about him – a combination that could be quite devastating. She wondered if there was any chance he was a straight goer. She'd been performing in Soho clubs for long enough to know that wealthy businessmen and villains often had a need for each other and often socialised. Not that she was really interested. She couldn't afford to be interested in men; not when she had Tricia to think about.

To noisy applause she exited the stage, wondering how she could persuade The Centurion's management to give her a longer spot, one in which she could choreograph something that would really personalise her act and give it genuine class. She also wondered whether Tricia's temperature had begun to go down yet or if it was still worryingly high. Louise, the elderly neighbour who baby-sat Tricia, was well used to the child's fevers and knew at what point the doctor should be called. Even so, Rusty wanted to get home as soon as possible. The Centurion was her last club of the night and her one intention was to scramble into her street clothes as fast as possible and to grab a cab and hightail it home, not to enjoy a night on the tiles with one of the punters.

'Hi and bye, Charlie,' she said, dashing past the black stand-up comic about to take her place on stage. 'See ya.'

'Bye, sugar. Keep it hot for me.'

Despite her worries where Tricia was concerned, she was grinning as she reached the cubbyhole that passed for a dressing-room. Charlie's request wasn't one to take seriously. Like Ronnie Kray, he preferred boys to girls.

'There's a party tonight at blonde Susan's,' one of The Centurion's cigarette-girls said, watching her as she peeled off her false eyelashes and wiped fluorescent pink lipstick off with a tissue. 'It should be a laugh. Are you coming?'

'Nope.' She tugged white leather trews up over her hips, zipped them up and pulled a sleeveless black sweater over her head. 'My little girl isn't too good,' she said, anchoring her mane of hair away from her face with two tortoiseshell combs. 'I'm heading straight back home.' She crammed the bits and pieces that were the tools of her trade into a travelling vanity-case and snapped it shut. 'See ya.'

'Sure. Bye.' The girl stubbed out the cigarette she'd been smoking, aware it would be folly to extend her illicit break any longer. Rumour was that there was something not quite right with Rusty's little girl. She was certainly sick with monotonous regularity. She couldn't for the life of her imagine how Rusty put up with the inconvenience of it all. If she'd been in Rusty's shoes, she'd have parked the kid with its granny, or a child-minder, yonks ago.

Rusty stepped out of The Centurion's service entrance into a little Soho back alley and sucked in her breath sharply. One of the punters, a regular she'd had run-ins with before, was standing at the end of the alley, waiting for her.

Her fingers tightened around the handle of her black patent vanity-case. God, but some men were a pain in the arse. No matter how swiftly or surreptitiously she made an exit from a club, they would be laying in wait, determined not to take no for an answer.

Walking as swiftly over the cobbles as her suicidally high, flamingo-pink suede shoes allowed, she hoped to God the bloke in question wasn't going to be a problem. She just didn't have time for an argumentative brush-off, not when Tricia was fretting for her.

Bryce rose from the table. As clubs went, The Centurion was pretty cosy, but it wasn't a gambling club and those were the only sort of club he was interested in these days.

'I'm going to split, mate,' he said, clapping a hand on Frankie's shoulder. 'Gunter's bringing a lorryload of copper piping into the yard sometime before dawn and I want to be there when it arrives.'

'Christ, Bryce! It's only two thirty in the morning!'

Bryce grinned. 'Can't be helped. Work's work. Know what I mean?'

Frankie grunted assent and Bryce's grin deepened. It was all a load of bollocks about his having to be at the yard to receive the load Gunter was bringing in, but any excuse connected, however indirectly, with his Uncle Chas always went down without argument with Frankie.

The comic delivered the punch line to the blue gag

he'd been telling and Frankie bellowed with laughter, his attention once again on the entertainment.

Bryce strolled out of the club and into Dean Street. Despite being half-past two in the morning it was still brightly lit and busy. He paused, wondering whether to head off home or to hit a friendly spieler for a game of poker or kalooki. Where gambling was concerned, he'd become an addict. He loved the atmosphere: the buzz of conversation competing with the clack of chips; the whirr of roulette wheels; the low calls of the dealers.

It had been a hot day and the night air was pleasantly warm, giving Soho a Mediterranean atmosphere. There were well-patronised Continental-style tables and chairs on the pavement outside a couple of the cafés and bars on the opposite side of the street and, on the corner nearest to him, a flame-haired girl and a big, beefy-looking bloke were indulging in a noisy lovers' tiff.

He tapped a cigarette from a packet of Players and lit up. God, but he adored London! Especially this particular patch of town. It throbbed with excitement and frenzied activity and, after six years' incarceration, he couldn't get enough of its bright lights, its sleazy clubs and its glamorously tarty girls.

He blew a thin plume of cigarette smoke into the air and rocked back on his heels, his mind still not made up as to whether or not he was going to go on somewhere, grateful it was a choice he was still able to make. For a couple of weeks after he'd laid Sandra's husband out flat he'd been on tenterhooks, expecting an unwelcome knock on the door and speedy arrest on a charge of assaulting a policeman. No knock had come and now, after an interval of almost two months, he knew no knock would come – or at least not to do with his having decked Malcolm Hurst.

The argument taking place a little way down the alley was still going strong, having gained momentum after the girl had tried to flag a black cab down and the bloke had sent it on its way before she could scramble into it.

It was the kind of public argument that was two-a-penny in Soho and, as he continued to reflect on the last few weeks, it barely impinged on his consciousness. Taking over the reins of Big Chas's scrap-metal business and keeping an eye out for an opportunity where a club of his own was concerned had meant he hadn't been able to spend as much time with Frankie as Frankie had wanted, but it had still been an eye-opener.

Frankie's routine – and that of his brothers and cousins – was to lie in bed till midday and then wander up to a meeting pub, which, for the Briscoes, was invariably The Spinners. Afterwards, with a bit of business done, they would drift into the West End to any one of a number of afternoon drinking clubs frequented by fellow villains. Then it was back to local Bermondsey pubs in the evening, followed by a long stint in Soho from midnight until the early hours. Hard-grafting nine to five it wasn't, and Bryce could well see the attraction of it.

He wasn't about to get sucked into it himself, though. At least, not entirely. He enjoyed work – if that work was wheeling and dealing. The scrap-metal business, for instance, wasn't just handling anything that came along, no questions asked. In the short time he'd been managing things for Big Chas, he'd secured a lucrative contract with a local council. True, palms had had to be greased, but as far as he was aware, even in the straight business world that was par for the course.

*'Will you fucking well leave me alone and piss off?'*

The argument taking place some yards away from him was growing more explosive by the minute. Saying, 'No, darlin', not tonight,' to a streetwalker who had been propositioning him, he looked towards the corner of the alleyway. The verbal battle was showing signs of becoming physical. As the girl tried to circumnavigate him, the burly bloke grabbed her by the arm and swung her hard against the stone of The Centurion's street wall.

Bryce's interest stirred. With the club's neon lights now flashing full on her face he realised, for the first time, just who the girl was. Wryly amused by how different she looked in street clothes – and with her hair held away from her face – he continued to watch the tussle she was having with her boyfriend, his thoughts returning to business matters, but this time not scrap-metal business matters.

Over the last couple of months he'd sussed out lots of gambling clubs, from the high-flying joints in Mayfair and Knightsbridge where hundreds of thousands of pounds regularly crossed the tables, all the way down to the one-man run spielers in Soho.

Of all the clubs he'd visited, the most interesting, to him, had been one owned by Frankie's mates, Ronnie and Reggie Kray.

Apart from a billiard hall that had served the Twins as a headquarters for years, The Double R had been the first club they had opened; or, more precisely, that Reggie had opened, for it had first seen the light of day while Ronnie was doing bird.

What intrigued Bryce about it was its location. Situated in the East End, in Bow Road, it wasn't a very likely spot for a club that was West End in style – and he knew that any club he opened would have to be in an equally unlikely area, though in his case it would be south of the Thames, not north of it.

'Reggie don't put up with any nonsense in here,' Frankie had said to him when they had strolled in together. 'No hooligans, know what I mean? He likes blokes to be able to bring their ladies wiv 'em. Quite respectable in his own way, is Reggie. He has this place as well run as the Ritz.'

Remembering the conversation, a smile tugged at the corners of Bryce's mouth. The Ritz analogy wasn't one he'd have come up with, but he'd had to admit that The Double R seemed remarkably well managed. It had also been spawned with next to no capital, and that was the aspect that really interested him.

'It was just a large derelict house,' Frankie had said, waving acknowledgement to half a dozen people simultaneously. 'Reggie paid the landlord a visit, came to an amicable arrangement about the rent, kitted the place out with red flock wallpaper, a bar, a stage, furniture and a jukebox and Bob's your uncle. He was up and running, and, where clubs are concerned, he ain't looked back since.'

To date, without Frankie in tow, he'd looked at several likely properties south of the river in the hope that he could pull off something similar. So far, his trawl was zilch. Properties that were suitable in size and location were just too costly. He could always borrow, of course. Big Chas would lend him the money. But that would mean taking Big Chas on board as a partner and he didn't want that. When he opened his club, he wanted it to be exactly that – *his* club and no one else's.

His train of thought was broken as the noisy altercation taking place a few yards away increased in intensity. Despite all the burly bloke's attempts to prevent her, Rusty Daniels had managed to flag down yet another black cab, but her chances of actually stepping into it were no higher than they'd been with the last one.

'Stop fuckin' pretending you don't want to know, 'cos I know fuckin' different!' the bloke was saying belligerently as he continued to stop her from crossing the pavement. 'All this Lady Muck stuff don't cut no ice wiv me, Rusty, know what I mean?'

Bryce tossed his half-smoked cigarette to the ground. The bloke's technique with women was like Frankie's – it left an awful lot to be desired.

'*I'm in a hurry, you brain-dead animal!*'

As she shouted at him and as he slammed her yet again

against The Centurion's street wall, Rusty Daniels was both kicking her tormentor and hitting out at him with her hard-edged vanity-case. She might as well have been kicking and hitting the wall. Built like a brick shit-house, the bloke was impervious to every blow that landed.

'*Get your fucking paws off me!*'

One of her shoes went flying and there was a near hysterical break in Rusty Daniels voice. Bryce could well understand why. Accustomed to Soho barneys, the cabbie was still waiting for her, but there wasn't a hope in hell of his coming to her aid – and very little likelihood of anyone else doing so.

Knowing it, Rusty spat full in the bloke's face. The effect was only partially what she had hoped for. He released his iron grip on her with one hand, but only in order to slap her open-handedly so hard that her head nearly left her shoulders.

Seconds later, as Bryce's arm whipped round his neck, he let go of her with such suddenness she was sent sprawling to her knees, her vanity-case skidding in the same direction as the shoe she had lost.

'You're being a nuisance, mate,' Rusty heard her rescuer saying as he hauled her tormentor away from her by means of a crucifying headlock. 'Your company ain't wanted. Got it?'

Being dragged backwards, choking and struggling, her assailant was unable to make a coherent answer. For a brief second, as the pressure on his windpipe was released and he was spun around, he managed to utter something that sounded like, '*Bleedin' fuck* . . . !' and then he was crashing backwards into the waiting taxi-cab, propelled by the force of a fist smashing into his chin.

While he slid unconsciously down against the cab's door and into the gutter, Rusty scrambled to her feet, aware that Bryce was the very fanciable bloke who had been seated in the club with the Briscoes.

'Ta,' she said, retrieving her shoe and hopping on one leg in order to slide her foot into it.

Bryce grinned, appreciating the way the manoeuvre was causing her gorgeous breasts to jiggle and bounce. 'Do you still want your cab?' he asked, abandoning the idea of a game of poker or kalooki. 'It won't wait for ever.'

Rusty scooped up her vanity-case from the pavement. 'Yes, I do.' Her hair had spilled free of its combs and she pushed a mane of waves away from her face and back over her shoulders. 'Is that stupid prick going to be all right, do you think?'

Bryce glanced down at the still-comatose heap lying in the gutter. 'Yep,' he said, not caring too much one way or another. 'More to the point: are you OK?'

'Apart from now being late getting home,' she said drily, 'yes.'

Her voice had a husky quality to it and was as alluring as everything else about her. As he walked with her across the pavement, towards the cab, he quirked an eyebrow. 'D'you have a husband waiting for you?'

Despite her still bubbling fury at the way she had been manhandled, Rusty spluttered with throaty laughter. 'No, thank God, but I do have a little girl and she's sick.'

Turning away from him, she reached for the handle of the passenger-seat door and bent her head slightly in order to speak to the cabbie through his half-open window. 'Number 46 Lee Gardens, Deptford,' she said as the prone figure by her feet stirred slightly and gave a groan.

Bryce spared his victim another glance. He was going to be conscious and struggling to his feet in another minute or so.

'I'm going to Bermondsey,' he said to Rusty, not particularly wanting to have to punch the bloke's lights out a second time. 'Do you mind if we share?'

Out of sheer force of habit she hesitated – but only

for a split second. For one thing, she owed him. If he hadn't come to her assistance her face would be black and blue by now. For another thing, he was the most attractive geezer to fall across her path for a long time. She'd always had a weakness for boxers – and she was sure that that was what he was. Only a professional fighter could have dealt with a bloke of her assailant's size and strength with such speed and finality and economy of effort.

'No problem,' she said, a pulse of sensuality going up like a flare inside her as he opened the cab door, his body brushing hers.

'So what's wrong with your kiddie?' He sat beside her on the cracked leather seat and the cab, at long last, pulled away from the kerb. 'And how old is she?'

Rusty drew in a breath, about to tell him what she told everyone: that Tricia wasn't strong and that she fell for every cold and fever going.

In the dark interior of the cab his face was all planes and hard, jutting angles. The cab sped past a strip-club and in the fleeting illumination of its neon lights she saw clearly how long-lashed his eyes were and how disturbingly intent his gaze was.

'Tricia suffers from osteoarthritis,' she said, speaking the hated word for almost the first time outside of a doctor's consulting room or a hospital ward. 'She's only five and she's more or less crippled with it. If she catches the slightest cold or chill it goes straight to her joints and then the pain she's always in gets even worse.'

He didn't say anything. He didn't offer any of the platitudes she was accustomed to hearing. It was almost as if he knew she was keeping something back; as if he knew she hadn't told him everything.

The cab swung out of Dean Street and into Old Compton Street. There were fewer neon signs now and his face, with its winged brows and, for a boxer, its intriguingly straight

176

nose, was in deep shadow. They were seated hip to hip and knee to knee. She could smell the faint lemon tang of his aftershave and, even in the darkness, knew exactly how thick and springy his hair would feel beneath the palm of her hand.

They began heading towards Cambridge Circus, the sexual electricity between them so strong she could practically hear it crackling.

'And she's mentally retarded,' she said, speaking the words for the first time.

He still hadn't reached out for her, but she knew he was going to, and she knew she was going to let him. In telling him that Tricia was mentally as well as physically disabled she was emotionally exposing herself to him in a way she'd never done before with anyone.

She'd known he was pretty special when she'd first caught sight of him from behind the spotlights on The Centurion's stage. Even from that distance, she'd registered his look of intense virility and powerful, careless charm. Now, as the lights of Cambridge Circus illuminated the cab and their eyes held, she was overcome by a sensation of being on a precipice and, at any second, of being about to step off it into infinite space.

He made a noise in his throat that could have meant anything she wanted it to mean and then he leant towards her and his hair was coarse beneath her fingers, his hands hard upon her body, his mouth dry as her tongue slipped past his lips.

He never did go to Bermondsey that night. By the time the cabbie drew up outside 46 Lee Gardens they were both so confounded by desire that Rusty was, for the first time ever, beyond thinking about Tricia, and Bryce was beyond being coherent about cash. Instead of stuffing just one crisp note into the cabbie's open palm, he peeled off an uncounted number from the wad he always carried, leaving behind, as he took a flight of stairs two at a time in Rusty's wake, a very happy man.

Rusty's place wasn't a house but a maisonette and, as he swung into the sitting-room, his tie was loose and he was already unbuttoning his shirt. The unexpected sight of an elderly woman seated comfily on a sofa stopped him dead in his tracks. Was it her mother? A babysitter? Either way, it meant an excruciating delay before he and Rusty could hurl themselves into bed.

'Hi, Louie.' Rusty's voice was far more breathless than the run up the stairs justified and with a flash of amusement he realised she'd forgotten about the woman's presence. 'How is Tricia? Did she wake? Has she still got a temperature?'

'There's not been a peep out of her.' The woman heaved herself to her feet. 'And she doesn't look to have a temperature to me, Rusty love. I think this time you've been worrying over nothing.'

'That's good, Louie. I'll straighten up with you in the morning. Is that OK?'

'Course it is.' The woman ambled out of the room without troubling to put on a coat or to show any curiosity at his presence, and, the next minute, the front door had closed behind her.

'She lives in the ground-floor flat,' Rusty said in explanation and then, as Bryce's tie and shirt went skimming on to the nearest chair, she was sending her own clothes flying with a speed that would have left her audience at The Centurion roaring appreciation.

It was one o'clock the next day before Bryce heaved himself out of Rusty's bed. She had reluctantly done so on a couple of occasions earlier, in order to give her little girl breakfast and something to play with. He'd heard the kiddie chattering to her in the kitchen whilst he'd been lying in bed and it had been the oddest feeling he'd ever experienced. He'd never before slept with anyone who'd had a kiddie, and he'd certainly never had it off with anyone when there'd been a kiddie in a nearby room.

He'd rolled over, smiling to himself. Hell, even though he'd put himself about quite a lot since he'd come out of prison, he'd never slept with anyone like Rusty Daniels, kiddie or no kiddie. She was completely shameless, enjoying sex with a zest and an expertise that had nearly blown his mind. 'Christ!' he'd panted as she'd initiated a variation he'd never imagined acrobatically possible before. 'Where did you learn all this stuff?'

She'd given a throaty chuckle but had been too breathless, at that precise moment in time, to tell him.

Later, as they'd lain coiled together in a tangle of sheets, she'd been starkly honest. 'I turn tricks sometimes,' she'd said as they'd shared a cigarette. 'Not often, owing to Tricia – and I never bring punters back to the flat. This place is strictly off limits when it comes to my earning anything extra.' She'd raised herself up on an elbow and looked down at him speculatively, her lion's mane of hair so fiery red it was almost sparking. 'Is my sideline going to be a problem for you?'

He'd cracked with laughter, amused both by her assumption that what had happened between them wasn't going to be a one-night stand, and by her diverting, almost masculine frankness.

'Nope.' It was true, it didn't. He and Rusty were never going to be walking off into the sunset together. Those kind of idiotic expectations where emotional relationships were concerned had died a death in Sandra's marital front garden. He'd given his heart, mind, soul and commitment once and had had it thrown back in his face. It wasn't a mistake he was going to make again – ever. Still smiling, he'd said, 'And is my being an ex-jailbird going to be a problem for you?'

The throaty, unchained laugh he liked so much had

spluttered out. 'Nope,' she'd said, pushing her hair away from her face and echoing his own reaction. 'I guessed you'd either done time, or, if you hadn't, should have done, when I saw who you were with in The Centurion. The Briscoes aren't exactly known for honest citizenship.' Her eyes, cat-green, wide-spaced and black-lashed, had held his. 'Are you one of the family? And is that why I've never seen you around with them before, because you were in the nick?'

'My surname isn't Briscoe,' he'd said, so aware of the magnificent heaviness of her breasts compared with the delicate narrowness of her waist that he was beginning to harden again with a vengeance. 'But I am family – sort of.'

It hadn't been the time for explanations. If he'd wasted time in explaining, Tricia might have started calling for her and then a replay would have been off the cards altogether. 'Let me show you something,' he'd said, his voice rough with heat as he'd twisted her beneath him, 'something you're going to really appreciate.'

It was nearly two o'clock before their cab drew up outside The Spinners. Louie was again babysitting Tricia and Rusty's day, at least until mid evening when she began her round of the clubs she stripped in, was her own.

The reaction in the pub, when they strolled in together, was one Bryce wished he'd sold tickets for.

'Christ Almighty!' Ginger said, his eyes nearly popping out of his head. 'You ain't doin' a strip 'ere Rusty love, are yer?'

'I wish she was,' Curly said fervently from behind the bar where he was carefully pulling Terry a pint of Guinness. 'My takings would rocket sky-high!'

Jack Wilkinson was seated on a bar stool wearing a black linen jacket, heavy jewellery and shades. He looked

180

the dog's bollocks and Bryce, remembering him as a ragged-arse kid who'd always hated the fact that he was the youngest in their gang, grinned. Now Victor was no longer a mate that could be openly acknowledged, Jack was fast becoming a kid brother to him – the kind of kid brother he'd never had.

'Hi, Bryce,' Jack said now, his attention riveted on Rusty. 'I have some news about a club that's on offer. Are you interested?'

Bryce was, but was still enjoying the goggle-eyed reaction far too much to want to pitch into a discussion immediately. Poor old Frankie looked like a bloke who'd simultaneously had the rug pulled from beneath his feet and been hit on the head with a bottle. Jimmy merely looked perplexed. 'When the hell did you two meet up?' he said, taking advantage of Bryce's obvious intimacy with her to slide his arms around her waist and give her a kiss on the cheek. 'And wherever it was, what are you 'aving to drink, Rusty darlin'?'

'A G and T, please,' she said, easing herself away from him with long-practised ease. She was wearing her tight-fitting white leather trousers and a coffee-coloured blouse. The sleeves were cuffed just below her elbows and it was open at the throat displaying her quality cleavage, the shirt-style collar standing high and flicked. Her hair was away from her face again, this time twisted into a heavy, waist-length ponytail.

'I ain't never seen yer with yer 'air like that before,' Terry said, his hand so unsteady as he lifted his pint of Guinness that he slopped its foaming head all over the back of his hand. 'But then, I ain't never seen you with so many clothes on, either.'

'You won't be seeing at all if you don't watch your mouth.' Bryce's voice didn't rise even a smidgen, but it didn't need to. There was steel in it and it spoke volumes. It was clear to everyone that he and Rusty were a number and that leery jokes and snide remarks about her profession were out of order – or else.

'Hello, darlin'.' The tension in the bar was palpable as Frankie greeted her like an old and intimate friend. 'I hear there was a spot of trouble outside the club last night, as you left. When me and the boys came out, an ambulance was just carting the bloke away. You should have let me know about it, 'specially seeing as who the bloke was, and I'd have sorted it for you.'

Something flashed into Bryce's eyes and was immediately suppressed. If the bloke hadn't been a run-of-the mill punter and his identity was going to be an issue, Frankie shouldn't be arsing around with the knowledge, he should be telling him straight. It had also never occurred to him there might be history between Frankie and Rusty, but Frankie's manner was indicative there had been and he was obviously jealous as hell. Determined not to dance to Frankie's tune, he ignored both lots of bait, merely saying, 'What's it to be, mate? A Remy?' and then, Rusty close by his side, he turned his attention fully to Jack.

'What's the club that's up for offer? Is it a likely or just a long-shot?'

'It's red-hot if the money can be sorted.'

Jack knew exactly what sort of premises he was looking for, and where, and at the certainty in Jack's voice Bryce felt excitement tightening in his belly. This was going to be it. He knew it as sure as he'd known, before they'd spoken, that he and Rusty were going to be an item.

As for whatever money was needed, he'd already made up his mind where that was going to come from. He, Jack, Gunter, Curly and Georgie were going to pull a bank job. It was the kind of stunt Big Chas had been pulling for years and that Jimmy was well into, and if they could get away with it, so could he.

# Chapter Nine

'It will mean being tooled up, Bryce,' Jack had said baldly when he'd broken the news to him. 'You've just done six years. Are you sure you want to take the risk involved? If things go boss-eyed, you'll be looking at a sentence of eight or ten.'

Bryce had grinned, amused that Jack, who was reckless to the point of near insanity, should be showing such caution on his behalf. 'It's because of the time I've done that I need to pull a couple of stunts,' he'd said equably. 'I haven't got years to waste trying to put money together for a casino. If I had, Big Chas's scrap-metal business would give me it easy. It isn't going to give me it in one big lump sum *now*, though – and so there's no alternative. I'm going to have to put my education of the last six years to good use. Are you coming in with me, or not?'

It had been a ludicrous question. Jack would be with him whatever he was planning and both of them knew it.

Three days later, before he'd even arranged the first meet for the job, Frankie waylaid him in The Pickwick on Woolwich Lower Road.

''Ave yer run into difficulty yet over Denny Gerard, the bloke whose lights you punched out in Soho?' he asked, cradling a balloon glass of Remy.

'Nope.' Bryce clocked the name away, glad to have it at last. 'What's the matter, Frankie? You ain't worried about me, are you?'

Frankie didn't grin back. Instead he pulled thoughtfully

at his ear-lobe. 'W-e-ll,' he said musingly, 'mebbe some-body should be, mate. Rusty was a bit out of order over Gerard, if yer don't mind me sayin' so. She should 'ave put you wise about 'im. The Islington outfit he runs with are hard buggers. They're not just going to forget about it, know what I mean?'

Bryce shrugged. After serving over six years in prison, he knew exactly what Frankie meant. It was an unwritten rule that if a member of a mob came off badly in a run-in with a member of another mob, he would be revenged in style. If he'd been a straightforward punter, he'd have had no reason for concern. The task of tracking him down would have required too much effort and, besides, mobsters didn't make a habit of beating or cutting straight members of the public. Such activity inevitably entailed police action, and the light wasn't worth the candle.

He bought a Remy for himself and another for Frankie, knowing that Gerard's friends wouldn't be viewing him as a straight member of the public. He'd served time for manslaughter and, in the months since his release, he'd become well known in the pubs and clubs of south-east London and Soho. He was a player and every other player knew it. Denny Gerard would, by now, most certainly know his identity and would have his card well and truly marked. In the very near future he was going to swan into a pub or a club and find Gerard and his mates waiting for him like alligators at feeding time.

'I'll cope,' he said briefly, once the Remy had hit the back of his throat. 'But thanks for the info, all the same.'

This time it was Frankie's turn to shrug. 'We go back a long way, don't we?' he said, his squint intensifying as it always did when he came on the Mr Sincerity bit. 'Problem is, you don't go in for walkin' around tooled-up – and fists and feet ain't going to sort things when you run into Gerard and his mates mob-handed. So I thought I'd 'elp out. Take yer down to my hidey-hole and fit you up with a weapon, know what I mean?' He drained his brandy glass and grinned. 'You'll be the first person I've taken there. Even the rest of the family don't know about it.'

Only with great difficulty did Bryce keep his sudden interest from blazing in his eyes. He didn't want a weapon. If he'd come to any sensible decision in prison it was that unarmed combat, commando-style, was always going to be his best bet in personal confrontations. He was, however, intensely curious about Frankie's 'hidey-hole' – especially if it was one even Jimmy wasn't aware of.

'OK, Frankie,' he said easily, ignoring a long-legged blonde seated nearby who was giving him welcome signals. 'You're on. When did you have in mind?'

'No time like the present.' Frankie flashed him a cracked-tooth grin. 'I've got a Roller outside. Let's give it a bit of hammering, shall we?'

Forty-five minutes later they were on a windswept caravan site on the Isle of Sheppey.

'I use it as a stow for cash and gear,' Frankie said as they walked between a seemingly endless row of innocent-looking holiday caravans. 'And I don't want anyone else knowing about it, right? This is a serious secret, Bryce. Dead serious.'

From the outside there was nothing whatsoever to distinguish Frankie's caravan from the rest.

'Put the kettle on for a cuppa,' Frankie said as they stepped inside. Even though it was only early afternoon, he turned on a light and drew frilly-edged curtains. 'And while we're waiting for the water to boil, I'll show you my little collection.'

Deeply intrigued, Bryce stood by whilst Frankie lifted off settee-like cushions that formed the seating down both sides of the caravan, and then raised the lid of one of the long and wide box-like bases.

He expected to see a reasonable collection of weapons.

Frankie had, after all, been collecting guns ever since they'd been kids. What was revealed, however, wasn't a reasonable collection. It was an arsenal that had him sucking in his breath so deeply, he nearly choked.

Choppers, machetes, swords and a crossbow were packed tightly together with heavy and light machine-guns, rifles, shotguns, a whole gamut of handguns – Smith and Wesson .45s, Walther PK38 automatics, Lugers – and what looked to be a home-made Gatling gun.

'Jesus, Frankie!' he exclaimed when he could finally trust himself to speak. 'What's this little lot in readiness for? World War Three?'

Frankie bared his teeth in deep satisfaction. 'I'm like a good boy scout, Bry. I'm always prepared.'

'No bleedin' kidding.'

'Most of the handguns are 100 per cent clean.' Frankie eyed his collection lovingly. 'I buy them, decommissioned, from a regular dealer. Then I rebuild the chambers and replace the barrels myself. It only takes a couple of hours, if you know what you're doing. And I never ditch anything. These guns are my children, know what I mean?'

'What about the Lugers?' Bryce asked, wondering if Frankie also had a rocket launcher stashed nearby. 'Are they from the war?'

'Yeah. Do you remember Ted Craven, Curly and Georgie's older brother? The one that emigrated to Australia when we were still kids? He brought them home with him from Italy. They still feel great to handle – real war on the Eastern front stuff. What do you think of this? It's a Tanfaglio. Italian self-loading. Nifty, ain't it?'

It was nifty and, aware he hadn't any gloves with him – and knowing that even if he had brought any, it would have looked bloody strange his putting them on – Bryce fought down the desire to handle it.

'I'm impressed, Frankie,' he said truthfully, 'but I've got a gut feeling about not going around tooled up and, if you don't mind, I'm going to stick with it. Have you any biscuits to go with the tea? I could murder a packet of chocolate digestives.'

The next day he turned all his attention to the planning of his first robbery.

'What about Frankie and Jimmy?' Gunter asked him as, with pints of light ale to hand, he, Jack, Georgie and Curly lounged on a variety of battered chairs and a sagging sofa in a room above The Spinners. 'If we're going to pull a big job, surely they should be in on it with us?'

Seeing by the expressions on their faces that Curly and Georgie shared his concern, Jack, sprawled full-length on the sofa with a lighted cigarette in his hand, cocked an eyebrow quizzically in Bryce's direction.

Bryce surveyed the hard core of his childhood gang. For years, even before he'd been sentenced for killing Roy Clarkson, they had followed him and run with the Briscoes as if they were all one unit and, during the years of his imprisonment, Jack and the others and Frankie's mob had been indivisible. Now, however, he was out of the nick and on the streets again, and things were a little different, especially as the Briscoes were no longer the tight entity they'd once been.

Frankie spent as much time on the other side of the water, acting as an enforcer for the Krays, as he did in South London. Ginger and Terry were still making themselves similarly useful to the Richardson brothers in Peckham, and it was hard to imagine two more dissimilar gangs.

The Krays were basically thieves' ponces who fed off the criminals and club and restaurant owners they blackmailed and terrorised. The Richardsons were more like Big Chas, mixing criminality with legitimate business, running scrap-yards, dabbling in government surplus and floating hookey companies.

Both outfits needed a lot of foot-soldiers for their operations, and the foot-soldiers in question regarded each other with deep suspicion and bitter jealousy. When push came to shove and the friction that already existed between the two gangs erupted into full-scale warfare, as it was bound to before much longer, Ginger and Terry and Frankie were going to be faced with a grave problem of loyalties. And it was a problem he, Bryce, wanted no part of.

'Not necessarily,' he said now in answer to Gunter's query. 'Big Chas and Jimmy don't always include Frankie in their operations. Why should they? They don't want the Twins muscling in on their takes, do they? And you know Frankie. He isn't a team player. He'll be wanting to call all the shots and there'll be arguments over every damn thing.'

'And Jimmy?' Georgie, who had become something of a porker, was tubbily ensconced in a chair near a window that looked out over the Old Kent Road. 'You've been away a long time, Bry. You've got to realise that Jimmy's regarded as being "the man" where banks and wage snatches are concerned.'

'Bring Jimmy in on it and Big Chas is in on it,' Jack said, saving Bryce the trouble of explaining the obvious. 'And you want to keep this tight, Bryce, don't you?'

Bryce nodded. He had no track record of armed robbery – nor of thieving of any kind – but in his years inside some of the top blaggers in the country had become his best mates and he knew exactly what he was about, and the first rule was that the fewer the players, the tighter the security.

'Frankie's too involved north of the river,' he said, putting into words what he knew they all felt. 'Jimmy's too big to let us have our own way over things. He'll want whoever he usually works with to be brought in on the action. Besides, we can't cut Jimmy in and not Frankie.'

He didn't bring Ginger and Terry into the equation. They simply weren't worth the trouble. 'So it's the five of us,' he said with a note of finality so that this time no one argued. 'And the job isn't a bank. It's a wages snatch.'

All of them shifted position, beginning to take real interest. Curly leaned forward in his favoured armchair, secure in the knowledge that the barmaid he was sleeping with was standing in for him downstairs behind the bar. Jack swung his legs off the sofa, allowing The Spinners guard dog, a huge Alsatian, to heave itself up on to the cushions beside him. Gunter rested one foot akimbo on the knee of his other leg, revealing a louche, purple silk sock. Georgie lifted his T-shirt, scratching his beer belly.

Bryce grinned, reminded of the scores of military-type planning meetings he'd held with them when they'd all been ragged-arse kids playing on local bomb sites. 'We've Richard to thank for this piece of work,' he said, enjoying Curly's choke of disbelief. 'Not that he's aware of it.'

'Naturally.' Gunter's thin, wolfish face was amused. Of all the drop-outs from their childhood gang, Richard was the prissiest. Robert and Billy were straight goers, but they did at least occasionally venture into The Spinners to have a drink and rehash old times. Richard never did so. He kept very firmly to his friends in the print and the respectable pubs local to the house he had bought in Greenwich. 'So what information has Richard inadvertently passed on, and who did he tell?' he asked. 'Was it Jack?'

'Nah.' Jack cracked his knuckles. 'It was Mum.'

There were hoots of laughter all round.

'Mum told me about how pissed off Richard was, now he's moved into management in the print, at having to sort out the transport when it goes pear-shaped. Back-up vans are garaged at the same place repairs are carried out, so that if a van is off the road for any length of time another is there to replace it. My Richard apparently believes that frigging about with the transport is beneath him.'

'So – OK – we know where to get our hands on an empty newspaper van,' Georgie said, not seeing where the information was leading. 'We simply nick it from where it's garaged. I don't see what bleedin' use it will be, though.'

'When the wages van delivers, it drives into the bay used for loading up the papers,' Bryce said patiently. 'Loading up isn't carried out, of course, at the same time the wages are delivered, though there'll be empty vans parked up. When the wages van enters the bay, the doors are rollered down and locked so that no one crashes in on things.'

Gunter, seeing exactly where Bryce was going with this information, whistled appreciatively through his teeth. Thanks to his long association with Jimmy and Big Chas he'd been on several wages snatches and knew instinctively, right from the moment one was mooted, whether it was viable or not.

'So what do you plan that we do?' he asked Bryce rhetorically. 'Nick a back-up van from where they're garaged and drive it into the bay when there's lots of activity going on?'

Bryce nodded. 'Three of us will be in the back, tooled up and well hidden. Then, when the wages van trundles in and the doors are down, we jump out, do the business, hit the button for the doors and then away to a waiting getaway car. We'll need a second change-over and I reckon the best place would be beneath one of the arches near London Bridge, all nice and unobtrusive. From then on we're south of the river and on home turf. It's neat and tidy and, best of all, it's uncomplicated.'

It was the uncomplicatedness of it that had attracted him to it. What the haul would be, having no informant in the wages office, he had no way of knowing, but considering the huge number of highly paid people employed in the building it would be enough to make the exercise – and the risk involved – worthwhile.

'It's a cinch.' Gunter's flint-grey eyes were alight with anticipation. 'Have you recceed it out, Bryce, timing the wages van and other vans in and out, or is that still to do?'

'I've recceed it. Delivery van movement is slapdash, at least when it comes to the vans returning to the bay, but we'd need to drive in fairly tight to the time the wages van is due, to make sure we don't turn up while newspaper loading is going on. We don't want someone flinging the van doors open to chuck a parcel of papers on top of us, do we? So first of all we have to get the timing right. If whoever is driving is geared up like the other drivers he can stroll out of the bay, a clipboard under his arm, no problem. Then it's pretty smartish to wherever the getaway's parked so that he's ready and waiting for us with the engine revved. We're too small a team to run to two drivers.'

'When do we steal the van from the garage?' Though jobs hadn't yet been allocated, Georgie was fairly sure he'd be the one doing the driving. On jobs with the Briscoes he'd always been the wheelman. 'The evening before? Or is that leaving it too late?'

'We'll do it the evening before – at the last minute possible.'

Now that the plan had been accepted in principle, there were only relatively straightforward matters to settle:

'We'll need to dump the spare wheel of the getaway,' Georgie said practically. 'We'll need the room for the dosh.'

'And let's have a few names up our sleeve as to who'd be willing to be a "witness", just in case our luck runs out and we get pulled for an ID parade,' Gunter said, smoothly professional. 'I like to know there'll be someone on the scene who says they can identify us and who will breeze past us in a line-up without a flicker of recognition.'

191

'What about the ringer?' Georgie asked. 'Have you got one sorted, Bryce?'

Bryce nodded. 'I've garaged up a dark green Rover 2000 – very police-looking. I suggest we take the hubcaps off. I don't think it will come to a chase – we'll be away too fast – but if it does, we don't want hubcaps flying off and laying a trail.'

'And the cash?' Curly asked. 'Where are we going to stow it? The pub is too dodgy. I'm always being raided, though it's a liberty considering the amount I pay local cozzers in backhanders.'

'Lee Gardens, Deptford.' Bryce pushed a tumbled fall of hair away from his forehead. He hadn't yet mentioned this little fact to Rusty, but that she might not be OK about it didn't even enter his head.

It was an address that meant nothing to anyone else in the room, but none of them queried it. Ever since his release, Bryce had been acknowledged as the man in charge, just as he'd always been when they were kids. If he thought Lee Gardens a safe stow, then they trusted his judgement.

'I think that's it for today,' he said, rising abruptly to his feet. 'If you're doing the driving, Georgie, you'll need to plot out some alternative back doubles between Fleet Street and Lee Gardens, and you need to recce the garage. We don't want a hitch when it comes to nicking the van. Gunter, rig your favourite shotgun using salt instead of pellets in the cartridges.'

'Why?' For once Gunter was mystified.

Bryce lit a cigarette. 'Because we're not going in armed with pellets. We're not risking anyone being hurt, no matter how cock-eyed things might get. Live ammo on a raid slaps an automatic ten on any sentence and we'd have to be barking mad to run that kind of risk.'

'So what's with the salt?' Curly asked, intrigued.

Bryce blew a thread of smoke into the air. 'If any

would-be hero tries to tackle us we can shoot and he'll think he's been hit. It will give us time to get away – by the time the truth dawns, we'll be long gone. I know Gunter only ever uses his own tool. What I want him to do is to make quite sure it behaves as it should. Any more questions?'

'Yep.' Georgie heaved himself out of his armchair. 'What date are we going for? Next week? The week after?'

'The week after. I want you, Curly and Gunter to have a chance at timing the wages van and of becoming 100 per cent familiar with the territory. That means you recceing this coming Friday. Is that it? Does everyone know where they stand?'

'Yep.' Georgie said again, answering for everyone. 'I'm off downstairs to get a round in. Who's coming?'

Bryce had been the only one not to join him. Now that the proposed job was well in hand he had other matters to attend to. The club he was already in negotiations to buy, for one thing. He strolled out of The Spinners and across the pavement to where his yellow Ford Zodiac convertible was parked. It was going to be a cash transaction – for anyone with his kind of record and present lifestyle it was the only kind there was.

The premises in question were in Catford – a little off his manor, but still very definitely south-east London. It had already had two previous existences as a club. In the early fifties, it had been an ex-servicemen's club and, later, a working men's club. Two years ago, when a road-widening scheme had been on the cards, the council had sold it to a private property developer who, if its present condition was anything to go by, had carelessly forgotten its existence.

He turned left to cut down towards Jamaica Road. He and the developer had already reached an under-standing agreeable to them both. Now all he needed was plenty of cash so that he could follow through on it.

August had been hot and muggy ever since it had begun and there was the scent of a long-heralded thunderstorm in the air. Dextrously and with eye-catching panache he tooled the open-topped Ford Zodiac in and out of heavy traffic, heading back to Swan Row so that he could shower and change before meeting up later in the day with Rusty.

The second he turned out of Jamaica Road and into the side street leading down into Swan Row, he saw her. The very fact she was on her own was sufficient to attract his attention. Hilda Clarkson had never allowed those she ruled the slightest freedom. She'd certainly never allowed Roy any – it was one of the reasons he'd grown up such a weirdo. That six-year-old Debbie should be strolling unconcernedly down the street in her distinctive red gingham dress – and with Hilda nowhere in sight – was enough to make him slow down and pull in beside the kerb.

'Hi, Debbie,' he said, stepping out of the car and leaning against it as she approached. 'You're not lost, are you?'

She halted three yards or so away from him and eyed him witheringly from beneath a badly cut, mousy fringe. 'No. Course I'm not.'

Seeing her up close she looked so like Sandra as a child that Bryce felt he was in a science-fiction time warp.

'I knew your mum,' he said starkly, wanting to engage her interest so that he could keep hold of the sensation for a little longer. 'Her hair was just as straight as yours, only not quite so fair.'

A look of puzzlement flashed through Debbie's eyes. 'My mum has sausage curls and her hair is bluey-grey,' she said, making no move to step any nearer to him and still speaking in the same curiously sullen manner.

He was about to laugh and to put her straight when

194

it suddenly dawned on him that she was talking about Hilda. A tide of rage roared through him. How *dare* Hilda Clarkson pass herself off as being the mother of Sandra's kiddie?

'Now just listen to me carefully for a few minutes . . .' he began, no longer lounging against the car but taut with tension, his arms folded. 'Your mother . . .' But then he stopped.

Her mother had never known her. She had never wanted to know her in the past and was unlikely to want to know her in the future. If he started putting a kiddie as young as Debbie in the picture as to the truth about her parentage, he'd be opening a real can of worms. For the first time it occurred to him that even attracting her attention had been way out of line on his part. He was responsible for the death of her dad, for Christ's sake – what sort of a man was he, chatting to her now as if he were a family friend?

The grossness of the situation hit him like a sledgehammer. Did Debbie know about her dad and how he had died? As soon as the thought occurred to him, he rejected it. If Debbie believed that her grandma was her mum, then she'd also believe that her granddad was her dad. Most of her neighbours, of course, knew differently, but presumably they, like him, felt that Debbie was too young to be carelessly faced with a truth that could do nothing but bewilder her.

'Well?' she said to him now, scowling for no reason he could see, other than that it was obviously an ingrained habit. 'What about my mum?'

'I bet she's told you not to talk to strange men,' he said, concerned he might be setting a dangerous precedent.

'I do what I like,' Sandra's daughter said with a toughness Sandra, at the same age, had never been capable of, and probably still wasn't. She cocked her head slightly to one side, looking at him speculatively. 'Are you the bad man that's come back to live in the row and that I haven't to talk to?'

Feeling fairly sure that he was, Bryce nodded, amused by her comically adult self-assurance. Debbie might look like a young Sandra, but that was as far as the similarity went.

His admitting that he was the bad man she'd been told about didn't disconcert Debbie in the slightest. The speculation in her eyes deepened to interest. 'What did you do? Did you frighten little girls? Did you . . .'

Before she had time to finish her questioning and before he had time to say that he would never, under any circumstance, frighten a little girl, Hilda Clarkson came steaming round the corner of the street, a bulging string-bag of shopping in either hand, and all hell broke loose.

'*Get away from her*!' she screeched, dropping both bags of shopping and breaking into a lumbering run. '*Get away from my little Debbie*! *You shouldn't have been let out of prison*! *You should have hanged*!'

In retrospect, Bryce found Debbie's stony lack of reaction the most significant part of the ugly incident. Whilst he balled his hands into fists and fought the urge to throttle the woman who'd given him and Sandra so much grief, Debbie merely remained with her feet planted square on the pavement, refusing to be swept up into Hilda's protective embrace, her sullen eyes continuing to hold his.

'Yeah, right-on, Hilda,' he said sarcastically, refusing to give vent to foul language in front of a child. He yanked open the Zodiac's door and slid behind the wheel. 'I should be careful of your mouth, though, if I was you . . . *Mummy*. Otherwise things might be said that you don't want saying. Know what I mean?'

Hilda knew exactly what he meant. Again she tried to hug Debbie protectively to her, this time so that if Bryce said Sandra's name, she'd be able to clap her hands over Debbie's ears.

Bryce gunned the engine into life and slewed the Zodiac out on to the crown of the road, glancing in his rear-view mirror as he did so. At what he saw he felt a surge of wholehearted rapport. Debbie was mutinously struggling to free herself of Hilda's embrace and he didn't blame her. He didn't blame her one little bit.

'Fuck off, Frankie,' Rusty said, not remotely surprised at his having barged in on her cubby-hole of a dressing-room and wanting him out of it double-quick.

'Nice to see you, too, darlin'.' Frankie dragged a chair towards him and, turning it back to front, straddled it, resting his arms on its back. 'It's especially nice seein' so much of you,' he leered, his squint intensifying.

It was only mid afternoon, but mid afternoon stripping at The Centurion was a popular, well-established pro-gramme. Rusty, her hair piled high in a loose tumble on top of her head and wearing a choker made from a squillion silver bugle beads, stiletto-heeled shoes and not much else, glared at him with loathing.

He and she had never been a number, but fending him off, and keeping him off, hadn't been easy. Frankie Briscoe was a force to be reckoned with – the kind of heavy villain many women were mesmerised by.

People were frightened of him – and they had good reason to be. She had been present enough times to know that when Frankie was in a certain mood a hush fell across any room he entered. It was the same in any bar he drank in. If Frankie was in a mean frame of mind there would be tension all the while he was there and palpable relief when he'd gone.

Angrily she snatched a very unglamorous towelling robe from a hook on the door and rammed her arms into its sleeves, wrapping it round herself and knotting its tie-belt savagely tight so that it couldn't possibly come adrift.

Frankie was uncaring. He'd seen enough, at very close

quarters, to keep his prick in a state of throbbing erection all day. For weeks Jimmy and Terry had had bets as to whether Rusty's sizzling hair colour came out of a bottle – and that her pubic hair was dyed to match. It was a speculation he could now end. He'd just been within sniffing distance of her springy, spicy-red pubic curls and they were natural – no doubt at all.

He clenched his jaw, fancying her so much his throat was crackly dry and his front teeth ached. 'What's the low-down on you and Bryce, then?' he asked, knowing she wouldn't shout for anyone to come to throw him out; knowing she was well aware it was a job no one would willingly take on. 'He seems to think you and he are pretty much a hot item.'

Rusty cast a surreptitious look at the dressing-room's battered wall clock. Frankie had walked in on her just as she'd exited from the stage. By rights she should now be scrambling into her street clothes, the rest of the day her own until early evening when her working day truly began.

'So?' she said, determined not to start dressing until she'd got rid of him, turning her back on him as she removed her outsize false eyelashes.

'So, I thought you didn't like giving it out to heavy villains,' he said, his eyes on her rump. 'I thought you were too much of a fucking princess.'

'I don't like thugs.' Rusty's smoky voice was tight. 'I don't like people who hurt people.' She paused meaningfully, looking at him through the grimy glass of the dressing-table mirror. 'People like you, know what I mean?'

'Oh yeah. I know what you mean.' He smiled evilly. 'Which is why I can't quite figure the Bryce and you scene. I mean, Bryce doesn't just hurt people. When Bryce gets narked with them, he plunges them in the ticker.'

She spun round to face him, dropping the false eyelashes

she was holding. 'What do you mean? What the *fuck* do you bleeding well mean?'

Frankie gave a rasp of laughter, enjoying himself hugely. He might not be furthering his own chances too much where Rusty was concerned, but he sure as hell was putting an end to Bryce's bedtime frolics with her.

'I mean he's a killer, Rusty darlin'. He's served time for it. Six years out of a nine-year sentence. Clarkson was only a weedy kid of seventeen and when he got in Bryce's way, Bryce knifed him straight in the heart. Poor Roy was dead before he hit the floor. Leastways, they think he was dead. Hard to tell when he died, really, 'cos Bryce didn't trouble about getting him to a hospital or nothing. He was too busy shagging the girl who was with him.'

Rusty sucked in her breath. She'd had Bryce marked down as a Jack-the-lad crim from the first moment she'd seen him – if he hadn't been, he wouldn't have been out with the Briscoes. She'd also seen for herself that he was as tough as he looked, but had assumed his style of violence was the smack-in-the-mouth variety – a variety she had no quibble with, especially when the occasion was as deserving as it had been when he'd slugged the bloke who'd been pestering her. If he was a raging psychopath, though, that was a very different matter. Raging psychopaths, no matter how criminally handsome, she could do without.

'I don't believe you.' The words were automatic. She didn't *want* to believe him, but she was really stalling for time. What on earth would she do if he were telling the truth? She'd fallen for Bryce like a ton of bricks. He possessed two qualities she'd never come across in a man before, at least not together. Toughness and tenderness. Though there had been times when their love-making had been as violent as a battle – when he'd taken her on the hard floor of the kitchen, for instance – there were also times when his tenderness, and his concern for her pleasure, had taken her breath away. Not in a million years did she want to stop seeing him and sleeping with him.

'I don't believe you, Frankie,' she said again. 'Bryce is brilliant with his fists. I've seen how brilliant he is. But he isn't a killer. He doesn't have a killer's eyes. He's fantastic with my little girl and . . .'

She stopped short. If there was even a shred of truth in what Frankie was telling her, she couldn't take the slightest risk. The kind of violence Frankie was talking about was the kind that erupted out of nowhere and she couldn't expose Tricia to that kind of danger. Panic welled up in her throat. Frankie wasn't telling her the truth. He couldn't be.

'You're just out to split Bryce and me up!' She hurled the words at him in sudden, fierce, conviction. 'That's what this is all about, isn't it, Frankie? You can't stand seeing me with him, can you?'

Frankie was no longer grinning. His large-boned face was as taut and tense as a mask. 'No, I can't,' he said savagely, his knuckles whitening as his hands gripped the back of the chair he was straddling. 'But I ain't lying about Brycie-boy. He's served time for manslaughter – and it ain't a killing he's ever grieved over. If you don't believe me, Rusty, ask him.'

She looked into his disconcertingly off-centred eyes and felt the floor rock beneath her feet. Though telling the truth wasn't something Frankie made a habit of, she knew with sickening certainty he was doing so now.

'Get out!' There was a crack in her voice she couldn't control. She wanted to be on her own; had to be on her own in order to deal with the chaotic emotions she was feeling.

She was wasting her breath, just as she had been when she'd told him to fuck off. He rose abruptly to his feet, sending the chair toppling out of his way, filling the tiny cupboard of a room with his hard-muscled bulk.

'I want you, Rusty darlin',' he said, moving in on her. 'I always 'ave. I always will.'

Rusty tried to side-step him and failed. From deep in the club there came the faint rattle of beer crates as, with the club now closed, members of the bar staff began re-stocking. There was not the slightest point in shouting and trying to attract their attention. All that would happen, if she did, was that someone else would get hurt.

'There are some things in life you can't have!' she hissed, her eyes flashing fire as, unable to escape round him, she stepped backwards, banging against the dressing-table and sending a make-up bottle toppling.

'Not me, Rusty. I always get what I want.' The lust in his eyes was coupled with a sense of purpose that had her stomach heaving.

'You lay one hand on me, Frankie, just one hand and you'll live to regret it! The world and its brother may be scared to death of you, but Bryce isn't!'

He paused, breathing hard, his nostrils pinched and white.

For one heart-stopping moment, as she stood with her hands splayed against the wall so that she could give herself good leverage to ram a knee hard into his balls, she thought she'd said something that counted with him, and then his tension evaporated and he flashed one of his rare grins.

'I don't think you'd want me and Bryce falling out, Rusty darlin',' he said with amused certainty. 'Your lover boy's got enough on at the moment waiting for Denny Gerard's friends to pay him a call. You wouldn't want my friends, Ronnie and Reggie, to be unhappy with him as well, would you?'

As the blood drained from her face he moved swiftly, seizing hold of her hair, pinioning her against the wall with one hand, yanking her towelling-robe open with the other.

'This is going to be a revelation to you, sweetheart,' he panted, prising her legs apart with his knee. 'Brycie-boy can't have too much experience – he was only a kid when he went in clink and he can't have packed that much in since he came out. Now, me . . .' His free hand slid down to where it had always wanted to be, her spicy-red pubic curls springing against his palm. 'Me . . . I'm very experienced. V-e-r-y.'

As his big ugly fingers invaded her body and she cried out in revulsion and protest, he covered her mouth hard with his, his tongue silencing her as brutally as a gag.

# Chapter Ten

'So, you're happy with everything?'

Bryce flashed Jack a grin that stretched from ear to ear. 'As a king,' he said, his hands in the trouser pockets of an immaculately tailored mohair suit. 'Wouldn't you be?'

It was lunchtime and they were strolling into one of their regular haunts, The Pickwick, the subject under discussion: the nightclub Bryce had acquired in nearby Catford.

'Yeah.' Jack grinned. 'Especially now we've settled on a name.'

Christening the club had been a headache of mammoth proportions. Georgie and Ginger had been in favour of something evocative of the protection era in America, Georgie favouring The Kentucky, even though it was a name the Kray twins had already appropriated for one of their clubs, and Ginger rooting for Chicago Nights or The Palm Springs. Even Gunter's suggestion – The Lucky Strike – had sounded American.

Bryce had rejected all their suggestions out of hand. Anything American-sounding in the heart of Catford was, in his opinion, pathetically out of place. He didn't want anything French, either, despite Curly's conviction that names such as The Pigalle and Club Can-Can were 'dead classy'.

'It's going to be The Renegade,' he'd said decisively, believing it down to earth enough not to sound pretentious. It was also how he thought of himself, though he'd no intention of admitting it.

'Two lagers and two Remy chasers,' he said now to the

pretty barmaid they were both on exceedingly friendly terms with, glad to see that the pub was near empty. It meant they would be able to talk undisturbed, a luxury never allowed them in The Spinners.

'I want to get the staff side of things settled,' he said, sliding on to a bar stool. 'Billy Dixon's missis wants a job. She's bored out of her head in the corner shop, but she's competent business-wise. I reckon she could run the bar easily. Robert Wilkinson's other half wants in on the cloakroom and –'

The pub doors blasted open and Denny Gerard stormed in, flanked by four bruisers built like brick shit-houses. All of them wore knuckle-dusters; two of them had knives.

The barmaid screamed and ran for the phone. The handful of regulars ran for cover. Bryce and Jack – with not a weapon between them – had their backs to the bar.

For a split second Bryce's reaction was one of stunned fury. He'd known for weeks that this confrontation was on the cards, but he'd never expected to be ambushed on home turf – and The Pickwick was almost as much his home turf as The Spinners was.

Riding hard on his fury was fear. Not for himself, but for Jack. This battle was his. It had nothing to do with Jack – and if Jack came to grief because of it, he'd never forgive himself; not in a hundred years.

'What the *fuck*?' he heard Jack say as Gerard slammed on the door locks and the four gorillas hurled themselves towards them.

'*Leave Gerard to me!*'

It was the only command he had time to utter. A blade was coming straight at him and he deflected the blow with his right arm, slamming a left hook with such almighty force he knew he'd broken his attacker's jawbone. He'd certainly destroyed his ability to fight any further. As he wheeled on a second attacker he was aware of the bloke keeling over, half-conscious and helpless, blood pouring from his mouth.

He was aware, too, that feet away from him Jack was fighting for his life.

Knowing he had to get to Jack's side he blasted a right hook with demonic ferocity, aiming for the point of the chin. It connected with sledgehammer strength, propelling his victim inches into the air. As he fell, Bryce grabbed for his shirt collar, butting him in the face. It wasn't necessary. He was already out cold.

There was still Gerard to deal with and Gerard was coming at him with a knuckle-duster on one hand, a six-inch knife in the other. He was also coming at him with an expression in his eyes that Bryce read loud and clear. Gerard hadn't intended this to be a one-to-one confrontation. He'd expected his heavyweight mates to be doing the dirty for him and, now that two of them were sprawled on the floor in pools of blood and broken teeth, he was a very unhappy bunny.

Seeing Gerard hesitate, knowing he was uncertain of which way to come at him, Bryce took full advantage, ramming a terrible uppercut to his gut. Gerard hurtled backwards, landing on the floor. Aware that Jack was still defending himself from a knife attack with his fists and feet and a bar stool, he wrested Gerard's knife from his hand and, as Gerard rallied, regaining his feet and hitting out at him, he grabbed him by the throat.

He wasn't by nature a sadistic fighter, but as Gerard threw another punch at him with a knuckle-dustered fist, he blocked the blow with his right arm and increased the pressure with his left. He had no intention of being kind to Denny Gerard.

As far as he was concerned, Gerard should have accepted what had happened to him outside The Centurion with good grace. The way he'd been treating Rusty had, after all, been way out of order – and he'd only been knocked out, not beaten to a bloody pulp. His seeking revenge for such a trivial incident was seriously annoying, but having his friends taking Jack with knives as well as fists was in another, altogether different category.

As he forced Gerard to his knees and as Gerard's eyes began to bulge, he was aware of the barmaid still screaming and of pandemonium coming from the small group of unwilling witnesses.

He took not the slightest notice.

Feverishly Gerard tried to dislodge Bryce's fist from his throat and, failing, began slugging futilely at his arms and side.

Bryce continued the pressure, aware that behind him Jack had sorted one of his assailants and was near to sorting the other.

Gurgling sounds began coming from Gerard's throat.

All background shouting ceased.

Frantically, Gerard's eyes sought help from the handful of people keeping well out of the way at the far end of the room, but it wasn't forthcoming. No one had the remotest intention of getting involved, not even Jack, who was leaning against the bar, panting and bleeding, but victorious.

A few seconds before Gerard would have lost consciousness and no more than thirty seconds or so before he would have died, Bryce let go of him.

The battle was over.

All that mattered now was Jack.

'How bad is it, mate?' he asked as, leaving the semi-conscious and the unconscious behind, he half-carried him out to the Zodiac.

'Dunno.' Jack's speech was dangerously indistinct. 'I've been punctured somewhere in the gut and I'm near blinded in one eye. I can hardly see a fucking thing.'

Heaving him as gently as he could into the car, Bryce wasn't surprised. There was a gaping knife wound slicing down over Jack's left eye and it was pumping blood at a terrifying rate.

He scrabbled in the glove compartment, finding only a chamois wash-leather. As Jack slumped in the passenger seat he made a pad out of it, fearful as to whether Jack was going to have the strength to hold it in place for the length of time it was going to take to reach a hospital clear of their home area.

'And your gut, Jack?' Frantically he dragged Jack's bloody shirt out of his pants.

This time the only possible pad was his own shirt. Shrugging himself out of his jacket and yanking his shirt over his head, he strapped it into place with his trouser belt.

'The cozzers are on their way,' Jack said weakly as they both registered the wailing sound of police sirens. 'Let's get out of here, eh?'

Looking at the ghastly mess that was – or had been – Jack's eye, Bryce hesitated. Hard on the heels of the police cars would be an ambulance – and if there wasn't, the cozzers would soon have one on the scene. The price that would be paid, though, for Jack being so swiftly conveyed to a Casualty Department, would be their arrest. It wouldn't matter that Gerard and his gorillas had been tooled-up and they hadn't, or that Gerard and his mob had come looking for them and that they hadn't been the aggressors. He knew enough of the police by now to know they'd both be risking charges of GBH – and with his track record another prison sentence would be a cert.

'Don't even think about it, mate,' Jack said blurrily, sensing his indecision. 'Let's jus' get the hell out.'

He had. A casualty doctor at the Middlesex Hospital had saved Jack's eye, and his only lasting souvenir of the fight was a scar that rakishly sliced his left eyebrow. His own souvenir was an enhanced reputation for being someone it was wisest not to take liberties with. Denny Gerard's cronies certainly weren't going to do so again. Via an intermediary, they'd let him know that they didn't rate Denny as being worth dying for.

'There was a time, in The Pickwick, when I didn't think I was going to live to see this place open,' Jack said with a grin as he strolled with Bryce through the newly carpeted, freshly decorated rooms of The Renegade. 'It looks a treat, don't it?'

Bryce nodded, his satisfaction bone-deep.

He hadn't had the slightest experience of what he was about when he'd begun re-building and refurbishing what had been a very run-down property, but it hadn't mattered. Living on champagne and pure adrenaline, and fuelled by the cash stolen in the wages snatch, he'd brought in local workmen and let his imagination run riot. The result was, as Jack said, 'a treat'.

There was an opulently furnished gaming-room, a dance area with a sensational glass floor and mirrored ceiling, a long, curved bar, and a restaurant.

Evelyn Briscoe, Frankie's mum and someone who, after the long years he'd spent beneath her roof, was something of a mother-figure to him, had agreed to act as chef. After a near lifetime as a school-dinner cook her repertoire was basic but, as he knew from personal experience, it was also amazingly good.

He'd poached his croupiers from the various Soho clubs he frequented, with Sheree, Big Chas's second ex-wife – a lady who'd once been a croupier at the prestigious Churchill's in Bond Street – acting as croupier-in-chief. He'd wanted Ginger and Terry on the door, but both said that, though they intended being a highly visible presence in the club, they had too many commitments elsewhere for him to be able to rely on them as doormen.

'We can recommend someone, though,' Ginger had said,

ever helpful. 'There's a bloke known as the Gorilla who trains in the boxing gym down at the Thomas à Becket. He's built like a brick wall and he isn't running with any local gangs. He says he isn't interested in anything dodgy and he's too big to argue with so he gets left alone. You wouldn't get a squeak out of anyone with him on the door, and as it's a straight number he'd probably go for it.'

He'd gone down to the Thomas à Becket with Rusty, made himself known to the Gorilla, instantly taken a shine to him and had come away knowing that The Renegade was going to have the best possible protection against trouble-makers.

All in all, where his staff were concerned, he felt he'd come to some very satisfactory arrangements. There was a family, friendly feel to The Renegade, which would, he hoped, be apparent to its clientele. As for what kind of clientele that would be, he had no illusions. A Catford-based club certainly wouldn't attract the out-of-town businessmen who were so regularly ripped off in Churchill's, or the really high rollers who frequented West End clubs and casinos such as The Claremont, above Annabel's night-club, and The 21, off Berkeley Square.

'We'll be up to the eyeballs with nothing but crooks, villains and local layabouts treating it as a second home unless we take a leaf out of Reggie Kray's book,' he'd said to Jack when he'd first shown him the run-down, dilapidated property. 'So what I don't want it to be is a straightforward gambling club. I want it to be somewhere blokes will bring their ladies for a night out. There's going to be a dance floor, music, good food, swish décor.'

With the most up-to-date sound system installed that hookey money could buy; ducts around the dance floor for dry ice to be blown up and around the dancers legs; an overall colour scheme of soft smoky greys and deep dramatic purples, he felt he had achieved his objective. He had only one problem left. It was a problem that hadn't raised its head as yet, but which he knew would do so the moment the club opened: protection.

'Ron and Reggie won't trouble you,' Frankie had said with a certainty that came of his being a Kray henchman. 'You're south of the river and way off their manor. The Richardsons may have a word, although protection for protection's sake isn't really their scene.' He'd cracked his knuckles and given one of his rare grins. 'To tell the truth, old cock, if you and me weren't practically family, I'm the bloke you'd have to be paying.'

'I won't be paying anyone,' he'd said with steel in his voice. 'And you can put the word round that I won't. OK, Frankie?'

Frankie had given a careless shrug of his massive shoulders. 'It's always worth a few quid to make sure everything's sweet, Bryce. You don't want a customer getting razored, do you? Blood all over the place. Cozzers on top of you like a ton of bricks. Punters too shit-scared to come near. Once that happens it's closedown time, then where are you? You and Jack may have sorted out Denny Gerard's mates, but it doesn't mean the two of you can take on the whole bleedin' world, know what I mean?'

It had been a long speech for Frankie and Bryce had taken note of it. Maybe, if he was leaned on really hard, he'd have to pay protection. But he wasn't going to start out doing so, not when he was already having to dig deep in his pocket for another, quite different kind of insurance.

As he strolled with Jack into the bar area he glanced down at his watch. His meeting with Detective Inspector Somerville had been arranged for two thirty and it was now twenty past. 'Give me the low-down again on Somerville,' he said, going round the back of the chrome-edged bar and helping himself to a couple of bottles of light ale. He cracked the tops off and, not bothering with glasses, handed a fizzing bottle to Jack. 'How long have Big Chas and Jimmy had him in their pockets?'

'Yonks.' Jack took a couple of deep swallows from the chilled bottle and then wiped his mouth with the back of his hand. 'They have him on a retainer.' He leaned comfortably against the bar. 'When Jimmy was in the frame last year for the Post Office van job, Somerville neutralised the evidence, no problem at all. Whenever Big Chas needs a record pulled, he delivers. He's corrupt as they come, but he doesn't look it.'

He ran a hand through his straw-coloured hair, inadvertently drawing attention to the livid scar slicing his eyebrow. At the moment it was too raw to be sexy, but it was obvious that by increasing his aura of danger and toughness it would eventually emphasise, not mar, his James Dean-like good looks. 'He's a big bloke,' he said, as Bryce remained silent. 'When he pats you on the back he nearly knocks you over. And he kills pints. I'd get a few set up in advance, if I were you.'

Bryce chewed the corner of his lip. Every villain worth his salt had a tame bent copper in his pocket, even those as low in the pecking order as old Jug Ears. At the other end of the scale it was said that the Kray twins had so many senior policemen bribed or blackmailed that they knew immediately if information about them was offered to Scotland Yard. As this meant the name of the informant also becoming known, informants, where the Krays were concerned, were in very short supply.

His need of police protection was a little different, but no less vital. Without it, he'd never have advance warning if The Renegade was about to be raided – and all such clubs, even well-run ones, suffered police raids with monotonous regularity. Straight, middle-class clientele would be scared off at even the suggestion of police interest and, as that was the kind of clientele he was hoping to attract, he needed a highly placed cozzer on his payroll. Detective Inspector Somerville, if everything he'd heard about him was correct, sounded as though he'd be just the man.

'And you reckon he's a serious high-flier?' he asked Jack, acutely conscious of the knife wound that had nearly cost Jack an eye.

'Somerville's a career copper. He was only thirty-two when he was promoted to detective inspector and Big Chas reckons he's going to go right to the top of the tree – detective chief inspector, detective chief superintendent, assistant commissioner, maybe even to commissioner.' He chuckled, the idea of one day having a corrupt Metropolitan commissioner in their pockets amusing him vastly.

Bryce glanced down at his watch again. DI high-flying Somerville was on the verge of being late.

'What are your plans after we've met with Somerville?' Jack asked. 'Do you fancy shooting down to the West End for a couple of hours?'

'No. I'm off back to Lee Gardens. I've fences to mend with Rusty.'

Jack snorted with laughter. 'I'm not bleedin' surprised, the amount of time you've been spending with Big Chas's ex-missus. Playing away from home is never a good idea, mate. Not when the little lady at home is such a fire-cracker.'

Bryce flashed a rueful grin. 'You're telling me,' he said, still smarting from some of the well-aimed blows Rusty had delivered that morning after finding one of Sheree Briscoe's earrings in his trouser pocket. 'But, much as I love the lady in question, I've no intention of changing my ways. I've too much catching up on lost time to do.'

He was speaking the simple truth. The years when he should have been satisfying his curiosity about women, the years between his eighteenth birthday and his twenty-fifth, had been years of enforced, bromide-aided celibacy, and there were times when he felt he'd never be able to compensate for them.

He and Rusty were a great double-act. He was seriously in love with her – and in a way quite different to the way he'd been in love with Sandra. It didn't mean he was faithful, though. Ever since the day he'd moved in with her, he'd spent money on other women, out of curiosity as much as anything else. He wanted variety. He wanted to sleep with them all – good girls, bad girls, tall ones, short ones. Sheree Briscoe was leggy and doe-eyed and, though he didn't like admitting it to himself, the fact that she'd once been married to Big Chas – and still lived beneath his roof – was an extra turn on.

'Take the smile off your face and stop thinking dirty thoughts,' Jack said, suddenly relaxed no longer. 'The door bell's ringing.'

Seconds later they heard the door being opened and then the distant, unmistakable sound of the Gorilla growlingly greeting their expected visitor.

'Get a couple more bottles opened, Bryce,' Jack said tensely. 'I can't have a meet with a cozzer without something to deaden the pain.'

Later, driving home, Bryce reflected that the meeting hadn't been nearly as painful as Jack had feared. Somerville had proven to be in his mid thirties, a big, bulky bloke with a moon face and ponderous manner. For what he termed 'the usual sweetener' – a hefty weekly payment of ready cash – he was happy to ensure that The Renegade would meet with a smooth run where the police were concerned.

As he tooled the Zodiac down Lewisham High Street in the direction of Deptford, Bryce reflected that, except for his pre-breakfast spat with Rusty, it had been a very satisfactory morning. Immediately he had set eyes on Somerville he had sensed his ability, ambition and amorality. Taken together, they were character traits he was going to be able to exploit to the full over the coming years – and not only where clubs and casinos were concerned.

His mouth tugged into a smile as he negotiated the heavy Christmas traffic and turned left at Deptford Bridge. All he had to do now was to sweeten Rusty. As Tricia would be at her special nursery school, and they'd have the house to themselves, it was a task he was looking forward to.

In a state of highly charged sexual tension he opened the door of Lee Gardens to be met, seconds later, by a scene so totally unexpected that for a moment he wondered if he was hallucinating.

'What the bleeding hell . . .' he began, so goggle-eyed he knew he must look an absolute dick.

Victor set his cup of tea down and rose to his feet, the armchair cushions so squashed it was obvious he'd been comfortably seated for some time.

From the other armchair, with her legs curled beneath her, Rusty shot him a look that could have meant anything. Her body language, however, was totally relaxed. She and Victor had quite obviously been getting on very well together.

'Try and look pleased to see me, mate,' Victor said, giving him a hug and a slap on the back. 'I had the devil's own job tracking you down. Old Jug Ears told me to fuck off when I called at number 5. Said he'd no forwarding address for you and wouldn't give me it even if he had. He seems to think my becoming a copper has disgraced the entire neighbourhood.'

'It has.' Bryce's voice was full of dry amusement. Victor's manner was making it obvious there was nothing sinister behind his visit, and as long as Victor wasn't looking him up out of professional interest he was happy to see him. 'Who gave you the address?' he asked. 'Just as a matter of interest.'

As Victor returned to the comfort of the deep armchair that was twin to Rusty's, Bryce flopped down on the sofa, resigned to the fact that sex was, for the moment, off the agenda.

'Curly.'

Bryce's eyebrows rose slightly and Victor shrugged his shoulders.

'Curly knows me well enough to know I wouldn't have an ulterior motive,' he said, picking up his cup of tea again. 'I told him it was to do with Sandra and he gave me the nod as to where I'd find you.'

That Victor was still in touch with Sandra was no great surprise. They had, after all, lived next door to each other from the time Sandra had been born until the day she'd gone into the Salvation Army mother-and-baby home and, as Victor was now a detective sergeant, he was one childhood friend her policeman husband couldn't possibly disapprove of. What did surprise him, though, was Victor's mentioning Sandra's name in front of Rusty. How the hell could he possibly have known that it wouldn't cause problems?

He flicked her a look to gauge her reaction. She was wearing a black turtleneck and black trousers and her strong, slender feet were bare, her toenails unlacquered. As always when she wore black, her skin looked paler than usual, the flame-red of her hair intensified to a colour that was almost incandescent. She was so beautiful and so damned sexy that just looking at her made it difficult for him to breathe. How Victor had remained so relaxed after sharing a cup of tea with her on his own, he couldn't even begin to imagine.

'Vic knows I know about Sandra,' she said, her eyes meeting his, answering his unspoken query.

There was something in her voice and in her eyes he couldn't pin down. She wasn't still mad at him; if she had been, he'd have sensed it immediately. It was almost as if there was something amusing her – something she had no intention of sharing with him. The cosy friendliness between her and Victor was definitely odd. Victor never let anyone call him Vic. Not even his mum. He wondered if Victor had broken the news to her that he was a policeman and, if he had, whether that was what was so amusing her.

'What's the news on Sandra?' he asked, returning his attention to Victor and trying to get to the heart of the reason for his visit.

Whenever he and Victor had met up in the past he'd never let the fact that Victor was a cozzer intrude on their relationship; he'd certainly never allowed himself to feel uncomfortable with him. He was uncomfortable now, though. He didn't know if it was because of the newspaper wages snatch – what Victor's reaction would be if he knew about that didn't even bear thinking about – or whether it was because he'd just left the company of a man who was such a disgrace to Victor's profession.

'When did you last see Sandra?' he asked, glad he'd put Rusty in the picture about her and making an immense effort to forget all about Somerville.

'Today.' Victor leaned forward, resting his arms on his knees, his hands clasped. 'She wants to see you, Bryce. She's expecting a baby at Easter and she isn't coping too well. She's all weepy. I don't think her marriage to Malc Hurst is any great shakes and she needs old friends . . .' He paused awkwardly.

Bryce didn't blame him. It was impossible to talk about Sandra having a baby without remembering the horrors of seven years ago, and Victor labelling him an 'old friend' – done, presumably, out of respect for Rusty's feelings – was pathetically inadequate.

'That's OK,' he said, coming to a decision about something he had been mulling over, on and off, for ages. 'I want to see her as well.'

Rusty cleared her throat.

He flashed her a look of reassurance. 'It's to do with Debbie, the kiddie I told you about,' he said truthfully. 'Sandra's always refused to have anything to do with her. She hasn't seen her since the day she left the mother-and-baby home. Now that I have some idea of what it's like having a kiddie around' – for Victor's benefit he indicated the photograph of Tricia that stood on top of the television – 'I think she's out of order. Leastways, I'm not going to allow her to *forget* her daughter's existence. Debbie is so like her in looks, it's unreal.'

'Christ, mate!' Victor's alarm was instant. 'She's unhappy enough about the baby she's having now, without you giving her grief about the one she had to Clarkson!'

Even just thinking about Sandra's first pregnancy made him want to retch. The merest memory of her sweat-sheened thighs, exposed genitalia, and the monstrous, medieval-looking hook the abortionist had inserted high into her vagina brought him out in goose pimples. From that day on he'd never been able to regard a woman's private parts as being sexually exciting and knew that if any one event was responsible for his present state of celibate homosexuality, it was his having witnessed the botched and bloody attempt to abort Sandra's child.

'Where was Sandra hoping to meet up with Bryce?' Rusty asked, mercifully breaking in on his thoughts. 'She won't want her husband knowing she's meeting him, will she? Bryce once decked him, or didn't you know?'

Not knowing whether to be relieved or disconcerted at how much Rusty knew of Bryce's past, Victor avoided admitting he knew about the fracas between Bryce and Malcolm Hurst. In answer to her question, he said, 'She's hoping to meet up with him now. I'm parked at the bottom of Lee Gardens and she's in the car.'

As Bryce swore and erupted to his feet, he added lamely, 'She'd be with me anyway, today, because once a month

I take her over to Nunhead Cemetery to visit her mum's grave.'

'And she's married to a cozzer and she now knows where I live!' Bryce was so blazingly angry his hands had balled into fists. 'Christ, Victor! You're a cozzer yourself! You should have more sense!'

Victor rose stiffly from his chair. 'And it matters?' he asked abruptly. 'I know you associate with villains, Bryce. I didn't know you'd become one.'

'Oh, for goodness sake!' Rusty bounded to her feet. 'What is this? Stand-off at the OK Corral? No one likes people from their past knowing too much about their present, Vic. You should know that. Plus you should have considered how I might feel about you parking one of Bryce's ex-girlfriends outside my door. As it happens, I don't give a stuff. If Bryce still fancied his childhood sweetheart, I'd know – and he doesn't.'

Her eyes flashed from Victor to Bryce. 'Which isn't to say he doesn't sometimes have trouble keeping out of other beds,' she added, steaming with renewed anger, knowing damn well Bryce knew whose bed she was referring to, 'because he does.'

'Did,' Bryce corrected, grateful for the way her intervention had glossed over a sticky moment. He slipped an arm round her waist. 'Past tense, sweetheart. OK?'

Their eyes held and for a moment the atmosphere was so sexually charged Victor found himself loosening his collar.

'Don't you think you'd better go out to your childhood chum and find out why she wants to see you?' It was Rusty who finally broke the silence. 'I think that would be better than her coming in the house, don't you? I don't particularly want to meet her and I don't suppose she's mad about meeting me. And whilst you're out there chatting to her, I'll make a fresh cup of tea for me and Vic.'

'Victor,' Bryce automatically corrected. 'His name is Victor, sweetheart. No one calls him Vic.'

Rusty followed him out into the small hallway. 'You're wrong, Bry,' she said, leaning against the newel-post at the foot of the stairs, her arms folded, one leg crossing the other at the ankle, her torrent of fiery hair tumbling waist-long. '*I* call him Vic.'

She waited until he had opened the door and was halfway out of the house before adding tantalisingly, 'I always have.'

He turned, shooting her a grin that told her he'd known all along she'd been amusing herself with some kind of a secret where she and Victor were concerned and then not giving her the satisfaction of seeing just how intrigued he was, he continued down Lee Gardens to the corner where Victor had parked his car.

Rusty returned to the sitting-room, laughing huskily. 'Poor Bryce,' she said as Victor looked queryingly towards her, 'I've given him the nod we know each other, but he's never going to be able to figure out how. Come into the kitchen with me whilst I put the kettle on. I'd like to know a bit more about Sandra. Was it really serious between them when they were teenagers?'

Victor put the photograph he'd been looking at back on top of the television. 'I'll tell you about Sandra, but first I want to know if you're going to tell Bryce the truth about how you came to know me, or if we're going to tell him a porky-pie.'

'Lie?' Rusty pushed her mane of hair away from her face, her cat-green eyes rounding in feigned disbelief. 'And you a policeman, Vic! How can you even suggest such a thing?'

'OK, less of the mickey-taking.' He was amazed at how relaxed he felt in her company. 'But surely it isn't necessary to tell him the raw truth?'

'Why not?' She ignited a gas hob and set a kettle down on top of it. 'Bryce and I have always been able to tell each other anything and everything about our pasts. He's well aware that ages ago I did a bit of tomming.' She spooned two caddy-spoonfuls of tea into a prettily decorated china teapot. 'It's history, though. Hell, I don't even do as much stripping as I used to. I'm into photographic modelling now – upmarket modelling with Pirelli, the tyre people. You would not *believe* the kind of money they pay.'

'You soliciting, and me having once busted you for it, are two different things,' he said drily. 'Bryce isn't over fond of being reminded that I'm a policeman.'

'And is what Bryce thinks so very important to you?' she asked, keeping the suspicion she was beginning to entertain from showing in her voice.

He turned away from her abruptly, opening the fridge and taking out a bottle of milk, but not before she'd seen the faint flush of colour that had touched his cheeks.

'Bryce and me are mates,' he said, his voice as studiedly careless as hers had been, 'so of course it matters what we think of each other. Until his mother was run over and killed we were best mates, more like brothers really.'

He handed her the milk. 'Then he went to live with the Briscoes and it got a bit awkward. The Briscoes are scum and my parents were very respectable, as were Bryce's. Did you know that Bryce's dad was a war hero? Anyhow, it got difficult for me to spend quite as much time with him because of the company he was keeping – which is exactly how things are now – but we've always been central to each other's lives. We always will be.'

She nodded as if understanding – which she did; though not quite as Victor had intended.

Because of the way he'd always reacted to her – or rather because of the way he *didn't* react to her – she'd long ago suspected that, where sex was concerned, he preferred men to women. Being a policeman he couldn't betray even the slightest glimmer of sexual deviancy – and didn't. That she'd picked up on it at all had been down to feminine intuition and nothing more.

Now another suspicion was beginning to grow: Victor's feelings for Bryce weren't quite as uncomplicated as Bryce's were for him.

'What's the situation with you and Bryce?' he asked, breaking in on her thoughts so suddenly that she spilled some of the boiling water she was pouring into the teapot.

She put the kettle down hastily, grabbing for a cloth. 'The situation between Bryce and me is that I'm crackers about him and I want to marry him,' she said, gingerly mopping up the water. 'He's also crackers about me, the difference being he doesn't want to marry me – or he thinks he doesn't.'

She tossed the dishcloth back into the sink and put the lid on the teapot.

'And so it's stalemate,' he said as they waited for the tea to brew.

She spluttered with laughter. 'No, Vic, it isn't. Bryce doesn't know it – and won't know it till the car pulls up outside the Registry Office – but a wedding, as they say in the best circles, has been arranged.'

His eyes widened.

'The booking has been made at the Registry Office. The dress has been bought. Tricia is looking forward to being my bridesmaid and the flowers have been ordered. It's all set for two o'clock Christmas Eve afternoon and the opening of The Renegade is in the evening. As all his mates, and mine, will be at the party Bryce has arranged, I thought it could double up as a brilliant wedding reception. What do you think?'

'What do I think?' His incredulity was comic. 'I think you must be certifiable! What if he refuses to play ball? And how are you going to get him to the Registry Office in the first place?'

Rusty poured the tea into the cups. She, too, thought she was probably certifiable. 'I'm going to make sure his car won't start when he leaves for the club – and I'm going to make sure there'll be a phone call from The Renegade with a problem that needs his immediate attention.'

'There are more holes in your plan than there are in a sieve.' Victor poured milk into the cups. 'How are you going to make sure the Zodiac won't start?'

'The Zodiac won't start because I have an uncle who is a car mechanic and he's going to make sure of it. Trust me.'

Looking at her, Victor found it impossible not to. At the thought of Bryce's face when, instead of finding himself at The Renegade, he found himself confronted with a bride, bridesmaid and registrar, he cracked with laughter, wishing to God he could be here to see the fun.

Handing him one of the cups of tea Rusty said, as if reading his thoughts, 'And I'd like you to be there, Vic – as Bryce's best man.'

Their eyes met and Victor knew she had sensed the way he felt about Bryce and that she both understood and sympathised. Relief at the knowledge he had finally found a friend who accepted him as he was, without his having to hide behind any kind of façade, was monumental.

'I'll be there, Rusty,' he said, knowing that if Bryce were to marry anyone, he wanted it to be Rusty Daniels. 'There isn't money enough in the world to keep me away!'

# Chapter Eleven

*August 1965*

'So you know what this is about, then?' Ronnie Kray asked in his peculiarly low, soft voice.

Bryce was in an upstairs room in The Regency, a club-cum-restaurant in Stoke Newington owned by two brothers who paid protection money to the Krays. He didn't particularly want to be there. For the past four years, despite the half-dozen gambling clubs and the casino he had opened, he'd managed to steer clear of heavy trouble.

His reputation was such that small-time gangs left him and his businesses well alone, and he'd been clever enough never to have run foul of either of London's two biggest gangs, the Richardsons, south of the River, and the Krays, north of it. Now, with the long simmering antagonism between the Richardsons and the Krays reaching boiling point, he was being put in a position of taking sides, and once he did so he knew that his smooth run would be well and truly over.

'I know you're unhappy about the way certain people have taken over the fruit machine market in the West End, but with all you've got going for you at the moment, Ron, I'd have thought it was small-time aggravation.'

His voice and attitude were laconic, which wasn't easy, even for him. Not when Reggie Kray was sitting on the edge of a table, one leg swinging, and three Kray henchmen the size of walking doors were standing nearby, feet apart, arms folded.

'I don't like aggravation, Bryce – any aggravation.' The voice was so whisper-soft as to be spookily sinister. Bryce didn't spook easily, if at all, but he'd had happier moments than this.

From out of the window he could see down into the street where his pale blue Rolls was parked. He'd traded the Zodiac for the Rolls to celebrate the opening of his casino in 1963. Rusty regarded it as pathetically flash, but he got an enormous buzz out of owning it. It was the sort of motor he wished his dad had been alive to see him driving.

'I'm not quite sure how I can help, Ron,' he said, wishing to God he was behind the Rolls's wheel now and not cooped up with a couple of psychos. Reggie wasn't too bad – or at least he wasn't when he was on his own. Ron was different. There was just never any telling which way he was going to jump – as many people, battered, bruised and brutalised, had found out.

'I don't run an outfit, Ron,' he said now in a tone of sweet reason, 'you know that.'

It was a monumental lie, but he certainly didn't run an outfit the way Ronnie and Reggie did. Instead, like a skilled businessman, he masterminded the infrequent but huge heists that Jack, Gunter, Curly and Georgie carried out. And he ran his clubs and the casino, and still did Big Chas favours where his scrap-metal business was concerned.

'And the people you have a particular grudge against aren't associates of mine,' he continued, wondering how the hell Frankie managed to retain the Krays' trust when two other Briscoes, Ginger and Terry, were known Richardson men. 'Just in case you're under any impression to the contrary.'

'Me and Reg know you run a tight ship, Bryce.' Ronnie was being placating and Bryce wondered if he was going to be able to walk away from the meeting without being pinned down as to where, when warfare broke out, his loyalties would lie. 'What we want is for you to steer clear of business with any of our competitors – I'm talking now about the blue-film market and the fruit machines, right?'

Bryce gave a careless shrug of his shoulders. The lucrative blue-film market, where an apartment was rented in or near the West End and kitted out with a projector and screen, was one he'd never touched and had no desire to. Touts would garner up large numbers of men, charging them a fortune to view the kind of films it was impossible to see without travelling to somewhere like Amsterdam. It was the kind of operation Frankie would happily run, but which was of no interest to him, nor to Jack.

The fruit machines were a different matter. With those he was going to run into difficulty where his clubs were concerned – but not a difficulty that couldn't be overcome.

'There's no problem, Ronnie,' he said, hoping he sounded convincing. 'And as things are sweet between us,' he added, trying to bring the rambling meeting to a close, 'what say we leave it that way?'

Whether things were sweet or not was debatable, but it seemed a sensible idea to try and plant.

'Yeah, well, someone said last week that you were the biggest dark horse going.' Ronnie's soft, sneering voice was beginning to be a serious annoyance. 'And if push came to shove you could find more armed men in half an hour than the Metropolitan Police. Now, if that were true, things wouldn't be so sweet between us Bryce, would they?'

With not a little effort, a deep chuckle rumbled up from Bryce's chest. 'I'm a businessman, Ronnie – not a gangster. Ask Frankie.'

'You ironed a bloke out once and served time for it,' Reggie said, unexpectedly intervening in the conversation.

'And you nearly did for that prick Gerard. We just want you to know where you stand with us, Bryce. Know what I mean?'

'I stand easy, Reg.'

'Yeah, well . . .' This time it was Ronnie who was speaking and who, much to Bryce's relief, seemed to be indicating he was happy with the situation and that nothing more remained to be said.

Five minutes later, walking across the pavement to his Rolls, he was breathing a deep sigh of relief and trying to figure out what the hell it had all been about.

'Keep Ronnie happy at all costs,' Jack had advised him when he'd told him where he was going. 'We've come off light so far where interference from the Twins is concerned. Don't scupper things now.'

He hadn't had any intention of doing so, but he'd had a worry Jack knew nothing about. A week previously Frankie had burst into his office at the casino in a state of barely controlled panic.

'I've shot a copper,' he had said, panting harshly. 'And I think my motor was noted. Take care of this for me, there's a mate.' He'd drawn a Walther PK38 automatic from the waistband of his trousers. 'Dump it where it won't re-surface.'

Far more careful than Frankie, who had been gloveless, he'd used his handkerchief to drop the weapon in a desk drawer and then, a day later, motivated by nothing other than instinct, he had deposited it, wrapped in a carrier-bag, in his usual stow.

Frankie had turned out to be wrong about his motor's number having been noted. He hadn't been picked up and he hadn't asked what had happened to the gun. Only when the summons had come from the Twins had Bryce begun wondering if the shooting which had involved the copper had had Kray links.

He opened the door of the Rolls and slid behind the

wheel. His fear had been unfounded. Whatever the reason for Reg and Ronnie's sudden interest in him, it had nothing to do with the gun incident.

He pulled out into the traffic, fairly sure that, where his clubs and casinos were concerned, he'd scuppered nothing – and nor had he been dragged into the Krays' feud with the Richardson gang. The only thing was, everything had been so ambiguous that he couldn't be absolutely sure.

He drove off in the direction of central London. He'd intended spending the day at the races and was still hoping to make it down to Ascot for the afternoon. Rusty had already been in her best togs when he'd left home an hour or so earlier and as he glanced down at his Omar Picquet watch he knew she would, by now, be steaming with impatience.

At times like this, Lee Gardens would have been quicker and, where traffic was concerned, easier to reach, but Lee Gardens was now little more than a dummy address. For the past three years home for himself, Rusty and Tricia, had been a luxury apartment in Mayfair, acquired from a punter who'd had no other way of settling a gambling debt.

As he drove out of the meanness of East End streets into the plate-glass office-land of the City he wondered how Rusty would want to spend Christmas. Because Christmas was also the date of their wedding anniversary, they always did something special. Last year they'd gone on a Nile cruise, taking Tricia with them. The year before they'd gone to Antigua.

He grinned to himself as he remembered the sheer insanity of their wedding day. Rusty and Tricia had left the house early in the morning, dressed as if for a trip to the shops. A half-hour later he'd received a phone call from Tina, Billy Dixon's wife, saying there was a problem she couldn't sort and would he please get down to The Renegade pretty damn quick.

As the opening party was that night he'd been on the point of driving down there anyway and, immaculately suited and booted as always, had left the house immediately. He'd been stymied, however, by the Zodiac refusing to start. The cab he'd rung for had arrived quicker than was usual but, with his head full of The Renegade's opening, he hadn't given it much thought.

Lewisham Registry Office was on the way to Catford and so there was nothing odd about the route the driver took. There was nothing odd at all until almost the very last moment when, cruising down Lewisham High Street towards Catford, the driver had suddenly taken a sharp right-hand turn – straight into the forecourt of the Registry Office.

For a brief second he'd thought there must be a problem with the car and that the driver was ducking quickly out of traffic in order to sort it. Then he saw that the small crowd of wedding guests milling about on the Registry Office's forecourt looked disconcertingly familiar. First he'd seen Ginger and Terry, red carnations in their buttonholes, and had wondered which of their friends was getting hitched. Then he'd seen Gunter and Jack and, as they were both supposed to be at The Renegade, had known immediately that something was adrift.

Jack, a wicked grin on his face, had walked swiftly towards the car to open the door, but he'd been out of it long before Jack, or anyone else, reached it.

'What the fuck is going on?' he'd demanded as nearly every close mate he possessed had regarded him with a mixture of vast amusement and trepidation.

Rusty had stepped from behind the combined bulk of Curly and Georgie. 'A wedding is going on,' she had said, her voice thick with nervousness. 'At least, darling, I hope it is.'

As she was dressed in a lace wedding-dress and was wearing a white rose in her hair, it hadn't been too hard for him to figure out the identity of the intended groom.

Their eyes held.

Despite the nearness of the main road and the heavy traffic, a pin could have been heard dropping.

His first, instantaneous reaction had been that no way was he going to be set up in such an outrageously flagrant fashion. Then he'd seen Tricia, holding tightly to Tina Dixon's hand, pretty as a picture in an ice-blue dress with a frilly skirt, a small posy of flowers clutched in her free hand, her eyes shining with excitement.

'Please, Bryce.' Rusty had been as taut as a drawn bow.

Beyond her he had seen the most amazing collection of people. Victor was standing in close proximity to Evelyn Briscoe and old Jug Ears. Behind them had been Big Chas, a cashmere and vicuna topcoat slung casually round his shoulders, a new dolly-bird on his arm. Gunter Nowakowska's aged parents had been there, as had Jimmy Briscoe and Frankie, both of them wearing dark glasses despite the fact that it was a cloudy December day.

Even Tommy Briscoe, recently released from Gartree and displaying a distinct prison pallor, had been there, as had the Wilkinson family: Robert and his wife and two little kiddies; and Richard. Even the Wilkinsons' mum had been there, a small spray of ornamental red cherries decorating her hat. She was elderly and arthritic now, but whenever he saw Joan Wilkinson, memories of his mother rushed up out of the past, grabbing him by the throat.

They had done so as he'd stood surrounded by friends and the only people he regarded as family, Rusty's eyes fixed on his, her anxiety palpable.

'Bryce?' she had prompted again, her tension so acute he had been able to feel it. He'd sensed everyone else's tension, too. The amusement in Jack's eyes had turned to apprehension. Gunter, the collar of his black Crombie overcoat turned up at his throat, had begun to look uneasy. Victor had looked distinctly stressed. Worst of all, Tricia's eyes were no longer shining but bewildered.

As he'd looked around at them all he'd suddenly felt his own tension evaporate. If everyone who was part of his life was so happy at the thought of his marrying Rusty then what the hell, he had thought; why not?

'Give me a spare carnation, someone,' he'd said, slipping his arm round Rusty's waist. 'And let's get this show on the road.'

Even now, just thinking about that moment, the whoops and cheers that had gone up rang in his ears. He grinned to himself as he turned into Piccadilly. The only person who hadn't been pleased at his becoming a married man was Sheree. She, however, was way in his past – though infidelity, much to Rusty's steaming exasperation, wasn't.

He drew to a halt at the traffic lights at Berkeley Street, continuing his trip down memory lane. Sandra hadn't been at the wedding, of course, nor at the party later that day at The Renegade. He still saw her intermittently and whenever he did he couldn't suppress a pang for what so easily might have been, if only she'd had the strength of character to remain loyal to him when he'd been inside.

The day Victor had brought her to Lee Gardens and he'd gone out to Victor's car to talk to her had been a difficult meeting for both of them. She'd cried and said again and again how sorry she was she hadn't continued to visit him when he'd been in prison; that she still loved him and that her marrying Malcolm Hurst had been a mistake.

He'd felt desperately sorry for her, but had had the sense to know that the time for responding to her, as she wanted him to respond, was long past. As he'd hugged her close and her sobs had eventually subsided into tearful sniffles, he'd told her how like her Debbie was.

'There's nothing of the Clarksons in her at all, Sand,' he'd said. 'She's a comical little thing, really. Very direct and sure of herself, and I suspect she gives Hilda Clarkson a real hard time of it.'

'I don't want to know!' Sandra had clapped her hands over her ears, fresh tears spilling down her cheeks. 'If it wasn't for what happened with Roy Clarkson we'd be together now! And if she'd never be born I wouldn't have had to leave Swan Row! And if I'd never left Swan Row I wouldn't have met Malcolm and I wouldn't be pregnant with another baby that I don't want!'

It had been emotionally wearing, to say the least. And whenever they infrequently met, the scenario was the same. She would tell him that she wasn't in love with Malcolm the way she was still in love with him. She wouldn't allow him to talk about Debbie. She would cry. He would comfort her as much as he was able. Then they would talk about the old days – the days before Roy Clarkson had raped her. They would talk about her mother, and his; about Tigger; about their long conversations perched high in the branches of Swan Row's lone tree.

Then, no longer crying but still pale and wan, she would return to her steadfastly dependable husband and he would return to a life that was so different from the past they had talked about as to be on another planet.

He turned into Curzon Street, parked and pressed the palm of his hand on the Rolls's horn. In the few seconds before Rusty grabbed her hat and handbag and ran out to join him, he reflected that the odd thing about having so much money at his disposal was how, the easier it came in, the easier it was to get rid of it.

This afternoon's drive down to Ascot was a case in point. He loved horse-racing. He loved it so much he was thinking of buying into a racing stables. Whatever he won, though, he soon lost. The luck that always clung to him when he gambled in a casino, be it his own or someone else's, abandoned him in spades the instant he set foot on a racecourse.

As Rusty came hurtling out of the Georgian townhouse, as leggy as a colt in a cream shantung, Mary Quant mini-skirted suit, a hat festooned with roses and veiling, and wearing shoes with heels that would immediately impale her on Ascot's grass, he grinned. He didn't give a damn how much he lost, the fun was worth it – besides, he always had plenty of money rolling in.

He flung the passenger-seat door open so that Rusty, in a scented cloud of Chanel No. 5, could slide in next to him. If the heist he was now planning came off – and he was having a meet with Jack late that evening to discuss the pros and cons of it further – there would be money enough to last a lifetime.

'You mean break into the bank vault from the street sewer?' Jack's eyebrows rose so high they nearly disappeared into his blond hair. 'Is that possible? I mean, what happens to the sewerage when we've broken through the sewer wall? And then how far would we have to tunnel? And how do you know that there is a main sewer-pipe running so near the bank?'

'Taking your last query first, I know because I've seen the shaft leading down to it.' It was just after midnight and they were in his private office above the main gaming-room in his Mayfair casino. 'Come over here.'

He strolled across to the window and pulled up the blind. The room they were in was on the fifth floor and outside, in the darkness, the lights of London glittered like diamonds in a tiara.

'From here you can see clear down to the corner and to the north side of the square. A month ago the road and the square were sealed off so that maintenance work to the sewer tunnel could be carried out.' He took a sip of the Scotch he was nursing, and grinned. 'I had a bird's-eye view. I'd never seen a main sewer-pipe shaft before. Their size is amazing.'

He let the blind fall. 'The really interesting thing,' he said, strolling back to the leather sofa he'd been seated on, 'is that the Al-Bakara Arab Bank is on the north side of the square. Even more interesting, it's a mother bank, supplying other Arab banks in London. The sewer-pipe in question runs so near it that the bank had to close down whilst the maintenance work was being carried out. I have a deposit box there and I was very inconvenienced, as were lots of other local people, nearly all of them mega wealthy. A lot of the casino's Arab punters bank there and the number of private safe-deposit boxes in use is huge.'

Jack flopped down into a nearby winged chair and hooked a leg over the arm, letting it swing. 'Yeah. Well. I can see the way your mind is working, Bryce, but it just isn't possible, is it? We can't gain entrance to the sewer by posing as workmen, not if getting down and into it entails such massive roadworks that the street and square have to be sealed off. The police would be on to us in a flash. Plus, even if we could – and even if we knew the exact location of the bank's vault in relation to the pipe – we would still have to tunnel from there into the bank and into the vault. It would take days, maybe even weeks, and there's no way that kind of drilling and excavating could be carried out without it being heard.'

Bryce took another swig of his Scotch. 'Don't come to hasty conclusions, Jack. The workmen I watched simply erected road barriers up around the place in the road where they climbed down to the sewer. As you say, there's no way we could get away with that – not for long enough to be able to break into the bank. What we could do, though, is to convert a large van – a removal van, for example.'

'Convert it?' Jack looked blank. 'How?'

'We take out the van's flooring. From the outside it will

233

look regular enough, in reality it will be a shell. Then, when traffic is light, late evening or early morning, we park the van over the spot in the road that gives access to the sewer. The actual removing of the sewer entrance cover will take only minutes with the right tools. From then on it's straight down the ladders that are permanently in place and into the pipe at the access point at the ladder's foot. Because we'll be working in the dark, unlike the genuine workmen who had the entrance open to the sky, we'll need some mining gear. Hard hats with lamps attached, etc.'

'And the van . . . ?'

'The second we're safely in the shaft leading down to the sewer, our driver replaces the entrance cover and then drives off, leaving no sign of anything amiss.'

'And comes back at a pre-arranged time to remove the cover and to let us out?'

'You've got it in one.' Bryce's grin stretched from ear to ear. 'Tunnelling from the sewer into the bank vault will take time and can only, of course, be carried out when the bank is empty. I reckon three days should be enough, though.'

Jack let out a long whistle. 'And so we do it at Christmas?'

Bryce nodded.

'Christ!' Jack was no longer lounging nonchalantly. He was on his feet and back at the window, a corner of the blind lifted so that he could see down to the darkened square. 'And how do we locate the walls of the vault? We don't want to be still tunnelling away, looking for it, this time next summer.'

'Credit me with a bit of sense.' A deep chuckle rumbled up from Bryce's chest. 'I had a chat with the foreman when he and his crew were taking a tea-break. Just showed general interest in what they were doing. It didn't look suspicious. Half the world and his brother were stopping to watch and to do the same. I made a joke about them accidentally crashing into the bank. Mr Know-it-all was only too eager to tell me it couldn't happen because the bank lay left off the third conduit down from where they were working and no maintenance work was needed on it.'

Jack cracked with laughter. It was always the same. Intentionally or unintentionally, it was usually info from straight geezers that enabled a job to be put together.

'And let's face it,' Bryce continued, rising to his feet and crossing the thickly carpeted room to a half-moon cocktail bar, 'we have to come up with something on these lines. The days when robbing a bank was as easy as jumping over a sweetie counter are gone.'

He poured another healthy slug of Black Label over the ice-cubes in his glass. That kind of robbery, where there was a high risk of members of the public being involved, had never been his style. The new-fangled security vans carrying money not just for one bank but for several, were, in his view, more sensible targets. Even they, however, were beginning to become harder to hit.

With the banks, the difficulties were the security screens that were now commonplace – and which were getting higher and higher. With the security vans it was the fact that the police now monitored many of them with radar. All in all, life was getting tougher for crims like Big Chas and Jimmy who, for years, had relied on a straightforward approach of direct confrontation where banks were concerned and a wait, watch and pounce technique when it came to tackling security vans.

He, however, was in a different class to Big Chas and Jimmy. He used his brains – and not only for jobs he personally led or that Jack led. Behind a persona that even Jack knew nothing about, he indulged his love of meticulous military-style planning by masterminding heists carried out by gangs who never knew he was their Mr Big. He bankrolled all such operations from casino profits and, when they were successful, raked off a healthy percentage of the take.

'Bank closures at Christmas aren't always that long,' Jack said, chewing the corner of his lip. 'Easter might be a safer bet. If Christmas falls mid-week the bank will only be closed two days.'

'It falls on a Saturday.' Bryce's grin was now as wide as the Cheshire Cat's. 'So it looks as if Christmas this year is going to be one to remember. We'll be up to our knees in shit and piss on Christmas Eve, tunnelling for England on Christmas Day and away with the biggest present of our lives on Boxing Day. I think it deserves a bottle of Louis Cristal, don't you?'

Next morning, suffering from a mild hangover, he'd driven over to Swan Row to visit Evelyn Briscoe. For years she'd been the only person in his life remotely resembling a mother figure and he was very fond of her.

Normally he could pay her a visit simply by calling in at The Renegade, where she ruled the kitchen with an iron hand. She was off sick at the moment, however, with a trapped nerve in her shoulder, and so for the first time in quite a while he found himself driving down Jamaica Road and taking a left-hand turn in the general direction of the river.

The minute he walked into the house and heard Tommy Briscoe's sniggering laugh coming from the direction of the kitchen he knew his sense of timing had let him down. Despite pretending differently, Tommy didn't like him. He knew why, of course. It was the same reason his relationship with Frankie was no longer what it had once been. Unable to emulate his financial success where clubs and casinos were concerned, they were jealous and, unable to lose face by letting their jealousy show, they let it fester instead.

'Soddin' hell!' Tommy said in mock amazement as he

walked into the kitchen. 'It's a long time since you've bin here, innit? Did yer need a road map, or did your chauffeur bring yer?'

Bryce didn't respond to the sarcasm. He couldn't. He was too stunned by the identity of the other person seated with Tommy at Evelyn's kitchen table.

''Lo,' Debbie said in her usual sullen way, her hands wrapped round a steaming mug of tea. 'You won't tell my mum you've seen me here, will you? I'm not supposed to have anything to do with Mrs Briscoe.'

She was ten years old now and, because of her oddly mature manner, could easily have passed for being twelve, or even thirteen.

'Well, as I don't have anything to do with your mum, it's not likely to be a problem,' he said, looking across to where Evelyn was one-handedly turning freshly baked scones on to a wire tray, her hair scraped up hedgehog-like in pink plastic curlers.

Aware she was being silently asked for an explanation, Evelyn shrugged the shoulder that wasn't paining her. 'Debbie often comes in 'ere for a cup of tea and a chat, Bryce. I don't mind. She's good company.'

'She's 'ere now 'cos she's pissed off with old man Parry,' Tommy said, his thin weaselly face vastly amused. 'He keeps tellin' her he's her granddad and she won't believe him.'

'I don't believe him because it isn't true!' There was no distress in Debbie's voice, only cross exasperation. 'People are always telling me stupid stories about my mum not being my mum and my dad not being my dad. My mum says they're wrong in their heads and I should take no notice.'

She looked across at Tommy, the inference that she thought he, too, was wrong in his head, obvious. Despite all the unpleasant sensations he felt whenever Debbie referred to Hilda as her mother, Bryce felt a smile tug

237

the corner of his mouth. Over the years he and she had struck up an easy, if odd, acquaintanceship and she always entertained and intrigued him.

'So, how is school?' he asked, leaving the tricky subject of her parentage well alone and sitting down at the table as Evelyn poured him a mug of tea. 'Is it still boring you to death?'

In a way he couldn't quite define, he felt he had some kind of a part to play in her life; as if he were a distant elder brother figure, or an uncle that she didn't see too often.

'It's rubbish,' she said flatly. 'My mum says I'll be going to a grammar school soon and that I'll like it better than where I am now, but I don't think I will. I'm going to be an actress when I grow up and I don't need boring old lessons in history and geography for that.'

As Bryce tried to put a different point of view forward, a point of view that would have had his own mother gasping in disbelief, he couldn't help reflecting how odd it was that, childless himself, he somehow felt surrogate responsibility for two pre-pubescent girls.

Tricia, of course, was his step-daughter and so the interest he took in her welfare was understandable, especially so considering her physical and mental handicaps. Not that either kind of handicap was always screamingly obvious. There were long periods when her arthritis was controlled and relieved by the drugs she took, particularly now that she was on a drug called phenylbutazone.

As for her mental disability . . . just thinking about it, and the consequences it had had on his life and Rusty's, gave him a deep pang. Tricia wasn't severely retarded; she simply had a very low IQ and her physical co-ordination was poor – and not helped, of course, by her arthritis. As if in compensation, she'd been blessed with the sunniest, most affectionate nature of any child he'd ever met and, as her trust in people was so dangerously total, it was natural that both he and Rusty were fiercely protective parents.

Rusty's protection was, however, carried to an extreme he didn't share. She refused point-blank to become pregnant again, saying that Tricia needed undivided love and attention. He disagreed, believing a younger half-brother or -sister would be beneficial to Tricia. It was an argument that, on and off, had run for years and that was presently in a very familiar position: complete stalemate.

'Tommy may be going into prison again,' Debbie said suddenly, startling Bryce so much that as Evelyn passed him his mug of tea he almost dropped it. 'It isn't a secret. Everyone knows, don't they, Mrs Briscoe?'

'Well, they will do when you've finished spreading the news,' Evelyn said drily. 'For a little girl, you've got very big ears.'

'You don't go in and out of prison, do you?' She looked at Bryce across the kitchen table, her head tilted slightly to one side, her fair, straight hair skimming her shoulders. 'My mum says you do, but I don't believe her.'

Evelyn cracked with laughter. 'God, child! You are a pill and no mistake! What will you be wanting to know next?'

As Bryce was making no attempt to answer her question she said, taking Evelyn literally, 'I want to know if Tommy's wife minds him always being away in prison.'

'Nah,' Tommy said, surprising Bryce by being almost pleasant. 'She's learned to live with it. She could have married a bloody sailor and then where would she have been?'

'A damn sight better off!' Evelyn hadn't enjoyed herself so much for ages. 'And as it looks as if you'll be enjoying Christmas in one of Her Majesty's prisons, the lady in question is coming here for her Christmas dinner.' She turned her attention to Bryce: 'I suppose it's useless asking you if you'll be here, seeing as how you always swan off somewhere exotic. Where is it going to be this year? The bleedin' Caribbean?'

'No.' Bryce thought of the giant sewer-pipe he would be spending Christmas in and struggled to keep the laughter from his voice. 'I'm thinking of going down under this year, Evelyn.'

'Australia?' Evelyn was unimpressed. 'A hundred years ago our Tommy would have been there with you – whether he wanted to be or not!'

# Chapter Twelve

The bed he was in wasn't his own – as was often the case. For the last five years the quality of the sex he enjoyed with Rusty had never flagged, mainly because her zest, imagination, and deep commitment to their marriage had never allowed it to. They had a relationship that, considering the raciness of their individual lifestyles, was amazingly stable. It wasn't monogamous, though – at least it wasn't on his part. Nor, considering the impudent way she had dragooned him to the altar, did he see any reason why it should be.

In the world he inhabited an extra-marital girlfriend was as essential as the right clothes and the right car. Image was everything in crim circles, and both clothes and car – and often girlfriend – had to be blatantly expensive.

Even for heavyweight gorillas like Ginger and Terry, thick gold wristwatches and cashmere and vicuna topcoats were *de rigueur*. Frankie favoured crocodile shoes and silk socks. Jimmy was a really snazzy dresser. With Jimmy everything matched: shirt, handkerchief, socks. Frankie used to say that all his cousin was short of was a nice little handbag.

When it came to his own gear, Bryce went for top-notch class. Silk shirts, all with his initials on, came from Turnbull & Asser, or Sulka. His shoes were handmade from Maclaren's in Albemarle Street. His personal jewellery was from Vacherin & Constantin, or Cartier.

Cars, sometimes, were a little trickier to get just right. When he'd buoyantly driven home his first Mercedes Benz, Rusty had witheringly pointed out that in Tel Aviv –

where she had spent a season stripping in the city's most prestigious nightspot – the taxi-cabs were all Mercedes. Even though he'd been damn sure the taxis weren't pukka Mercedes, it had taken the gilt off the gingerbread. Now he had a Rolls Royce Corniche and, though Rusty hated it and said that whenever she was seated in the back of it she felt like the Queen Mother, he didn't care. No city in the world boasted taxi-cabs made by Rolls Royce.

He rolled off the nubile body lying beneath him and reached across to the bedside table for his silver cigarette case and lighter. Girlfriends, for him, had never been a problem. He spent more time fighting women off than he did looking for them, and he always kept to well-established crim rules. In the afternoon drinking clubs they all patronised, girlfriends were in force Monday to Friday and weekends were exclusively for wives. It was a system that worked well. Wives enjoyed a status that was rarely encroached on and consequently jealous scenes were few.

That even the most unprepossessing crim usually had an adoring mistress hanging on his arm had once been a mystery to him – until Rusty had put him wise.

'There are a lot of women who like to be around heavy people,' she had said when he'd remarked on the amazing number of glamorous birds Ginger and Terry were always knee-deep in. 'And generally speaking they're not tarts, they're just attracted to danger and excitement. Being fancied by a tough villain can be quite a turn-on.'

She had paused, her eyes darkening. 'And some women even go for Frankie, though God knows why. He gives me the heebie-jeebies.'

She hadn't been joking, and he had known it. One of the reasons he now saw so little of Frankie was Rusty's refusal to tolerate his company.

'I think a little bit of that again, in another five minutes, would be fine, sweetheart, don't you?' his present companion said now in low, cut-glass tones, turning on her side so that she could slide a long leg that had been suntanned in the Caribbean, between his.

As she began brushing his chest with her lips he made a noise in his throat that could have meant anything and, safe in the knowledge that her attention was engaged elsewhere, raised his eyes to heaven, wondering if all Benenden-educated girls were as frenetically sex-mad.

Not that she was at Benenden now. She'd left in the summer, a week after her seventeenth birthday and five days after she had seduced him. His relief, when he'd learnt that her finishing school in Switzerland didn't label its pupils as schoolgirls, had been vast. Somehow it made him feel less like a cradle-snatcher bordering on the verges of paedophilia.

Her interest had now moved a little lower than his chest and he folded his arms behind his head and closed his eyes. God knows, he hadn't intended cradle-snatching – and nor had he intended accessorizing himself with a girlfriend for whom Rolls Royces were ten a penny and for whom the Queen Mother was an elderly lady she'd been taught, as a small child, to address as Ma'am.

It had all come about because, like the Krays – who had an outwardly respectable and influential Member of Parliament in their pockets as well as an even more outwardly respectable and influential Member of the House of Lords – he had wanted involvement with a name that, where Establishment figures were concerned, had clout.

Sir William Denster had filled the bill admirably. A gambler whose luck at the tables was abysmal, he was in constant debt and constantly in need of ready cash. In return for a generous amount of it, he was more than happy to accept the title of 'Associate Director' and to have his name emblazoned prominently on the headed notepaper Bryce used when conducting straight, or near-straight, business ventures.

All in all, it was a very satisfactory – and uncomplicated – arrangement. The complications had arisen when Willie had brought his daughter to one of their monthly lunches at Simpsons.

'It's her school hols,' he had said by way of explanation. 'She's always having 'em. It's a rip off, when you consider what the fees are.'

Bryce felt as if he'd been sledgehammered in the chest. *This* was a *schoolgirl*? Dark-haired, dark-eyed and dazzling, she was as coolly soignée as a French catwalk model. With not an ounce of spare flesh on her, her legs reached up to her armpits and her neck was as long as a swan's.

She wasn't classically beautiful. She was too *gamine*. Her face was too short and square, her nose too blunt and her mouth too wide. It didn't matter a jot. She was more than beautiful. She was ravishing.

Like a sleek, perfectly groomed cat, she had exuded an air of boredom throughout the meal, barely deigning to speak to him and bestowing only an occasional, contemptuous glance in her father's direction.

Bryce had found himself amused, intrigued and enthralled.

He hadn't, though, contemplated seducing her. She was the daughter of a man who, if not a close friend, was a close acquaintance, and though she was on the verge of her seventeenth birthday, she wasn't seventeen yet. Even for someone as carelessly amoral as himself, a line had to be drawn somewhere.

Three days later, in his office above the gaming-rooms of his Mayfair casino, it became obvious that Nina didn't share his scruples.

'I've never been to bed with a heavy villain,' she'd said, her Vidal Sassoon-cut hair as black and glossy as a medieval helmet, sunglasses hiding her eyes, a Courrège's scarlet mini-dress skimming her bottom and white boots with heels so high they looked as if they'd come out of a pantomime. 'I'm curious. I'd like to give it a try.'

He'd felt like a piece of meat on a rack.

'You're out of order,' he'd said brusquely, aware that the sledgehammer was once again affecting his ability to breathe normally. 'This is a casino, not a schoolroom. Who the hell let you in?'

'A cleaning lady.' She'd removed her sunglasses, talking as if speaking to a child. 'It is only mid morning. And why are you being so stuffy? I thought heavy villains lived dangerously.'

'Let's get one or two things straight.' He'd thrust the yellow legal pad he'd been making notes on into his desk drawer, slammed the drawer shut and locked it. 'One: this is my private office and I only see people in it by appointment. Two: I am not a heavy villain. Heavy villains hurt people. Three: I do not take under-age girls to bed. Got it?'

She'd shrugged her shoulders, saying with Gallic indifference, 'I don't make appointments with anyone – not even my hairdresser. My father says you're a heavy villain and as his name is on your notepaper, he should know. And I'm not an under-age girl. I'll be seventeen in two days' time and I'm very sexually experienced.'

Looking into her near-black, knowing eyes, he hadn't doubted her for a moment. 'You deserve a good spanking,' he'd said grimly, and it was then, when he'd read in her eyes her amused, lascivious response, that he'd given up all thought of drawing lines.

Neither of them had said anything. Both had moved swiftly. She had pulled her dress over her head, revealing crimson-nippled breasts as small and hard as under-ripe apples. He had covered the distance to the door in three strides, ramming the bolt home. Seconds later, without preliminaries of any kind, he had slammed her against the wall and taken her where she stood.

There was no way he could have known it at the time, but it was the kind of rough, off-hand sex Nina revelled in

– and sex with Nina was the kind of sex he found himself rapidly becoming addicted to.

His intention had been a one-off escapade. Now, five months later, it was an affair so full-blown that the unthinkable was happening and it was beginning to threaten his marriage.

Even though he was now, thanks to her expert ministrations, beginning to harden again, he pushed her away and swung his legs abruptly to the floor.

He didn't want things to come to an end between himself and Rusty. They had too much shared history together – and there was Tricia to consider. He had other things on his mind, too. The heist he was now planning was the biggest and most complex he had ever undertaken, or was ever likely to undertake. Outsiders were going to have to be brought in, for he and his team simply didn't possess the mining skills that were going to be necessary.

He had places to go and people to see and the last place he needed to be was in bed with a teenage nymphomaniac mistress who had never, in all the months he had known her, shown a spark of real warmth towards him, or, as far as he knew, towards anyone else.

'I'm off,' he said, reaching for his jeans, enjoying the knowledge that she was furious with him. 'I'm going to be gone for a few days.'

It was a lie. What he was going to be, though, was busy.

Very busy.


'I'm told you're a sewer-tunnel ganger and that you can put me in the picture about what will be needed for a short trip through the tunnels. Is that right?'

The sallow-faced man seated opposite him and Jack in The Spinners, nodded. 'Yeah,' he said, taking a deep drink from his pint and wiping his mouth with the back of his hand before adding, 'I run a team of five flushers.'

246

'Flushers?'

There was a very unsavoury smell coming from their companion and Bryce hoped to God the same smell wouldn't linger on him and Jack after their own stint underground.

'Yeah.' There was another long pause while the man took another drink. 'That's my team, see. Five blokes. We keep the sewers clear – shovel up all the muck when it forms blockages in the system. That's why they call us flushers. We've got this trolley and it's got a couple of skips on it. We just load up the skips with the muck and push the trolleys to the nearest manhole. Then a bloke up top winches the skips up and unloads 'em and sends 'em down again. Then we shovel another heap of muck into 'em.'

'Christ!' Jack looked as if he was going to be ill. 'And that's all you do all day, every day? Shovel up shit?'

'Yeah – well, not quite. Sometimes we 'ave to rebuild the sewer walls. That's skilled work, that is, 'specially as you're often doin' it wearin' breathing equipment. Breathing equipment don't 'alf get in your way when you're building.'

'Will we need breathing equipment? We're not going to be underground for long.'

'Yeah, well, you might be,' the sewage worker said unencouragingly. 'It's a bleedin' maze down there. Blokes whose livin' is workin' down there 'ave been known to get lost for 'ours on end. It's the gases, see? You get pockets of gas unexpected like and if you ain't prepared for 'em they're lethal, 'specially the carburetted hydrogen. Carburetted hydrogen explodes. Then there's the sulphurated hydrogen – that's the product of putrid decomposition. Nasty, that is. And then if you're really unlucky there's the choke-damp.'

'Choke-damp?' Bryce asked, half wondering if the sewage worker was sending him up.

'Yeah.' The unprepossessing little man took another long drink and this time wiped his mouth on the back of his sleeve. 'Choke-damp is carbonic acid. Any of that and your safety lamp goes out and though you need to get the 'ell out double quick, it's iffy, 'cos you're in the bleedin' dark.'

'Christ!' Jack said again expressively as Bryce made a mental note that breathing apparatus was a necessity.

The sewage worker looked towards Jack and, well experienced in recognising claustrophobic tendencies, said with malicious relish, 'The gases are useful for keepin' down the rats and eels, though. There's 'undreds of rats and eels down there, whole bleedin' armies of 'em.'

Jack rose to his feet so abruptly that Bryce had to steady his pint glass. 'I'm getting another drink in,' Jack said, so white about the mouth that it was all Bryce could do not to let his amusement show. 'What do you want, Bryce? Another light and bitter?'

'A Remy,' he said, knowing very well that a stiff Remy was what Jack was in need of.

'And what else are we going to need?' he said, turning his attention once again to his informant.

'You'll need waist-high waders; thigh-length wool socks; some of the strips of chemically treated paper that we carry and that change colour when gases build up to danger point; torches; belts and safety harnesses for getting down into the sewer; lifelines, safety helmets and two-way radios.'

'And you can get the whole lot for us?'

'Yeah.' The sewage worker drained his glass. 'If the money's good enough.'

'The money will be good enough.' He waited until Jack was out of earshot at the bar. 'Now, tell me why we have to have a two-way radio with us? We aren't going to be splitting up into groups.'

'You 'ave to be in contact with someone above ground

who's receiving regular weather forecasts,' the sewage worker said, his tone of voice indicating that he felt he was pointing out the pathetically obvious. 'That little bit of information can be the difference between life and death when you're in a tunnel. That's what sewers are for, after all: storm water and waste water. Get a flash rainstorm and a tidal wave runs through the whole bleedin' system, heading for the Thames. That's why you need lifelines down there. Just in case, see?'

Bryce saw. He'd expected the negotiating of the sewer to be a straightforward operation – or at least straightforward in relation to the tunnelling work that was going to be needed when it came to breaking through the pipe and across to the bank. Now he was realising that even the sewer part of the operation was going to be far trickier than he had thought.

Jack returned with the drinks and Bryce took a deep swallow of his Remy. He and Jack were meeting with a hookey Kent miner later that afternoon. He only hoped that the miner's information was going to be more cheering than the sewer tunnel ganger's info had been.


'Getting all this specialised mining equipment down into the sewer isn't going to be easy, is it?'

The speaker was Gunter. It was coming up for ten o'clock at night and the entire team – or at least all the regular members of it – was in The Spinners, seated around a corner table at the back of the saloon bar.

'It isn't going to be easy, I'll give you that,' Bryce said fairly, 'but it can be done. The ganger's info was that huge skips were continually being hoisted in and out of the sewer via manhole entrances. Where a skip of muck can go, mining equipment can go.'

'Muck?' Georgie asked queryingly, scratching his beer belly.

'Shit,' Jack said flatly. 'Don't ask for any more details

about it, Georgie. Take it from me, mate, you don't want to know.'

Curly glanced over to the bar, checking that his barmaids had everything under control and that there was no one in his pub he didn't want in it. Satisfied that everything was tickety-boo, he said, 'And just how deep is the climb down the manhole? Is there a ladder fixed to the side, or iron struts, or what?'

'There are iron rings driven into the sides.' Bryce took a drink of his Remy. He'd been on it, on and off, ever since his and Jack's meet with the ganger, and, though he was far from being drunk, had a very pleasurable buzz going. 'The first drop is about twenty feet and then there's a concrete landing. From there we lower a spiral safety lamp to check for the gases I told you about. If there are any, the lamp goes out and we're in shit creek – literally.'

No one laughed.

'What will we do if that happens?' Georgie asked. 'Put on the breathing equipment and carry on, or get the hell out?'

Bryce didn't answer because, for once, it was something he was still unsure about.

'And after the landing?' Gunter asked, pragmatic as always.

'After the landing there's a second shaft. That's the same drop: twenty foot. Then there's what our informant described as a small crypt which goes down at a walkable slope into the sewer itself. And though I'd thought the sewer would be big enough to stand upright in, apparently it won't be. Not unless you're a five-foot pygmy.'

'OK, I think I've got the picture.' Gunter's voice was dry. 'We're bent double in a tunnel full of shit and rats and eels. To avoid being killed by poisoned gas we're wearing heavy breathing equipment, and to avoid being swept away by a tidal wave we're wearing lifelines. We've also got mining equipment with us and, just for good measure, oxyacetylene torches and gelignite so that we can break into the vault.'

'That's about the measure of it.' Bryce grinned. 'And as gelly is unstable in damp conditions, we're going to have to go carefully, aren't we?'

'Christ!' Jack ran a hand over his perfectly smooth blond hair. Normally he was game for anything, but he didn't like dark enclosed spaces and ever since the sewer ganger had mentioned rats and eels he'd been having serious second thoughts about the job under discussion.

'I don't like this too much, Bryce.' The speaker was Curly, and Jack could have kissed him. 'Things can go haywire on any job, but if they go haywire on this we could end up dead. Tunnelling through from the sewer to the bank vault is going to be a really heavy number. How do we know we'll be able to do it in the time we've got? How do we know the noise and vibrations won't be heard at street level?'

'And how can we be sure that we strike out from the sewer at exactly the right point and that we'll fetch up at the bank at the right level?' Georgie chipped in, picking up on his brother's unhappiness. 'We're forty feet down, right? OK, so you know the bank vault is in a sub-basement, Bry, but how do you know exactly how many feet down it is? We'd only have to be a couple of feet out and we'd be tunnelling under and beyond it. Fuck! We could be burrowing like moles for bleedin' weeks!'

Bryce shook his head in mock despair. 'Have a bit more faith,' he said, reflecting that things hadn't changed much since they'd all been kids. Then, as now, he'd been the sole instigator of their scams – and always the one who'd done not only all the planning, but all the coercing and convincing as well.

He drank the last of his Remy and then said patiently, 'The bank in question is a bank I use. I've had a deposit-box in the vault ever since I opened the casino. I know *exactly* how many feet below ground level the safe-deposit box vault, and the other vaults, are.'

'Yeah, well, if we were getting down there in the usual manner – a couple of us holding everyone down on the floor upstairs while the rest of us zoomed down to the vault in the lift, I'd be happier.' Gunter's thin, wolfish face was seriously perturbed. 'I'll vault over a bank counter any time, anywhere, you know that, Bryce, but serious mining work where everything could, quite literally, cave in on us, is another matter. Without meaning to be funny, I reckon we'll be completely out of our depth.'

Georgie sniggered. Bryce's grin deepened. 'Any kind of a straight robbery is a no-no these days, Gunter, and you know it. Even an Olympic athlete can't vault a counter when it's fitted with a ceiling-high security screen. The days of carrying out bank heists with just a minder, a goer and a driver are long gone – which is why we're now looking at a completely new approach. The miner who –' The pub door swung open and he broke off abruptly.

Gunter swivelled his head to see who had just entered.

It was Tina Dixon, all bust and beehive hairdo, and she was on the arm of a muscular well-known villain.

'Hi, fellas!' she called across perkily, not remotely put out at being seen with a man not her husband. Aware that they were probably having some kind of a meet, she didn't come over to them but steered her companion straight across to the bar.

'Is he Tina's latest?' Georgie asked with interest. 'Because if he is, someone should tell her he's a paid-up, cards-in member of the Richardsons.'

'I'll put her in the picture.' Curly crushed a cigarette butt into an ashtray that badly needed emptying. 'Not that I imagine it'll cut much ice with Tina. All she'll be interested in is how big a bulge he's got in his wallet and his pants.'

Over the years that Tina had worked for Bryce at The

Renegade she'd come to be regarded as one of their own in a way her old man had long since ceased to be and, as no one regarded Billy as being a proper mate any more, no exception to her flightiness was ever taken.

'What were you saying, Bryce?' Gunter prompted once it was obvious Tina's friend wasn't going to be sitting or standing too near to them.

As casually as if he was talking about Charlton Athletic's last win on home ground, Bryce said, 'I was saying that the miner who's coming in on the job knows exactly what he's about and as he's also bringing in all the equipment we need, there isn't going to be a problem. Trust me.'

They did. They had, after all, trusted him for as long as they could remember and despite the doubts that had been expressed it was a habit too ingrained to abandon.

'Is this bloke going to be with us when we break through into the bank?' Curly's tone of voice indicated that the job itself was no longer a problem to him. 'Or do we drop him once the main tunnelling is done?'

'We drop him. Or more accurately, we drop them.'

'Them?' The speaker was Gunter, but at this last bombshell everyone had sat up very sharply.

Bryce lit a cigarette. 'As Curly has already pointed out, the tunnelling – getting the direction right, shoring everything up, etc, is going to be a heavy number and there's no reason why we should complicate things by attempting it ourselves. The bloke I've spoken to can be trusted absolutely. He and three of his mining mates will do all the main tunnelling in the couple of weeks before Christmas. We're going to have a variety of large vans with the floors removed and each in turn will be stationary over the manhole entrance long enough for them to be able to enter and exit. By the time we go in, late Christmas Eve, they'll have been paid off and will be out of it. All we'll need to do is to break through the last couple of feet into the bank itself.'

'And what about noise and vibration at street level?' Gunter asked, reminding Bryce of the one query he hadn't yet answered. 'Will there be any?'

'Not according to our mining friend. Forty feet is pretty deep.'

'Plus the area in question is heavily trafficked,' Jack said, speaking for the first time. 'The corner the bank is on is a busy one. There are heavy lorries and buses trundling past all day long. Even if there was extra vibration, it wouldn't be noticeable.'

'Jeez!' Georgie sank back in his chair. 'This could be a real goer, couldn't it?'

Bryce nodded. He, too, thought it was going to be really something. The haul would be huge – it was bound to be. In an area dense with rich residents, many of them Arab, the safe-deposit boxes alone would be worth the effort involved.

'It's not going to get better than this,' he said, sure he had everything under control and that he'd covered every angle. 'This is –'

What else he thought, none of them found out. The pub door slammed open with such force that even the drinkers at the bar broke off their conversations to see who the hell was making an entrance.

It was Rusty – and that she hadn't dropped by for a friendly drink was blazingly obvious.

'You *fucker*!' she hurled at Bryce as the door rocked behind her on its hinges. 'You absolute *shit*!'

She stormed towards him, a raging Amazon in a white leather miniskirt and purple patent slingback shoes, her magnificent breasts stretching a skimpy crocheted top to the limits, her lion's mane of hair tumbling over her shoulders and down her back.

To say that the attention of every person in the pub was

riveted on her – and tensely awaiting Bryce's reaction – was an understatement. Lots of heavy villains patronised The Spinners and though Bryce's reputation wasn't for dark villainy, everyone knew he was big-time. For a woman – any woman, even a wife – to be so publicly out of order with a man of his reputation was an event not often seen.

As she reached the far side of the table he was on his feet facing her, tight-lipped and cobra-eyed. He knew what it was about, of course. It had to be Nina. It couldn't possibly be anything else.

'We're in the wrong place for this, sweetheart,' he said tautly, barely able to control the fury he felt at being forced to conduct a private row so publicly. 'Let's leave it till later, shall we?'

'Like hell I'll leave it till later!' If it hadn't been a corner table, and if he hadn't been seated at the far side of it, where she couldn't easily reach him, she would have hit him. 'You said you were going to stop seeing that rich bitch teenage nymphomaniac!' There was a break in her voice and her eyes were bright with more than just fury. 'She's a *schoolgirl*, for Christ's sake – and you were seen out with her last Monday at Churchill's!'

Jack and Gunter and Georgie remained frozen in their seats, desperately struggling to avoid eye contact with either Rusty or Bryce. Curly, aware that as the pub landlord he should at least be attempting to bring the situation under control, had reluctantly risen to his feet. He was well experienced at breaking up nasty situations on his premises, but this one was different. For one thing a woman was involved – and Rusty wasn't just any woman. Rusty was an international artiste, a woman whose nude photograph adorned calendars in places as diverse as America, South Africa and Japan. She was a friend of long-standing and she was also – though he wouldn't have said so to Bryce's face – completely in the right where this little argument was concerned. Neither he, nor any other of Bryce's friends, liked Nina Denster one little bit.

'Er . . . I think perhaps we should cool it, Rusty darlin',' he said awkwardly, wishing every last one of his avidly watching customers in hell.

He might as well not have spoken.

'She's at a fucking finishing school,' Bryce was saying through clenched teeth in answer to Rusty's last barbed accusation, 'not a fucking nursery school!'

'I don't care what kind of a school she's at! She's *seventeen*!' There wasn't just a break in Rusty's voice now, there was a sob.

If the row had been private, Bryce would have had the grace – and sense – to have tried to calm her down, but the row wasn't private. There were thirty to forty people in the pub and all he could think of was getting her out of it pretty damn quick.

Swiftly he moved around the table towards her, taking hold of her arm so that he could frogmarch her to the door. Trembling violently, she wrenched herself away from him. 'Don't touch me! Don't touch me ever again!' He could see the struggle in her eyes as she fought the temptation to slap him across his face and then, beside herself with anguish, she spun away from him, making blindly in the direction of the ladies' toilets.

'Crikey,' Georgie said, letting his breath out and trying to lighten the tension. 'She comes on a bit strong when she's riled, don't she?'

Jack rose to his feet. 'I'll get another round in,' he said, still avoiding eye contact with Bryce, wondering why he couldn't at least have denied the Churchill's allegation. That way Rusty might well have simmered down. As it was, he couldn't help feeling that it was going to be a row with far-reaching repercussions. Rusty wasn't a run-of-the-mill wife. She was a high-earning top-class nude model; a lady who didn't have to take grief from anyone – not even Bryce; a lady more than capable of calling all her own shots.

As he crossed to the bar, where conversation was picking up again, he saw Rusty whirl out from the passageway that led to the loos with what looked to be a half-pint glass of lager in one hand.

He turned round to see if Bryce was also aware she was back in the bar, but Bryce was now seated in the chair he had just vacated and his back was turned towards Rusty.

'Look, Rusty . . .' Jack began tentatively as she marched past him, heading in Bryce's direction. 'Don't you think . . .'

Rusty wasn't remotely interested in what he thought.

With lightening speed she covered the distance to where Bryce was sitting and then – while, far too late, Curly and Georgie looked up, saw her and opened their mouths to warn Bryce – she poured the contents of the pint glass over Bryce's unsuspecting head.

As he erupted to his feet, blaspheming and drenched, an unmistakable steaming aroma left no one in the pub in any doubt as to what the contents of the glass had been.

'I never knew women could piss that much in one go,' Georgie said admiringly as Jack and Curly launched themselves on Bryce, using all their considerable strength to hold him fast until Rusty had not only escaped from the pub but the distinctive sound of her souped-up Mini Cooper could be heard roaring away down the Old Kent Road. 'She should start doing it as part of her act. It'd be a knock-out.'

# *Chapter Thirteen*

'Is there any chance of the two of you getting back together, Bryce?'

Wearing overcoats against the December chill, Bryce and Victor were strolling along the Embankment with Tricia, her gloved hand trailing along the riverside wall, walking with her awkwardly arthritic gait a little way behind them.

Bryce quirked an eyebrow wryly. 'After she poured half a pint of piss over me in full view of everyone? No, mate. Not a hope.'

Victor glanced over his shoulder towards Tricia. 'She's a nice kiddie, isn't she? And she calls you daddy. Didn't that make you think twice about ending things?'

Bryce shrugged; his hands plunged deep in the pockets of his camelhair coat. 'Tricia calls me daddy because in every way that counts I am her daddy,' he said, wondering why so many people found it hard to comprehend just how deep his feelings and sense of responsibility for Tricia ran. 'Me and Rusty may have come to the end of the line, but the situation where Tricia is concerned is the same as it is in any marriage when it breaks up and a kiddie is involved. I have regular access to her and I take full advantage of it. End of story.'

Victor looked across at him, feeling the usual lurch in his loins, and, as always, clamping down on the emotion fast and hard. 'And do you still see Sandra's little girl?' he asked, envying Bryce his easy manner with children – and not just children. Bryce was equally at ease with anyone and everyone: old people, rich people, poor people, the whole bloody world. He only wished to God that he'd been blessed with the same ability. Emotionally, his life was so buttoned-up it was a wonder he was still able to breathe.

'Yes.' Bryce flashed him a grin. 'Though somehow I never think of Debbie as being a little girl. That little madam came into the world old.'

Victor summoned up an answering smile. His meetings with Bryce were so rare these days, and so short, that he didn't want to spend time talking about Debbie Clarkson. Even the mere mention of her name catapulted him back into the fear-filled kitchen where the sluttish abortionist had so bloodily and hopelessly tried to terminate her life.

He never saw Debbie himself. His parents had moved out of Swan Row and into a semi-detached house in New Eltham years ago. Nowadays his only contact with that early wodge of his life was via his continuing friendship with Bryce and, where some of his other childhood acquaintances were concerned, via his work.

He still saw Sandra occasionally. Her marriage to Malcolm Hurst was lasting and she now had two young-sters, both boys. Whether she was happy or not, he found it impossible to tell. All she ever wanted to do was ask questions about Bryce. Who was he living with? What was he doing? Did he ever ask about her? His answers were nearly always fudged. What Bryce was doing, apart from being a highly successful club-owner, he didn't know and nor, bearing in mind his rank of detective inspector, did he want to know.

'Look!' Tricia called out from behind them. 'A big birdie! Isn't he pretty?'

A seagull swooped low over the pale grey glitter of the Thames.

Bryce came to a halt so that he could watch the bird with her, suddenly remembering the time when, as a kid, he'd dragged Frankie free of the quicksand.

'He's lovely, sweetheart,' he said indulgently.

Victor turned his coat collar up, intrigued as always by

the way Bryce communicated so easily with his physically and mentally handicapped step-daughter. She was eight now, and an exceptionally bonny child. Her hair was the same fiery red as her mother's and her eyes were a soft smoky green.

'I'm being promoted,' he said suddenly, breaking the silence that had fallen between himself and Bryce. 'I'll be a DCI at thirty. Not bad, eh?'

For a long moment Bryce didn't respond. Victor's career as a copper had been a stumbling block between them nearly all their adult lives and, on the occasions when they met up and had a drink together, was a topic of conversation they usually fought shy of. The prospect of having Victor assigned to a case in which he himself was the suspect under investigation was one he lived in dread of.

Acutely aware that, even as he and Victor were talking, his mining friends were beavering away, tunnelling their way towards the bank he was about to rob, Bryce felt the muscles along his jaw line tightening. If the need arose, there certainly wouldn't be a hope in hell of paying Victor off. Victor was the exception to what was, in his experience, the general rule. A 100 per cent straight, absolutely incorruptible copper. There was always Somerville, of course. He still had Somerville in his pocket and he carried a lot of clout. Even more of a high-flier than Victor, he'd been a DCI for nearly two years now, the only snag being that he was in the Vice Squad. For the majority of incidents involved with the running of his clubs and casinos Somerville's placing was invaluable. When it came to the bank job, however . . .

'I need your help.'

The request was so unexpected, so sudden, that Bryce forgot all about Somerville and even, temporarily, about the bank.

'What kind of help? Personal?'

Victor's personal life had always been a mystery to Bryce, but being a man who didn't like people prying into his own

260

private affairs he'd always steered clear of noseying into Victor's.

'Nope.' A little to the left of them, Tricia was cooing at the seagull, which had obligingly landed on the Embankment wall. 'Professional.'

Bryce swung his head towards him so swiftly his neck cracked. 'No,' he said savagely. 'Not on, Victor! Never in a million years. You know how I feel about coppers and grasses. Christ! I can't believe you'd even think such a thing, let alone fucking ask it!'

Victor turned round, leaning his back against the freezing-cold wall, holding his collar closed beneath his chin. 'Hear me out, Bryce.' There was weariness in his voice and something else – deep, deep depression. 'It's not straightforward and, whether you finally see things from my point of view or not, it's something we should talk about.'

'Can I give the birdie some of my crisps, Daddy?' With cheeks rosy from the cold, Tricia was struggling to retrieve a packet of half-eaten potato crisps from her pocket.

Bryce nodded, knowing from the tone of Victor's voice that he was going to say his piece come hell or high water.

'OK.' He turned so that his back, too, was against the Embankment wall, one foot negligently crossing the other at the ankle. 'Spit it out and get it over with.'

'Indirectly, it's about the Krays. It's been a hell of a year where they and their friends have been concerned.' Victor's face and voice were grim. 'I know you keep well clear of them, Bryce, but you must know what's going on. Frankie Fraser is out on the streets again. He's 100 per cent for the Richardsons and he hates the Twins and the Twins hate him.'

'Yeah. So?' All-out war between the Krays, their tame gorillas and the Richardsons' mob, had been on the cards for so long that the subject, from his point of view, was a bore.

'So, we have it on good authority that Ronnie Kray is

busy making a death list,' Victor continued, looking across the broad, deserted pavement to a line of leafless trees. 'The Richardsons and Fraser will be on it. So will Myers, though he isn't going by that name now. He's hitched his star to the Richardsons and changed his monicker to Cornell.'

Bryce heaved an exasperated sigh. Myers was an East End thug well known both sides of the river. 'OK. Fine. As you said, Victor, I know what's going on, or at least there's been enough gossip around for me to have a good idea. Ever since Ronnie and Reggie were brought to trial in April and then walked free, word's been out that Ronnie's battier than ever. It's nothing to do with me, though. I don't rattle their cages and they don't rattle mine. If you're wanting any info regarding the Twins and their private wars, you've come to the wrong man.'

'No, I haven't.' Victor kept his eyes fixed on the distant trees. 'Not if you and Frankie are still in each other's pockets.'

A tight, closed expression came down over Bryce's face. His relationship with Frankie was now almost at breaking point, for it had been Frankie who had dropped the information in Rusty's hearing that he had been seen at Churchill's with Nina and, as it had led to the break-up of his marriage, it was an act of malice he had no intention of forgiving or forgetting.

It didn't mean, though, that he would now discuss Frankie with Victor – not when Victor's interest was professional. Grassing was a cardinal sin and nothing on earth would ever make him commit it.

'Frankie is off-limits as far as you and me are concerned and you know it,' he said flatly.

'The Krays are in with the American Mafia now,' Victor continued, just as if Bryce hadn't spoken. 'The Americans want to muscle in on the London gambling scene. They're already investing heavily in new clubs and casinos . . . But then, you know that, don't you?'

It was a rhetorical question and Bryce didn't bother to answer it. Mafia interest in his owns clubs and casinos had been rife for the last year and, considering the money under discussion, not entirely unwelcome.

'The Americans want to ensure they have a trouble-free run here,' Victor continued, telling him nothing, as yet, that he didn't already know. 'Which is where their liaison with Ronnie and Reggie – and Frankie – comes into play.'

The seagull engaging Tricia's attention had been joined, much to her delight, by its mate.

'This isn't a conversation that's going anywhere.' Bryce abandoned his relaxed position and stood upright, signifying that as far as he was concerned the conversation was at an end.

Victor made no answering movement. 'That's because I haven't yet got to where I'm going,' he said, his voice hard-edged. 'It's Frankie's involvement with the Mafia, via the Krays, that's of real interest to me, Bryce. It may not seem like it, but the Krays' days are nearly over. Once Ronnie starts working his way through his little list we'll get the pair of them – and when we do, Frankie will step into their shoes. It's what he's planning, Bryce. It's what he's working towards.'

Bryce gave a mirthless laugh. 'You can't really believe that, Victor! Frankie's to be reckoned with, but that's only because he's got the Twins behind him. On his own he'd be just another nasty villain.'

Victor shook his head. 'That's where you're wrong,' he said emphatically, 'and that's why I need your help. Everyone underestimates Frankie . . .' he paused and then added: 'including the Twins.'

Bryce stared at him, his attention now riveted. 'Are you saying Frankie's agreed to help the Met put the Krays behind bars? And that if he does, the understanding is that he'll be left well alone?'

Even as he asked the question he knew it was one Victor couldn't possibly answer.

'I'm saying Frankie is serious bad news and that you should start realising it. And you should be especially aware just how deep his Mafia connections have become.'

Bryce swung away from him. Tricia's gulls had flown away and as she began hurrying awkwardly down the Embankment, looking for more, he began to stroll in her wake, aware that Victor still hadn't come to the nub of what it was he wanted from him and wishing to God he'd hurry up and get it over with.

Victor eased himself away from the wall and fell into step beside him. 'I have a personal reason for going all out for Frankie, Bryce.'

Bryce had thought as much all along. Though he was now closer to Jack than to anyone, he still thought of Victor as being his best mate and, though he never forgot that Victor was a copper, he usually enjoyed their occasional meetings. He wasn't enjoying this one, though. This one was growing increasingly tricky and he wanted it over.

'Whatever the reason, I'm not going to be able to help you,' he said as Victor continued to wait for some sort of a response from him. 'You're on one side of the line, and whatever the differences between me and Frankie, we're on the other side of it – together. When push comes to shove, my loyalty will always be to Frankie, Victor. Not you.'

'Really?' There was barely reined-in bitter anger in Victor's voice. 'Even if I tell you that we have Frankie down for two murders – one of them a policeman?'

Bryce stopped walking, his face carefully expressionless. 'Was the copper in question Frankie's contact?' It was a guess, nothing more.

'And if he was?' Victor's eyes were blazing with an emotion he was no longer able to control. 'What the fuck difference does it make? No policeman would be bent if it wasn't for the likes of the Briscoes always thrusting wads of cash into their palms!'

For a second, Bryce couldn't believe what he was hearing and then he gave a shout of mirthless laughter, well aware that they were on the verge of a full-scale fall-out and beyond caring. 'Christ! It's the villain's fault if a copper is bent – is that it, Victor? Is that where you stand and how you think? Or have you served with bent colleagues for so long that you're not averse to a little back-hander yourself these days?'

It was a taunt too far and the instant it was out of his mouth he knew it.

'Fuck you!' The skin had drawn so tight across Victor's cheekbones that it looked like parchment. '*Fuck you!*' He stumbled a step or two backwards. 'I've stuck with you through everything! Through all the years you were in prison! Through all the years you've fraternised with Frankie! I always felt *you* were honourable even if the company you kept wasn't! Well, I don't fucking think that any fucking longer!'

Tricia had stopped her search for another seagull and, alarmed and frightened by their shouting, was walking uncertainly towards them.

Acutely aware of her presence, acutely aware that they were hurling their abuse at each other in a public place, Victor stumbled another step backwards, so enraged and distressed that, much as he wanted to bring himself under control, he was quite incapable of doing so. 'I've never thought of you as being a really bad bastard Bryce, but seeing you've put me straight as to where your loyalties lie, even when murder is involved, then it's a mistake I won't be making again! From now on I'll be out to nail you, just as I'm out to nail Frankie! There isn't a line between us now! There's a fucking great canyon!'

Unable to cope with the situation any longer he turned,

breaking into a run, heading blindly back in the direction of Westminster Bridge.

Bryce stared after him, too deeply shocked to move. Where the *hell* had all that come from? For years now their relationship had been full of tensions and strains, but their shared history – their deep friendship as children – had always been enough to enable them to paper over the cracks. Now, if Victor's extreme reaction to his taunt about corruption was anything to go by, the cracks had become way too deep.

As Tricia slid her hand into his, he felt a bleakness almost as bad as the bleakness he had felt when Rusty had moved her clothes out of their Curzon Street home.

'Are you all right, Daddy?' Tricia asked, her voice a little wobbly. 'You're not upset, are you?'

'No,' he lied, squeezing her hand reassuringly. 'And you mustn't be either. Shall we go to Hamley's and visit Father Christmas?'

'Oh *yes*!' she said ecstatically, the bewilderment she had been feeling instantly forgotten.

He flagged down a black cab, wishing his own feelings could be put to rights as easily. In the last few days he'd lost both his wife and his best friend. Even to him it seemed like carelessness on a grand scale.

A cab slid to a halt and he helped Tricia climb into the back of it, reflecting that at least the heist was still on course. Over the last few days his mining friends had proved that access in and out of the sewer system via a van over a manhole entrance was viable. Nina was out of the way, spending Christmas in the Caribbean with her father. And, in three days' time, on Christmas Eve, he and the hard core of his childhood gang would break into the vaults of the Al-Bakara Arab Bank.

# Chapter Fourteen

'How are we fixed, Tom?'

Tom Craven, Georgie and Curly's cousin, continued to allow the van's engine to tick over. 'Great, Bryce, the road is practically deserted. Everyone's either at home stuffing pressies into their kids' Christmas stockings, or they're in the boozer filling themselves with good cheer. Get going. The miners had the entry down to one minute thirty flat.'

Bryce, who, along with Georgie, Curly, Jack and Gunter, had been strap-hanging in order not to lose balance on the strip of van floor still remaining, an edging barely deep enough to stand on, eased his arm down and flexed it.

'Right,' he said, as they all exchanged swift glances. 'This is it. Let's go.'

A foot and a half beneath them lay the tarmacked road and, dead centre, the giant manhole cover.

No one else spoke; all knew what they had to do.

Bags of heavy tools and electrical equipment were heaved down from the meat hooks on the inner sides of the van. With gloved hands Curly and Georgie inserted the appropriate iron rods into the slots on the manhole cover, twisting it clockwise and then lifting.

'You're still OK!' Tom shouted back to them from his vantage point behind the wheel as the manhole lid noisily scraped the tarmac. 'No one's about. I can hear some Christmas carollers somewhere nearby, though. Christ, but they're murdering "Away in a bleedin' Manger"!'

No one in the van area behind him was remotely interested in the carollers. 'You're down first, Gunter,' Bryce said tersely, the buzz he always got once a job was underway roaring through him. 'Then Georgie. You got your safety harness on right, Georgie? I've seen turkeys trussed up neater.'

With a safety light slung over his shoulder, Gunter began climbing down the narrow circular shaft via the iron rings that were driven in its sides. Seconds later, Georgie squeezed his bulky figure down after him.

'You're still doing OK!' Tom said to Bryce without turning his head. 'There's no cozzers about and no one noseying as to what we're up to, though with Thames Water Board lettering plastered all over the van, that isn't too much of a surprise, is it?'

Tom was a notorious windbag and Bryce didn't bother to reply. He and Jack were now lowering the bags of tools, one after the other, down the shaft.

'Which bag has the gelly in?' Jack asked, an edge of nervousness in his voice. 'We don't want it getting damp, do we? What if it falls into water, or piss, or . . . ?'

'It's safely tinned and it was in the first bag down.' Bryce glanced at his Rolex. So far they were running at three minutes thirty seconds and needed to speed up. Another bag was rope-lowered down. And another.

'Go careful with the last one,' he said, passing it across to Jack. 'It has the grub and the beer in it.'

The inner sides of the van were now empty. On one side of them, only feet away, a late-night bus trundled past, a lorry in its wake. On the other side a lone pedestrian was walking towards them, heavily laden with parcels. The carollers were still singing, 'Away in a Manger' having given way to 'Silent Night'.

'And the ciggies?' Jack asked, delaying the moment of entering the shaft by another precious second. 'I know you say the air's too stale to be able to smoke down there, but I'll feel happier if we have some with us – just in case of emergency.'

Well aware of what a nightmare the next fifteen hours or so were going to be for Jack, Bryce suppressed his impatience and leaned forward into the cab area, stretching past Tom to grab hold of the packet of cigarettes laying on the dashboard.

'Merry Christmas,' the dark-raincoated pedestrian said, taking him by surprise. 'Not much fun if you're having to work though, is it?'

Leaving Tom to make a friendly response, Bryce ducked back swiftly, tossing the cigarettes to Jack. 'Right,' he said tautly. 'No more stalling, Jack. Get the fuck down there.'

Jack blanched. He was known as a bloke who had ice-water in his veins, but it didn't feel that way at the moment. He couldn't abide enclosed dark places – and nowhere was more enclosed or dark than a sewer-pipe forty feet below Mayfair.

'Christ, but I'll be glad when this lark is over,' he said through gritted teeth as he levered himself into position over the shaft, beginning the climb down. 'Why don't we do something easy next time? Hijack an aeroplane carrying bullion, or rob a transatlantic liner or Buckingham Palace?'

Bryce flashed him a grin. 'Go on, Goldilocks,' he said as Jack's blond head of hair disappeared down into the darkness. 'Be careful of the rats.'

Jack's reply was mercifully too muffled to be intelligible. Still grinning, Bryce checked he had all his equipment on him and then said: 'OK, Tom, it's all yours. Don't make a hash of lowering the manhole cover back into position, and garage the van pronto.'

'Don't worry, Guv. Will do.'

Even as Bryce was easing himself down into the shaft, Tom was scrambling from his seat and into the rear of the van – or what would have been the rear of it, if it had still had a floor.

Aware of Jack descending immediately beneath him,

Bryce took the climb down nice and steady. Above him, the manhole cover clanged into place, cutting off the moonlight as violently as a blow.

'Fucking *hell*,' he heard Jack mutter and then, a second or so later as his feet touched the solid concrete of the first subterranean landing, 'Thank Christ!'

Seconds later he was standing beside him and Curly in the dull pool of light given by their torches.

'The miners have done their stuff and left a couple of trolleys for us at the bottom of the second shaft,' Curly said, immediately putting Bryce into the picture. 'Georgie and Gunter are down there now, loading our gear on to them.'

'And you checked for gases before they went down?'

'Yeah.' Curly swung the spiral safety lamp with its long length of chain. 'I wouldn't have my kid brother climbing down into any nasty hydrogens or acids, would I?'

It was a question that didn't need an answer.

'Right,' Bryce said, aware that one of the most difficult parts of the operation – now that they were in the sewer and so was all their gear – was safely over. 'Let's get down and join them. You first, Jack.'

Jack shot him a look that meant he was going to make him pay, later, for every second they spent underground. Then, wearing thigh-high waders, he began the descent of the second shaft.

As he followed, Bryce, who had been down to the main sewer level several times with the miners, had to admit that it was a pretty spooky environment. The sweaty brickwork of the shaft was as claustrophobic as a tomb and the pungent, foetid smell he thought he had got used to was growing stronger every minute. This time there was a kind of mist with it. He hadn't come across mist before and the flushers' ganger hadn't mentioned mist. What if the mist indicated gas? What if they were climbing straight down into it? What if . . . ?

'Pongs dahn 'ere, don't it?' Georgie said cheerily to him as he stepped off the bottom rung of the iron ladder into a cavern that resembled a small crypt. 'It's a good job these trolleys float. Gunter's down in the sewer proper and he says the shit and water is knee-deep.'

'He should have stayed with you.' Bryce's voice was sharp. The last thing he needed was any of them getting lost. He led the way down a slope towards the sewer, his torch illuminating pillars and arches and buttresses so vast that, as always, they took his breath away. It was like an entire city – but one built underground, inhabited only by rats and eels.

Through the murky gloom they came to the sewer itself. 'Come on in,' Gunter said sarcastically, 'the water's lovely.'

'It looks like the Stiss,' Jack said as Curly and Bryce waded into it. 'You know, the river of death.'

'The Styx,' Bryce corrected as a large rat swam past him. 'Now get the hell in here, Jack. We're robbing a bank, or have you forgotten?'

For a long time, as they began negotiating the tunnel, Bryce in the lead, none of them spoke. Not one of them was enjoying the experience – not even Georgie, who normally wasn't stymied by anything. The height of the tunnel was too low for them to stand completely upright and in a very short time their necks and backs ached. Their torch-lit shadows on the tunnel walls were of grotesque, distorted Quasimodos.

Every so often the mist they had encountered earlier would rise again, shrouding them so that they could barely see each other. Worse, the chalk markings left for them on the tunnel wall by the miners would be completely impossible to see. Every few hundred yards, dark, slime-encrusted smaller tunnels opened out from the tunnel they were in, all of them at different angles, all of them bringing in main and local sewer tributaries.

'You're sure we're still in the right tunnel, ain't yer, Bry?' Georgie asked as a pack of rats scurried over an outcrop of brickwork. 'You're sure we ain't lost?'

'We're nearly there.' Bryce didn't need chalk markings to keep to the route. He knew exactly how many tunnel entrances they had to pass to find the one they were looking for, and he'd been counting them with great care. The tunnel that ran practically beneath the bank was what the flushers' ganger had described as being a man-entry one – though because of its positioning there wasn't an entry to it.

'All man-entry tunnels are no more than three feet high, and a foot of that will be shit,' the ganger had said to him dourly. 'I wouldn't tell your mates that, though. Not until you actually go into it.'

'We've cleared out most of the muck,' his mining friend had said after he and his mates had completed their first weekend's work breaking through from it towards the bank. 'And it isn't a long stretch – only a few yards. You'll all be able to manage it – though Georgie Porgie might wish he was a little slimmer.'

The miner's main concern – and his own – had been of seepage from the man-entry sewer, once they'd broken through its wall, so noticeable that the Thames Water Board would be on to it and that flushers would be sent down to investigate the cause. If that had happened, the cat would have been well and truly out of the bag and the miners might well have been caught red-handed. Even if they had escaped, it would have been obvious that the damage was man-made and the heist would have had to be called off.

The danger, of course, still existed, but Bryce was banking on the fact that only a real emergency would have the Thames Water Board calling out flushers over the Christmas holidays.

'Here we go,' he said, as his torch picked out the

murky entrance to the tunnel in question. 'We're nearly there now.'

'Christ, but it's about bloody time.' Like all of them, Curly's massive shoulder and arm muscles were aching from the effort of half hauling, half carrying their water-proofed bags of equipment. 'I swear to God, if we break into this fucking vault and find it fucking empty, I'll fucking kill someone!'

One after the other they slithered first through the narrow tributary sewer and then arduously into the upward-sloping tunnel the miners had excavated for them. Their mining friends had done a good job. The tunnel was firmly shored up and large enough for even Georgie to be able to crawl along it on his hands and knees. They had excavated passing places in it and the rope pulley system they had installed, so that bagged-up debris could be hauled back to the sewer and dumped, was still in place.

'We couldn't have dug this – not in a million years,' Curly panted, nose to tail behind his brother. 'And even if we could – I wouldn't have been here helping, not for all the tea in bleedin' China!'

'It ain't tea we're digging for,' Jack said grimly. 'It's dosh.'

'And jewels,' they heard Gunter mutter from the rear. 'Think of all those deposit boxes. They'll be stuffed with 'em.'

'OK.' Bryce's business-like tone silenced them. 'It's time for a strategy meet. Can you all squeeze up here next to me?'

The tunnel had been hacked out into a semicircular area that, with a little squeezing and a lot of swearing, accommodated them all. At Bryce's back was brickwork. Lots and lots of it.

He shone his torch over the geometrical lines of the mortaring. 'This is where we really start to work,' he said, his voice tense with anticipation and an excitement impossible to contain. 'There's isn't room to swing a pick, so it's going to be a long, slow job.'

'That's it? That's the foundation wall of the bank?' Georgie took a glove off and wiped his sweating face with the back of his hand.

'Sling the beer and grub bag up front,' Bryce said to Gunter, and then to Georgie, 'Yeah. This is it. And if our mining friends have done their work spot on, breaking through here will bring us in under the flooring of the vault.'

Gunter slung the lightest of the waterproof bags into the centre of the circle they had formed, and unzipped it.

'Now, the only problem,' Bryce continued as Gunter began handing out cans of beer, 'is which vault?'

'Christ Almighty!' Jack said with devout passion. 'We're forty feet in the bowels of the soddin' earth and now you say there's a problem. It would have been nice if you'd thought of it before, Bry, 'cos I ain't enjoying this. I ain't enjoying any of it.'

In the torch-lit gloom, Bryce's teeth flashed vividly white. 'You will when I tell you the nature of the problem.' He sat cross-legged, Indian-style. 'We can come up in the deposit box vault and sack it clean, but once we're in there, we can't break out of it into any of the other vaults. The alarm system is too complicated. If we want to do the cash vault, we have to do it the same way we do the deposit vault. Up into it via the foundations and the floor. Back out the same way.'

'Jesus God, he thinks we're bleedin' moles.' Georgie hitched his safety harness to one side so that he could scratch his belly. 'How many bleedin' tunnels are you wanting us to dig, Bry? One into the deposit vault, one into the cash vault – what about one into the lavvies, just for good measure?'

'Stop the crap, Georgie.' Curly took a swig of his beer. 'It is a bit of a problem, ain't it? If we dig two routes upwards, how can we be sure the second one will bring us out where we want to be? We had a mining engineer figure this one out for us – and just looking at all his and Bryce's calculations gave me a headache that lasted a week. If we come up in the wrong place, say a corridor, we'll have all sorts of alarm systems firing off.'

'And if we don't give it a try, we'll never forgive ourselves,' Gunter said, terse and matter-of-fact as always. 'So how do we go about it? What's the next step, Bry?'

Bryce drained the last gulp of beer and crushed the can in his hand. 'First off, we break through these foundation walls. We're then in place to break up through the floor of the deposit vault. I'm not anticipating that being much hassle. Only the cash vault is likely to have a steel-plated floor and to need the oxyacetylenes. While Curly and Georgie do the straightforward business with the deposit vault, the rest of us are going to tunnel for a further eight yards, in a direct angle east.' He dropped the can back into the bag and took a small silver compass out of his pocket. 'I can't promise that when we then strike upwards we'll be in the cash vault, but a bloke who knows far more about surveying than I do assures me we'll be in with a very good chance.'

Curly looked down at his wristwatch. 'It's dead on midnight. Happy Christmas Day everyone.'

'Santa is going to be very good to us this year,' Georgie said with a chuckle as Gunter began sorting out the slime-covered toolbags and divvying up the equipment. 'It must be because we're such good little boys.'

'Let's cut the crap and get to work.' Bryce, too, was looking at his watch. There was no telling what depth of concrete would be beneath the steel-sheeted floor, or how long it was going to take them to cut their way through it. One thing was for sure, though: time wasn't on their side and they were going to have to move fast.

\*　　\*　　\*

Six hours later, bathed in perspiration, they had succeeded in breaking through into the bank's foundations and were well on their way to both their final objectives.

Curly and Georgie, working in practised unison, had excavated up to the concrete base of the safe-deposit vault's floor.

Bryce and Jack and Gunter had tunnelled out a narrow passage, eight yards long and, taking a well-deserved break, were praying to God that the cash vault was now directly above them.

'Do you reckon we're going to be OK where security staff are concerned?' Jack asked, so focused on trying to control his claustrophobia he could hardly remember anything any more.

'Yeah.' Bryce sounded far more relaxed about the question than he actually felt. 'It's Christmas Day. They'll be skeleton and, as there are no cameras actually *in* the vaults, only in the corridors leading to them, we're going to be fine.'

Neither Jack nor Gunter said anything though both of them knew, as did Bryce, that things weren't quite so cut and dried as he was making them out to be – not when it came to the oxyacetylenes and gelly. Gunter was a gellyman par excellence, but even he couldn't make the operation a completely soundproof one.

'Come on.' Bryce checked his compass reading once more, and then slipped the compass back into his pocket. 'Rest break is over. From now on, we're going upwards.'

It was a sweating, painful, chokingly laborious process. The earth and the rubble they excavated had to be man-handled into the same kind of sacks the miners had used when excavating the access tunnel. Then, via the pulley, it was hauled down their own tunnel, down the access tunnel, to be deposited in the sewer by whichever one of them was taking a rest from the actual digging.

Bryce knew the moment Curly and Georgie broke

through the flooring into the nearby deposit vault, not because there was distinctive noise, but because a puff of blessed fresh air found its way into their own shaft. His elation was euphoric. With luck, all Curly and Georgie would need to break into the deposit boxes would be crowbars.

He shone his torch on his muddily begrimed Rolex. It was ten o'clock in the morning. As far as time was concerned, they were doing well. The trickiest part was still to come, though. If the floor above him proved to be lined with steel, and he was fairly certain it would be, then they would need to oxyacetylene their way through it – and the thought of using torches in such a cramped, confined space was giving him heart failure.

'Shit!'

The ringing sound was unmistakable. Stripped to the waist, labouring for breath, Bryce and Gunter slumped in the stinking darkness in utter exhaustion. The floor was steel. They were going to have to use the torches.

'Shall I give Jack a tug on the pulley to let him know?' Gunter asked at last.

'Nah.' Bryce coughed up a lungful of brickdust. 'It's not as if he can help out here, there's no soddin' room. Let's leave him on rubble-dumping duty where he can at least walk about a bit.'

Gunter struggled into another position and hauled on the rope fastened round his waist. Attached to the other end of it, a heavy toolbag began inching its way cumbersomely towards them.

'How are we going to do this?' he asked Bryce as he grabbed hold of the bag and unzipped it. 'Both together or one at a time?'

Bryce took out the torches and the oxygen bottles. 'One at a time.' He checked one of the oxyacetylene cylinders and clipped an oxygen bottle securely on to his back, putting the mask on, then he gave Gunter a thumbs-up sign.

Once Gunter had scrambled clear, he took a deep, steadying breath and turned both knobs on the cylinder. As the gases began to mix he put a match to the nozzle, adjusted the flame, and set about burning his way through the metal above his head.

'Happy Christmas, little brother!'

Curly stood in the centre of the safe-deposit box vault as Georgie heaved himself with difficulty through the hacked-out flooring.

'Christ All-bleedin' Mighty!' Finally on his feet, Georgie arched his aching back and looked around him at the tiers and tiers of deposit boxes. 'Is this really 'appening, Curly?' he asked, an expression of beatific joy on his face. 'Or am I dreaming?'

'It's really happening.' Curly wanted to fist the air with triumph, but was far too professional to waste time in doing so. 'Haul the toolbag up, Georgie. There's a good two hours work here. Let's get cracking.'

Under normal conditions, Bryce knew he'd have cut through the steel plating in five minutes, perhaps even less. The conditions weren't normal, though. He barely had room to manoeuvre and, even with the benefit of the oxygen, he felt as if he was going to start choking to death at any minute.

When he was nearly halfway to his objective he had to hand over to Gunter. And when Gunter couldn't continue any more, he summoned up what felt to be all his remaining strength and, his arm muscles in spasms of pain, finished the job off.

Through the two-by-two-foot jagged hole they had opened up, they could see up into the strong-room. No alarm bells could be heard; the only noise was that of their own harsh breathing. They had done the near impossible. They had gained entry to the heart of a bank via what had felt to be the bowels of the earth.

'You go first,' Bryce said, still panting for breath. 'But for Christ's sake, don't cut yourself to ribbons on the edging. Bleeding to death isn't part of the deal.'

Gingerly, Gunter eased himself through the opening into the cash vault. With a slamming heart, Bryce followed him.

The sight that met his eyes was better than he'd hoped for in his wildest dreams. There were no safes needing to be gellied open. The space they had surfaced into was the strong-room itself and it was shelved floor to ceiling – and on the shelves were wads and wads of neatly banded notes. In one section, old notes. In another, new notes.

'Haul the empty bags up,' Bryce said on a long, drawn out breath of wonder. 'And give the pulley a tug. We need Jack in here for this – and Curly and Georgie when they're finished bagging-up next door.'

After the grimness of the digging, the actual stashing of the money into old mail bags, and the dragging of the bags down the tunnel to the point where they could be hooked on to the pulley and hauled down to the main sewer, was sheer unalloyed pleasure.

As Curly disappeared down the shaft with the last bag, Bryce keeled over in the cash vault in mock exhaustion that wasn't far from the real thing.

Gunter, his face still as black as coal from their tunnelling work, cracked with laughter.

'We've done it! It's only five o'clock and we're on our way out. We'll have the whole lot safely loaded into the van by midnight.'

Bryce rocked back up into a sitting position and for a brief moment hugged his knees and gazed at the empty shelving where the old notes had been stacked high. If security men had visited the building during the day, they obviously hadn't heard anything. Because they had gone nowhere near the door of either vault, no alarms had been triggered. They were going to face no complications on their return journey via their own roughly hewn tunnel, or the miners' tunnel, or the sewers because, short of a cave-in, nothing could go wrong. It was the best Christmas he'd ever had. It had been a Christmas he would never forget.

'Is everything cleared?' he asked Gunter, who always acted as their unofficial quartermaster.

Gunter nodded. 'There isn't so much as a crisp packet in either tunnel. The only thing I didn't fancy lugging back with us was the gelly. I thought we'd leave it as a present for the bank manager when he opens up.'

Bryce grinned. 'Pity we don't have any ribbon to tie the tin up with. Come on, let's get the hell out. The sooner I see the back of the tunnels, the better I'll like it.'

Easing themselves over the hammered-down edges of the hole in the flooring, they wriggled down, feet first, towards the steeply sloping tunnel, burrowing along it for the last time.

Jack and Georgie were waiting for them at the junction of the man-entry sewer and the main sewer.

'We've ferried one trolleyload of bags up to the crypt,' Jack said, referring to the church-like structure above the slope leading from the entry shaft to the sewer. 'But it was back-breaking and I'm knackered.'

They were all knackered, but Bryce knew that Jack was, quite literally, at the end of his rope. He'd been underground for sixteen hours and the panic he had been fighting, for all of that time, was now beginning to show.

'When you go up with this next one, there'll be no need for you to come back.' He wasn't making an exception for Jack. There was going to be no need for Curly to come back either. Though the trolleys were fuckers to manoeuvre through the sludge and the slime, they were purpose-built for the task and would easily take three bags a trip. 'It's going to be one final trip only for all of us, with me and Gunter bringing up the rear. So come on, let's get moving one last time.'

It was three in the morning before all the bags of dosh, both from the cash vault and safe-deposit vault, and their bags of tools, were neatly stacked in what they had all come to refer to as the crypt.

Curly looked at his watch. 'Two hours to go until we can be sure Tom is up top with the van. Anyone fancy a game of cards?'

'Piss off,' Georgie said, more elated than he'd ever been in his life, and also more exhausted.

Jack wasn't even sitting with them on the torch-lit dry stone slope. He was hunkered down at the foot of the first vertical shaft, as near as he could possibly get to the starlight and fresh air beyond the manhole cover, forty feet above him.

Gunter wasn't a card man and never had been, apart from which he was busy making mental lists of all the things he was going do and buy with his share of the take.

Jack, however, had never turned down a game of cards in his life and wasn't about to do so now. Easing off gloves rock hard with dried mud and shit, he came over to them. 'I'll play you. What about a hand of three-card brag? And don't worry about the stakes. I can meet whatever you raise.'

First Gunter began to roar with laughter, and then Curly, and then they were all laughing, rolling all over the place, utterly convulsed. The sound echoed and re-echoed around the cavernous crypt and the nearby sewer, and none of them gave a toss. They'd robbed a bank more thoroughly than anyone they knew had ever robbed one, and all they were doing now was waiting for their transport home.

Everything had gone so smoothly that it wouldn't have surprised Jack if there'd been a hiccup with Tom and the timing of the van's arrival, but there wasn't.

Dead on the stroke of five o'clock, when he tapped the underneath of the manhole cover, Tom tapped back and, seconds later, hoisted the cover to one side. The filthy, smelly bags were all laboriously heaved up and out of the shaft, and then heaved yet again on to the many meat hooks fitted on the inside of the van. No one passed the van in the street while they were carrying out the final part of their operation, not even a cat.

'Christ, but that was one perfect job!' Curly said as Tom drove at decorous speed through the silent, pre-dawn streets in the direction of the London Bridge lock-up. 'There's only one thing in the world I need now and that's a bath!'

'And a shag,' Georgie said, cradling his nuts. 'I always like a shag when I've pulled a successful job.'

'You'd be lucky to get a sheep to shag you, the state you're in.' Gunter's rare wolfish grin creased his dirty face. 'When are we going to do the divvying up, Bryce? Before you crush the van, or after?'

'There's going to be two divvies,' Bryce said as the van cruised across Waterloo Bridge towards their own patch of London. 'Curly and Georgie are going to take everything they hauled from the deposit boxes and give it the once-over at the pub. You, me and Jack, after the van and the toolbags are crushed, are going to take the dosh bags to the casino to do a count there. Whatever happens, neither me nor Jack are going to get involved in the deposit box haul. Most of it will be jewellery and that isn't our line. If Curly's fence doesn't think it's going to bring in what our third share of the cash is, we'll balance it up. Or vice versa.'

It was a decidedly loose arrangement, but no one quibbled. They'd been trusting each other – and Bryce in particular – since childhood and knew that, however their haul was divvied up, it would be divvied up fairly.

'There's three motors standing by at the lock-up, Guv,' Tom called over his shoulder. 'I wouldn't fancy getting in any of them after you, though. If you don't mind me saying so, you all pong something rotten.'

This was the understatement of the year and by the time the van slid into the lock-up garage, they were all helpless with laughter again.

It was later, back at the casino, as he stripped out of his obscenely filthy, shit-and-mud-caked clothes, that the smile was wiped from Bryce's face.

His compass was no longer in his pocket.

He stood very still, stark bollock naked, his heart racing. He'd last had it in his hand immediately prior to tunnelling upwards to the floor of the vault. He certainly hadn't needed it after that. It could easily have fallen out in the sewer, when he and Gunter were hauling and pushing one of the bag-laden trollies through knee-deep muck. If it had fallen out then, it would never be found.

But what if it hadn't fallen out then? What if it had fallen out of his pocket when he'd been in the bank vault?

He remembered his mock fall of exhaustion, his half roll on the strong-room floor. Was that when the compass, thick with his fingerprints, had fallen out of his pocket?

His heart felt as if it had quite literally ceased to beat.

'Oh God,' he whispered, clenching his hands into fists, the knuckles white. 'Oh Christ. Oh *hell*!'

# Chapter Fifteen

When he rejoined Jack and Gunter, who were already showered and in tracksuits and busily at work in his office gleefully dividing the wads of old notes from the new, Bryce was once again coolly calm and in perfect control of himself.

He'd made a gaffe of stupendous proportions, but he was the only one who would, if the worst came to the worst, have to pay for it. No one else's fingerprints were on the compass. As a piece of evidence, he was the only person it could nail.

'It's wedge, Bry,' Gunter said, pausing in his task to flash him an ear-to-ear grin. 'It's nearly all fucking wedge!'

He was kneeling on the floor and he leaned back, resting his weight on his heels. 'The new is in the bags to the right, the old we're stacking to the left, in three equal piles. We can divvy up further when Curly and Georgie let us know what they want to do. I reckon they're going to want to stick with the jewellery. Curly said that, even at first glance, it looked to be a mammoth haul, and Curly likes the wheeling and dealing of fencing stones. It keeps his adrenaline high.'

Bryce squatted down on his haunches, his hands loosely clasped between his knees.

'Yeah, well, mine's still high and I wish to God it wasn't.'

At the flat, bitter tone in his voice they both instantly tensed.

'What's wrong?' Jack asked sharply. 'Have you had the radio on? Has there been a news bulletin?'

'Nah.' Bryce shook his head and a cowlick of dark hair fell over his forehead. 'I might . . . just might . . . have incriminated myself. My compass is missing. If it dropped from my pocket when we were in the tunnels there's a chance it might be now in the Thames. On the other hand . . .'

'Sweet Christ!' All Gunter's glee vanished. Jack's face, which had only slowly returned from being tunnel-induced ashen, was fast draining white again.

'. . . on the other hand,' Bryce continued, 'I could be well and truly shafted. If I am, and I'm pulled in, the rest of you will also be in the frame. As you're my known associates, you're bound to be.'

'So what do we do?'

The question came from Jack.

'We continue dividing the cash up – fast. Then when Curly and Georgie get here we seriously reconsider our plan of sitting tight.'

Three hours later a buzzer on Bryce's desk indicated by its tattoo that Curly and Georgie were at the door of the building.

'Christ, but Curly isn't going to be happy,' Gunter said as Bryce left the room to go down to the door. 'He was hoping to sit it out and to fence everything from London. It's not going to affect Georgie too much. Georgie's plan has always been to head out to Mallorca and live in the sun. All this means is that he'll be leaving sooner rather than later.'

'And you?'

Gunter shrugged. 'Canada, I think. And pretty damn quick. There's no use sitting around waiting to see if Bryce is collared or not, is there? If he is, the rest of us will be under the kind of surveillance that will make leaving the country impossible. Best to get out now, before the shit hits the fan.'

'Don't talk about shit . . .' Georgie entered the room, Curly and Bryce behind him. 'I've had three showers and I still feel as if I'm knee-deep in it.'

'We are if Bry's lost his compass in the bank vault.' Curly stood for a moment, gazing at the piles and piles of money stacked on the carpeted floor. He'd entered the building fisting the air in exultant triumph. Bryce's news had cut the moment short, as it had for everyone else. The timescale for the plans they had made now needed drastically speeding up and, as he was the only one of them, apart from Bryce, who had a legitimate business to wind up, he was going to be the most affected.

'The way I see it, is this . . .' Bryce half sat on the corner of his vast desk, a cigarette between his fingers. '. . . We've got another few hours – if we're lucky – before bank staff enter the vault. Once they start screaming blue murder – and once the CID is crawling all over the scene – the compass will either be found pretty quick or it won't be found at all. Now I know we said that if any of us disappeared immediately after such a job was pulled it would attract unwelcome attention and that it would be more sensible to sit tight, but the odds have shortened and I now think differently.'

He took a long, deep pull on his cigarette. 'I think all four of you should leave the country now, before morning. And that means, where the cash and contents of the security boxes are concerned, making a lot of very fast plans. The final divvying of the cash is going to be complicated because Curly and Georgie don't yet know the value of the security-box haul . . .'

'That isn't a problem for me and Georgie, Bry,' Curly said, speaking for both himself and his brother, as always. 'Leastways, not if what's worrying you is whether me and Georgie should be cut in on some of the cash. A few readies would be appreciated to tide us over until some fencing is done, but basically we're happy with the original division. The jewellery, bonds, etc, down to us. The cash, new and old, down to you and Gunter and Jack.'

Gunter's relief was palpable.

Jack was near indifferent. For him, the value of their haul was now of little interest. His concern was Bryce and what would happen to Bryce's cut and to his business interests, legitimate and not so legitimate, if he was collared and sent down. Someone would have to look after things for him and, as Jack knew nearly as much about the running of the clubs and casinos as Bryce did, it would have to be him – which meant he wouldn't be jaunting with the others out to Heathrow.

'Georgie is going to leave now, right this minute,' Curly continued, not even bothering to look in Georgie's direction. 'He has a hookey passport – we both have – neither of us were ever going to risk leaving any other way. He'll be in sunny Puerto Pollensa by the time anyone walks into the bank vaults. All he needs is enough cash to be able to open a beach bar and, until the hard stuff is sorted and fenced and I'm out there with him, he'll be as happy as the day is long.'

'So is that it?' Georgie asked, his gut straining beneath his winter anorak. 'Am I off and is this goodbye?'

'Yep,' Bryce said succinctly, glancing down at his watch as Jack handed Georgie a wad of notes thick enough to choke a pig. 'Scarper, mate.'

Georgie unzipped his anorak, stuffed the money inside it and zipped it up again. 'OK,' he said obligingly. 'See yer.'

'One down, four of us to go,' Gunter said as Georgie ambled from the room and the door slammed behind him. 'What are you going to do now, Curly? Go to ground whilst you sort things, or stash it to be fenced later? And if you're going to stash it, do you know where?'

'Do me a favour, mate. I ain't a bleedin' child. All my arrangements are already in hand. The only thing that's different about 'em is that I ain't going to hang around the pub.'

'Don't hang around here, either,' Bryce said, moving away from the desk and reaching for a couple of hefty wads. 'These will tide you over until you sort things. The less contact we all have with each other now, the better.'

'Yeah, well. Good luck, Bry.' Curly sought for the words to express how he felt about the rest of them having no real problems when Bryce was probably facing a barrow-load. 'Don't worry about me or Georgie – or the gear. It's as good as fenced already. Trust me.'

Bryce did. Curly was a very canny operator and he had implicit faith in his ability not to cock anything up. The only person so far, who had done that, was himself.

'I'm leaving with you,' Gunter said as Curly began walking towards the door. He picked up the bulky cricket bag crammed with his share of the divvy. 'My plans have been in place for weeks,' he said. 'Canada and a new life. I might even go straight from now on. If the shit doesn't hit the fan, I'll be in touch, Bryce. If it does, I'll lay low. Did you know Canada allows you to acquire a Canadian passport when you've been resident for three years? And Canada is a great back door into America. Perhaps you and Jack should follow me out there.'

'Yeah, well. We'll see how things pan out.' Bryce stubbed his cigarette out in a giant onyx ashtray and, as Curly and Gunter left the room, said to Jack, 'You too, mate. On your bike. Under the circumstances, it's the only sensible thing to do.'

Jack shot him a crooked smile. 'It's the only sensible thing for *you* to do – and while you're doing it, I'll look after things here. Don't fucking argue with me on this one, Bry. If you're collared, *someone* has to look after things till you're out and about again, and I don't like the idea of it being Frankie, do you?'

Their eyes held and there was a long, taut silence.

'No,' Bryce said at last, having speedily assessed a dozen alternatives only to reject every one of them. 'But do one thing for me now, straight away. Get your divvy out of here and get it stowed – and make sure it's stowed somewhere ultra-safe. If I find myself in the frame, the cozzers will know you were in it with me and they'll be over every drum you've ever had like locusts.'

'Will do.' He picked up two bulging sports bags. 'I'll be back in a few hours – early morning. Will you still be here?'

Bryce nodded. He had a mountain of money to stash away, and because of Boxing Day falling on a Sunday and Monday consequently being a Bank Holiday, his regular stash wouldn't be available to him until 9.30 a.m. on Tuesday. By then the robbery would have been discovered and, by not already having gone to ground, he'd be cutting things very fine indeed. He gave a shrug of his shoulders. It couldn't be helped. Years ago, he'd gone to a lot of trouble to find a perfect stow and not to use it, on this occasion, would be to run the risk of losing the bloody lot.

He remained in the room until his desk buzzer indicated that Jack had left the building and then he strolled into the small adjoining room that was kitted out as a shower-room. The only productive thing he could do, until Boxing Day dawned properly, was to have another go at soaping away the lingering scent of decaying shit.

He was on the settee in his office, deep in a sleep of utter exhaustion, when the buzzer went again. He flicked on the nearby standard lamp and glanced at his watch. It was four thirty. Certain that his caller was Jack, he pulled on a pair of Levi's and padded barefoot down the three flights of back stairs that led to the casino's service entrance.

'Jack?' he checked, his hand on the strong inner bolt.

'No, you lucky bastard.' Nina's voice was amused.

For a second he hesitated, but only for a second. He

would need to see Nina before he went to ground and so her showing up now was probably fortuitous – plus he had a day and a half to kill and he couldn't think of a better way of whiling away the time than of spending it with a nubile nymphomaniac.

He opened the door. She was lounging in its recess, buried deep in an ankle-length fur, a leather suitcase at her feet.

'Hello, lover,' she said in her cut-glass voice, moving forward and winding her arms round his neck. 'Barbados was the pits.' Her lips brushed his neck and then the corner of his mouth. 'All sun and sand. Daddy's on a bender of rum and dusky maidens and so I thought I'd do a runner. Do you want to fuck on the doorstep or wait until we get upstairs?'

Even though his naked chest was crushed against her fur, the icy air was piercingly biting. 'Upstairs, you silly bitch,' he said, slinging the suitcase inside and sliding his arm round her waist, hauling her across the doorstep after it. As she wound a colt-like, miniskirted leg through his, he slammed the bolt back on and re-secured the locks, reflecting that Nina's unexpected arrival was the perfect icing on the best Christmas cake of his life.

'Did you come here straight from the airport?' he asked as they went upstairs thigh to thigh and hip to hip, her hand already inside the top of his Levi's.

'Yep. I knew you'd be here – when are you ever anywhere else? You're wedded to the place.'

He thought of the Mafiosa he was in business negotiations with regarding its sale and wondered, if the dice fell the wrong way and he found himself serving a hefty prison sentence, if it might not be better to hand it over to Jack.

'So with no horse-racing on Christmas Day, what did you do?' she asked as they emerged on the private corridor that led to his office. 'Play a day-long game of poker?'

'No.' He pushed his office door open, knowing the

290

sight that would meet her eyes. 'But I did hit a lucky streak.'

The old notes were bagged and not in evidence but the new notes, the notes that were too dodgy for them to handle and that it had been agreed he would sell to a dealer for two shillings in the pound, were stacked in a pile six feet high.

'What the –' She came to an abrupt halt, sucking in her breath, her eyes wide.

He grinned, enjoying the sight of her being well and truly lost for words.

It was a moment that didn't last for long. 'So *that's* why you were so unconcerned when I said I would be spending Christmas in Barbados!'

She darted across to the immaculately neat tower of wadded notes. 'My God, Bryce! These are all wads of tens! How much is there altogether? A quarter of a million? More?'

She was being a little ambitious in her estimate, but as she ripped the band off one of the wads and whirled round, showering the notes confetti-like in the air, Bryce didn't care. The fizzing elation he'd felt, before concern over the compass had cut it abruptly short, came thundering back in great roaring waves. He'd masterminded and carried out a heist of mammoth proportions and, by Christ, he was going to begin enjoying the sensation!

As Nina flung her coat to the thickly carpeted floor he crossed to the fridge beside his desk, taking out two bottles of Louis Cristal and two champagne flutes.

'Can I tear open more?' she was asking, ripping open another wad even before he replied. 'I want to feel them on my skin, Bryce darling! I want to roll naked on them! I want to *fuck* on them!'

As the second wad went showering high in the air, she pulled her Mary Quant dress over her head and he poured bubbling champagne into the frosted glasses.

Whooping with glee, spilling far more of the champagne than they managed to drink, they rolled together on the carpeted floor, five-pound notes and ten-pound notes clinging to their skin.

The champagne was on her crimson-nippled breasts and flat, sun-kissed stomach. It was the best Louis Cristal he had ever tasted.

'Fuck me, lover,' she said unnecessarily as he unzipped his jeans and she lay beneath him, her long legs splayed, one hand knotted in the thick curling hair in the nape of his neck, the other clutching a fistful of champagne-soaked ten-pound notes. 'Fuck me beautifully, *earth-shatteringly* senseless!'

He had obliged spectacularly – and more than once. By the time the buzzer on his desk heralded the morning and Jack, he was beginning to wonder how the hell he could get through yet another day on so little sleep.

The minute Jack walked in the room and saw Nina, a tight, closed look shuttered his face. 'I thought you were in Barbados,' he said curtly, not hiding the fact that, like many of Bryce's friends, he didn't approve of her and wished to God Bryce was still with Rusty.

'You thought wrong,' she said, still stark naked and not caring an iota about being so, or about his opinion.

Bryce prodded an empty champagne bottle with his foot, sending it rolling across the carpet, threw her fur coat towards her and said, 'Get some shut-eye on the settee, sweetheart. Jack and me have a few things to discuss.'

As the office door clicked behind them and they began to walk along the corridor towards the stairs leading down to the still-deserted gaming-rooms, Jack said, 'Why didn't you tell her to leave? And why did you let her see the money? It looked like a bleedin' snow storm in there.'

What he was biting back from saying was: How the hell

could she be trusted enough to be left in the room with so much cash?

Knowing very well what Jack's main concern was, Bryce said easily, 'The only money still in the office is the two-shillings-in-the-pound stuff. If she wants to play with it, it's no big deal.'

In the main gaming-room they helped themselves to brandy from the bar and then sat down at one of the roulette tables.

'You've got your whack safely stowed?'

Jack nodded. Like Bryce, his plans had been in place for a long time. 'Yeah, sweet.' He ran a hand over his slick blond hair. 'There is a problem though, Bryce, and it isn't to do with our little bit of business – or not directly. I ran into Ginger on my way over here. He says Frankie's got the right hump. He says he's mouthing off to all and sundry that you don't treat him with proper respect – that you've become a liberty-taker. Ginger says Frankie's in an ugly mood and that you should watch your back.'

Bryce made a noncommittal noise in his throat. Where Frankie was concerned, he'd always watched his back. 'Don't worry your head about Frankie,' he said, knowing that one of Frankie's beefs with him was the certainty that major jobs were being planned and carried out and that he wasn't being called in on them.

It was a valid gripe, for it had been a long time now since he had wanted any real involvement with Frankie. Whenever he acted as a clean-hands operator, bankrolling heists for other gangs, raking off a percentage when the operation was successful, bearing the burden on the occasions when it wasn't, he never stipulated that Frankie be in on things.

Frankie was too uncontrollable and too gun-happy. Thanks to his disastrous pre-Christmas chat with Victor, he knew the Met had Frankie down for killing the copper – but he also knew there'd been other occasions when

Frankie's gun obsession had led to fatalities. The victims had all been fellow crims of the kind who hadn't been much missed – but that didn't make Frankie's psychotic instability any less dangerous.

As for his other gripe . . . Frankie was as nuts about women as he was about guns, and his jealousy about the women Bryce shacked up with was legendary. For years he'd been obsessed with Rusty – and still was. Now he was also obsessed with Nina.

'Frankie's the least of our problems,' he said. 'For now let's discuss how you're going to get some of your bank dosh into circulation.'

'Same way I've always done, I suppose.' Jack flashed his cheeky grin. 'I'll do it through the casino. There's no sudden problem, is there?'

'Nope.' Bryce grinned back. The casino was the best laundering service in the world. As its boss he was almost a banker. He cashed cheques, exchanged foreign currency, paid out large sums in cashier's cheques and gave credit. They'd never yet had trouble reducing the bulk of a haul; if it was all in small notes, they'd simply change them in the gaming-room for something bigger. Jack and the others would buy five hundred pounds' worth of chips, play for an hour or two, cash out and tell his bank manager they'd won fifteen thousand. If there was ever a query, he substantiated it for them. It was easy-peasy.

All he did himself was shove the cash in the till and make sure his accountant listed it in the profit column when filing his tax returns. Unless the amount was ultra-ridiculous – as it was at the moment – it couldn't be easier.

'I'm selling the new notes on tomorrow morning,' he said, reaching for the bottle of brandy in order to top up their glasses. 'You can have your third straight away if you like, or I'll stash it away with Gunter's third. What do you want to do?'

'Stash it.' Jack said equably, having enough to deal

with without having more. 'And now we've settled that, can we both get a bit of shut-eye? I'm absolutely knackered.'

So was Bryce and, even though it would mean taking Nina with him, like Jack, all he wanted to do was to head home and make up for all the sleep he'd lost.

Despite telephone calls from Georgie, Sir William Denster and Big Chas, he managed to do so – just.

Georgie's phone call had been from Puerto Pollensa – though knowing that phones could be tapped, Georgie had said only that he'd arrived at his intended destination and everything was hunky-dory.

Nina's father's telephone call hadn't been an anxious one enquiring as to her whereabouts but a request for funds. He was staying at Barbados's exclusive Sandy Lane Hotel and finding it, and the company he was keeping there, 'a trifle expensive. An advance on my next quarter's directorship fee would be much appreciated, dear boy,' he said.

Big Chas's phone call had been a shade more worrying. He'd heard a whisper that a big tickle was in the offing and had wanted to know whether or not the rumour was true and, if it was, why had no Briscoes been called in on it?

Bryce had smoothed him over saying that there was no big tickle being arranged – which, as the tickle had already been pulled, was perfectly true. He'd been left with a problem, though. Had Chas simply been playing a hunch, or had someone been unable to keep their mouth shut? Jack, Gunter, Curly and Georgie wouldn't have blabbed, but one of the miners, or the sewer ganger, might have been unable to resist sounding big in the presence of a bloke like Chas – and if they had, it meant they'd be bound to grass if pulled in by the police.

On Monday evening he met with the nameless man who,

paying two shillings in the pound for the privilege, took all the new notes off his hands.

On Tuesday morning, leaving Nina asleep in bed, he loaded two large and bulky tin trunks into his car and, wearing a dark pinstriped suit, drove off in the direction of the City, his nerves tense.

So far there had still been no news reports of the robbery, but it was a silence that couldn't last for much longer and, once the news broke, he'd soon know whether or not his compass had fallen from his pocket in the vault.

He glanced at his Rolex. All his plans for leaving the country were in place and in three hours' time he'd be on a plane flying out to the sun. The first thing he had to do was to stow the bulk of the cash; the second was to say goodbye to Tricia.

He turned out of the Strand into the Aldwych and felt the jolt he had long been expecting beneath his breastbone. The news was out, plastered all over news-stand bulletin boards: '*Mammoth haul for sewer-rats!*' '*Robbers' Christmas Day Bonanza!*'

With difficulty he kept his speed down, turning left into Chancery Lane which was, as always at that time in the morning, crammed with briefcase-carrying, pinstripe-suited solicitors and barristers all making their way to their offices and chambers.

Unhurriedly, he slipped on a pair of horn-rimmed glasses and parked. Seconds later he was off-loading the trunks on to the pavement and then, cumbersomely, into the entrance foyer of a large building housing a great many barristers' chambers.

'Keep an eye on these for me, will you, Martin?' he said to the young man on duty in the small reception room. 'I'll be back in a jiffy.'

'Yes, Mr Malling, sir,' the young man said obligingly. 'Will do.'

Bryce returned to his car, slid behind the wheel and three

minutes later was parking it in a nearby underground car park. Another two minutes and he was back outside the building again, this time remaining on the pavement. He flagged down a black taxi-cab and, with the help of the cabbie and the obliging Martin, he ferried the trunks he had left in the foyer out across the pavement again and into the cab.

'Temple Court West, Cabbie,' he said, tipping Malcolm and stepping into the rear of the cab.

'Right you are, sir.' The cabbie pulled out into heavy traffic. 'Tedious amount of paperwork you've got there, sir. I took three trunks full of legal documents down to the Temple vaults a day or so ago for Mr Carnham. Gawd knows when they'll see the light of day again. Never, I expect!'

He turned left into Fleet Street and Bryce smiled wryly, saying in an accent imitative of Nina's father's: 'That nothing must ever be destroyed is a cardinal rule in the legal profession, Cabbie. What I'm now putting into storage may prove very useful to me some day.'

'I don't believe that for one moment, sir,' the cabbie said, chortling. 'If I was you, I'd put a match to the lot!'

As the cabbie passed the scene of the newspaper wages heist, taking a right-hand turn out of Fleet Street into the warren of narrow cobbled streets that ran down towards the Victoria Embankment, Bryce fought back a crack of laughter.

The cabbie was oblivious. 'Here we are, sir,' he said, coming to a halt outside a building of age-blackened Victorian grandeur. 'I don't envy you heaving this little lot into a storage vault.' He opened the rear door. 'Paper weighs a ton, don't it? It's enough to break your bleedin' back. Do you want me to wait, sir?'

Bryce hesitated. He was crucifyingly short on time and very tempted. He didn't, however, want to push his luck by once again having to go through the Mr Malling routine at the Chancery Lane chambers.

For weeks past he had entered the building's foyer and ridden up and down in the antiquated lift that lay beyond it, making sure each time that young Martin assumed him to be a visiting silk who had business with one of the barristers resident in the building.

So far the ruse had worked perfectly. Martin had come to recognise and accept him, and hadn't thought it at all odd that he had temporarily off-loaded legal document storage trunks in the foyer.

Black taxi-cabs were accustomed to ferrying barristers and their trunks of legal documentation to and fro, so the cabbie hadn't given a second thought to either him or the trunks. Which was exactly the way he wanted it.

Deciding to play it ultra-safe and stick to his original plan of walking away from the building and then picking up a second cab in Fleet Street, he said easily, 'No thanks, Cabbie. I have some paperwork to check up on whilst I'm here and it may take some time.'

In actual fact, his business at the archive vault took just under ten minutes. Once inside the building he was courteously greeted as Mr Malling and given help loading his bags on to a trolley. Then, unescorted, he descended with them in a lift to a musty-smelling basement that was devoted entirely to large private storage vaults. A short walk down a canyon-like corridor brought him to a vault bearing the name Malling, QC and, using the key he had been provided with when he'd first rented the vault, he opened it up and wheeled his cargo inside.

Minutes later he off-loaded the trunks and took a slim packet from his breast pocket. The packet contained a passport, driving licence, medical card, several credit cards and a birth certificate, all in the name of Malling. He

298

slipped the packet into one of the trunks, gave the rest of the contents of the vault a quick check and then re-locked the door and returned the trolley to the ground floor.

Ten minutes later he was walking in chill December sunshine towards Middle Temple Lane's junction with Fleet Street. Twenty-five minutes later, at eleven o'clock, he was again behind the wheel of his car, heading out of the City towards Blackfriars Bridge.

The shrill ringing of the bedside phone woke Nina a minute or so after eleven.

'Bryce?' a male voice said urgently. 'They're on to you. Get the hell out *now*!'

The line clicked and went dead.

Totally unconcerned, Nina sleepily replaced the receiver. Bryce's world was one in which people were always on each other's tails for something or the other. If a disgruntled punter was wanting to take it out on him for having lost a fortune in Bryce's casino, Bryce would be able to handle him. She wondered if Jack had been the unknown voice delivering the tip-off. It hadn't sounded like Jack. Not caring who it had been, she closed her eyes and drifted back to dreamland.

A half-mile or so away, in a telephone box not far from Scotland Yard, Victor swore savagely, his hands clenched into fists. How could Bryce have been so carelessly, so *unforgivably* stupid? It had taken no time at all for the prints on the compass found in the bank vault to be matched with those of Bryce Reece, a man who had served time for manslaughter and who, since his release, had long been suspected of leading a host of bank and security-van robberies, and masterminding many more.

'Jesus!' he said, pushing the telephone-box door open and sprinting back to where his men were waiting to take

299

instructions from him regarding Bryce's arrest, aware he was now in the middle of the nightmare he had long dreaded. 'Jesus! Jesus! *Jesus*!'

Bryce took the familiar route from the south side of Blackfriars Bridge through Southwark and towards Deptford. There'd been no earthly reason why Rusty should have returned to her old home. He'd offered to pay the rent on a Mayfair flat, or even a house, but Rusty had been pig-headedly adamant. She'd finished living off his money, she had said, and she was never going to live off it again. The fact that she earned high amounts herself had cut no ice either. 'Deptford is where me and Tricia feel at home,' she had flared, green cat-eyes flashing fire. 'And where we live is our business, not yours! How is your teenage nympho mistress, by the way? Has she started robbing you blind yet? Christ, but you make me sick, Bryce! We had it all going for us! Everything! And you threw it away for a schoolgirl rich bitch who doesn't give a damn about you!'

Even just remembering the confrontation had him clenching his teeth so hard that his jaw hurt.

He veered out of Jamaica Road, turning right. The worst part of such scenes was that they invariably took place in front of Tricia. He clenched his jaw even harder. Tricia was a little sweetheart and whenever an ugly scene between him and Rusty resulted in Tricia crying her eyes out, he felt the greatest brute alive. He overtook a Ford Consul, turned left and then right and then right again into Lee Gardens, wondering how on earth he was going to break the news to her that he was going away.

Hopefully, of course, he wouldn't be away for long. If the cozzers weren't on his tail within the next few days, they never would be, no matter what suspicions about him they might harbour. On the other hand . . . He slid the car close to the kerb and switched off the engine. On the other hand, if the compass was found and a full-scale search for him was mounted, he wouldn't be in Lee Gardens again for a long, long time.

Grim-faced, he strode to the front door and knocked once, loudly.

At the speed at which it was opened, he knew Rusty had seen his car pull up.

'Yes?' she spat as she opened the door, her flame-red hair piled high on her head, a white towelling bath-robe wrapped tightly around her magnificent body. 'I work nights, remember? This is the crack of dawn for me. Just what the hell do you want?'

'I want to see Tricia.' Brusquely he strode past her, taking the steps to the maisonette two at a time. 'It's still the Christmas holidays, isn't it?' he said as she began running up the stairs behind him. 'She's here, isn't she?'

'Yes, she's here, but it's not a Saturday and the arrangement is that you only take her out on Saturdays . . .'

'Tricia!' he called, pushing open the glass door that led into the open-plan sitting-room, knowing he hadn't time to get involved in a row, wishing to God Rusty would, for once, just cool it.

'Daddy-Bryce!' Tricia trilled, coming down the stairs that led to the sitting-room from the bedrooms as fast as her arthritically afflicted legs would allow her to. 'Daddy-Bryce! You're here and it's not a Saturday! Thank you for all my Christmas presents! Thank you for the –'

He didn't give her the chance to go into a long list. He simply put his arms round her and lifted her high in the air, swinging her around. 'Did you have a good Christmas, Trish?' he asked, his throat tightening at the thought of how upset she was going to be in another few minutes time. 'Did you go to a pantomime . . . ?'

'Why are you here, Bryce?' Rusty's voice cut across his, sharp with tension. 'It's not because you're about to do a disappearing act, is it?'

He set Tricia unsteadily back on her feet. 'Three hundred years ago you'd have been burnt as a witch,' he said tightly, his eyes meeting hers. 'How the fuck did you guess?'

'Because the radio's been on all morning and I listen to the news.' Her outraged aggression was now naked concern. 'Were you in on the raid that took place over Christmas? Is that why you didn't see Tricia Christmas Eve or Christmas Day? Is it why you're here now? Because you have to do a runner?'

'Yes to all four questions, but could you be careful what you say?' His arm was around Tricia's shoulders. 'I don't want to be the chief topic of conversation in the school playground.'

'But, Bryce, the amount was huge! Gi-normous! If you're swagged in for it you'll go down for years and years and years!' The blood had drained from her face. 'Think of the sentences the Great Train Robbers got! Thirty years each. *Thirty years*!'

'I don't really need this, Rusty,' he said, for once almost grateful that Tricia was too mentally slow to realise the real gist of what was being said. 'I just want to say goodbye to Tricia and . . .'

They both heard the police sirens at exactly the same time.

'Oh God!' As Bryce stepped swiftly away from Tricia and towards the corner of the window, Rusty's face was as white as a sheet. 'They're not coming here, are they? They can't be! How would they know you'd be here? How . . . ?'

An entire squad of cars screeched into Lee Gardens.

From his first-storey vantage-point, screened by the curtain, Bryce remained immobile whilst his brain screamed into gear, considering and then rejecting plan after plan of action.

He wasn't armed and, even if he had been, he couldn't

become embroiled in a shoot-out with Tricia and Rusty in the house. He wasn't in a block of flats. In high-rise flats it would take the cozzers several minutes to charge up the stairs and, whilst they were doing so, he might have been able to have put a waste chute or central-heating duct to good use.

As the cozzers spilled out of the half-dozen police cars and neighbours the length and breadth of Lee Gardens rushed to their doors and windows for a look-see, he sucked in his breath, his top lip flattening against his teeth. Christ, but there were enough cozzers to take a beach-head! Dressed to kill in flak jackets, guns clearly in evidence, bloody great Alsatians at their heels, they were racing towards the maisonette, their car doors open behind them, their sirens still wailing.

Vaguely he was aware of Rusty screaming and yanking Tricia protectively into a corner as far distant from the glass door at the top of the stairs as she could get.

In the pocket of his pinstriped trousers his fingers closed around the storage-vault key. They were going to take him – there was no way, in the circumstances, that they could fail to. They weren't going to get their hands on the cash, though. The cash wasn't just his. There was a huge wodge of Jack's divvy amongst it, plus Gunter's divvy from the sale of the new notes.

As the front door was broken in and heavily booted feet began charging up the stairs, he lifted a corner of the curtains. They had once belonged to Rusty's mother and, though they were made of uninspiring brown velvet, they had hung in his bedroom in Curzon Street because Rusty insisted on taking them with her wherever she went.

'*Freeze*!' A half-dozen voices shouted in near unison as the safety-glass door was punched open with such force that the glass cracked. '*We're armed police officers. We have a warrant for your arrest! Stay where you are!*'

He shrugged and faced them, letting the curtain fall back

303

into place. 'So what's with all the hardwear?' he asked with negligent insolence as he was leapt on by half a dozen of the Met's finest and his arms were wrenched behind his back, his wrists locked in a pair of handcuffs. 'What did you think you were going to find? A commando unit?'

If anyone replied to him he couldn't hear it above the din. Every copper in the room was either yelling at him, at each other, or into a mobile radio. Rusty was screaming the most filthy kind of abuse possible – presumably at them and not at him. Tricia was sobbing hysterically, terrified out of her mind.

Wanting for Tricia's sake to bring the grotesque scene to a halt as speedily as possible, he made no attempt to struggle as, with unnecessary force, he was manhandled towards the maisonette's access stairs.

'Daddy-Bryce!' Tricia shouted as, surrounded on all sides, he was half pushed and half pulled down the stairs. 'Daddy-Bryce! *Daddy-Bryce!*'

It was a moment of unimaginable hideousness – and then came one even worse.

'We're bringing him in, Guv,' he heard the driver of the car say over his radio as he was bundled ignominiously into it, armed coppers hurtling in on either side of him.

'OK, Tango Two,' a voice replied tersely as all around them police-car engines began to rev, 'over and out.'

The voice had been devoid of an accent and bereft of all emotion, but it was one Bryce would have recognised anywhere.

Victor was the DCI in charge and the man who had nailed him. Victor, who could have given him the nod and who hadn't done so. Victor, who had been his best friend ever since he could remember and who was a friend no longer.

As the car careened out of Lee Gardens, the centre of a siren-wailing convoy, Bryce clenched his teeth. Victor wouldn't have the satisfaction of nailing any other old friends. Georgie, Curly, Gunter and Jack were either clear away or, where evidence was concerned, untouchable. The money was untouchable, too. No matter how many years he went down for, it would be waiting for him when he came out.

He bared his teeth in a rictus grin.

Where he and Victor were concerned, he was going to have the last laugh, for even if Victor lived to be a hundred he'd never have the kudos of finding the money and returning it to the bank. Never. No way. No how.

# Chapter Sixteen

*September 1966*

He lay on his back on the narrow metal bed, his hands behind his head. In a little over an hour it would be visiting time and he was expecting Frankie. It wasn't a hell of a lot to look forward to, but it was better than nothing.

The cell he was in was indistinguishable from the cells he had been incarcerated in when serving time for Roy Clarkson's manslaughter. There were the same cream-painted walls; the same sparse furnishings: a bed, wash-stand, table and chair; the same small, barred window. The only difference was that instead of a photograph of Sandra being pinned next to the one of his mum and dad, there was a photo of Tricia.

He stared at the small patch of sky visible beyond the bars, wondering what news Frankie would have for him – wondering if he cared. All he could think about was his sentence. Twenty-one years. *Twenty-one fucking years.* And all he'd done was rob a bank, without hurting a fly in the process.

From the moment of his arrest there had been no doubt that he was going to go down. The CID had too many other jobs with his name on them to screw up now they'd finally got some evidence with which to nail him. The compass had been his Nemesis – helped for good measure by the late-night Christmas reveller who had caught a glimpse of him when he'd ducked into the van's cab to reach for Jack's cigarettes.

The reveller had proved to be a small-time punter who

had played the tables in his clubs and casino. Not a member of the criminal fraternity and seemingly unaware that there was a God-given command 'Thou shalt not grass', he had trotted forward of his own volition to state that he'd seen and recognised Bryce Reece on the night of 24 December, in a van parked over the manhole which had served as the Al-Bakara Bank robbers' point of entry.

Considering how dark it had been, his evidence, if it had stood alone, could have been discredited – but it hadn't stood alone. There had been the compass, found in the vault and thick with his fingerprints, and that had decisively done for him.

His eyes narrowed as he continued lying on his bed, re-living the weeks that had led up to his trial. At least no other charges had been laid against him – though it hadn't been for the want of trying.

'We know you've been bankrolling jobs for years,' Victor had said at one of their tediously long, agonisingly tense interviews. 'And you're the only name on the sheets for the newspaper wages heist in '61.'

'Prove it,' he had said, his eyes as hard as granite.

Every word had been noted, of course. Victor had never seen him, even for a second, without having everything recorded. And there had always been other coppers in the room with them.

Nothing personal had been said between the two of them, not even anything personally abusive. Neither of them had revealed by so much as a look or a gesture the history they shared.

As his known associates, Jack and Curly had both been pulled in and questioned, and there had been long, hard, abortive searches for Gunter and Georgie. Jack's girlfriends had done their stuff, two of them stating he was with them for a three-in-a-bed romp over the entire period in question.

A whole gamut of drinkers at The Spinners had vowed

that Curly was doing his stuff as a landlord on the night of the twenty-fourth and that he was the host of a private party that went on into the early hours of Christmas Day. Victor's men had arrested Curly when he'd been walking the pub's guard dog down the Old Kent Road. The dog had been taken with him to London Bridge police station and it was there, after sixteen hours of fruitless questioning, that Curly had said memorably, 'You can't keep my dog here any longer. Either charge him or let him go.'

Afterwards, when Victor had had no option but to release him, the tale had gone round every pub in south-east London, making Victor a laughing stock.

Then there'd been the trial.

Bryce reached in his denim shirt pocket for a roll-up. When his trial had opened Rusty had been in the public gallery and she'd continued to put in an appearance every day, much to the glee of the press boys who had salivated over her figure-hugging, miniskirted outfits.

Nina – perhaps fortunately – had been back at her Swiss finishing school. She hadn't written to him and, even now, he didn't want to remember how he'd felt about that. Other people had written to him, though. He'd received letters from people he'd known when he'd been a kid; letters from the regular punters at his clubs and the casino. One letter, given to him by Jack when he'd still been on remand, had taken him completely by surprise.

'It comes with a packet of sweeties,' Jack had said, obviously amused. 'I know you've got yourself a repu-tation as a bit of a cradle-snatcher, but don't you think a ten-year-old is going it a bit, even for you?'

The card had been from Debbie.

'*I know you've been bad and stole a lot of money 'cos I read it in the paper,*' she had written in unnervingly confident joined-up writing.

*My mum says you shud have been hanged years
ago but wont tell me why. I am eleven this year
and I have to go to a new school. I dont want to
go to it. I want to go to a stage school to learn to
be an aktress.*

*Debbie*

*PS Mrs Briscoe says you probly did stole the
money but that unlike a lot of people she could
menshon you're a ray of sunshine and shes going
to miss you. So am I.*

'Evelyn brought it round to my flat the other night,' Jack
had said to him as his throat had tightened. 'Let's hope it
brings you luck, eh?'

It hadn't.

After a two-week trial, with the final speeches made,
the jury had retired. The ensuing wait had been ominously
short. Within two hours he had been recalled from his cell
beneath the courtroom.

The Clerk of the Court had faced the foreman of the
jury and asked if a verdict had been reached.

The foreman had replied that it had and then, keeping
his eyes firmly averted from the dock, had said: 'Guilty.'

Though it had been hard not to, he hadn't flinched. It
was, after all, the verdict he had been expecting.

What he hadn't been expecting, though, was the sav-
agery of the judge's remarks – or the barbarity of his
sentencing.

'Bryce Joseph Reece, you played for high stakes and you
have lost,' the judge had said, directing his glasses and gaze
towards him. 'You have been convicted of a crime of gross
impudence and enormity and I propose to do all within
my power to ensure it will be your last crime, for your
outrageous conduct constitutes an intolerable menace to
the well-being of society.'

Somewhere in the public gallery a woman had begun crying and, though he hadn't turned his head to look, he'd known that it wasn't Rusty. Rusty wasn't a crier. Sandra was, though. He'd clenched his handcuffed hands, wondering how long she had been in the courtroom.

'When a grave crime is committed it calls for grave punishment,' the judge had continued, ignoring the disturbance. 'Not for the purpose of mere retribution, but so that others similarly tempted shall be brought to the sharp realisation that crime does not pay and that crime is most certainly not worth even the most alluring candle.'

He had been acutely aware of Victor's presence. All through the two weeks of the trial they had scrupulously avoided making eye contact with each other. Now, as the judge reached the point they had all been waiting for, Victor's head was bent low and his hands were clasped between his knees.

Incredibly, considering how tense the moment had been, he'd felt a surge of triumph. Victor had got nothing from him. Nothing. Victor might have been certain enough that Jack, Gunter, Curly and Georgie had been with him on the robbery for him to have gambled his life on it, but he hadn't got an admission of that from Bryce – and neither had he a clue as to where the stolen millions were.

'I therefore,' the judge had continued, 'find myself faced with an unenviable task.'

It had been a moment that had seemed to last an eternity.

'Bryce Joseph Reece, you have been convicted of robbery. The consequence of this crime is that the vast booty remains entirely unrecovered. It would be an affront to the public if you should be at liberty in anything like the near future to enjoy your ill-gotten gains. I therefore sentence you to go to prison for a period of twenty-one years.'

He'd heard a concerted intake of breath from both sides of the courtroom; an agonised cry of disbelief that he knew had come from Rusty. A dazed shout of, *'You're off your rocker!'* from Jack, who had been on his feet, uncaring of the court ushers sprinting towards him. *'He robbed a bank, you old fool!'* Jack had continued to shout, as they had seized him. *'He didn't kill anyone!'*

As he'd been hustled from the dock he'd flashed a last look towards the public gallery. If Sandra was still there, he hadn't seen her. He'd seen only Rusty, a shocking-pink miniskirt skimming her bottom, a white silk blouse displaying her quality cleavage, her torrent of fiery hair framing a face drained white.

He had flashed her a wink and given Jack a shrug of his shoulders. Then he had turned and, outwardly cool and composed, stepped from the dock, the words 'twenty-one years' beating in his ears like waves on a beach.

He lit his roll-up, inhaling deeply.

Twenty-one years. *Twenty-one years.* Even with parole, he was looking at fourteen years. He would be forty-five when he came out. He couldn't imagine being forty-five. Forty-five was old. Forty-five was a lifetime away.

How he'd remained so outwardly unperturbed as he'd been driven under police escort from the court to the special unit in Brixton to await transfer to Parkhurst, he still didn't know. He remembered, though, what his first concern had been.

It had been for Tricia.

Tricia was going to miss him like hell. Even though he and Rusty had no longer been living together, he'd continued to be a very caring step-dad. Aware of Tricia's special needs, he'd always given her a lot of his time. Coming to grips with the knowledge that he would only now see her if Rusty received permission for Tricia to visit him in prison, had made him feel sick to the pit of his stomach.

It still did. He swung his legs off the bed and crushed the roll-up out in the sweetie-tin lid that served him as an ashtray. There'd been other grim realities to come to terms with. One of them had been the knowledge that he was leaving Jack in a very tricky situation. Rightly or wrongly, he'd decided not to sell out to the Americans, but to hand over all his business interests for Jack to run. He knew that Jack could do it, of course. Jack had been in on the running of the clubs and casino right from the very beginning and it wasn't Jack's business ability that had worried him. It was Frankie, and whether Jack was going to be able to cope with him.

And then there was the sex situation. When he asked himself how, in the name of God, he was going to do without sex for the next fourteen years, he would break out in a cold sweat. His six years celibacy while serving time for Roy Clarkson's manslaughter had been bad enough, but at least then there had been an end in sight. This time the end was so far away as to seem non-existent.

Thinking about sex made him think about Nina. He didn't have a clue as to whether she would hop a ferry and visit him when she returned, finally and for good, from Switzerland. Even if she did, he was pretty sure it would be a one-off novelty visit and not the beginning of a long-standing routine. Nina playing the part of a loyal girlfriend, waiting patiently through the years for his release, was too bizarre an image even for him. After all, when he'd been imprisoned before Sandra hadn't waited for him – and if Sandra hadn't waited, no one would.

'So 'ow's it going, old cock?'

Frankie was the only person Bryce knew who seemed to relish prison visiting conditions – not that the conditions were as hard to cope with as they'd been his last time round. The barbaric glass partitions were a thing of the past and kiddies were charging around between the various tables as if in a playground.

'Surviving,' he said drily. 'Just.'

Frankie cracked with laughter, sprawling his huge form across the hard chair as if it were a sofa. 'You've copped for it well and truly, Brycie-boy, ain't you? How the hell could you gamble for such high stakes and come a cropper over something as naff as leavin' your calling-card on the bank floor? I hate to say it, old son, but your leavin' that compass behind beggars fuckin' belief.'

'Yeah. Right. I don't need you to tell me that,' he said, unamused, knowing Frankie wouldn't have made the trip across the Solent out of the goodness of his heart and waiting for him to get to the real reason for his visit.

He didn't have long to wait.

A warder standing nearby moved away, continuing his patrol of the room, and Frankie said, lowering his voice: 'You should 'ave sold to the Eyetie-Americans when they wanted you to, Bryce, not handed things over for Jack to run. He just ain't up to it, know what I mean?'

Behind the chummy friendliness his eyes were hungrily speculative. Bryce knew exactly what he meant. The proposition now coming his way was one he'd been expecting for quite some time.

'Yeah?' he said, wondering just how he was going to deal with it.

'Yeah.' Frankie grinned, showing his cracked front tooth. 'Now, wiv me it would be different.' He leaned forward as far as was possible without a screw's attention being attracted. 'I got friends, Brycie-boy. Big friends. They thought they had a deal wiv you and you went and let 'em down. Americans don't take easily to being let down – especially not when they speak Italian. They want to fly in big organised gambling parties and they want to use an up-and-running casino they've got a stake in and that they know will stay free of aggro.'

He paused as a warder once again came within earshot.

'And so how is Auntie Evelyn?' Bryce asked. 'Still got back trouble, has she?'

Frankie, never quick on the uptake, blinked and then, cottoning on, said, 'Yeah. She's suffering somefink terrible wiv it. I reckon she should see an osteo-whatever, but you know what she's like, Bryce. Stubborn as a mule.'

The screw resumed his patrol of the room.

'My friends are trusting me to keep everything sweet this end,' Frankie continued, keeping his voice low and trying to look as casual as if he was still talking about his mother. 'If we had the use of your clubs and casinos, we could operate smooth as silk, no problem, and you'd 'ave a nice little nest-egg to look forward to when you get released.'

'I already have,' Bryce said wryly, knowing that Frankie would sell his soul to learn where the missing bank money was stashed and unable to resist the opportunity of teasing and tormenting him.

The cast in Frankie's eye became so pronounced he looked almost cross-eyed. 'Yeah . . . well . . . that's another thing we need to talk about, Brycie,' he said, rising to the bait in a manner that gave Bryce the most pleasure he'd had for a long time. 'Yer must 'ave worries there and I can sort 'em for you.'

He had looked over his shoulder to check on the where-abouts of the warders. 'It's not as if you an' me are simply mates, is it?' he continued, having ascertained that they were all at a safe distance. 'Ever since you moved in wiv my family when you was a kid, we've been like brothers. If yer can't trust me, who can yer trust?'

With great difficulty Bryce managed not to burst into laughter. 'Who indeed, Frankie?' he said, wishing Jack was with him to enjoy the fun.

The bell signalling the end of visiting time brought the entertainment to a sharp conclusion.

As he returned to his landing, his amusement died. For all his guff to the contrary, Frankie didn't give a stuff about friendship, or even family. He'd been daggers drawn with Ginger and Terry for yonks, and he regularly bad-mouthed Jimmy and Big Chas. If he wanted the casino, he wouldn't let old childhood ties stand in his way.

He walked into his cell, tension building in his neck and shoulder muscles, knowing the situation was one he should have anticipated way back. Even at the time of his trial there'd been rumours that, via the Krays, Frankie had established links with New York's top Mafiosi. He'd certainly become big-time – and seriously dangerous.

If Frankie was out to make trouble, Jack was facing a problem – and with Curly now in Majorca with Georgie, and Gunter in Canada – he was facing it alone.

He bunched his fists, his sense of impotence total. Jack had become like a kid brother to him – the kid brother he'd never had – and the only good he could now be to him was to warn him to mind his back.

'Frankie pulled a box out and began sharing out enough weapons to start a war,' Jack's informant said to him as they walked through Deptford's crowded street market. 'Swords. Knives. You name it, 'e 'ad it. 'E threw a sawn-off shotgun in my direction. "Tuck it in your coat," 'e said, "and leave the safety on till we get there. It's already loaded." Christ, but I nearly shat myself. I'm a thief, Jack. You know that. I ain't a bleedin' gangster.'

Jack side-stepped a box of lettuces. 'And all this was to put the frighteners on a North London mob who were getting a bit stroppy?'

'Yeah. And it worked. Well, it would do, wouldn't it? You want to give 'im a wide berth, Jack. 'E's a nutter. 'E's run with Ronnie Kray so long 'e's become just like 'im.'

Later, alone in Bryce's private suite of rooms above the casino, Jack stood at one of the giant windows looking out towards the distant greenery of Hyde Park, a tumbler of Jack Daniels in his hand.

Frankie had already begun leaning on him and, though it was done with a certain amount of 'old pals' tripe, it wasn't a pleasant sensation. He swirled the ice-cubes round in his glass meditatively. For one thing, he and Frankie had never been old pals. It had been Frankie and Bryce who had had a brother-like relationship – or at least, that was the way it had seemed when Bryce had moved in with Frankie's family as a kid.

Frankie certainly thought he was the one who should have been given control of Bryce's business interests – and it was quite obvious that he was eventually going to try and take what hadn't been freely given.

He took a deep swallow of his bourbon. The clubs and the casino weren't the only thing Frankie had his gimlet cross-eyes on. The whereabouts of Bryce's stash from the Al-Bakara job was a mystery tormenting the hell out of him, and Jack knew damn well that Frankie thought it was a mystery he held the key to.

What was going to happen when Frankie got tired of the old pals façade and pulled the gloves off? He'd been on the scene long enough to be able to call on a lot of people to back him up if he was ever in a tight corner, but heavy though the mob he'd be able to assemble was, they weren't loyal-to-the-death mates like Gunter and Curly and Georgie. And Bryce. He took another swallow of bourbon. If Bryce were at his side, he wouldn't give a shit about anything.

He rolled the ice-cold tumbler against his cheekbone. How the fuck was he going to manage the next fourteen years – more, if parole wasn't forthcoming – without Bryce? And how the fuck was Bryce going to endure fourteen years or more in the slammer?

The mere thought sent a roar of pain through his head. Bryce would, of course, have the advantage of being a celebrity – and in prison that was always a big help. He was a premier-league thief. The Al-Bakara job had been the biggest of the decade and he'd been the only one to go down for it. Everyone he'd taken in on it had got away scot-free.

There was also the gossip-column status he enjoyed as a club and casino owner. And last, but by no means least, there was his high-gloss reputation as a 'clean-hands operator'. At some time or another he'd arranged jobs for most of Parkhurst's inmates, though not the jobs they'd been nicked on. It had been rare for anyone to be nicked on a Reece-arranged job and, the few times anyone had been, it had always been because of their own stupidity and not through a fault in the planning.

Bryce would hack his time, just as he'd hacked it when he'd served his sentence for killing Roy Clarkson. He was already kingpin where the gambling scene was concerned. Gambling was, after all, Bryce's métier – and there was no higher status in a prison than to be the openly acknowledged gambling boss.

He turned away from the window, his glass empty. He had a business to run; Bryce's business. And though he'd need to keep Bryce informed of Frankie's activities – and of Frankie's friends' activities – he wasn't going to burden him with any personal worries. He'd deal with those by himself.


'So the lie of the land is that, though the Richardsons are now away, the Krays' war against everyone who ran with them is still continuing,' Jack said, next time he visited Bryce. 'Which means the situation between Frankie, Ginger and Terry is well tricky.'

Bryce ran a hand over his close-cropped hair. The Richardson brothers had finally been put away after a fatal shoot-out involving themselves and most of their top men, in a club in Catford. The Krays hadn't been directly involved, but the man who had died had been a Kray ally. Unlike previous shooting incidents, there'd been arrests and, with the Richardsons now away for what was obviously going to be a substantial time, the Richardson–Kray war had seemed to be over.

'Some of the Richardsons' henchmen went loco in Bethnal Green ten nights ago,' Jack continued, his voice carefully low. 'They fired shots from a car into a pub regularly used by Ron and Reggie. The Twins – and Frankie – had just left it. Then last week a car mowed down a bloke who looked like Ronnie. There's ructions on in Swan Row too. Eddie Briscoe reckons Frankie is gunning for Ginger and Terry. Jug Ears believes that Ginger and Terry fired the shots in the pub. The whole bloody family is walking around in bullet-proof vests, and takings at the casino are down because everyone knows it's a Briscoe haunt.'

He'd known, of course, that Bryce wouldn't give a flying fuck about the casino takings – and he hadn't. Like himself, all he'd been worried about was what the outcome and knock-on effect would be if Frankie finally went completely loco.

All the way back across the Solent and on the drive from Portsmouth to London, Jack had pondered what the chances were of a head-on fatal clash between Frankie and Ginger, or Frankie and Terry. One thing was for sure, if Frankie did for either of them, his own chances would be much grimmer. Killing a childhood mate, especially one who had never fallen into the blood-brother category, would be a piece of cake after killing a cousin.

'There's a young lady waiting for you in your office,' a newly appointed male croupier said to him as he strode through the main gaming-room. 'She said she was a girl-friend.'

Jack sucked in his breath. He had girlfriends by the barrowload, but none of them would have had the temerity to assume they could wait for him in his office. Without wasting time on giving the croupier the bollocking he deserved, he quickened his pace towards the lift that connected solely with the private rooms on the casino's top floor.

She was sprawled on a white leather sofa, wearing a gold-on-black high-throated brocade poncho over skin-tight black jersey pants. Her sun-kissed feet were bare, her toenails painted the same blood red as her crocodile-wide mouth.

'Hiya, Jack,' she said negligently, not moving off her back as he let the door slam behind him. 'Long time no see.'

Her raven-black hair was as straight and glossy as a helmet, her sexuality so blatant it hit him like a physical force.

'However long it's been, it hasn't been long enough,' he said, crossing to the drinks cabinet and pouring himself a large Jack Daniels. 'Bryce is in Parkhurst, but then you know that, don't you? You must have known for months.'

'Is this a guilt trip you're trying to send me on, lover?' Her cut-glass voice dripped amusement as, ever so slightly, she moved her head on the white leather-covered cushions so that she could continue watching him. 'I've been in Switzerland. Making Daddy happy by being a good little girl at finishing school. Making lots of ski instructors happy, too.'

He drained the tumbler-full of bourbon without turning to look at her and then poured himself another one, adding a great chunk of ice to it.

'There's a postal service in Switzerland, isn't there?' he said, turning round when the bourbon had fired its way into his belly, knowing damn well Bryce hadn't received so much as a postcard from her. 'And don't call me "lover". Where you're concerned, Nina, I'm not even a friend.'

Her unnervingly wide mouth curved into a languid smile. 'Ah,' she said with apparent deep satisfaction. 'I affect you so strongly, do I, Jacko baby?'

'You don't affect me at all,' he said, keeping his distance from her, knowing it was a lie. Her sexuality was the most unnerving he had ever encountered. There was something almost reptilian about her. Her ice-cold indifference to everyone on the planet, other than herself, made his skin crawl. He liked nothing about her, because there was nothing to like. She possessed a hardness he found shocking in a girl so young. She was mercenary, conniving, deeply and unpleasantly disturbing. And his cock reacted to her with rampant, raging insistence.

It was reacting now and he knew that she knew it.

'So you're in England to finally visit Bryce?' he asked.

It was winter and he could think of no other reason for her being here. In winter, Nina fled to the West Indies and tropical heat.

'I might visit him, and I might not.' She tilted her head, regarding him thoughtfully out of eyes the colour of quartz. 'What happened to all Bryce's lovely Al-Bakara money, Jacko-baby? Is it all in your very safekeeping?'

For once in her company, he laughed with genuine mirth. 'Christ, but this is a little transparent for you, isn't it, Nina?' He drained his tumbler. 'Bryce is too old a hand to give his stash into *anyone's* safekeeping. I don't know what he's done with it, and I don't want to know.'

There was an infinitesimal movement at the corner of her mouth and he knew, with a surge of anger, that she was merely amusing herself with him.

'Get the hell out, Nina,' he said, his fingers tight round the empty tumbler, aware that despite his awesome reputation as a Lothario, where Nina Denster was concerned, he was way out of his depth.

She rose unhurriedly from the sofa, but she didn't move towards the door. Instead she walked towards him, draping an arm round his neck, pressing her sinuous body serpent-like against him. 'When we've fucked, lover,' she murmured, knowing how much he loathed her; knowing it was a drop in the ocean compared to the depth of his lust.

For the merest split second his gold-flecked eyes were so dark as to be unreadable and then, just as she was wondering if she had miscalculated, he hurled the tumbler across the room and, with a deep groan, laid hungry hands on her.

'I'm not sure I'm going to be able to keep Tricia's visits going, Bryce,' Rusty said when she visited in the New Year.

'What the *fuck* do you mean?'

Rusty bit the corner of her lip, uncaring about his having sworn at her. It was, under the circumstances, a reasonable reaction. 'I find it a nightmare,' she said bluntly.

She crossed her legs, clasping her hands together on her lap. She never dressed provocatively on a prison visit and she was wearing a cream-coloured tailored trouser-suit. Her shoes, though, were as raunchy as always: purple patent and high-heeled.

'Well of course you find it a nightmare! It *is* a nightmare.' He looked across the crowded visiting-room to where Tricia was chatting to one of the screws. She did it every time she visited, as artlessly friendly as a toddler, and the prison officers, realizing her mental backwardness, were nearly always gently kind to her.

Tricia wasn't a toddler, though. She was twelve years old and, dressed a little differently, could easily have looked sixteen.

'I'm talking to you, Rusty, for Christ's sake! *Why* is it suddenly such a nightmare that you're thinking of stopping Tricia's visits? She needs to see me just as much as I need to see her. You *can't* stop them!'

321

Rusty twisted the wedding ring on her finger and forced herself to look away from Tricia and back to Bryce. Her heart jarred against her breastbone. Even with his prison pallor and barbarically short haircut, he was still the handsomest, most vitally alive man she'd ever seen in her life. When she'd fallen in love with him, she had done so almost immediately – and she was in love with him still.

The situation was, however, utterly hopeless. There had always been other women. Women and Bryce were an inseparable combination. Before the arrival of Nina nymphet Denster it hadn't mattered – at least, not on a deep and dangerous level. In a way she rarely acknowledged to herself, his womanising, like his fearlessness and recklessness, was all part and parcel of what made him so fatally attractive. There was no caging Bryce in a monogamous relationship – and if it had been possible, she knew she would never have fallen so dizzily in love with him.

Like a lot of south-east London men, Bryce had a way about him, a swagger. He was a man to be reckoned with and he lived life in the fast lane. Easy money, fast cars, fast women, style and status. The package was one she'd found irresistible. Nothing could match the tension, excitement and sense of fulfilment she'd experienced living with him, and she knew that nothing ever would. There was an aura him about that, even in prison, captured attention. A strength one could sense even at a distance.

And from now on she was going to disassociate herself from it. Nina Denster's claws were sunk in him so deep she had no option. Ironically, she wondered how Nina would have coped if she'd been the one Bryce had been with when Victor's men had made their commando-style, heavily armed pounce on him. Would it have bothered her, seeing him with a gun to his head? Seeing him being dragged off in handcuffs and bundled into the back of a police car?

'Tricia's getting too old to bring into a place like

Parkhurst,' she said, knowing as she said it that she was making an excuse for herself; that the real reason was she could no longer endure the pain of seeing him in prison denims. 'She's already having to wear a bra and, though I make sure she doesn't wear the sort of clothes that draw attention to her figure, it's impossible to disguise that she *has* a figure – and on a girl her age, in a place like this, it attracts the worst kind of unwelcome attention.'

'OK, there's a problem. I accept that. I don't want Tricia coming in for unpleasant glances and remarks any more than you do. But it's easily overcome, isn't it? Just make sure she wears a coat or a jacket and that you keep that lion's mane of hair she inherited from you anchored down. Your visits, and Tricia's, are important to me . . .'

'Really?' She couldn't keep her hurt and anger in check any longer. 'I know seeing Tricia is important to you, Bryce, but I doubt whether my visits are. Not in comparison to Nina Denster's.'

She saw shock flare through his eyes and his jaw muscles tighten, and knew he'd thought she hadn't a clue about them.

'There was confusion over our visiting orders. Her name was written in where mine should have been,' she said bitterly, knowing she had to hurl her final thunderbolt and get the hell out.

She rose to her feet, every male eye in the visiting-room swivelling in her direction. 'I've decided to file for divorce, Bryce. I like things tidy and there's nothing tidy about our situation now, is there?'

She waited, hardly daring to acknowledge to herself what it was she was waiting for. Whatever it was, it didn't come.

'It was good while it lasted, Rusty,' he said at last, without rising to his feet.

She choked back the sobs rising in her throat, knowing she was already as much a part of his past as Sandra was.

'God damn you, Bryce Reece!' she spat, her green cat-eyes flashing fire, uncaring of who heard her. 'It would have lasted a damn sight longer if you'd kept your pecker in your pants!'

Frankie leered at her as he always had done, seeing no reason why Rusty's reaction shouldn't, now, be a trifle different. 'Yer need me, Rusty darlin'. Bryce is no longer a player. By the time 'e sees the light of day 'e'll be grey-haired and middle-aged. I know you ain't visiting him any more – except to take the kid in sometimes.'

He moved towards her, already anticipating Bryce's reaction when he heard that he, Frankie, had his feet well under the dining-table at Lee Gardens.

'I'm off to Vegas on Saturday, darlin'. Lots of serious bright lights and lots of seriously big people – and I'm one of 'em. So 'ow about it?'

They were in her small kitchen and she'd backed away from him as far as she could, her hands splayed against a yellow-painted kitchen unit. What passed for a chuckle rose in his throat. Even if she wasn't up for Vegas, this was going to be a re-run of their little encounter years ago in her dressing-room at the strip-club, and he couldn't wait. She was wearing a few more clothes now than she'd been wearing then, but he'd soon take care of that.

He thrust his hand in his back pocket, bringing out a wad of notes thick enough to choke a pig. 'Buy yerself some ritzy gear – money's no object where you're concerned, darlin'. Not wiv me.'

'Fuck *off*.' There wasn't even a tad of fear in Rusty's voice. Fear was something that turned Frankie on and she would have died rather add to his pleasure. 'I wouldn't go the end of the street with you, Frankie Briscoe, let alone Las Vegas.' Her husky voice dripped contempt. 'When I look at you, all I think of is shit. Do you get it?' Her eyes glittered. 'DO . . . YOU . . . UNDERSTAND?'

There came the sound of a car drawing to a halt outside the house.

'I'd rather be pawed over by a roomful of punters than have you put one of your ugly, gross fingers on me,' she was saying through clenched teeth, but he was no longer listening.

Two things were going through his head. One was that the occupants of the car were quite clearly about to enter the maisonette. The car doors had slammed and as well as two middle-class female voices, he recognised Rusty's daughter's voice.

The second was that he'd given Rusty Daniels too many chances. Who the *fuck* did she think she was? It was bad enough Nina fucking Denster coming the Lady of the Manor bit with him, but at least she was genuine upper drawer. Rusty fucking Daniels wasn't. Rusty fucking Daniels was south-east London scum, as he was, and he was going to make her pay for making his prick shrivel. He didn't know how, and he didn't know when, but one day he was going to make Rusty Daniels suffer mega-time.

'Mum! We're home! Miss Woods wants to have a word with you and she's got another teacher with her!'

Even as his thoughts were coming to a conclusion, Tricia was opening the glass door that led from the stairs into the open-plan sitting-room. From where he was standing he could see two middle-aged trouts following in her wake, all pearls, twinsets, tweed suits and dopily polite smiles.

As he stuffed his money back into his hip pocket, he registered Tricia's similarity to her mother, at least as far as the torrent of red wavy hair and green eyes were concerned – and he also registered that, for a kid her age, her tits were much in evidence.

'You'll regret giving me the cold shoulder,' he said, eyeballing Rusty steelily, his cast pronounced. 'One day you'll pay. You'll pay in squillions.'

As he turned away from her, pushing past Tricia and her startled teachers, anger pumped through his veins. It wasn't only Rusty Daniels who was going to pay for treating him as if he were shit on her shoe. Other condescending bastards were going to pay too; Jack Wilkinson being top of the list.

He erupted out into the tiny garden that served both the maisonettes and the flats beneath them and stormed across to his Roller. He'd never been able to stand Jack Wilkinson. He was too good-looking, a dead ringer for Steve McQueen. Just like Bryce, everything came easy to him; especially women.

Frankie gunned the Roller into life, seeing his reflection in the driving mirror. It wasn't a pretty sight. Every bone in his body was too big, and that included his jutting cheekbones, his jawbone and his massively prominent nose. He slewed away from the kerb, his mouth pulling into a grim smile. Though he may not have been pretty to look at, he was a geezer to be reckoned with, a geezer who scared the shit out of people. He needed to scare the shit out of someone now, just to relieve his feelings. Rusty Daniels and Jack Wilkinson were on the back-burner until the perfect opportunity presented itself, but his cousin Ginger wasn't.

He veered left out of Deptford High Street, heading towards the Elephant and Castle. His friends the Krays had had enough of Ginger tearing round their watering-holes with a shotgun in his hand. If Ginger wanted to play the part of the loyal Richardson henchman to the last gasp, then Frankie would help him out. He was, after all, a connoisseur of last gasps.

The sun was shining over the Bermondsey skyline as he cruised in vulgar grandeur down Jamaica Road. It made the world feel very spring-like. He began to whistle. It was going to be a good day, after all. It was going to be a day to remember.

# Chapter Seventeen

Parkhurst was the hardest prison Bryce had ever been in and the days between one monthly visit and the next dragged like centuries.

'For Christ's sake, give me some interesting news,' he said as he seated himself at one of the hated little tables opposite Big Chas.

'You won't like it.' Chas's hard-boned face was grim. 'Ginger's missing. Word is, he's dead – and if he is, you and I know who's fucking responsible.'

Even though Frankie doing serious injury to Ginger or Terry – or even to both of them – had been on the cards for a long while, the shock Bryce felt was pulverising.

'But, Christ Almighty, they're cousins, for fuck's sake!' His voice was raw with disbelief.

'You've no need to tell me,' Chas said savagely. 'I'm fucking uncle to both of 'em!'

For a long moment they stared at each other, each knowing exactly what the other was thinking. Whether Frankie had taken Ginger out because he believed Ginger had been a member of the raiding party that had shot up the pub in Bethnal Green, or whether he had done so because the Twins had ordered the death of a Richardson man to avenge the shooting of their ally in Catford, was impossible to tell. Whichever it was, though, if Frankie had killed Ginger, he had crossed a line of no return.

'I'm going to get him for it, Bryce.' The pupils in Big Chas's eyes were like pinpricks. 'When Ginger's body surfaces and I know for certain that he's dead, I'm going to do for Frankie. He may be my nephew, but so was

Ginger. My honour's involved here, Bryce. Know what I mean?'

A screw had begun walking too close to them for comfort and the subject had been abandoned, but Bryce had known exactly what he meant.

Where the older generation of Briscoes was concerned, Chas had always been the acknowledged clan leader. Though times had changed and neither Eddie nor Jug Ears was pursuing any criminal activity worthy of the name any more – nor, for that matter, was Chas – he was still the nearest thing to a patriarch that they had. Now that one of their offspring had turned rogue, killing a family member, it was down to Chas to see that justice, however rough, was done.

Over the next few months there were reports of a whole spate of killings, all of them attributable to the Krays and their cronies. Ronnie Kray's driver disappeared as did Teddy Smith, an erstwhile Kray man who had annoyed Ronnie. Next to vanish from the face of the East End was Jack the Hat, a villain who had often made himself useful to the Krays but who, like 'Mad' Teddy Smith, had fallen foul of them.

Via the prison-visiting grapevine, all such news reached Parkhurst quicker than it reached the Met. Jack was Bryce's most regular visitor – though Rusty continued to intermittently bring Tricia, and Nina had, at last, begun to occasionally show – but it was Jack who kept him up to date with news.

'Everyone running with the Krays is jumpy,' he said as Bryce's second Christmas in Parkhurst approached. 'Except for Frankie. That's a bit worrying, don't you think? It's as if Frankie has got lots of aces tucked up his sleeve and is just biding his time before showing them.'

Come Christmas, he received home-made cards from both

Tricia and Debbie. Tricia's Father Christmas had been clumsily drawn, which, considering her disabilities was, he supposed, only to be expected. Debbie's card had shown impressive artistic ability – and humour. She had sketched a Father Christmas, his hands on the bars of a cell window as he peered forlornly through them, and the resemblance to himself was unmistakable. On the other side of the cell door, amidst heavily falling snow, stood four pathetic reindeer. The caption read: 'If you can't come out, can we come in?'

Grinning broadly, he pinned both cards on the wall and, when Christmas was over, didn't take either of them down.

In February a crane-driver working on a Whitechapel building site unearthed Ginger's body.

'That's it,' Big Chas said when he visited a few days later. 'So help me, I'm going to do for him, Bryce. Murdering people who've crossed the Krays is one thing, but ironing out his own family for those bastards is quite another.'

'So what's going on, Bryce-baby?' Nina asked, her skirt so provocatively short it was a miracle she'd been allowed through the prison gates. She crossed mile-long legs, suntanned despite it being barely spring. 'When I was last in the casino I heard lots of intriguing rumours.'

'Such as?' His tone of voice was mild but he was taut with sexual tension, as always when he was within inches of her.

She gave a careless shrug of her shoulders. 'That Frankie Briscoe's responsible for the corpse that was dug up in Whitechapel and that he's having to look over his shoulder.' She tilted her head, night-black hair swinging satin-smooth. 'Word is, the corpse was his cousin. Is that true? Jack was his usual iffy self when Sholto-baby asked him about it.'

At the mention of the aristocratic chinless wonder she'd been spending her time with, his tension reached crippling proportions.

'Sholto Penhaligan is a fool!' he said savagely, wishing to God he could lay his hands on him. 'And so are you if you think Jack is going to chat about Frankie with him! Why the fuck do you spend time with the prick, anyway? His picture was in yesterday's diary column of the *Mail* and he looked young enough to be in nappies!'

A smile touched her blood-red mouth. 'He's twenty-one and heir to a fortune – though like everyone in my set, a large wodge of his millions will always be tied up in land.' Her eyes were speculative. 'Your millions aren't so inconvenienced, though, are they? Willie says unless you allow someone to launder and invest the cash in question, your former friends will get their hands on it and, like many another major bank robber, you'll come out of prison to bugger-all.'

'Willie' was how she always referred to her father. Immediately after Bryce's arrest, Sir William Denster had disassociated himself from him in every way, so now it was Bryce's turn to be amused.

'And does your father think he's the right man to launder and invest my cash for me?' he asked drily, already knowing the answer. 'Because if he does, he's an even bigger arsehole than I thought him.'

She shrugged again, as if she couldn't care less. Where his name-calling of her father was concerned he'd known her indifference was genuine. Where his bank stash was concerned, he'd known she was putting on a very good act.

Like everyone else in his world, bar Jack, she wanted to know where his share of the Al-Bakara money was hidden. In bringing her father into the equation she was simply trying to get information by a route not previously tried.

At twenty she was what she had been at seventeen: a completely self-absorbed, self-centred, sex-mad, cool, clever and money-loving bitch. He knew it, had always known it, and because just looking at her made his prick so engorged it hurt, he didn't care. All he cared about was that she continued her erratic, dramatic visits.

That she had bothered to take the ferry at all had seemed, when she had first visited him, a minor miracle. To begin with he had suspected she made the journey just for the novelty value. Parkhurst had, after all, the hardest villains in the country banged up inside it and he knew her well enough to know that the knowledge would be a sexual turn-on for her.

Her visits had, however, continued – though on her own terms. She dropped the names of the men she saw like confetti. Sholto Penhaligan was only one in a long, long line. Pick and mix seemed to be her motto where her sleeping partners were concerned. They were either upper-class shits from what she referred to as her own 'set', or low-life crims – some of them, from what his other visitors told him, being very low life indeed.

'Problem is, the Age of the Robber is more or less over, Bry,' Jack, who never mentioned Nina unless he was specifically asked about her, said on one of his visits. 'I reckon our scam was probably the last of its kind. It's the Age of the Dealer now. Everyone's getting in on the drugs racket. Frankie's never seen without a couple of Colombians in tow. The casino's high rollers all have his calling-card. The upper classes treat cocaine as casually as we used to smoke ciggies.'

Bryce knew immediately that Nina was one of the cocaine-users in question. He also knew that now Frankie was of use to her, her contemptuous attitude towards him would have changed. When he found out it had altered to such an extent that she was dating Frankie's friends, his fury and frustration had been almost uncontainable. 'Christ Almighty!' he'd raged to Jack. 'She'll be shacking up with Reggie Kray next!'

Jack, who knew that was exactly what Nina was doing, had kept silent. His own sexual encounter with her had been a one and only, not because that was the way she had wanted to play it, but because his self-loathing afterwards had been so deep, he knew he'd kill himself if it ever happened again.

In May, Bryce thought his and Big Chas's problems were over when the Krays and twenty-six of their henchmen were arrested in a massive co-ordinated dawn raid. The twenty-six henchmen weren't named, but it seemed impossible that Frankie wouldn't be one of them.

He hadn't been, though, and Bryce had wondered if perhaps Somerville had given him a tip-off.

Over the next months gossip as to how many of the twenty-six arrested would turn Queen's Evidence and go into the witness-box, was rife.

'If Big Chas is going to do for Frankie, he'd better stop pussyfooting around and get on with it,' was Jack's blunt opinion, 'because word is, all witnesses are being offered round-the-clock protection and, if Frankie goes for that, ironing him out will be an impossibility.'

At the thought of Frankie being given protection by the police, Bryce cracked up. 'Any Kray witnesses accepting protection are being protected *from* Frankie,' he said when he could trust himself to speak. 'Christ Almighty, he's the only top Kray man still on the streets. My bet is he's doing all the witness intimidation possible and any rumours that he's going to grass have been started by himself so as to give him some cover.'

When Jimmy Briscoe visited him, dressed like the dog's

bollocks but with a face as white as parchment, Bryce knew immediately what it was he'd come to tell him.

'My dad's missing,' he said. 'I don't need to spell anything out, do I?'

The expression on Bryce's face had been answer enough.

'Frankie's loco,' he said, his teeth clenched. 'First Ginger, now Dad. It's as if he's taking the whole bloody family out!'

Bryce, knowing that where Chas was concerned, whatever Frankie had done had probably been in self-defence, kept quiet. It was an observation Jimmy didn't need to hear.

'I need help dealing with him,' Jimmy continued. 'If you've got anything on him, Bryce. Anything at all . . .'

Bryce shook his head. He'd had bundles of respect for Chas, and he owed him for the way Chas had set him on his feet when he'd come out of the nick in 1960, but short of becoming a police informer he couldn't give Jimmy the kind of help he was asking for. For the right sum of money someone, somewhere, would probably grass on Frankie, but it wouldn't be him. Not grassing was a code he couldn't break under any circumstances. Not for anyone. Not even for a diamond geezer like Chas.


'The Krays have copped for thirty years!' a prison officer said with grim satisfaction the following May, tossing a newspaper into Bryce's cell. 'Serves the vicious buggers right!'

Bryce picked up the paper, shaking it open. '*Gangland bosses, Kray twins, jailed for life. Judge's recommendation thirty years*!'

It was a giant whack, but considering the murders the Twins were guilty of and the length of time they had terrorised London, it wasn't a surprising one – unlike his own. Even now there were times when he couldn't believe the sentence he was serving.

'Visitors are in,' the prison officer continued. 'And yours is the looker. Though why a bint like that comes all this way to see a fucker like you, is beyond me.'

Knowing very well that the bint in question was Nina, Bryce grinned, his ticker singing like a skylark.

She was wearing a scarlet linen shift dress, a host of gold bracelets and not much more.

'Hi, lover,' she said, her lashes impossibly thick and long, her exotic eye make-up Cleopatra black. 'I've thought up a great wheeze to bring some fun into our lives.'

He sat down at the table, aware that they were already the focal point of interest where everyone else in the room was concerned, other prison visitors and warders alike.

'Oh yeah?' He was getting a buzz out of just looking at her, but he didn't believe for one moment that under the present conditions even she could bring fun into his life.

She flashed him a smile, her wide, glossily painted mouth almost splitting her gamine-like face in two.

'I got the idea after reading about an American death-row prisoner who did it hours before he was executed.'

'Did what?' he asked, intrigued.

'Got married.'

Her bracelets shimmered and tinkled as she rested her arms on the shabby table and leaned towards him over the low wooden barrier that nominally separated them. 'Think about it, Bryce-baby. Willie will have heart failure. I'll have status amongst your friends. Sholto will be history. You could have one of the Great Train Robbers or Reggie Kray as best man. It will be the prison wedding of the decade. So what do you say, lover? Yes or no?'

He'd said yes. It was an act of insanity and, looking back on it, he'd known so right from the beginning. Jack, not Reggie Kray, had been best man. The bride had worn a miniskirted wedding dress designed by Zandra Rhodes. Despite taking place in prison, the wedding had received show-biz type attention from the press which, bearing in mind Nina's near Royal Family connections and the fact that every editor in Fleet Street still regarded the missing Al-Bakara money as a newsworthy item, hadn't been too surprising.

Billy Dixon had sent them a 'Congratulations' card. Jug Ears and Evelyn had sent an ornamental cruet.

Joan Wilkinson had written to him, bringing back memories of his mother so raw he was hardly able to bear them. He'd also received a wedding-card from Debbie. '*I didn't know you could get married in prison,*' she had written in her unnervingly strong handwriting. '*You should have waited a couple of years. I'll be sixteen in 1971.*' Vastly amused, he had put it in the shoe-box that held all the cards and notelets she and Tricia sent him.

The shit, of course, had hit the fan almost immediately.

'She's still spending time with Frankie,' Jack told him reluctantly when he pressed him. 'And she's dealing in drugs. The Knightsbridge set don't want face-to-face contact with a villain as heavy as Frankie, so Nina is the ideal go-between. The thing is,' he continued, looking even more uncomfortable, 'she's not only on terms with Frankie, Bryce. She's on terms with other drug dealers as well. She gets a high out of mixing with crims and whereas they used to be suspicious of her, now she's your missus they're not. She's got the status that comes of being married to a big-time face and word is she's milking it for all she's worth.'

There'd been nothing he could do. When she visited him, all she was interested in was the whereabouts of the bank money. 'I'm your *wife* for Christ's sake, Bryce-baby!' she would say, as if butter wouldn't melt in her mouth. '*I* should have care of it, not Jack. For all you know, Jack could already have robbed you of the lot!'

'Jack isn't taking care of it for me.' He said the same thing each and every time, knowing she didn't believe him; knowing that no one did.

The belief that Jack had care of his haul from the bank job was general. The police believed it; his crim friends believed it; his enemies were sure of it. It was a scenario he had never envisaged and, where Jack was concerned, it was potentially lethal.

Time after time, he wondered whether he should tell Jack where the money was stashed and where he had hidden the key. And time after time, he came down on the side of caution. For Jack to know the money's whereabouts could be as dangerous for him as not knowing. Either way it was a gamble – and it was one he could only pray that he'd got right.

It was impossible for him to think about the money without thinking about Rusty and Tricia and Lee Gardens as well. By 1970, Rusty's career was riding high. She did no stripping at all, only nude photographic modelling, but it was modelling of international repute. Sometimes it seemed that every con in Parkhurst had her Pirelli calendar photograph somewhere in their cell. What her income was, Bryce had no idea. He knew, though, that if she had wanted she could easily have moved out of Lee Gardens to a much smarter address – and he knew the reason she didn't was Tricia.

Tricia was now fifteen and, despite her disabling arthritis, a beauty. Having inherited Rusty's flame-red hair, stunning green eyes and eye-goggling figure, there was no way she could be anything else. She was also naively sweet-natured and mentally retarded, and the overall combination was one that caused Rusty – and him – grave concern.

'I'm not moving from Deptford for Tricia's sake,' Rusty

had once told him when he had asked whether she was thinking of taking her mother's curtains to a more upmarket home. 'Deptford, where our neighbours have known her ever since she was a baby, is much safer territory for her than Hampstead or Chelsea. I don't want the sharks and wolves that pester me to move in on her. Christ, Bryce. The very thought is enough to give me nightmares for a week.'

It was enough to give him nightmares, too. Through the years he had been inside, Jack had continued to be a good friend to Rusty and very protective where Tricia was concerned – as were lots of his other old friends. Robert and Richard Wilkinson both kept in touch with Rusty and Tricia; and Tina Dixon, Billy Dixon's ex-wife, had become almost a surrogate mother to the girl, moving into number 46 whenever a photographic assignment took Rusty abroad. There were times, now, when Gunter, Curly and Georgie felt safe enough to pay flying trips to London and, when they did, they would take Rusty and Tricia out on the town. In such a social circle, Tricia was safe. Outside of it, anything could happen.

The knowledge that his three ex-gang mates were in town and that there was no way they could risk putting even hookey names to a visiting order to see him, always drove Bryce wild with frustration.

'Curly and Georgie are going to join Gunter in Vancouver,' Jack reported in late 1972. 'Gunter says the west coast of Canada is the dog's bollocks.' He ran a hand through his straw-coloured hair and began to laugh. 'The crack is, the suburb Gunter lives in is home to a Brinks Mat gold bullion warehouse – Gunter can see it from his veranda!'

Bryce, too, had laughed, suppressing the bitter ache he felt inside, wishing to God he, like them, was living it up in Vancouver.

Later, though, with the jokes over, Jack had said: 'I'm having a fuck of a time with Frankie, Bryce. Thanks to his gorillas, all the regular punters are too shit-scared to come into a Reece-owned club or casino. I'm being tailed – I know it's by one of Frankie's lot, and I know why. Frankie's still convinced I know where the Al-Bakara money is stashed and he thinks I'm bound to check in on it eventually.'

Their eyes had held, both of them knowing what Frankie was capable of; both of them remembering what had happened to Ginger and to Big Chas.

'Christ, but I'm sorry for dropping you into all this.' His rage towards Frankie and his frustration at being so helpless had been so great he'd felt as if he was about to explode. What did the money matter if Jack were to be seriously maimed or to lose his life over it? It meant absolutely fuck all. 'Let me put you completely in the picture,' he'd said, making his mind up which was the safest option. 'The money is in a stow in Temple Gardens West, off Fleet Street. The building is a . . .'

'*No!*' Jack's protest had been so vehement that the prison officer patrolling the room's observation landing had shouted out: 'Oi, you two! Keep it down!'

'I don't want to fuckin' know where your stow is!' This time Jack's voice had been a fierce whisper. 'What fuckin' good would it do me? Do you think if I told him, Frankie would pat me on the head and let bygones be bygones? He'd simply kill me – because that's what he's wanted to do for ages – and he'd have the dosh as well! No way, Bryce. *No way*. When I want you to tell me where the cash is, I'll let you know. Till then, we'll go on as before. Right?'

'Right,' had been the only thing he could say. But he hadn't liked it. He hadn't liked it one little bit.

'Me Auntie Evelyn's dead,' Tommy Briscoe said bluntly

on a rare visit in 1973. 'I tried to come in and tell you on a compassionate, but they weren't 'avin' none of it – said Evelyn wasn't a proper relation to you, not being your real mum.'

'How did it happen?' The shock was so great he felt as if he'd been hit in the stomach. Ever since he'd been twelve years old and had moved into number 5, Evelyn had been part and parcel of his life.

'Heart attack. She'd bin tryin' to heave Jug Ears on to the sofa – he'd bin on one of his benders – and she just pegged it. Jug Ears didn't even come round. He was still in a drunken stupor when she was bein' carried out to the ambulance.'

'Frankie wasn't at the funeral,' Terry Briscoe said, months later when, fresh out of the nick himself, he made the journey across the Solent. 'Not surprising, under the circumstances. Everyone knows 'e did for Ginger and Uncle Chas. Do yer know, Bryce, I fink the only reason 'e 'asn't ironed Jack out as well is that 'e finks Jack knows where your Al-Bakara money is stashed and 'e's living in the 'ope 'e'll one day make Jack spill the beans.'

'Thanks,' he'd said wryly, not bothering to let Terry know this was yesterday's news, grateful that the tense stalemate between Frankie and Jack still hadn't broken out into open war.

'The Clarksons are dead.' It was 7 July 1974, and West Germany had just won the World Cup. His informant was Jack.

'*Debbie*?' A truly terrifying emotion had roared through him.

'Nah. Do you think I'd have broken the news like that if she'd snuffed it as well?' Jack grinned, seriously amused. 'Hilda and Norm died of food poisoning – after eating at home. Word is Hilda had served up a tin of corned beef that had been in her larder ever since the war. It must have been full of botulism. Whatever it was full of, it did them both in.'

'Poor old Norman,' he'd said, seeing the funny side of the Clarksons' deaths and shedding no tears for Hilda. Norman Clarkson, though, was a different matter. It had been Norman who had pumped the river water from his lungs and covered him with his coat after he'd nearly drowned rescuing Frankie from the Thames. He'd always had reason to be grateful to Norman Clarkson and any remorse he'd ever felt for Roy's death had always been solely on Norm's account.

Shortly after Jack's visit he'd been handed a visiting order application.

'Cast your eyes over that,' said a screw he was on friendly terms with. 'It's a different name to the usual. She says she's your niece.' He winked. 'And we believe her, Reece, don't we?'

The application form bore the name Debbie Clarkson.

He sat down on the edge of his metal bed, staring at it. She'd applied to see him before. The first time had been on her sixteenth birthday. Other applications had followed at the rate of two a year. He'd turned them all down. He didn't want Debbie visiting a prison and seeing him under prison conditions. It was bad enough Tricia doing so, but at least she didn't fully understand the situation. Debbie was a quite different matter.

He thought about Hilda and Norman Clarksons' deaths. They'd been the only family Debbie was aware of. What would she do now? He knew from the letters she had sent him that, ever since her mid teens, she'd had ructions with Hilda over her refusal to study for a place at university. '*I don't want to go to university*,' she had written in the violet ink she always used. '*I want to go to the Royal Academy of Dramatic Art.*'

340

She hadn't done so, though perhaps now, with Hilda and Norman dead, she would. She was still only nineteen years old. For an intelligent girl – from the moment he'd first spoken to her, when she'd been only five, he'd never had the slightest doubt as to Debbie's intelligence – the world was her oyster.

Whatever she decided to do, she would be feeling bereft at the moment and his refusing her permission to visit would not help matters.

With mixed feelings he OK'd the application – and then began counting off the days on his calendar.

His first reaction when, with deliberate nonchalance, he strolled into the crowded visiting-room, was that she wasn't there. There was the usual battery of care-worn wives with children in their arms or at their knees, the usual sprinkling of dollybirds, but no mousily fair, sulky-faced Debbie.

'Table 12, Reece,' a prison officer said as he paused, looking around. 'And if that's your niece, I'm Ronnie Kray.'

He looked towards table 12 and the floor shelved away at his feet. Crazy though he now realised it was, he'd been expecting to see the Debbie he had last seen; the Debbie who, in November 1965, had been ten years old.

The girl at the table was tall and slim and, considering her surroundings, remarkably relaxed. She wasn't dressed, as he knew most girls her age now dressed, either all hippy or all pseudo-countrified Laura Ashley. She was wearing a straight beige skirt and a white silk blouse, a cream cardigan draped around her shoulders. Her legs were naked and her high-heeled, cinnamon-suede sandals revealed pearly-pink varnished toes. Her hair hung down to her shoulders, lighter than he remembered it – so light it was wheat-blonde. She looked both timelessly elegant and sexy, and it was the sexiness that threw him.

341

He knew as he looked at her, that before she turned her head and her eyes met his, he must leave the room or be doomed.

He tried to retreat, but his feet wouldn't obey the commands he was giving them.

'*Table 12*, Reece!' the prison officer bawled out and as she heard his name, Debbie raised her head, her eyes meeting his.

'Hi,' he said negligently, walking forward and sitting down at the table opposite her. 'Long time no see.'

What her emotions were he had no way of telling. Her grey-green eyes were as unreadable as they had been as a child.

'Eight years, three months, two weeks and three days,' she said, deadpan. 'And you've put on weight. I thought they had gyms in prison. I thought you'd be fit.'

The amusement she'd always aroused in him took hold. 'There is a gym here and I spend every minute possible in it,' he said truthfully. 'And I am fit, you cheeky minx. It just happens that I'm also thirty-eight.' *And old enough to be your father*, he nearly added, but didn't.

'Mum and Dad are dead – did you know?'

He noticed that her fingernails were short and unlacquered, buffed to a pale pink sheen.

'It was food poisoning. Mum's fault. She was still feeding Dad food she'd hoarded in the war.'

As always, whenever she referred to Hilda as her mum he wanted to set the record straight. Now she was no longer a child he could, he supposed, do so. But not just now. Not today.

'Jack told me.' He paused, knowing he should be offering her some kind of condolence but completely, where Hilda was concerned, unable to. 'I was sorry to hear your dad had died,' he said at last. 'I don't suppose you know this, but when I was a kid he dragged me clear of the Thames and pumped gallons of water from my lungs.'

'Dad did?' Her eyebrows shot high. 'You're right. I didn't know. I bet Mum wasn't with him. Mum wouldn't have hauled you in. She'd have thrown you further out!'

He'd roared with laughter, realising how wrong he'd been in not allowing her to visit him before. Debbie could handle prison visiting. As he should have realised a long time ago, Debbie could handle anything. For the hundredth time, he marvelled over her dissimilarity to Sandra. When Sandra had visited him during the first couple of years of his manslaughter sentence she'd either been in tears, or on the verge of tears, the entire time.

As always, whenever it registered on him that he had killed her father and that she didn't know, shock blasted through him. Concern about breaking the news that Hilda had been her grandmother, not her mother, was nothing compared to the biggie of telling her she had been conceived as the result of a rape and that he had stabbed her father through the heart.

'What's the matter?' she asked in her stunningly direct manner. 'You were laughing a minute ago and now you look like Attila the Hun on a bad day.'

Though it was a crazy moment to become aware of it, he realised that her eyes weren't grey-green. They were sea-green. A sea-green that was now dark with concern.

'Nothing's the matter,' he said swiftly, knowing he could never tell her about Sandra, knowing she was going to have to go through the rest of her life believing the hideous Hilda had been her mother. 'Tell me what you're doing these days. Have you got a job you like? Have you got a boyfriend?'

How he got the last question past his lips was a miracle. If the answer was yes, he wouldn't want to know.

'No, and no.'

For the first time since they had begun talking there was a pause between them and, over and above his vast feeling of relief, he was aware of a growing tension.

'How is your wife?' she asked suddenly. 'I keep seeing her photo in gossip columns. She parties a lot, doesn't she?'

'Yes,' he said briefly, well aware of the extent of Nina's party-going. High society parties were where she discreetly did her drug dealing. The rows they'd had about it were as savage as visiting-room conditions allowed. Her response to his demand that she cut all ties with Frankie and the other drug barons she was in contact with was always the same: 'If you'd let me launder and invest the Al-Bakara money, I wouldn't need to be doing it, Bryce-baby. So . . . where is it? Are you going to tell me?'

Knowing now that she'd only married him because she'd hoped he would share such secrets with her, his answer was that he would sooner shoot himself in the head.

'How many more years do you still have to do?' Debbie asked, quite obviously following an agenda of her own – though he couldn't imagine quite what it was.

'Technically, another twelve. With parole, perhaps five and a bit.'

She made no comment and he hadn't blamed her. What could she say, for Christ's sake? That it was a pity? That he'd still only be forty-three if he got parole? That the time would soon pass?

'Now Mum and Dad are dead, I'm going to do what I've always wanted to do,' she said, moving her head slightly, the light catching her hair so that the gold was meshed with silver. 'I've got a place in a drama school in Toronto.'

'*Toronto*? Why the hell Toronto?' He was seized by panic. 'What's wrong with a drama school in London? There's a whole host of them, isn't there? There's RADA, there's the Central School . . .'

Vainly he tried to think of the names of more London drama schools. She couldn't go to Canada. If she went to Canada, she wouldn't be able to visit him again. What the fuck was it with that country, that everyone who mattered to him buggered off to it?

'I want a bit more of a challenge than simply going to a drama school in London,' she said, something unreadable in her eyes. It was as if she badly wanted to say something else and had reluctantly decided against it.

He drew in breath, about to tell her she didn't need any challenges, and then stopped himself. She was nineteen years old and he was a married man of thirty-eight with a divorce behind him and years of imprisonment ahead. How the hell could he possibly start telling her what she needed or didn't need?

The bell signalling the end of visiting sounded and the noise level, at tables that had children at them, increased.

'Is that it?' she asked, her eyes opening wide. 'Do I have to go now?'

His throat was so choked with emotion he could barely trust himself to speak. 'Yes,' he said with the outward appearance of it being no big deal, reflecting that he, too, would be a good candidate for a stage school. 'Good luck in Canada, Debbie. Write to me now and then.'

They were on their feet now, facing each other across the mean little table as, all around them, couples were hugging and kissing and saying their goodbyes.

He knew that he, too, should be saying goodbye, but he couldn't bring himself to say the word.

Neither, it seemed, could she.

Suddenly, with her eyes overly bright, she leaned across the table, kissing him full on the mouth.

'*Quit the liberty-taking, Reece*!' an authoritative voice hollered. '*I know who your missus is, and that isn't her*!'

Even before the prison officer reached him, Debbie had spun away, making for the visitors' exit at what seemed to be the speed of light, her pale-toned figure as unattainable as the moon.

\*　　\*　　\*

It had taken him days to recover. Even when Jack visited, a fortnight later, he still felt dazed just thinking about the effect her visit had had on him.

'So, as she flatly refuses to come and tell you herself, I've been detailed to do the dirty,' Jack said wryly, knowing the news about Nina wasn't going to devastate Bryce the way it would have done a few years previously. 'The bloke in question is a Colombian she met via Frankie, a real Mr Big. I'm surprised you've not already received the divorce papers. Mr Big is obviously a drug king worth millions and now that Nina has her claws in him you can bet your sweet life nothing on earth will make her let go.'

As Jack had anticipated, Bryce received the news with indifference. Whatever the feelings he had once had for Nina, they had long since turned to dross.

His next visitor, a month later, had been Jimmy Briscoe. Despite being as immaculately dressed as always, Jimmy had not looked the dog's bollocks. He had looked ten years older than his thirty-eight years – and ill with it.

'It's cancer,' he had said bluntly. 'And it's terminal. I ain't going to put up with it when it gets really bad. I tell you now, Bryce, I shall top myself before I'll die in some cunt of a hospital with tubes in every fuckin' orifice and little girl nurses wiping my arse every time I shite.'

'Somerville's about to be made a Chief Constable,' Jack said when he visited Christmas week. 'His patch is going to be in the Home Counties – which is a pity. I don't like the guy, but I'm going to miss him. He always earned his keep and did his stuff.' He cracked his knuckles. 'Victor's being promoted as well. I wonder if his and Somerville's paths ever cross and, if they do, I wonder if Victor knows how bent Somerville is?'

'Christ knows.' Not even with Jack would Bryce discuss Victor; nor did he particularly want to talk about

Somerville. The subject they needed to discuss was Frankie.

'I'm going to be down as MIA any moment,' Jack had been saying for months now. 'I'm looking over my shoulder even before I get out of bed of a morning. Christ knows why you ever pulled Frankie Briscoe from the Thames, Bryce. It was the worst day's work you ever did.'

'Frankie . . .' he said heavily. 'What's the latest, Jack?'

A spasm crossed Jack's face. 'The latest is he's finally beginning to believe I'm not care-taking your stash. The bad news is, he thinks one of your straight mates must be the minder. And you've only got three straight mates who fit the bill: my Robert and Richard, and little Billy Dixon.'

Bryce's stomach muscles cramped into knots. The nightmare scenario that was Frankie Briscoe was getting worse by the minute. The Richardsons and the Krays were off the streets but Frankie, who had learned every trick in the book from them, had replaced them with a vengeance.

At the thought of Frankie and his gorillas terrorising Jack's brothers or Billy, bile rose in Bryce's throat and he had to fight down the urge to be sick. If anything happened to his childhood mates and their families he would never forgive himself – not if he lived to be a hundred.

# Chapter Eighteen

Rusty swung out of the Arrivals Hall at Heathrow wearing mulberry-leather boots and an ankle-length fox-fur coat, her fiery hair piled beneath a matching Cossack hat. She had just flown in from a three-day photographic shoot in Zurich, where it had been cold but at least it had been a dry exhilarating kind of cold. London was simply cold and the pits.

With no luggage apart from a weekend bag, she strode Gulliver-like out on to the forecourt, heading for the short-term car park where her Volvo Coupé was waiting. It was already dusk and, as it was Christmas Eve, she wanted to be home as soon as possible.

Half the world and his brother seemed to have the same idea and the roads into Central London were choked with traffic. An hour later, crawling at a snail's pace over Westminster Bridge, she fought down the feeling of anxiety that had been threatening to swamp her for nearly a week.

Frankie Briscoe. How, in God's name, was she going to deal with Frankie Briscoe? He'd always been a thorn in her flesh, even back in the mid sixties, before she'd met Bryce.

With a surge of relief she saw that the traffic was opening up a little and, pressing her foot down, she cleared the bridge and began heading towards the Elephant and Castle roundabout.

Her marrying Bryce had made things worse, of course, where Frankie was concerned. Whatever Bryce had, Frankie wanted. It had been the same with the clubs and the casino, and the same with Nina Denster. Nina, though, had been too fast a bit of business even for Frankie.

At the thought of how Nina had, Lolita-like, ruined things between herself and Bryce, she took the roundabout so recklessly car horns were still sounding in her wake as she entered the Old Kent Road.

Narrowly missing a motorcyclist, she forced Nina from her mind. Now that she was living with a Colombian in a palatial hacienda outside Bogota, Nina no longer mattered. Even the damage that Nina had done, had, over the years, healed over. There was another man in Rusty's life now. A Swiss businessman who was ultra respectable and who would happily marry her, if only she would agree to live in Switzerland.

The traffic was crawling again. She couldn't live in Switzerland. Though Gregor had repeatedly said that having Tricia living with them would not be a problem for him, that was because he hadn't a clue as to the stresses and strains involved.

Tricia was still as sweet-natured as she'd been from childhood – but as a grown woman with a child's mental-ity, her frustrations were immense and, unable to deal with them, she had begun having terrible temper tantrums.

'It's her hormones,' Tina Dixon had said sagely. 'You've only to look at the way she's built to see she must be oozing with hormones. She wants to have a boyfriend like other girls her age and you can't blame her, can you?'

The answer had been, of course, that she couldn't. But neither had she been able to see a way round the problem. Tricia was simply not capable of being responsible about sex – out on her own with the kind of man who would be attracted by her bizarre mix of naivety and voluptuous-ness, she would be used and abused shamelessly.

Which brought her thoughts full circle back to Frankie Briscoe.

Her hands were so tight on the steering-wheel that

her knuckles were white. She'd been avoiding Frankie and, when failing to avoid him, fending him off, for what seemed to be most of her life. What she had never anticipated, though, was that the day would come when his attentions would turn from her to her daughter.

She overtook a lorry and then knifed right, down a shortcut.

It had been the day before she had flown out to Zurich that she had seen them together. The first thing she had recognised, driving through Blackheath Village, was Frankie's vulgarly distinctive American Lincoln parked outside one of the village's many restaurants. The second thing had been Frankie's massive figure, seated at a window table. Then she had seen who was with him.

She'd screeched to a halt so abruptly it had been a miracle the Renault driver behind hadn't ended up sitting in her lap.

Leaving the car in the road to cause a major traffic jam, she had blasted into the restaurant like a wild woman.

'*Out!*' she had shouted at a startled Tricia, uncaring of the startled looks from the other tables. '*And you, Briscoe – you try and take advantage of my daughter again and I'll swing for you, I swear it!*'

It had been a nightmare scene, made even more hideous by her having to physically manhandle Tricia from the restaurant and across the road into the car, with Tricia screaming every step of the way that she didn't want to go; that she wanted to stay with Frankie.

The row, when they had got home, had been horrendous. 'Frankie's like a brother to Daddy-Bryce!' Tricia had sobbed, time and time again. 'He told me so! He told me Daddy-Bryce would like it that he was taking care of me. And he told me I was beautiful! *Very* beautiful. And he told me that if you found out about us you wouldn't like it, and I know why. It's because you're jealous . . .'

It had been then, for the first time in her life, that she had slapped Tricia across her face.

As she swung out of New Cross Road towards Deptford High Street, the mere memory of it made her feel sick with distress.

Tina had come round to the house and, in her inimitable way, had calmed things down so that, by the time she had left for Zurich, Tricia's hysteria was no longer rocketing off the Richter scale. Tonight being Christmas Eve, the three of them were going to go out somewhere festive together and all her fingers and toes were crossed in the fervent hope that Tricia was looking forward to it.

She turned into Lee Gardens. There was a glorious lime-green dress in her holdall that she had bought for Tricia in Zurich. Tina was always fun on a night out and, all girls together, the evening ahead was one that would, with a bit of luck, put all thoughts of Frankie Briscoe from Tricia's mind.

She drew to a halt, turned off the engine and, before she had even stepped from the car, knew that all her optimism had been pointless.

'Thank Christ you're back, Rusty!' Tina was running out of the house, her face nearly as white as her bouffantly peroxided hair. 'I don't know where the fuck Tricia is!'

She hared round to Rusty's driving door. 'I went to the hairdresser's at eleven o'clock and when I got back, she'd gone. She hasn't been back. I've rung everywhere I can think of, but no one's seen her.'

'Get in!'

As Tina hurled herself in the back of the car, Rusty slammed it into gear. She hadn't a clue where Tricia could be either, but she knew damn well who she was with.

'What watering-holes does Frankie use?' she demanded, screeching away from the kerb. 'And would he have taken her to one of them, or would he take her somewhere right off his manor? Where would he take her, Tina? For Christ's sake, *where*?'

It was two o'clock Christmas morning when they found her. It had been Tina's idea that they should the trawl the hospitals. 'Just so it puts our minds to rest that she ain't in there,' had been Tina's tactful way of putting it.

In St Thomas's, Bart's, Guy's, the casualty departments were all run off their feet.

'Haven't people anything better to do on bleedin' Christmas Eve than get blind drunk and cut each other up?' Tina had said as, after mercifully drawing yet another blank, they'd left the frantic activity at Bart's behind them. 'I know it was my idea, Rusty, but I think we're wasting our time.'

'No,' Rusty had said between clenched teeth. 'I don't think we are.' As the evening had gone on, a dreadful feeling of premonition had taken hold of her. 'Let's drive out to Lewisham Hospital. Frankie used to spend a lot of time in clubs Lewisham way.'

All along the Old Kent Road and in New Cross there had been parties of drunken revellers noisily making their way homewards. Once they'd hit Lewisham High Street things had been a little quieter.

Rusty had driven in tense silence. Lewisham Hospital had become a talisman for her. If Tricia hadn't been admitted into Lewisham's casualty department then it meant the dark fear growing and growing inside of her was nothing but over-reaction to a stressful situation. If Tricia wasn't on a trolley in Lewisham, then she wasn't on a trolley anywhere. Once they'd checked with casualty admissions, asking if a young woman of Tricia's description had been admitted and been given the same negative response they'd received at all the other hospitals they'd visited, she'd give up searching and simply go back home and wait.

'She looks a lot like me,' she'd said to the clerk on duty

at the admissions desk. 'She has red hair and green eyes and she's nineteen. She also suffers with arthritis and . . . and her mental age is that of an eight- or a nine-year-old.'

The clerk had not made eye contact with her. Keeping her eyes on the admissions book in front of her she had said, 'And your name is . . . ?'

'Mrs Reece. Rusty Reece.'

In nearly every situation she'd ever been in, whenever she'd coupled Bryce's surname with her Christian name, there had been amused comment. There hadn't been this time.

'Please take a seat, Mrs Reece,' the clerk had said, rising to her feet. 'Someone will be with you in a few moments.'

'But if she isn't here . . .' Wildly, Rusty had looked around the crowded waiting-room. There'd been so many wounded drunks accompanied by equally drunken friends, it had resembled a war zone. 'I don't want to wait if she isn't here. I don't want to give you extra work . . .'

She'd wanted out. She'd wanted to forget that the thought Tricia could be hurt had ever occurred to her. The clerk had gone. The only person listening to her was Tina.

'I think we'd better sit down, Rusty love,' Tina had said, her pretty, heavily made-up face looking suddenly almost wizened.

'Mrs Reece?' The doctor was impossibly young. 'Mrs Reece, I think we need to have a few words together. A young woman answering the description of your daughter was brought in here a short while ago and is now about to go into theatre for emergency surgery . . .'

'Oh God! Oh Christ!' This wasn't happening. It couldn't be happening.

'She's been in and out of consciousness and unable to identify herself. If you would come with me . . .'

Everything seemed to be thrown in sharp relief. The

doctor's young, angular face. The colour of the nurses' uniforms. The fierce brightness of the strip lighting.

She tried to answer him and couldn't. Her throat had closed with fear and there had been a sheen of perspiration on her skin. Feeling as if she was moving under water, she had followed him down the corridor, through swing doors, along another corridor, into a lift.

'This . . . young woman. She's not going to die, is she?' she managed to say as the lift doors opened and they stepped out into another corridor; a corridor lined with glittering steel trolleys and surgical instruments.

He didn't answer her. He was talking to a nurse. There were other nurses, too, all of them wearing dark green theatre gowns and boots. Ahead was a huge double door with lights above it and, then, by the door, she saw the trolley and on the trolley a sterile-wrapped figure.

'An identification . . .' she heard the young doctor saying to the nurse, and his voice seemed to be coming from a vast distance. 'Best, I think, under the circumstances . . .'

Her heart was slamming against her breastbone. She wouldn't have been allowed into the room next to the operating theatre unless there was a high risk of the girl on the trolley not surviving the operation. Under normal circumstances the doctor would, surely, have asked her to remain at the hospital and to make her identification when the girl had returned from surgery.

As if in hideous slow-motion, she saw him step to one side so that she could approach the trolley and see the face of the person lying on it.

'*No!*' she was screaming in her head as she forced her legs to move. '*No, God! Please don't let it be Tricia! I'll do anything if you don't let it be Tricia! Anything.*'

God hadn't listened.

In the cataclysmic seconds as she looked down at Tricia's face, almost nun-like beneath the white theatre cap covering her hair, Tricia's eyes had flickered open.

'Mama?' she had said, a child in a woman's body, her eyes focusing hazily on Rusty's face. 'Mama, he frightened me. He tried to get into my knickers and . . . and . . .' Her voice had been fuzzy and bewildered and indistinct, but not so indistinct that Rusty hadn't understood every word. 'And when I got frightened he got angry and . . . and . . .'

Her eyes had rolled up beneath her lids.

'Tricia? *Tricia*!' She had thought Tricia had been dead then, even before she had been wheeled into the operating theatre.

The doctor had taken hold of her by the arm, steering her away from the trolley as the lights above the double doors had flicked from red to green and theatre staff had begun wheeling the trolley forward.

'What's going to happen to her?' she had asked, fighting hysteria as the doors closed behind the trolley. 'What kind of surgery is she going to have? How is she injured? *How* was she injured? Who brought her into Casualty? Was it a man? Was it . . .'

'We need to go back to Admissions,' the doctor had said, still holding her arm. 'We'll need your daughter's full name and date of birth, etc, and the police will be wanting to speak with you.'

'*What happened to her*?' As she had stepped once again into the lift she had been near demented with distress.

'Your daughter has a broken back and severe internal injuries, Mrs Reece,' the doctor had said reluctantly, his hands now deep in the pockets of his white coat. 'I can't tell you how she came by her injuries – the police will do that.'

'She'd been thrown from a car travelling at speed towards the Well Hall roundabout, near Catford,' Rusty said two days later as she was allowed the special privilege of speaking with Bryce in privacy. 'Me and Tina were at the hospital all night waiting for her to come back from theatre and recover consciousness . . . but she didn't, Bryce.'

Her voice, raw with grief, cracked and she began sobbing. 'He killed her, Bryce! Tricia didn't say his name, but she didn't need to – it was Frankie Briscoe! From what Tricia said, it's obvious what happened – she had a childish panic attack and he pushed her from the car to shut her up! He didn't even stop to see how badly she was hurt! He just drove away and it was another motorist – one who didn't see what had happened – who found her lying in the road and called for an ambulance. There's no way the police are going to get Frankie. They only have my word for it that she was with him – and I can't *prove* anything. He's going to get away with it, Bryce. Just as the bastard's always got away with everything.'

Bryce didn't give vent to the crucifying rage and all-consuming grief he felt. His mind was racing and he knew he couldn't afford to. Not now. Not yet. There would be weeks and months in which he would rage and grieve – possibly years. What was vital now, in the precious few minutes of privacy left to them, was to make sure Rusty knew exactly what he planned to do – and that she understood exactly what he wanted her to do.

'I'm going to kill him,' he said tersely. 'I'm going to break out of here and kill him, Rusty. And I need your help.'

She didn't say he was mad. She didn't say it was impossible. She simply fought to control her sobs, her eyes holding his, the pupils so dilated there was no telling iris from pupil.

'Before you arrange for Tricia to be cremated, check out the men's toilet at the crematorium. If it's small and tiled and there's an outside wall with a window, measure the size of the window. If it isn't small and tiled and there isn't a window, find a crematorium that has a toilet that fits the bill, OK?'

He was speaking fast and low, his eyes burning hers.

She nodded, her breathing shallow, terrified that at any moment a prison officer was going to enter the room to escort her from it.

'When you've got the measurements, get a chippie to cut a piece of hardboard that will fit in the space and that will hold there without being nailed. Have it tiled *exactly* as the rest of the wall is tiled, right? Immediately prior to the funeral, have someone put it in place for you. Arrange to have a bicycle near the toilet window, a car parked at the rear entrance to the cemetery, a diversion of some sort at the crematorium for exactly five minutes after my arrival. Rent a safe house in an unlikely area. And, Rusty – the car, make sure there's a gun wedged behind the brake and accelerator pedals. Jack will sort one. That's all you have to do, understand? And if I run into difficulties getting permission to attend the funeral, you have to pull out all the stops. *I have to be there.*'

'Christ Almighty, tell him *I'll* shoot the bastard!' Jack said, listening to Rusty in horror. 'Bryce is more than halfway through his sentence. If he breaks out now and is recaptured before he does for Frankie, he'll lose all chance of parole and it'll be another twelve years before he's back on the streets. If he breaks out and kills Frankie, he'll *never* be back on the streets, he'll be banged up for life! *I'm* the one who should be sorting Frankie – I need to get him anyway, before he gets me.'

'No, Jack.' Rusty's face looked as if it had been carved from marble. 'This is something Bryce has to do himself. He owes it to Tricia. He saved Frankie's life when you were all kids and all Frankie has done with his life is to terrorise and kill. If Bryce hadn't saved Frankie from drowning, Ginger wouldn't be dead and Big Chas wouldn't be dead and Tricia wouldn't be dead and God knows how many others who we don't know about wouldn't be dead. So just help me to do what Bryce has asked me to.'

Jack ran a hand through his hair, more sick at heart and fearful than he'd ever been. Bryce thought he knew Frankie; had the measure of him; could handle him. But Bryce had been inside for eight years and, though he knew in theory how powerful Frankie had become, he didn't know in practice. Big Chas hadn't been able to sort Frankie out and had ended up dead. What if the same thing happened to Bryce?

'I see you've got another sympathy card,' said one of the prison officers who Bryce was on reasonably friendly terms with, indicating the card Jimmy Briscoe had sent him. 'It's a terrible thing to lose a child – and they're still children even when they're in their teens, aren't they?'

The remark was well meant, but Bryce didn't trust his voice enough to be able to reply to it. Tricia had been more innocently childlike than any average teenager.

'Glad to know you've got permission to attend the funeral,' the prison officer continued. 'Sometimes, when it's step-family, the powers-that-be are iffy. You'll be cuffed all the time, of course. Time was when cuffs weren't used on the ferry, then a tearaway by the name of Virtue made a successful escape from one, so now, if the ferry goes down and you drown with your wrists cuffed, you know the bleeder to blame!'

Bryce had forced a wry grin – and why not? He was going to the funeral and once there, he'd make damn sure everything went his way.

When his cell door opened and the Prison Governor walked in, he knew instantly, from the expression on the Governor's face, that his grief was about to be compounded to a point impossible to bear.

'No!' he said, not wanting the Governor to speak; not

wanting to hear his news; the blood draining from his face in such a tidal wave it was a miracle he was still standing.

'I'm sorry, Reece.' The Governor stepped inside the cell, flanked by a couple of minions. 'I wouldn't normally break such news in person, especially when the circumstances are gangland, but I know how close you and Jack Wilkinson were and two bereavements in a week is grim news for anyone.'

It was news he'd been fearful of receiving for years and yet he wasn't remotely prepared for it. He couldn't speak. Couldn't breathe. Jack couldn't be dead. No one had been more alive, more cocky and cheeky and devil-may-care than Jack. Who else would he be able to laugh with till the tears ran down his face? Who else would fight by his side, to the death if need be, in a tight corner? Jack wasn't just a friend, not even just a best friend. He was the family Bryce had lost the day his mum had been killed. He was the kid brother he'd never had.

'He was mown down in broad daylight,' the Governor was saying, laying a couple of newspapers on the bedside locker. One headline screamed, '*Casino chief in Kray-era killing!*' Another proclaimed: '*Ex-Reece man shot in back.*' 'The shooting took place from a speeding car and there have been no arrests – nor, according to the press, are any expected.'

Bryce was barely listening to him. He didn't need to. Frankie had gunned down Jack, and Frankie's murders never culminated in his arrest. This one was going to culminate in his death, though. For Tricia, for Jack, Frankie Briscoe was going to die.

Hours – days – had gone by, and he'd been like a man deaf and dumb and blind, the words JACK IS DEAD, JACK IS DEAD, JACK IS DEAD hammering in his head like a mantra.

When at last he'd been able to force his brain to function, his grief had been racked to even new levels by terror. The newspapers were full of speculation that the killing was linked to the missing Al-Bakara money. What if, because of the way his name was being bandied about in the press, his release for Tricia's funeral was called off? He wouldn't be able to live. Unless he killed Frankie, he simply wouldn't be able to live with himself.

His tension was such that no one, cons or screws, came near him. Somehow the hours passed. Somehow the morning of Tricia's funeral dawned without his release being cancelled.

On the morning of 2 January 1975, he stepped through Parkhurst's gates handcuffed to two prison officers and accompanied by a third.

Three prison officers was one more than he'd bargained for and the lines around his mouth were white with tension. He hadn't been able to speak to Rusty since their vital few moments of privacy and he had no way of knowing if all the arrangements he'd asked for had been put in hand. If they hadn't been – if the gun wasn't in place and the get-away arranged – then he was going to be completely fucked. Even if everything was laid on, he'd no way of knowing it was going to be sufficient. Arranging an escape in two minutes flat hadn't exactly been the easiest of tasks and he knew there were holes in his plan big enough to drive a fleet of buses through.

On the ferry, visibly handcuffed, he attracted a lot of curiosity from holidaymaking passengers and was uncaring of it. Casually and contemptuously, Frankie had murdered the two people in the world Bryce had loved most and he was going to see to it that Frankie paid in the only coin he understood.

Twice on the short ferry journey he asked to go to the

loo. 'I've got the trots,' he had said to the exasperated screw he was handcuffed to. 'Not surprising, under the circumstances, is it?'

Each time, the smallness of the boat's head had meant the prison officer he was handcuffed to couldn't possibly accompany him inside, and so each time he'd been unhandcuffed whilst all three officers stood guard on the far side of the john's door.

On his own in the john, the only window a mini-size porthole, he'd patted his breast pocket. Inside it was the faded wedding photograph of his mum and dad, a photograph of Tricia and the last letter Debbie had sent him. He hadn't wanted to leave these items in his cell; they were far too precious to him. He took the letter out and re-read it.

*'I've been here six months now and I love it,'* she had written in her strong distinctive handwriting using the florid violet ink she was so fond of. *'The atmosphere in Canada is different to that in England. There's a feeling that anything is possible. When I was a kid and I used to tell Mum I wanted to be an actress, she always used to say, "People like us don't do things like that." A Canadian mother wouldn't say that – especially not if the kiddie in question is as talented as I was! That's another thing about Canada – you soon learn not to have any truck with false modesty! I go to stage school during the day and waitress in the evening. In another four years, when you finally walk through those frigging gates, there'll be a transatlantic star waiting to welcome you back to the world – hang on in there. I am.'*

There was a loud banging on the door. 'Hurry it up, Reece, for Christ's sake! We're nearly at bleedin' Portsmouth.'

Wryly refolding the letter and putting it back in his breast pocket, Bryce flushed the loo. If his plans for the next few hours went to plan, he wouldn't be walking through any prison gates in four years' time. Pain at the thought, on Debbie's behalf, knifed through him. He wasn't going to alter his plans, though. Not even for Debbie. He owed it to Tricia and Jack to make Frankie pay the price. If he didn't, in or out of prison, he wouldn't be able to live with himself.

The drive from Portsmouth to London was fast. Squashed between two of his three escorts, still handcuffed, he saw enough of the passing scene out of the rear windows to be made acutely aware of how long he'd been banged up. The style of advertising on the billboards was different. Fashions were different. Car designs were different.

When they began speeding into the suburbs of south-east London he was seized by homesickness. He wanted to be out there, on the streets, going in the pubs and clubs, meeting up with his mates.

His mouth tightened. He'd never be meeting up with Jack again, though. Not anywhere. Not ever.

They were nearly at the cemetery now and his stomach was coiled tight with nerves. Everything depended on Rusty having carried out his instructions to the letter – and luck being on his side.

As they turned in through the cemetery gates, all the indications were good. It wasn't the cemetery nearest to Deptford – which meant that Rusty had ruled that one out as not being suitable for his needs.

'Once we're out of the car, there's to be no fraternising with anyone. You can have a few words with your ex-wife and that's it, understand?'

'Yeah. Fine. Thanks for your sympathetic understanding.'

As the car slid to a halt he saw a scattering of other cars and a small group of mourners. Rusty was on the crematorium chapel steps, waiting for him. Dressed starkly in black, she was holding on to a wide-brimmed hat that framed her face as it shadowed it, her hair drawn back into an incandescent twist in the nape of her neck. Tina Dixon was with her.

He stepped from the car, manoeuvring with difficulty thanks to the handcuffs shackling him to his escorts, and saw with utter incredulity that Gunter and Curly and Georgie were standing beneath the chapel's porch.

His mind raced frantically. He appreciated their extraordinary show of sympathy, but as all three of them were strongly suspected of being crims who had got away with a big one, their presence might very well have attracted the attention of the police – and police presence at the crematorium was the last thing he needed.

He did as much of a recce as he could in the brief seconds that it took him to walk, escorted, from the car to the chapel steps. Jimmy Briscoe was there, a shockingly diminished figure who looked more like a man of sixty than one in his thirties. Bryce wondered if he'd discharged himself from hospital. Whether he had or not, Bryce appreciated the enormous effort that being there had cost him. There were other people he recognised: friends of Rusty's, and neighbours, but, to his vast relief, no police.

'I'm so sorry about Jack.' Rusty's voice was thick with pain and his frustration at not being able to hug her tight was almost more than he could bear. Then she said: 'I thought I was going to be late for my own daughter's funeral, Bryce. My blue Volvo packed up halfway down the Old Kent Road and I nearly had to cycle here via back doubles.'

He knew she was telling him which car was the ringer; that it was in place at the rear entrance to the cemetery and the bike was in place also. Their eyes held, saying a lot more – that she, like him, knew that Jack's death was down to Frankie; that she'd done everything he'd asked her to do; that the five-minute countdown he'd asked for was now under way.

As their small party began to walk into the chapel, Bryce started counting seconds away in his head. Now that the time had come, the knowledge that he wouldn't be seated when the hearse arrived and Tricia's coffin was carried in and laid on the waiting bier was like a physical blow. Why hadn't he arranged for things to happen *after* the short service? Doing so surely wouldn't have made much difference to the outcome.

Fifty seconds, his mental time-keeping said. One minute. One minute two seconds . . .

Though Billy Dixon hadn't known Tricia, he, too, was inside the chapel – as was a tall, mature figure he had never seen before and whom he knew instantly to be Rusty's Swiss boyfriend.

One minute six seconds. One minute eight seconds . . .

The piped music being played was Tricia's favourite hymn 'All Things Bright and Beautiful' and he knew Rusty had arranged to have it played now because he wouldn't, if God was good, be around to sing it during the brief service.

One minute twelve seconds. One minute fourteen seconds . . .

Even though it was early January the flowers decorating the chapel were all spring-like and child-like. Posies of violets and snowdrops. Flutes of cowslips. Vases of pale yellow African daisies.

One minute twenty seconds. One minute twenty-two seconds . . .

'Sorry, fellas,' he said to the two men on either side of him. 'I've got to get to a loo again. Fast.'

One minute thirty-five seconds. One minute thirty-seven . . .

His heart was slamming, his tension far worse than anything he had ever experienced in the seconds before going into action on a job.

One minute forty seconds. One minute forty-two . . .

'Christ Almighty, Reece! Can't you put a cork in it?'

Bryce eyeballed the prison officer in question. 'Just mind your frigging language!' he exploded savagely. 'This is my step-daughter's funeral, remember?'

Two minutes. Two minutes two seconds . . .

With one of them seriously wrong-footed and the other seriously disgruntled, the two prison officers did an about turn, Bryce wedged between them.

Two minutes ten seconds. Two minutes twelve seconds . . .

'The loos are off the entrance porch,' one of them said as they began walking out of the chapel, the third prison officer a pace or two behind them.

At the chapel door, Rusty's eyes again met his, her face cameo-white. Not by a flicker did either of them reveal the excruciating tension they were under.

Three minutes. Three minutes two seconds . . .

'In we go,' the officer on his left-hand side said, pushing open a door emblazoned with the word GENTS.

Bryce was unable to keep a count of the minutes any longer. Knowing there were beads of perspiration on his forehead, knowing it was now or never, he cast a swift look at the three blank, tiled walls and said, 'I'm not Houdini. Give me a break, will you? I don't want my family witnessing the humiliations I live with.'

Both officers glanced around the lavatory, so small it boasted only one loo and two stalls.

'Be a damn sight quicker than you were on the bleedin' ferry,' one of them said as he uncuffed him. 'And you'd better see the doc when we get back to Parkhurst. You need a heavy dose of kaolin, mate.'

The door slammed shut and he was on the inside and they were on the outside. How many minutes and seconds had gone by since the countdown had started? It must now be three minutes easy; perhaps even four.

In two swift strides he crossed to the only wall that could be an outside wall. Close to, the grouting between

365

the hardboarded tiles and the other tiles showed clearly. Praying to God the section wasn't going to be fixed in so tightly that he couldn't, without tools, remove it, he gave the lower edge a short, sharp knock.

His relief as the entire three-by-two-foot section tilted away from the wall was so vast he knew he would never forget it. The window beyond was closed and he pushed it open. A bicycle was propped against the wall below.

The two screws he had been handcuffed to were standing guard outside the lavatory door. The third would, no doubt, be keeping a watchful eye on things from the porch itself. His only problem now was whether the window was going to be big enough for him to wriggle through it. He wasn't as limber as he'd been in his youth and, despite all his denials to the contrary to Debbie, he'd piled on quite a few extra pounds during his years inside.

He glanced behind him towards the door. What was the timing now? It had to be nearly five minutes. If no diversion took place within the next few seconds he was going to have to make a run for it without one. He just couldn't afford to wait any longer. Another minute, perhaps less, and an exasperated prison officer would be striding into the toilet to see what the hell was keeping him.

He flushed the loo and re-crossed to the window, putting his hands on the high window-sill and prising himself up so that he could wriggle through the window head-first.

Then he heard a car approaching the chapel. From where he was he had no view of the entrance drive – all the side window looked out on to was a narrow pathway flanked by large bushes of laurel.

The tone of the engine wasn't right – the car was being driven far too fast and, though he couldn't see it, he was also sure it was being driven erratically.

His throat was dry. The five minutes were now surely up and instinct told him that the car was the diversion

Rusty had planned. Whether it was or not, he could wait no longer.

With the noise of the refilling toilet cistern giving him background cover he thrust himself out of the window, falling in a rolling foetal position to minimise the impact of the drop.

The unseen car was still going full pelt. As Bryce snatched hold of the bicycle, there was a screeching of tyres and the God-Almighty sound of metalwork crashing into stonework.

The screams and shouts, as he began pedalling furiously down the narrow path that wound away at the rear of the chapel, were music to his ears. Everyone would be running to the scene of the impact to render what assistance they could – and that would include the prison officer he hadn't been handcuffed to and perhaps one, or even both, of the two standing guard outside the loo door.

Unseen and unmolested, he whizzed through the old part of the cemetery, coming to a small side-entrance. Beyond it, parked at the kerb, was a blue Volvo. Knowing there would be a key in the ignition, the address of a safe house in the glove compartment and praying to God the gun was where he'd asked for it to be, he jumped from the bicycle and sprinted for the car.

Thanks to Rusty and whoever had been driving the unseen car, he was away.

Now all that was left was for him to find Frankie.

And to kill him.

# Chapter Nineteen

Wedged behind the accelerator and brake pedals had been a .38 Webley pistol. The address of the safe house was in the glove compartment as he had expected, but he hadn't driven straight to it. Knowing how soon his description would be with every copper in the city, knowing he had very little time in which he could look for Frankie without fear of being found, he'd headed the Volvo in the direction of Bermondsey and all Frankie's old haunts.

The problem was, of course, that most of Frankie's old haunts were also his old haunts and the attention he aroused, as a prison escapee, was colossal. By the time he had drawn a blank at Frankie's London Bridge flat and the south-east London pubs he habitually used, Bryce knew that, wherever Frankie was, he would know he was being hunted – the grapevine would have seen to that.

When Bermondsey had yielded nothing, he'd sped through the Rotherhithe Tunnel into the East End – it had been Frankie's patch all through the years he'd run with the Twins. He was as likely to run Frankie to earth there as anywhere.

Luck was against him and, as the hours had ticked by, he knew the risks of his being swiftly recaptured were increasing by the minute. He needed to be able to continue his search 'guised up, and that meant re-planning in a safe place – and the only safe place open to him was the house arranged by Rusty.

The address was Lee Green, an area sandwiched between middle-class Blackheath and working-class Lewisham.

As night had fallen he'd joined the crawl of commuters travelling southwards through the Tunnel and over Blackheath and then down the hill towards Lee Green crossroads. Outside a newsagent's an evening-paper billboard screamed the headline: '*Major Bank Robber Escapes Parkhurst!*'

It wasn't strictly accurate – he hadn't, after all, escaped from *within* Parkhurst, but it was near enough the truth as not to matter.

Turning left at the crossroads, continuing to follow the directions Rusty had left in the car's glove compartment, he knew with a tightening of his stomach muscles that his luck had definitely turned. Now there was a full-scale manhunt on for him, his search for Frankie was going to be risky as hell.

He drew to a halt outside a trim box-like little house on a newly built housing estate.

He needed to get a message to Gunter – and he needed to do so fast. For all he knew, Gunter and Curly and Georgie could be booked on a flight out of the country that very evening. They certainly wouldn't be staying around for Jack's funeral. Jack's funeral was going to be thick with plain-clothes cozzers and would be a risk too great for them to take.

Controlling his feelings with difficulty, he let himself into the house, knowing Rusty would have made quite sure that there was a telephone, well aware that, compared to the problems of hunting Frankie down, his escaping had been a piece of cake.

'Any luck?' The phone had been ringing even before the front door had closed behind him and the taut, nerve-wracked voice was Rusty's.

'No. Are you speaking from a phone-box?'

'Yes.'

That established, his voice relaxed an edge.

'Speak to Gunter for me. Fast,' he said, knowing he should be asking her about Tricia's funeral service and completely unable to bring himself to do so. If the two of them began talking about Tricia, neither of them would be able to think straight. 'Now the hounds are out, my wings are clipped. I need someone to locate Frankie for me, then I can make a move. Understand?'

'Yes. Things aren't easy. Number 46 is under heavy surveillance and so am I. Terry Briscoe's gaff has been searched and so has Connie's. Even your straight friends' places have been turned over: Richard and Robert Wilkinson's, Curly and Georgie's mother's place. The Old Bill are combing south-east London for you as if you were an escaped serial killer. I've made this call by dodging from train to train on the underground and using a call box at Old Bond Street station. If I haven't stocked in everything you need there's nothing I can do about it. I can't get over to you. They'd be on me every inch of the way.'

'Everything's fine,' he said swiftly, not knowing if it was or wasn't as he hadn't yet had a chance to vet the place. Even if it wasn't, though, he wouldn't put extra stress on Rusty by telling her so. 'Who was driving the diversion car? It sounded as if it went into a wall at a fair lick. No one was hurt, were they?'

'No.' Despite the circumstances a smidgen of wry humour entered Rusty's voice. 'The driver was Louie. She really put her heart and soul into things, shrieking that her legs were trapped. She's well into her eighties now and anyone who hadn't run to help her would have stuck out as being right fuckers. The prison officers were immediately in there, all three of them.'

'Thank her for me,' he said, and then, his throat tightening, 'Rusty, about Tricia . . .'

'No!' There was no longer even the faintest vestige of humour in her voice now. The hysteria she'd been fighting to control ever since Tricia's coffin had slid away from view at the crematorium rose thick in her throat. 'I can't talk about Tricia, Bryce. Get Frankie for me. That's all I ask. *Get Frankie*!'

Now that Frankie knew he was being hunted – and was in no doubt as to why – getting him was no easy task. Despite every copper in London having his description, Bryce was up at dawn next morning, driving out of London and into east Kent. Though it hadn't been mentioned between them for years, he was fairly sure Frankie still used the caravan on the Isle of Sheppey as a stow for goods and guns.

The caravan was still there, almost impossible to distinguish amongst the hundreds of others packed on the site. There was no sign of Frankie himself, though, and nothing to indicate he'd been there in the past few hours. For several minutes he debated whether to break in or not. If he did, there would be no way of disguising the fact that he had done so; if he didn't, Frankie would be under the happy impression that the caravan was still an unviolated bolt-hole.

Instinct told him that Frankie still believing the caravan could be of use to him would be the most useful option.

From the caravan site he'd motored into nearby Maidstone, parking up and strolling into a large branch of Boots the Chemist. There he'd bought hair dye and, at a market stall in the High Street, a flat cap, a scarf and a woolly hat and, at another stall, a pair of cheap, weak-lensed, horn-rimmed reading glasses.

There was a highly visible police presence in the High Street and as he'd returned to his car he'd walked past a shop window stacked with televisions and stereos. It wasn't a pleasant experience. From a dozen different televisions, in a dozen different screen sizes and colour tones, his image confronted him. He glanced at his watch. It was a minute or so after one o'clock. The programme was the news and he was the lead item.

At a painfully decorous speed, knowing if he were pulled over by the police for the slightest infringement his goose would be cooked, he drove back to the Lee Green house.

That afternoon he lightened his hair several shades, put on the glasses and cursed himself for not having had the forethought to ask Rusty to stock the house with a couple of wigs and false moustaches.

His next phone call from Rusty told him what he needed to hear: Gunter and Curly and Georgie were doing their stuff for him. 'But you're on your own, Bryce,' Rusty added, her voice fraught. 'Everyone you've ever had contact with is under surveillance. None of us can get to you. The risks are just too great.'

For the next two days he saw himself on every television news broadcast and in every newspaper he bought. Disguised to the best of his ability, grateful for the fact that it was winter and therefore it would not seem odd for him to be wearing a hat and scarf, he racked his brains as to where Frankie could be hiding. Whenever a new possibility occurred to him, he checked it out despite the risk.

'The police know damn well you're out to get Frankie,' Rusty said when she next made contact with him. 'You'd think, under the circumstances, they'd be happy to let you get on with it, wouldn't you?'

'Not while the Al-Bakara money is still missing,' he had said drily. 'It's the missing money that's ensured I'm still such a high priority. You're not moving house for a while yet, are you?'

'Not till after what has to be done has been done.' Rusty's voice was brittle and totally bereft of the bounce that had always been in it before Tricia's death. 'Once Frankie's been dealt with, I'm going to move to Zurich and become Mrs Gregor Zimmerman. I'm not going whilst

Frankie's still alive, though. Until that bastard pays for having killed Tricia, my life is on hold.'

His next phone call had been one that had left him totally gobsmacked.

'Rusty give me the number,' Connie Briscoe said the instant the receiver was at his ear. 'When I tell why, you'll understand.'

'I hope so. I'm not exactly wanting this number advertised.'

'It's Debbie,' Connie said succinctly. 'The minute she saw the news about your escape in the Canadian papers she hopped a plane. She arrived at my house this morning. She wants to see you, and she's being bloody fierce about it. When I told Rusty what the scenario was, she said for me to give you a bell. Thing is, Bryce, the Old Bill don't know Debbie from Adam. She can visit and bring you in things and there's no way anyone will be following her. What d'yer think?'

What did he think? The blood was pounding so hard in his ears and his heart was slamming so hard that he couldn't think – at least not clearly.

'Yeah,' he managed at last. 'Fine, Connie. Tell Rusty that where Debbie's concerned everything is sweet.'

'I thought it would be,' Connie said drily and then, her voice changing: 'And Bryce . . . get that bastard Frankie for me. I know me and Chas had been divorced a long time, but we was always good mates. You're the only one left who can sort Frankie out. My Tommy ain't clever enough and neither is Terry. Frankie would get them long before they got him. And poor Jimmy ain't long for this world, Bry. He can't even get out of bed any more.'

'I'll get Frankie,' he said quietly in a voice of steel, his head again filled with the image of Tricia's coffin. 'He won't get me first, Connie, I promise you that.'

He put the receiver down, his heart still pounding.

Debbie had flown from Canada the instant she'd known he was on the run. Of course, she could have done so for a variety of different reasons – none of them being the reason that would matter to him more than any other.

He made himself a cup of coffee and sat down at the kitchen's breakfast-bar, pushing a newspaper with his own image on the front page to one side. It was yesterday's paper and the article accompanying his photograph was full of speculation as to who his accomplices had been on the Al-Bakara job and whether he had escaped because his share of the haul had been, or was about to be, filched from him.

Debbie. Not for the first time he tried to get his head around the fact that she had been fathered by Roy Clarkson. How could he possibly feel like this about someone with Roy Clarkson's genes? And, nearly as bad, how could he feel like this about someone so closely related to hideous Hilda?

He swallowed a mouthful of scalding Nescafé. There was Sandra. He mustn't – couldn't – forget that Debbie was Sandra's daughter as well as Clarkson's. The problem was – did that make the situation better or worse?

He'd loved Sandra and, even now, after all these years and though he seldom saw her, he still had deep, complex feelings for her. If Sandra had been different – if she'd had the strength necessary to stand by him and wait for him, then his entire life since being released for Roy's manslaughter would have been different.

Perhaps, and perhaps not.

He swallowed another mouthful of coffee. Speculating about what might have been was a bloody pointless waste of time. It was the situation in the here-and-now that he needed to address – and the situation was that Debbie would be telephoning him at any minute.

She didn't do so.

Half an hour later – the telephone still silent – he paced through the small house for the hundredth time. Had she changed her mind? Had it been a mistake having her contact Rusty for his address? Why the fuck hadn't he simply told Connie to give her his telephone number? Rusty was in love with someone else now and wasn't likely to have thrown a jealous tantrum over Debbie, but Debbie's age would certainly have been against her where Rusty was concerned.

He thought back to Rusty's barbed and bitter remarks about cradle-snatching when he had begun his affair with Nina. Debbie was nineteen, not seventeen as Nina had been, but as he was now thirty-eight and not twenty-nine he couldn't imagine Rusty seeing things differently. What if Rusty had . . .

There came the sound of a car pulling up outside the house.

Seconds later he heard a short, sharp knock on the front door.

He rushed to open it and there she was: sea-green eyes meeting his, wheat-gold hair falling waterfall straight to her shoulders, a beautifully cut black wool coat fastened high at her throat.

'A crim on the run needs a moll!' she said in her disconcertingly direct manner. 'So here I am.'

In the seconds before the door closed behind her and he pulled her into his arms, he experienced an emotion that utterly confounded him. He loved her. Really loved her. Despite her being Roy Clarkson's daughter, despite his having loved her mother, despite his having known her since she'd been a sulky child, he was totally committed to her. For the first time in his life he knew that fidelity was, for him, going to be the name of the game. Where Debbie was concerned, anything else was absolutely unthinkable.

\*　　\*　　\*

She was a virgin. They were lying amidst tumbled sheets in the only bed in the house when the realisation dawned on him. Appalled, he tried to pull back.

She wouldn't let him.

'No!' Her gorgeously long legs were high and crossed at the ankles behind his back, her arms were around his neck and her fingers were knotted deep in his hair. 'It doesn't matter, darling. *It doesn't matter*!'

'You should have told me.' It was much later and he was holding her gently in his arms, his mouth against her hair. 'I would have taken more time . . .'

She turned slightly, her eyes meeting his. 'I didn't want you to take your time,' she said, her voice full of amusement, her eyes full of love. 'I'm nineteen and I've thought of nothing else since I was fifteen – perhaps even younger.'

Her candour, as always, devastated him. 'We need to talk,' he said, knowing the moment he'd put off for years could be put off no longer.

'About why you escaped?' She turned a little more against the pillows so that she was facing him full on. 'I already know. Connie told me. She told me about Ginger and Big Chas.' Her eyes were dark with compassion. 'And about Tricia and Jack.'

He imprisoned her hands in his. 'I have to talk to you about how your history, though you don't know it, is bound up with mine.'

It seemed suddenly very still and quiet in the room. It was early afternoon and a winter sun streamed through the window in pale shafts.

Something flashed through her eyes and he wasn't sure what it was.

'Does this have something to do with the secret my mother always hinted at but never spoke about when she said you should have been hanged? I've always known that, before I was born, something happened to make her hate you, but she'd never talk about it and I never cared what it was. And I don't care now.'

'The rumours about your mum and dad not being your mum and dad are true, Debbie.'

She frowned, opening her mouth to speak.

He continued swiftly, knowing he couldn't let her silence him; knowing he had to tell her everything before he lost his nerve: 'Hilda and Norman were your grandparents. Their only son, Roy, was your dad. Your mother . . .'

He was seized by a memory of Sandra as she had looked before Roy had ruined her life. Sandra wearing a white blouse with the collar flicked up, a kingfisher-blue skirt swirling around her legs, black velvet ballet pumps on her feet.

'Your mother . . .' he continued, his voice thick with emotion, 'was my girlfriend. Her name was Sandra Parry and she lived next door to me and my mum and dad when I was a small kid. Later, after my dad was killed in the war and after my mum was killed . . .'

He broke off. He'd always known this was going to be hard but it was even worse than he had anticipated. How many years had it been since he had spoken to anyone about his mum's death? And he couldn't do so even now. Later, perhaps, but not now. His mum's death was a tragedy separate from the one that affected Debbie so deeply.

'Later I moved in with the Parrys,' he continued, blotting out memories of Len Parry beating him on an almost daily basis and of little Tigger being kicked across the kitchen so hard that he bled to death, 'and later still I moved in with Frankie Briscoe's family.'

'But why didn't my mum . . . Hilda . . . ever talk to me about my dad? If he was her son, she could have talked about him easily, couldn't she? Did something happened to him? And *where is my real mum*?'

The enormity of the dreadfulness of what he was about

to tell her hit him full force, but there was no way back now. He'd started and there was no option but to see it through.

'Roy was a . . . a strange kid. He never mixed with the other kids in Swan Row. He was always bookish and always under Hilda's thumb. The summer we were all seventeen he became obsessed by Sandra – not that anyone knew about it at the time. If Sandra suspected he had a crush on her she never said anything – not even to me.'

He paused. She didn't say anything. Her eyes were fixed on his and she was so still that even her breathing seemed to be suspended.

'It was an early evening in 1954. I was waiting outside what was Tucker's the Butchers, for Sandra. We were going to go over the water to a ballroom called the Royal, in Tottenham. Sandra was walking down the row to meet me . . .'

He paused again. In another few seconds she was going to know that she was born as the result of a rape. There was no way he could fudge that – not if he was also going to tell her that he had killed Roy. And even if he didn't tell her, she knew enough now to be able to find out the circumstances of Roy's death for herself.

'Hilda and Norman were out on a church outing and Roy asked Sandra if she'd help him with a cat that was stuck on the top of a wardrobe.'

His hands were so tight on hers now that her skin, beneath the imprint of his thumbs, was white.

'There was no cat . . . he just wanted Sandra in the house. And when he'd got her there . . .'

His eyes were no longer holding hers.

'. . . when he got her in the house, he raped her.'

He heard Debbie's sharp intake of breath and still he couldn't look at her.

'I was walking back up the row to see what was keeping her and I heard her scream. The Clarksons' door was open and I rushed straight in there. Roy was . . .' He broke off, then forced himself to keep going: 'It was obvious what had happened . . . I went for him. It was a fist fight . . . or it would have been.'

For the first time in twenty years he relived the moment at the top of the Clarksons' stairs when his foot had slipped on the carpet and Roy had jumped on to his back.

'I half fell . . . Roy jumped on my back, trying to throttle me. We were at the very top of the stairs and I couldn't shake him off: I had no room to manoeuvre. I was a ted – a teddy boy – and in those days it was part of a ted's job description to carry a flick-knife.'

He could hear his heart beating and nothing else.

'I didn't mean to kill him. I didn't like him and, yes, I wanted to hit him into the middle of next week for what he'd done to Sand, but I never meant to kill him.'

At last his eyes met hers again.

'So, now you see why Hilda hated me so much. She had every reason to. I was sentenced to nine years for Roy's manslaughter and served six. You were born nine months later – and there was never the remotest chance of your being my child. Sandra and I never . . . she wanted to be a virgin when we got married . . . And when you were born Hilda and Norman adopted you.'

It was over. Everything that had to be said, if they were ever to have any kind of a future together, had been said.

Her pale, ivory face was like a mask.

'My mother,' she said, *'where is my mother?'*

It was, incredibly, her only real concern. His relief was so vast he hardly knew how to give expression to it. That evening, downstairs and in a room lit only by the flames of an old-fashioned fire, he told her, in detail, about Sandra. He told her about the fear and misery in

Sandra's life after her father came home from the war. He told her about Tigger's death. He told her how, when it became obvious she was pregnant, Sandra was sent to a harshly regimented mother-and-baby home about as far from London as it was possible to get.

'To understand her attitude to you, both before and after you were born, you have to understand the trauma of what she went through,' he said as, seated beside him on the hearthrug, she rested her back against his knees. 'What happened to her would have been terrible for any girl her age, but Sandra . . . Sandra was always terribly vulnerable. She always needed someone to look after her.'

She said nothing and he knew it was because she accepted what he was saying totally; that she understood exactly how deep her mother's trauma had been.

He told her about the scene the morning after his release from prison, when he had traced Sandra to the Romford police house and learned of her marriage to Malcolm Hurst. And he told her that she had two half-brothers.

When he had finished, she said quietly: 'I understand why she's never wanted to see me or know anything about me, but now I know of her existence I have to go and see her. You understand that, don't you, darling? If, when I do, she still doesn't want to have anything to do with me, then that's down to her. But I have to see her. I have to give her the chance.'

It wasn't a scenario he could look forward to but, in relation to his other problems, it was practically a doddle. The police search for him was showing no signs of losing momentum and so long as it continued the risks he ran in looking for Frankie were enormous. Every second he was out on the street he was also running another kind of risk. Just as he was looking for Frankie, so every henchman Frankie possessed was looking for him – and they were doing so with shooters rammed through their trouser belts.

He was fixing a false blond moustache to his upper lip, intent on running the gauntlet once again, when the telephone rang. He answered it swiftly, knowing his caller would be Rusty.

'Has Gunter had any luck?' he said tersely. 'Someone must know where Frankie is lying low. What about . . .'

'Victor's been on the blower to me.' Rusty's voice was fraught with tension. 'He wants a meet, Bryce. Strictly off the record. It isn't a set-up, he swore it on his mother's life. He has a proposition – and it's to do with Frankie.'

From where he was standing, he could see across the small lounge and through the window to where an almond tree was rimed with January frost.

There had been a time, before his arrest for the Al-Bakara job, when he would have trusted Victor's word implicitly. He couldn't do so now, though. Victor was no longer a friend. He'd ceased to be a friend when he hadn't so much as given him the nod before the raid on Rusty's. Given an hour, perhaps only half an hour, he could have been away, out of the country. That he'd been denied that chance, that he had instead stood trial and been sentenced to twenty-one years, was all down to Victor.

'No,' he said at last, his voice bitter. 'I don't trust him, Rusty. It's not on.'

There was a short, tense silence and then she said: 'If it's to do with Frankie, Bryce, I'd like to know what the proposition is. I can't endure the strain much longer. Every waking moment I'm terrified you're either going to be recaptured before you've found Frankie, or that Frankie and his gorillas will kill you before you kill him. If Victor's got a proposition, let's at least listen to it.'

Debbie was out, doing some grocery shopping, and the house was very still and quiet.

'OK,' he said reluctantly. 'For you, Rusty. Arrange it.'

After he had replaced the receiver he stood for a long time staring out of the window at the almond tree. What proposition could Victor possibly have for him? And how were they to handle any kind of a meeting after the history they had shared?

Both questions were impossible to answer and he frowned, turning his mind to the more practical matter of the location for the meet. It needed to be somewhere out in the open where it would be harder for him to be taken by surprise and where, if he *was* taken by surprise, he stood a chance, however remote, of getting away.

They met in Bermondsey on a stretch of walkway beside the Thames. Not far away, across the oil-slicked water, he could see the spot where, thirty years ago, he had hauled Frankie from the quicksand.

'This is no easier for me than it is for you,' Victor said bluntly, his overcoat collar turned up against the biting wind. 'You're on to an absolute loser, Bryce. You know that, don't you?'

'I know you're a cunt.' Bryce couldn't even bring himself to make eye contact with his former friend. Twenty-one years. That was what Victor had let him in for. Twenty-one bleeding, fucking, shit-miserable years.

Victor flinched, the skin so tight across his cheekbones it looked like parchment.

'Let's cut the pleasantries, shall we?' He rammed his hands deep in his coat pockets. 'And let me repeat myself. You're on to a loser. If you were picked up today without even having committed a traffic offence since absconding, you'd be looking at losing all possible parole. If you do what you intend doing, you'll lose everything. There'll be no release – not even twelve years down the line. You'll be banged up for life, Bryce. Literally.'

'It'll be worth it.' Tight-lipped and hard-eyed, he finally turned to look at Victor. 'And don't tell me when I sort Frankie that you and your mates won't be raising a God-Almighty cheer, because I won't fucking believe you.'

'Frankie's a cop-killer. The cheer will raise the bleeding rafters. But why do it this way, Bryce? There's another way – a way that won't entail you losing your liberty until you're so old and grey there'll be no point in having it; a way where we'll all be doing ourselves favours.'

Bryce eased the zip a little higher on his black leather bomber jacket. 'Yeah? Surprise me, Victor.'

'Nail Frankie the legal way. Give us something on him that will stand up in court. That way there'd be no question of you losing parole . . .'

'I'm not grassing.' His voice was flint hard. 'I'll kill the bastard, but I won't grass on him. Any more prize suggestions?'

'Give us what we need on Frankie, tell me where your wedge from the Al-Bakara job is and in return we'll see to it that you don't serve any of your outstanding sentence. Not a day of it. For public consumption, you'll be a successful escapee. In reality, you'll have witness protection status. A new identity in the country of your choice. Plastic surgery. The whole works.'

Bryce was stunned by the magnitude of the offer, but he didn't let his reaction show. 'And have you and your mates on my back for the rest of my life?' he said jeeringly. 'Have you knowing everything about me – the name I'll be living under, where I'll be living? Have you able to pull my strings whenever it suits you? Have you able to pick me up at a moment's notice, knowing you'll be able to do so for the rest of my natural? No bloody thank you, Victor.'

The wind blowing off the river had grown even colder and stray snowflakes had begun to fall.

'Incontrovertible evidence from you where Frankie is concerned will have scores of lesser fry feeling safe enough to testify against him,' Victor continued relentlessly, as though Bryce hadn't spoken. 'Past victims. Bullied gang members. Anyone and everyone wanting to save their necks. With a bit of luck, we'll get someone talking about the night Tricia died and he'll answer for her death in court. One thing I can promise, when Frankie goes down, he'll go down for good. Why kill him when you could make him suffer ad infinitum? Especially when, if you kill him, you'll pay for it by having to serve every single day of your present sentence – and with a fresh sentence for Frankie's murder bunged on top.'

Bryce gave a mirthless laugh. 'Nice try, Victor, but I'm not going to be in your pocket till the crack of doom. Also, aren't you forgetting something? I might not be recaptured after I've ironed Frankie out. I might just be away on my toes, never to be seen again.'

This time it was Victor's turn to give a scoffing laugh. 'You haven't a hope in hell, Bry. The only reason you're still on the streets is because the powers-that-be don't care too much how Frankie is removed from the scene. Your killing him would save a lot of people time, trouble and expense. The deal that's on the table at the moment won't stay on the table. I've had to work my bollocks off to get it and I've done so because I still give a flying fuck about what happens to you!'

'Oh, you give a flying fuck all right!' Bryce's anger was unleashed and so intense the tendons in his neck stood out in knots. 'Twenty-one years I went down for! All because you were too much the honourable policeman to give me a word of warning! Minutes, that was all I needed! Just a few bleedin' minutes!'

Victor sucked in his breath, his pupils dilating. 'I gave you more than minutes! I gave you a good half-hour, at least!'

Their eyes held, the moment so taut and tense it could have been cut with a knife.

'When?' Bryce asked at last, white lines edging his mouth.

'The morning of the swoop. Before I gave the team the

order for the off. I phoned your Curzon Street number from a call box.'

'And didn't get through?'

'I got through and I gave you the word – or I thought I did. Who the fuck else would have been answering your phone at that time in the morning?'

Even before Victor had finished speaking both of them knew the answer.

'Nina.' Bryce's voice was unemotional. Just because Victor had, after all, made an attempt to give him a running start, it didn't put them back on the old footing. Nothing could do that.

'So what's it to be?' Victor asked, snowflakes settling on his hair and on the shoulders of his overcoat. 'A new face and new identity in sunny Spain, or re-arrest and the next twenty years or so sewing mailbags for the Queen?'

# Chapter Twenty

'What was your answer, Bryce?' Rusty felt as if her whole life was on the line as she waited for his reply.

'I told him to stuff it.'

'But that's insane!' Panic fizzed in her throat so thick she thought she was going to choke. 'It would solve everything – Frankie would be dealt with and you wouldn't be behind bars! Grassing on Frankie wouldn't be like grassing on any other crim. Frankie's a torturer and a murderer, for Christ's sake – and he's murdered within the family. If you have anything on him, Bryce, anything that will stand up in court, use it. Otherwise . . .'

Tears blinded her eyes.

'. . . otherwise I'm going to have to live the rest of my life knowing you're behind bars – and that you're there because you avenged Tricia for me.'

Sobs choked her voice, the strain of the last few weeks finally overwhelming her. 'I know I said I wanted Frankie dead, Bry, but it's too high a price for you to pay and it's unnecessary now!'

'I'd rather live out the next twenty years behind bars than have Victor controlling my every movement,' he said tersely, 'and that's what his offer would mean. I'm sorry, Rusty, but it can't be done.'

'Why can't it be done?' Debbie faced him across the breakfast bar as heavily falling snow misted the kitchen window.

Bryce ran his fingers through his hair. 'I'll spell it out in detail when you tell me exactly what Connie said when she phoned, and when you've given me a blow-by-blow account of your meeting with your mum.'

Debbie curled her hand round a steaming mug of milky hot chocolate. 'Connie says Jimmy is refusing any more treatment and that he's going to kill himself.'

Bryce sighed heavily, knowing there was nothing he could do for Jimmy. 'And the bit about Frankie?'

Her eyes held his, dark with tension. 'She says Frankie is in Essex. A straight businessman he's been terrorising has vacated his property leaving Frankie king of it. It's a sixteenth-century manor-house on the outskirts of Upminster, and Frankie is making out he's part of the county set, riding and shooting and fishing and enjoying the fact that you're chasing your tail trying to find him.'

A deep surge of satisfaction ran through every vein in Bryce's body. Now he knew where Frankie was, he needed nothing else.

'And your mother?' he asked, wondering if it had been wise to allow her to drive out to Romford unaccompanied. 'What was her reaction when you told her who you were?'

'She cried,' Debbie said simply. 'She cried and cried and cried.'

'I don't believe you!' Sandra had tried to slam the door shut but it had merely met with the resistance of Debbie's foot.

'I haven't come to cause a scene or to upset you,' she had said swiftly as Sandra had clung to the door, tears beginning to course down her cheeks. 'I simply want to say hello. My mum and dad are dead now and I live in Canada. I'm only here for a short visit.'

It had been a lot of information in a short time – all of it intentionally non-threatening – and it had done the trick.

'Hilda Clarkson is dead?' Sandra had wanted Hilda dead for so many years that even though Debbie had pointedly referred to Hilda as her mum she couldn't pretend the news was anything other than welcome.

'And I know you're married and have a family,' Debbie had continued, wanting to calm any anxiety Sandra might have. 'If they don't know about me, that's fine – I'll make sure it stays that way. I haven't come because I want anything from you – I've come because . . . because I couldn't *not* come. Not when I knew about you. Not when Bryce told me.'

The instant she uttered Bryce's name she had been aware of a sea-change in Sandra.

'Bryce? Bryce told you?' The hands clutching hold of the door visibly relaxed and the pressure of it against Debbie's foot had eased. 'Did he bring you here? Is he waiting for you?'

Her eyes had flown to the street and the handful of cars that were parked in it.

It had been the most disorientating moment of Debbie's life. She had ridden the knowledge that Bryce had been responsible for her father's death with remarkable composure. After all, she had never known Roy Clarkson. As far as she was concerned, Norman had been her father and always would be. She had also accepted that Bryce and her mother had been childhood sweethearts. It had seemed to be something that didn't really affect her and she certainly hadn't seen it as something that affected her own relationship with Bryce. Now it suddenly hit her full force that she was in love with the man her mother had been in love with – a man her mother obviously still had deep feelings for.

'No,' she said, severely disconcerted, 'Bryce isn't with me. I came alone.'

'And I don't know why, but after that it was easy.' Her hot chocolate had cooled to the point where a thin skin had formed on the surface of the milk and she pushed the mug

388

to one side. 'She invited me in and made me a cup of tea, and cried all the time she was making it. She said she knew it was a wicked thing to say to me, but that if I hadn't been born, her entire life would have been different.'

Bryce frowned. 'I don't see . . .'

'If I hadn't been born she wouldn't have left Swan Row.' Debbie had understood her mother's lopsided logic perfectly. 'And if she hadn't left the row, she would never have become so daunted at visiting you in prison, because she would have had people like Connie Briscoe giving her support and telling her how to manage. And if that had been the case . . .' she paused, stretching her hand across the breakfast bar-top and sliding it in his '. . . if that had been the case she'd never have got so lonely that she started dating Malcolm Hurst – and she would never have married him.'

His hand tightened on hers. 'But she did,' he said, sensing the new difficulties she was struggling to come to terms with and terrified they were suddenly going to become an issue between them. 'She could have waited for me and she didn't. That was her choice, Debbie. No one else's.'

His eyes were brilliant with passionate intensity and answering sensuality flared within her.

'Now, please tell me why you can't go along with the offer the police have made you,' she said, so fearful of his not accepting it she couldn't control the unsteadiness in her voice. If he didn't accept it, all they would ever have was the time they had spent together over the last few days. There would be no future for them. He would kill Frankie, or die trying, and, after either a short or a long period on the run, alone, he would be re-arrested and re-sentenced – and the sentence would be long. Longer than she could possibly endure.

'I'll tell you in bed.' His voice was husky as he rose to his feet, drawing her to him, as aware as she was of how little time was left to them.

\*　　\*　　\*

Their love-making in the sparsely furnished bedroom had, for both of them, taken on an almost surreal quality. Every second was precious; every minute a minute to be treasured. There were times, as he reached out gently for her, touching her breasts with his powerful yet tender hands, when the world outside ceased to exist and even Frankie was forgotten.

Later, as they lay against the tumbled pillows sharing a cigarette, he finally answered the question that was so tormenting her.

'I can't accept the offer Victor's made to me,' he said, exhaling a thin blue plume of smoke, 'because it comes with too many unmentioned strings.'

'Such as?' She moved slightly, resting her weight on one arm, her eyes fixed on his face.

The lines about his mouth deepened. How, when accepting it would mean they could be together in Spain or Australia or anywhere else that they fancied, could he explain why it had to be refused?

'There's more than one kind of prison, Debbie,' he said at last. 'Victor's offer would mean that, though Frankie's friends wouldn't know my new identity, Scotland Yard would. My new identity, my whereabouts, every aspect of my life would not only be known to Victor and his guvnors, it would be controlled by them. I'd have to forfeit the Al-Bakara cash . . .'

He took back the cigarette he had handed her.

'Not that I give a stuff about the cash if forfeiting it is the price I have to pay for our having a life together. But I have to know I'll have the freedom to replace it, and the deal with Victor would mean never having freedom. They'd have me by the short and curlies, and the gloating would be enough to make a cat sick. Plus . . .'

He drew in a deep lungful of smoke and passed the cigarette back.

'. . . plus they'd want more information from me. Once

I'd grassed on Frankie they'd want me to grass on a hundred other people – and they'd have a lot of leverage. It would be a case of: "Tell us what you know about X, Y and Z or we cancel the present deal and you're back inside." So, though I'd be more than happy to see the judiciary sending Frankie down for an eternity in Parkhurst – or Broadmoor, which is where he belongs – it can't be done.'

His voice was raw with bitterness. Victor didn't know about Debbie but it was almost as if he did, for having her in the equation made the offer almost impossible to turn down. Almost, but not quite. He couldn't have Victor controlling his every movement for the rest of his life. He would rather be dead.

'If, after you gave them what they need on Frankie, they thought you were dead, it would work, wouldn't it?' she said musingly.

He took the cigarette from her and, one arm behind his head, stared up at the ceiling.

If he were dead, it would be a doddle.

'Canada is wonderful. It makes you feel as if, no matter what has happened in the past, you can start life afresh. What if you accepted the police deal . . . said you wanted to go to Canada, and . . .' She broke off, unable to continue as she thought of all the years they would have to live without each other. Possibly nearly all their lives.

He inhaled deeply, thinking of Somerville, now a Chief Inspector in the Home Counties; of Jimmy, waiting to see him before he topped himself; of Connie Briscoe's passionate desire to avenge Big Chas's murder; of Gunter and Georgie and Curly, all three of them still in London and intending to stay for as long as he was on the run. And he thought of the Al-Bakara money in the legal archive vault in Temple West.

His eyes narrowed.

If, after he had given the Old Bill the necessary on Frankie, Victor thought he were dead, he would be able to embark on an entirely new life with Debbie – and he would be able to do so in Canada, surrounded by all his old mates. Frankie would be away for good. Victor would be shafted. And he would be sitting pretty.

He moved swiftly, swinging his legs from the bed, adrenaline surging through every vein in his body. He had telephone calls to make – the most important telephone calls of his life.

'I'm returning your call from a safe line,' Somerville said drily. 'Though what use I can be to you now I'm no longer in London, I don't know. If you're hoping to hide out on my manor, the answer is that it can't be done.'

'That isn't what I'm after – and quit the self-righteousness. If the money is big enough, you're going to be interested, right?'

There was a slight whistling noise as Somerville breathed in deeply through his nose. 'Are you referring to what I think you're referring to?'

The whole tone of Somerville's voice had changed and, as he stood in the telephone-box at Lee Green crossroads, Bryce grinned. The mere mention of the Al-Bakara haul had hooked Somerville and with Somerville hooked, the rest was going to be plain sailing.

'I am. So paying for a favour is no problem to me, right?

'It depends on the favour.' Beneath the greed in Somerville's voice, there was caution. 'You're not exactly low profile at the moment. What is it you're after?'

Bryce's grin deepened. 'Sit tight,' he said, knowing the first hurdle was over, 'and I'll tell you.'

'It's an ace plan.' Jimmy's voice on the telephone was fatigued and raw with pain. 'And I'm with you all the way. Don't hang about with it, though. The sooner I see Gunter and the Cravens, the happier I'll be.

'Get what from where and give it to Gunter?' Rusty's voice was dazed. 'Jesus Christ, Bry! What if I was the kind of housewife who had her curtains dry-cleaned every year? Then where the fuck would we all be?'

'Will do,' Gunter said decisively. 'Once Rusty's given me the key and I've removed everything from the vault, I'll divide it into a quarter and three-quarters. Seems like bloody madness, though. Why hand over anything to Victor?'

'Because if I don't, he'll never believe I'm dead, no matter what the evidence. Besides, it's only money. Once the four of us are together again as a team, there'll be plenty more. Trust me.'

'I do.' It was true – trusting Bryce was a habit he'd never be able to break. 'And what monicker am I to use? Malling?'

'Another meet?' On the other end of the telephone Victor jack-knifed from his chair with such alacrity he jarred his desk and sent a pile of papers flying. 'Great. This is the right decision, Bryce. The best decision. I can't tell you how fucking pleased I am!'

'Frankie's playing games from a manor-house on the outskirts of Upminster,' Bryce said as Victor walked up to him on the embankment footpath. 'But you know that already, don't you? You just weren't going to give me the benefit of the info.'

'Fuck Frankie's whereabouts.' Victor rubbed gloved hands together in deep satisfaction. 'Finding Frankie has never been the problem – evidence that'll nail him is what we're after, and I've always known you had it, Bryce. Call it a gut feeling, call it what you like. For all his henchmen, Frankie's essentially a loner. You and he used to be like brothers, and if Frankie's ever confided in anyone, it's you. Right?'

Bryce didn't answer. The code of not grassing was so deeply ingrained in him that even at this late stage of the game he found it almost impossible to go through with it. With his overcoat collar turned up and his hands deep in his pockets, he turned away from Victor, looking out over the ice-cold Thames. And he remembered Tricia. And Jack.

'The deal is that you fix me up with a new identity; that you fund me in a country of my choice – which, incidentally, is Brazil. There is no question of my returning to nick to finish my outstanding sentence or any other sentence. Right?'

'That's one side of it, Bryce. And in return for letting you off a further twelve years in the nick, you give the Crown Prosecution Service what it needs to go ahead with a case against Frankie, and you hand over your share of the missing Al-Bakara money. OK?'

'What's the timing?' Bryce had turned so that they were once more face to face. 'When do I get my new identity and fly out of the country?'

'When you've given us all we need on Frankie.' Victor's cheeks were chapped red by the icy wind. 'So what have you got on him that will do the trick? It had better be good, because if it's blown out of court, or it doesn't do the job, you'll be on a plane back to England faster than it takes to spit.'

'Frankie's gun-mad. You know that from when we were kids. He never ditches a gun. They're his children. I swear to God he has conversations with them.'

'And?'

'And shortly after I came out of nick in 1960 he showed me his slaughter. It's a caravan on the Isle of Sheppey.'

Victor frowned. Frankie Briscoe's slaughter would be an interesting bust, but any guns in it would be clean as a whistle. Frankie was too fly for them to be anything else.

'They'll be clean,' he said. 'Which won't get us anywhere.'

Bryce shrugged. 'They may be, and they may not. One gun that isn't clean is the Walther PK38 automatic he used when he killed your copper friend.'

Victor sucked in his breath, his nostrils white. 'Are you telling me the gun that killed Pete Jowett is in the slaughter at Sheppey?'

'No.' Bryce looked out across the Thames again. 'It should be, but it isn't. Frankie was in a panic after the shooting. He was certain his car had been noted and that he was about to be pulled any second. He drove straight to the casino and asked me to get rid of the gun. As a favour to him, I promised I'd dump it where it would never re-surface – and when he handed it over he was gloveless.'

'And?' Victor prompted yet again.

'And I dumped it in my stow – the same stow the Al-Bakara cash is tucked away in.'

'Christ!' Victor's initial reaction was stupefaction at the realisation that Bryce's Al-Bakara money was sitting nice and tight and undispersed and was going to be so easy to recover, then euphoria at the knowledge that he had, at last, evidence with which to nail Frankie. 'Christ!' he said again, slamming a fist into the palm of his hand. 'I have him! *I have him*!'

'OK, what's the next step?' Debbie asked, as, in bed that night, he told her of the meeting.

'I have to make a statement – not just about the gun incident but everything and anything about Frankie, going back to the year dot. Victor and his guvnors want their pound of flesh and the kind of statement they want is going to take time to give – perhaps as long as a week.'

'I don't want to endure another week,' Jimmy said to him in a near whisper over the telephone. 'The gun will be enough to do for Frankie. Have you handed it over yet?'

'I've cleared the vault.' Gunter's voice was unruffled, as always. 'Frankie's little parcel is safe and sound. Where shall we meet for the handover?'

'Georgie and Curly are already in place at Jimmy's,' Rusty said, her voice thick with nervous tension. 'When the three of them head out of London, I'm going to stay with Connie. She'll need all the support she can get.'

'Dental records will be enough.' Somerville's Oxford-educated tones were those of a man utterly certain of his ground. 'The price is a quarter mill, though. To the penny.'

'The money will be a quarter million down,' Bryce said as, with gloved hands, Victor placed the plastic carrier-bag containing Frankie's gun into a forensic bag in the boot of his car. 'I had expenses before I was arrested for the job, but what's left will be enough to ensure your promotion.'

'Debbie's given us the ring and the photograph and we're heading out of London tonight, Bryce,' Curly said from a pay-phone. 'Jimmy insists on it. He says now Victor's got your statement regarding the gun the rest don't matter too much and he ain't hanging around any longer. Christ, but I hope I never cop for cancer. Poor old Jimmy's in a terrible state and he says if it was left to the doctors he'd be suffering in that condition for weeks yet.'

\* \* \*

'Bryce, does your becoming Mr Malling – having your passport and all your ID in that name – mean that when we get married I'll be Mrs Malling, not Mrs Reece?' Debbie asked, looking down at the passport Gunter had retrieved from the Al-Bakara trunk. 'I've been scrawling "Debbie Reece" on things for years – it's going to take me ages to get used to "Debbie Malling".'

'Ballistics are 100 per cent happy with the gun and Frankie's arrest is all set for tomorrow morning.' Victor's meet with Bryce was at the usual place, beside the Thames. 'Your new ID is all in place and we'll have you out of the country the minute the cash is handed over. It isn't that I don't trust you, Bryce. I just have to be careful.'

'Yeah, 'natch, Victor.' Bryce looked across at his former friend, knowing he would never see him again. 'The cash is ready and waiting for you at Rusty's,' he said, no longer giving a damn about the money; knowing he hadn't given a damn ever since Jack had died because of it. 'Al-Bakara are welcome to it. I wouldn't have enjoyed spending a penny of it.'

Victor remained silent, knowing Bryce was remembering Jack's murder, well aware that though he had always yearned to be Bryce's closest male friend that honour had been Jack's. With iron self-discipline he controlled his feelings as, where Bryce was concerned, he had always controlled them.

'Jack was a good mate to you, I know that,' he said, his voice flat. 'But your other mates – Gunter and the Cravens, are long in your past, Bryce, and they should stay that way. You have the chance of a complete new start in life now. I know you've stipulated Brazil as your country of choice, but when Frankie's court case is over my guvnors want to move you to Australia. You'll be able to live a straight life far easier in Australia. You'll be able to get a job ... meet a nice woman ... settle down ...'

'Yeah. Sweet. A straight life. What you've always wanted for me, eh, Victor?'

Victor wondered what Bryce would say if he told him exactly what it was he had always wanted for him. It was impossible, of course, but he could go halfway.

'Pete Jowett, the detective constable Frankie killed, was homosexual.' He looked away from Bryce. 'Like me.'

The silence was profound.

Victor cleared his throat, unable to turn his head. 'I don't have lots of relationships, Bryce. I'm not into rent boys and that kind of thing. Pete was a decent bloke. My kind of a bloke. So you know now why this is so important to me. Why I have to nail Frankie.'

Just when he began to think the silence was going to go on forever he felt Bryce's hand touch his shoulder. It was a gesture that meant far more to him than words could ever have done.

He cleared his throat again. 'I need to be off. I've a lot to tie up before dawn tomorrow. Once Frankie's gone before a magistrate and been refused bail – and he will be – we'll get down to the business of taking more info from you and fleshing out your new ID. Pollard will be your name, by the way. Barry Pollard.'

With great difficulty Bryce suppressed a broad grin. Pollard. He wondered who had come up with that little gem and strongly suspected it had been Victor.

Despite the gulf their different professions had gouged between them, Bryce felt a sudden surge of affection for his former friend.

'You were my best mate when I was a kid, Victor. Don't think I've forgotten. I never have and I never will.'

It was Victor's turn to be incapable of speech.

With a mix of feelings far too complex for him to analyse, Bryce turned abruptly on his heel and began walking away over the cobbles towards his parked car.

'Bryce!'

He came to a stop and looked back.

'One thing, Bryce! The key to the archive vault – where was it hidden?'

Bryce grinned, throwing his car keys up into the air and catching them. 'In the hem of Rusty's mother's curtains. Your boys could do with a lesson in turning places over, Victor.'

Cracking with laughter he raised his arm high, waving goodbye, and then, without another backward glance, walked the remaining few yards to his car.

'I've got your ticket!' Debbie couldn't keep the glee from her face and voice. 'Vancouver. From the day I landed in Toronto I was told Vancouver was the place to be. Only another twelve hours! God, but I'm counting every minute away! Nothing can go wrong now, darling, can it? Not now you've off-loaded the cash to Somerville and Victor's collected from Rusty's?'

'It's over.' It was early dawn and in the field behind the telephone-box Gunter was speaking from, an Austin Estate car was exploding in a sea of flame. 'He did it for himself, but he wedged the rifle in place and had a string attached to the trigger. As the gun won't be found with him, the distance and angle should fool the forensic boys into thinking it was murder.'

Frankie was in bed with a long-suffering girlfriend when a score of armed police officers, Alsatians at their heels, stormed in on him mob-handed.

'*We are armed police officers and you are under arrest!*' Victor bellowed unnecessarily through a loud-hailer as a police helicopter circled overhead, sirens wailed and, handcuffed and stark naked, Frankie was dragged out of the mansion and into the back of a police car, kicking and bucking and blaspheming every inch of the way.

'I strongly suspect the hunt for Reece is now over,' Chief Inspector Somerville said wryly over the telephone to the high-ranking Flying Squad officer who had been helping to co-ordinate the search for Bryce. 'The body was found in a blazing car early this morning. Signs are the victim died as the result of a bullet between the eyes. No gun was with the body and, even if it had been, the pathologist's opinion is that the bullet was fired from a distance that makes suicide unlikely.

'Of course, I can't be sure it's Reece, not till forensics have finished doing their stuff and there's been an autopsy. There are indications, though. A signet ring with the intertwined initials BR – and I don't presume that stands for British Rail – and a scorched photograph that was found several yards from the car, presumably blown there by the blast – it's of Reece and a deceased colleague of his, Jack Wilkinson. I've requested Reece's dental records from Parkhurst. When they arrive we'll know definitely one way or the other. Whoever the victim is, the killing smacks of gangland – not what I'm used to on my present patch and the sooner the matter is put to bed, the sooner I'll like it.'

When Victor received the news he'd been so stunned with shock he'd been robbed of breath. Bryce dead? The identification wasn't certain yet, of course, but if what Somerville was saying about the signet ring and photograph were true . . . Sweat had broken out on his forehead. If the body in the car was Bryce's, there were two possibilities. He'd been murdered for his Al-Bakara stash – which was no longer in his possession because Victor's men had already removed it from 46 Lee Gardens – or he'd been shot by Frankie or one of his henchmen. A shooting that might have been avoided if Frankie's arrest had come a day earlier.

He stared at the telephone on his desk, knowing all he had to do was to pick up the receiver and dial Rusty's number; knowing he should have had Bryce under much tighter surveillance; knowing that he had conducted the entire operation on a far too casual basis.

'Victor! Thank God!'

The second he heard the frantic anxiety in Rusty's voice he knew that his worst fears were about to be justified.

'Bryce has been out of contact for nearly twenty-four hours! Is he with you, Vic? Is he still making his statement for you?'

He had calmed her as best he could, not daring to put into words the fear he was gripped by; there would be time enough for that if Somerville's identification was confirmed.

He severed the connection, unaware just how blissfully calm Rusty really was.

With a feeling of finality she replaced the receiver on its rest and looked down at her wristwatch. It was 11.30 a.m. The flight into Vancouver Airport had been scheduled to land at 10.45 a.m. First-class passenger Malling would be leaving the airport about now, or would perhaps already have done so.

Curly and Georgie, who had flown out on an earlier flight, would have been there to meet him. Gunter was still in London and planned to remain there until Jimmy's corpse had been formally identified as Bryce's, then he would be flying back to Vancouver with Debbie.

Debbie. Thinking about Debbie, she turned away from the telephone and surveyed her near-bare sitting-room. Everything that mattered to her; everything of sentimental value, had been packed in the two cases she was taking with her to Zurich. Debbie Clarkson had been a real surprise for her. Until Connie had telephoned, saying Debbie was insisting on being put in contact with Bryce, she'd never given the girl a second thought. Debbie had never been anything more than a name to her; a child, very near to her own child in age, who, because of her history, Bryce had always taken a mild interest in.

She strolled across to the bare expanse of window – her mother's curtains, now invested with even more memories than before, were laying neatly folded in one of her suitcases. Discovering that Bryce and Debbie were madly, passionately and deeply in love, had been quite a facer. She'd long ago realised, of course, that she and Bryce had no future together, except as loving friends, and had come to terms with the knowledge – hence Gregor and the new life she was about to embark on in Zurich.

What had never occurred to her, though, was that Bryce was capable of falling in love with real commitment – and the commitment he felt to Debbie was staggeringly obvious.

She glanced down at her wristwatch again. The cab booked to take her to the airport would be arriving at any minute. She turned, picking up a coat that had been lying on the back of a chair. Whatever the outcome of Bryce and Debbie's love affair, it was certainly the oddest she had come across. Bryce had killed Debbie's father, been in love with her mother, and had hated her grandmother with grand passion. If their relationship could survive all those handicaps it deserved every good wish possible – including hers.

'Christ All-fucking-Mighty!' If Frankie hadn't been hand-cuffed to two police officers he would have torn Victor's head from his shoulders. 'No, I didn't fucking well kill the fucking bastard, though I fucking well wish I fucking had!'

'I don't believe you.' Victor's voice was stark, his normally ruddy face pale and strained. 'And you killed him too late, Frankie. We already have a statement from him and it's a statement that's going to put you away for a long, long time.'

'He fucking grassed on me and you think his making out he's dead isn't a scam?' As Victor turned to leave the interview-room, Frankie's off-centred eyes were bulging with such frustrated rage they were nearly out of their sockets. ''Course he ain't dead!' He erupted to his feet, dragging the police officers with him, sending the table he and Victor had been seated opposite each other at, flying. 'He's no more dead than I fucking am!'

As Victor walked out into the corridor, Frankie's demented voice continued to follow him. 'He's making a monkey out of you, you stupid cunt! *He's making a monkey out of you!*'

'So that's it, then,' Somerville said over the telephone to Victor three weeks later. 'The body *is* Reece's, though whether you'll ever be able to pin his murder on Briscoe would seem to be doubtful. Still, Reece coughed up nicely before he was silenced. When Briscoe comes to court there's no doubt he'll go down for the killing of DC Jowett – and for other things as well, considering his old cohorts and enemies are all scuttling from the woodwork, eager to help out. Did you say Reece was being cremated on the sixth? Seems a bit unnecessary, doesn't it, under the circumstances? Still, I suppose some ceremonial is called for to satisfy family and friends. I'll probably see you there – his body was found on my patch, after all, and I'd like to see who turns up to say goodbye to him. Should be interesting.'

It had been interesting. Numbed with grief as he was, as Victor motored slowly out of the cemetery he had to allow Somerville that. He certainly hadn't expected Nina to show her face – nor her father. And, as there were no warrants out for Gunter and the Cravens, he'd expected them to have turned up from Spain or Morocco or wherever else it was that they'd hared off to after the Al-Bakara job. That they hadn't done so both puzzled and disappointed him.

As his Wolseley slid between the cemetery gates, Victor's police radio clicked into life.

'I'm sorry, sir,' the young DC he had detailed to tail the Aston said unhappily. 'We lost the girl at Nunhead station. She parked up and went inside and, though DC Johns nipped in after her, he was a fraction too late – a train was just pulling out. As she hasn't returned to her car, we can only assume she was on it.'

'Sorry, sir,' another DC said over the radio a few minutes later. 'We've checked the registration, but the car's a ringer. The real MUW 639S is a Merc that was reported stolen a month ago. Odd, a ringer being taken to a funeral and then dumped. Makes you think, doesn't it?'

'Not really,' Victor said wearily. 'Not when you consider the kind of people Reece associated with.'

Overcome by a wave of fresh grief he pulled the Wolseley into the kerb and, coming to a halt, switched off the engine.

He hated referring to Bryce as 'Reece'. To him, Bryce was simply Bryce – and he was going to miss him. He was going to miss him terribly.

## Chapter Twenty-One

'Christ, but I missed you!' Bryce's voice was raw with emotion as Debbie hurtled into his arms, her face blazing with joy.

With his usual caution, Gunter had been adamant that when he and Debbie flew into Vancouver no one should be there to meet them, so their reunion was taking place on the glass-roofed veranda of Gunter's hill-top home.

'Crack open the champers,' Georgie said to Curly, as Bryce and Debbie's passionate embrace showed no sign of ever coming to an end. 'I didn't think this day was going to come for another bleedin' twelve years – and don't bring out Gunter's Moët et Chandon crap. I've stowed some Louis Cristal in the fridge.'

Later, as the cork erupted from a fifth ice-cold bottle of vintage champagne, Bryce, his arm close around Debbie's waist, asked: 'So what kind of a funeral did I have? Who was there?'

'Sandra,' she said, knowing that she would tell him just how deep her mother's grief had been, but not wanting to until they were on their own. 'And Connie.'

She stopped for a moment as a spasm crossed Bryce's face. For a few seconds no one said anything, all of them aware that the funeral had in reality been the funeral of Connie's son – and that Connie had known it.

'Both your ex-wives . . .'

Bryce's eyebrows shot high. He'd known Rusty would be flying in from Zurich, but it hadn't occurred to him for one minute that Nina would show.

'A whole host of people from your Swan Row days. An American who was doing a good imitation of Al Capone. Scores of blokes I didn't know who were obviously villains. Some Knightsbridge-types. Victor. Chief Inspector Somerville.'

'And did Rusty do her stuff where Victor was concerned?'

Debbie nodded. Rusty's simulated grief had been a lesson in acting she wouldn't soon forget.

'And Sandra didn't let me down for a second,' she said wryly. 'She never gave me so much as a flicker of recognition – though to tell the truth, Bryce, I don't think that was because I'd asked her not to. I don't think she would have anyway.'

'And Victor?' he asked, a shadow darkening his eyes. 'How did poor old Victor take it?'

'Badly.' Her arm tightened round his waist. 'I felt sorry for him, Bryce.'

'Yeah.' Bryce's voice was thick in his throat. He, too, felt sorry for Victor. The poor bugger had never known any real happiness or excitement – and he'd certainly never experienced the adrenaline rush that came from anticipating a big piece of business; the kind of adrenaline rush he was now experiencing.

'So what happens next?' The speaker was Georgie. 'Thanks to your being loco enough to have handed the Al-Bakara stash back to the bleedin' bank, you're broke. Me and Curly still have a heap of dough left, which you're welcome to. Gunter's in the same position and –'

'Whoa!' Bryce held up a silencing hand. 'Why is it you three never do any real thinking? We're a team again, right? None of us are carrying any baggage, right? And we're sitting on top of a gold-bullion warehouse, right?'

He was standing near the veranda rail, slim and supple in a black turtleneck sweater and blue denims, his dark hair falling low over his brow, a devilish gleam in his eyes – a gleam they were all familiar with.

Gunter dropped the bottle of Louis Cristal he'd been in the process of lifting from the ice-bucket. Curly swallowed his breath and began to choke. Georgie spilt his drink all over his trousers.

And then all three of them looked down into the bowl of the valley.

The Brinks-Mat warehouse lay in the centre of a high-security industrial estate not a quarter of a mile away. For years Gunter had joked about its proximity to his home. For years they'd laughed about it and never given it a further thought.

But Bryce had. Now, reading their minds, he said: 'In Parkhurst I had plenty of time to think about it and I've come up with a foolproof plan. I don't have to ask if you're going to be in on it with me, do I?' The corners of his mouth quirked into a wicked grin. 'The job is going to be big. Far bigger than the Al-Bakara.' His grin deepened, nearly splitting his face in two. 'And it's going to be a cinch. Trust me.'

# *Epilogue*

It was early afternoon and the traffic was light as Victor
drove away from the Old Bailey towards Ludgate Circus,
listening to the news on his car radio.

'Thirty-eight-year-old gangland boss Frank Briscoe was
today given three life sentences after being found guilty of
the murders of Detective Constable Peter Jowett, Patricia
Dracup and Jack Wilkinson,' the newscaster reported
in a monotonously flat tone. 'The judge, Mr Justice
Melford Stevenson, said he should not be released for
thirty years . . .'

With deep satisfaction Victor turned left towards Blackfriars Bridge.

'The British people have voted overwhelmingly for continued membership of the European Common Market . . .'

He turned right on to the Embankment. Once Frankie
had been safely behind bars on remand, a veritable army of
those he had maliciously wounded, terrorised and exhorted
money from, had come out of the woodwork. Victims and
former accomplices previously scared into silence had all,
when Frankie finally came to trial, trooped through the
witness box. The foot-soldier who had been driving the
car when he had shot Jack down, had turned Queen's
Evidence, as had the colleague who had been with him
the night he had hurled Tricia to her death.

That lesser criminals had been allowed to save their
skins by giving evidence against Frankie had been a small
price to pay in order to secure Frankie's conviction. As

far as Victor was concerned, it had been a price worth paying.

He cruised past the Law Courts, happily contemplating the wedding he was to attend in a week's time, in Zurich.

'. . . Eight years to the day after Egypt's crushing defeat by Israel, the Suez Canal reopened today for international maritime traffic . . .' the newscaster continued sonorously.

The sun was hot. On his left-hand side the surface of the Thames glittered like a burnished shield.

'A highly organised gang today carried out Canada's biggest robbery when they stole gold bars worth over $20 million from a Brinks-Mat warehouse in Vancouver . . .'

Bryce's presence was suddenly so real to him that he momentarily lost control of the wheel and the car veered.

'. . . Canadian police say the raid was so well planned that the four-man gang may have immediately melted the gold down and smuggled it out of the country . . .'

Even though no parking was permitted on the stretch of Embankment he was driving along, he pulled over, blinking against the fierce sunlight.

'. . . the bullion was taken from a Brinks-Mat security warehouse, where the gang broke through a formidable array of alarms and then held up the six guards inside. The three-ton haul was so vast, it took an hour for the gang to load it into a lorry . . .'

Twenty million dollars worth of bullion.

A smile touched the corners of Victor's mouth. It was the sort of stunt Bryce would have loved to have pulled.

He turned the key in the ignition, swamped by bitter-sweet memories. He and Bryce racing pell-mell through bomb-blasted streets, with Bryce waving high a bayonet flaunting Hilda Clarkson's bloomers. Bryce calling him his 'second-in-command' as they and the rest of the gang squatted on Swan Row's cobbles planning the strategy for their next fight with the Briscoes. Bryce, telling him only a few short months ago, that when they'd been kids he'd always thought of him as his best mate.

He edged the car back into the traffic, his eyes suspiciously bright, hoping to God the robbers in Canada got away with their crime; hoping to God they'd never be caught.